BIGFOOT ABOMINATION

DANE HATCHELL

SEVERED PRESS
HOBART TASMANIA

BIGFOOT ABOMINATION

ISBN: 978-1-925711-24-0

CHAPTER 1

Earth's Present

Darkness wasn't Cole Rainwater's friend, but he was drawn to it like a junkie hooked on heroin.

He was there again, hunting with his uncle in Owls Bend near Mark Twain National Forest. The fog was thick that morning. He could practically chew each breath of cold air. It tasted a bit like the funk of dried leaves and acid-resin pine needles. At least the mosquitos slept in for the morning. The cold did nothing to keep the spider's under the covers, though.

As usual, spiderwebs fanned across the trails in every direction. Cole hated spiders. There was something icky and flesh-crawling about those eight legs. With his rifle barrel in the lead, he cut through a silky arachnid's net. It split in half and whisked to either side. He looked in time to see the web's creator scurry from the edge onto a low-lying branch overhead. It was a Writing Spider, and it was huge! Had that beast been in the middle waiting to catch its breakfast, Cole would have found another trail to take. For a moment he thought about shooting it but knew better because Uncle George would get mad at him for scaring game away over a spider.

Cole lowered his head and looked for Uncle George, who had stepped somewhere out front out of sight. No matter, the two of them had hunted the area together before and knew where to meet up. They were hunting squirrels and would be firing up into trees, so there was no danger of shooting each other.

Déjà vu enlightened the moment. Cole had been here before. He had done all of this before. The spider web draped over his rifle barrel like strands of cotton candy and glistened in the morning sun. A quick wipe with his gloved hand cleaned it. Some chemical in the spider web could etch the bluing on the rifle's barrel if he left in on there.

Cole looked about, and an ominous feeling of dread held him in its clutches.

A squirrel a few trees over started barking.

The bad feeling evaporated as the thrill of his hunter instincts pushed it aside. Hunting was more than just something to do on a Saturday morning. There was something satisfying that words couldn't describe when stalking prey. His heart beat faster. His hearing amplified and eyesight focused clearer.

The squirrel chattered on. Nothing would enter its domain without getting a good tongue lashing and the threat of a whipping tail.

Stepping carefully toward the tree, keeping his head low and approaching with obstacles shielding his advance, Cole made his way to get off an unobstructed shot.

The squirrel was bad-ass enough to stand its ground. Good. It was a noble act but would soon lead to its death. Something that small should have been given enough sense not to provoke a larger animal. Cole knew that rats were smart and that squirrels were basically long-tail rats with a better publicist. But he couldn't remember one time a rat ever stood its ground. It was always 'head for the hills' when discovered.

A clear shot now opened before him. The squirrel's tail fluttered like a squirmy red worm cut in half. It was almost daring him to shoot! Cole was happy to take the invitation.

The rifle went up, and he carefully peered over the top until the front and rear sights aligned. He methodically pushed the button near the trigger, disabling the safety. As his finger reached for the trigger, the dreadful feeling returned and immobilized him.

Cole had been here before. He had done all of this before.

Then the smell wafted through the cool breeze, unleashing an avalanche of memories. A barnyard odor laced with other pungent notes that provoked primordial fears. The hairs felt prickly on the back of his neck, and his bum hole puckered a few times.

Cole was scared to look at where he knew the monster watched. But look he would, just as he had done the first time.

From a distance, it could have first appeared to be a tall, robust tree stump, rotting and without branches. Its form looked animal-like, though. Perhaps even like a bear standing tall to reach something good to eat from above. This was no bear because it was now obvious it was shaped like a man. A 'man' with long reddish-brown hair that covered its body, save for face and chest. Cole had watched enough of the Discovery Channel to know this creature could only be a bigfoot.

The bigfoot stood with its large eyes peering into Cole's very soul. He couldn't tell if it was contemplating an attack or if maybe he was there for the squirrel too. Knowing the rules of mother nature of predator and prey, making a dash for safety might inspire the monster to give chase. He racked his brain and couldn't remember ever hearing of bigfoot eating humans, but he was afraid to bolt and find out for himself.

Still, he couldn't just stand there and not do something. For a moment, his mind went down the path of pointing the gun at the creature *and shooting to scare it away. But what if that didn't work? His gun was a .22 caliber rifle and would be useless against a hulk like that.*

Fear had clouded his memory, but now the déjà vu returned.

He pushed the rifle's safety to 'on' and backed away. Soon, the bigfoot was out of sight. With no sign of pursuit, Cole turned and ran to find his Uncle George.

"Good morning Salem, Missouri. Time to get up and shave, shower, and get in ship-shape to start the day. This is your ol' pal Al on KQKY bringing you the best of Classic Rock of the '60s, '70s, and '80s. Guess what time it is? It's time to get the lead out!"

Cole reached over and slapped at the alarm clock until the music stopped playing. Hearing a Led Zeppelin song this early in the morning was too much even for him. Something like Kansas' "Dust in the Wind" would be better. As depressing as the lyrics were, it still was a soothing tune to wake up to and make the bed.

The reoccurring nightmare over, the mire of sleep released Cole from its chains. He had encountered the bigfoot some four years ago when he was ten. Of course, no one believed his story. Reports of bigfoot in the region were rare but not unheard of, usually told by some drunk hunter. His father blamed his *hallucination* on sugary cereal. Cole loved Froot Loops with marshmallows. He had eaten them for years without a similar incident. Regardless of what people thought from that day on, Cole had delved headfirst into the world of the paranormal, aliens, and cryptozoology.

He sat on the edge of his bed with his dangling feet hovering above the floor. The sheets were moist with sweat as was the hair on his neck. He ran his hand from the back of his head to the front of his high and tight haircut. Summer was coming, and he had let his dad talk him into getting a military-style haircut. At first, the short hair on his sandy-brown head made him look bald. But in less than a week enough had grown for him to look more like his hero, the wrestling champion, John Cena.

The floorboards felt cold as he slid from his bed. Socks were the first of the clothing to go on. Stepping into each one at a time, he stood before the mirror, with his elbows out and his fists near his belly button. Flexing in front of the mirror showed his time lifting weights was paying off. His pecs, deltoids, and biceps were coming along nicely. Although if he had to be honest with himself, his arms looked like toothpicks compared to John Cena's.

He imagined what he'd look like sporting Cena's *guns*. As he flexed, he realized he'd look stupid with arms disproportional to the rest of his body. Adding Cena's chest to his arms would make his head look three sizes too small. Plus, his legs would look like beanpoles. After a big sigh, he realized that it was going to take years and a lot of working out to look like Cena.

Pants and shirt went on next, and then a quick trip to the washroom before heading to the kitchen for breakfast.

The aroma of brewed coffee warmed the air as Cole went about his morning ritual. Grab a bowl and spoon and place them on the table. Get the cereal and drop it off while going to the fridge for the milk. Take the milk and pour it into the bowl until half-full, then put the milk back in the fridge. (His dad didn't like the milk sitting out to get warm.) Then, dump the cereal out of the box until it nearly spilled over. This week his dad had bought him Cheerios, which wasn't too bad for his liking. Of course, he hurriedly snuck in two spoons of sugar before his dad, who was in the washroom now, made his entrance.

A few oat-rich Os paratrooped to the table as the spoon went into the bowl and then up to his mouth. The cereal crunched between his teeth, and the sound reminded him of a horse feeding from a trough. When he wasn't able to slip extra sugar in bland cereal, he felt like he *was* eating horse food.

Slippers scuffing the hall carried into the kitchen. His dad had on his pajama bottoms and a tee shirt. Robotically, his focus never left the coffee pot, where he grabbed a mug from a hook under the counter and poured a cup. He brought the mug to his nose, and his eyes magically showed signs of life. "Morning." He shuffled over to the table and removed the sugar bowl top. Lifting the bowl, he sprinkled sugar into his coffee. Most of the sugar made it; some landed on the table.

"Dad, you ought to use a spoon," Cole said, and then crammed in another mouthful of cereal.

"Why dirty a spoon after one use?"

"We could just leave a spoon in the bowl all the time."

"That's unsanitary."

"We have a dishwasher."

"Yeah, that I load and unload. More work for me. You're lucky I don't make you do more around here." Mark Rainwater wasn't in bad shape for a thirty-five-year-old, but he could have taken much better care of himself. A widower and single dad for the last twelve years didn't afford much personal time. He was a lineman for Midstate Electric. His normal eight-hour shift often expanded during weather events and his co-workers calling in sick or on vacation.

"Uh, we need some more bananas," Cole said, hoping to divert his dad's train of thought.

"Oh, really?" Mark's sarcastic tone told Cole he picked the wrong thing to talk about.

"Yeah, you know. I take one for lunch."

"I was walking in the woods the other day and guess what I found?"

His gaze glued to the emptying bowl, Cole said, "I dunno."

"A banana, hanging from a string tied to a tree branch. Did you do that?"

Barely audible, Cole said, "Yes sir."

"Cole, you shouldn't waste food like that. There's no bigfoot so there's no need to leave bait."

"I had my wildlife camera set up in the woods. If bigfoot had taken the banana, I would have a picture of it. I'd be the first to prove bigfoot is real. Then, all the guys at school wouldn't make fun of me. I'd be a hero. We'd be rich. I bet I could sell the picture for a million dollars."

Mark's ire subsided, evident by his slumping shoulders, and his head tilting to one side. "Son, you should concentrate on more important things than bigfoot or UFOs or ghosts. Spend more time with your studies. If you want a good paying job, you'll need to go to college. You're a smart boy, but you'll have to make an effort. Don't go chasing rainbows. Work on your fastball. Who knows? You might be good enough one day to get a baseball scholarship to Mizzou."

"You really think!" Cole's face brightened.

Forcing a smile, Mark said, "Well…its possible. I wasn't good at sports, but your Uncle George was before he got in the car accident and messed up his shoulder. Who knows? You may take after him."

"Don't worry about me, Dad. I may be only fourteen, but I know how the world works."

Mark giggled. "You do?"

"Yeah. It's all about priorities. Do the important things first and then the fun stuff when you have time. I want a good job that pays lots of money so I can afford to look for crashed UFOs or go on hunts for bigfoot, and stuff like that."

"More power to you, son," Mark said, and then raised a thumb. "Oh, the school sent an email saying that old man Douglas is complaining that some boys from the school are playing pranks on him on his farm. You don't know anything about that, do you?"

"No sir, I don't."

"The prank, as Douglas called it, was leaving huge footprints and making a mess in his garden."

"You mean like bigfoot prints?" Cole said with excitement.

"No, he said they were shoe prints. I want you to be clear with that fact so you don't get any strange ideas about going over there. Stay away from the old codger. He spent some time in prison before buying his place. He doesn't bother anyone and doesn't like to be bothered."

"I don't have time to do anything like that," Cole said as he stood and took his bowl to the sink. "I'll be home a little later today. It's Tuesday, and I have baseball practice."

"Remember to do your stretching exercises before you throw any balls."

"Don't worry, Dad. I got this," Cole said as he raised a thumb up at his dad.

Something didn't sound right with Douglas' story. Huge shoe prints? That didn't make sense. What if Douglas altered the story so that bigfoot hunters would stay away from his place?

Cole had some thinking to do. If bigfoot was in the area, he would have to make an extra effort to capture it on his camera.

Chapter 2

Earth's Future

The mech-armor by the infirmary's door waited for the human to bring it to life. The *transmetal* shell was of *Skink* design and retrofitted for his smaller body. He needed the armor to make him their equal. Humans were squishy bags of flesh with bones easily broken. Skinks averaged seven feet in height, with thick skin, and ropey muscles hardening their bodies like steel. If Mother Earth had blessed the reptiles as She had done evolving the mammals, the Skinks would certainly qualify as cousins.

His name was Tarik. He was told his father was a recombinant mass of goo and his mother a petri dish. That was a strange answer to give a boy of four who had asked why he looked so different from everyone else, but it *was* the harsh truth. One of many harsh truths Tarik became aware of over the last twenty-five years. Life on Earth had changed drastically since the Skinks invaded and transformed humanity into a new species. Why had an alien race, after traveling hundreds of light years from their ancient planet, focused on genetic manipulation of the dominate species? It seemed that superior intelligence would have fostered benevolence, but the opposite was true.

Now, humanity's replacement, the Skinks referred to as *Nu-Mans*, were on a short path to extinction. Humankind's replacement had a genetic time bomb ticking that would explode before the next generation. Tarik wasn't one of the Nu-Mans. He was an anomaly and the last hope to save his home planet from an invading species.

Hudson lay uncovered, with his eyes half-open, on a ten-foot-long bed. His hairy, wide feet jutted up like small tombstones right at the bed's edge. The monitor to the side's tiny speaker pulsed in a dull rhythm as jagged colored lines etched against the black screen. The dim light and stale air in the room choked the moment. The scene defined hopelessness. A death sentence with no chance of parole.

"Tarik..." Hudson said weakly. His lips barely moved, and he continued to stare into the distance. The once sleek brown hair covering most of his body peppered now with gray, with coarse and matted patches like an animal in the wilderness.

"I'm right here, Hud." Tarik took a deep breath and lightly stepped toward his teacher, his friend. Did he have the right to call him his *father*? They were not blood-related. Their only connection shared DNA structures that all humanity had in common. Emphasis on *had*. Tarik was the last human on Earth, and Hudson was a Nu-Man.

The Skinks designed the Nu-Mans to be a hardier version of primate, genetically splicing homo sapien DNA with that of the rare creature known as sasquatch. An endeavor that had failed miserably, but with little consequence to the Skinks. Altering human evolution was more of a source of entertainment than meeting some beneficial objective. The Skinks had what they wanted. A Planet still vibrant with life, water, and plenty of precious elements and minerals, unlike on their now dead home planet.

"I'm sorry." Hudson lifted his left hand to the side of the bed, with an open palm.

Tarik took the invitation and placed a hand in Hudson's hold. The Nu-Man's gentle grip made him feel safe, despite the fact that if Hud made a fist, it would swallow Tarik's hand entirely and fracture bones. "Sorry? You don't have any reason to feel sorry for me. You're the one suffering."

"Yeah. I'm suffering all right. There's no way to sugar coat my condition," Hudson said, sounding stronger as if Tarik's touch commuted some of the human's life force. "I'm sorry that you're the only one. I can only imagine what it's been like growing up without anyone else of your kind. Why, I remember the day you asked me when your body hair would start growing like mine." A melancholy smile edged his lips.

"I've grown to appreciate my exposed skin. A fast toweling after a shower and I'm dry."

"Hair hides a multitude of imperfections. It helps when attracting the ladies, too."

"That's a *problem* I don't have." Tarik lowered his head.

"I know, and it's not like we didn't try. The Skinks doomed us as a race after their *refining* of our genetics. Our only hope to one day retake Earth was to recreate the human species. It took thousands of tries to produce you. After that, we thought we had the process perfected. You know the rest of the story. After thousands of more failures, we finally gave up."

"It's no more your fault that you failed than it was by your doing that I came to be. I'm just an accident, a *genetic abomination*."

"Maybe..." Hudson said. "I've thought a lot about that, and I'm reminded of something I once read. *Look not at the things that are seen, but at the things that are not seen.*"

"More philosophy? Philosophy did nothing to preserve the human race. The Skinks didn't care about human history or humanity's eons old struggle. Didn't give a damn about our Gods or revered men of history. The Skinks are so far advanced they have imposed themselves as Gods over us. You act as if fate owes mankind a chance to reclaim the planet."

"I am a scientist, as you well know. I trust in facts and not faith. Maybe my condition *has* softened my brain." Hudson licked his lips. His chest slightly rose as he took a deep breath. "A little voice in my head refuses to give up hope. What if...What if you weren't an accident? What if the Universe, in its inexplicable ways, intervened and created your birth?"

"We're back to the God argument now, aren't we? Why would the Universe want us to retake the Earth? The Skinks are the superior race. Compared to them we're no better than stupid animals. Don't they deserve the Earth?"

"All I know is that after the Big Bang every atom was set into motion. The path that each atom took determined the birth and death of the Universe. To me, our three-dimensional Universe is a book, and time turns the page."

"So everything that happens is destined to happen?" Tarik looked to the ceiling and smirked.

"Maybe certain events, but other factors determine the outcomes."

"You mean individuals?"

"Yes. There are two events occurring at the same time that are unique. Your birth, and the Skinks' time manipulation machine that's about to go online. We failed at recreating humankind, but we have you. If we can get you back in time before the Skinks' exploratory probe sends back Earth's data, we can prevent them from ever finding Earth."

Tarik didn't believe in God, faith, angels, or demons. He only knew the realities of life. In his case, his experiences were few. The Skinks would have either killed him or something worse if they had known he existed. So, he was forced to view life from within the confines of four walls. Running through a forest or swimming in a lake was out of the question. Foamy waves of water splashing sandy beaches never touched his skin. Virtual reality computers were his only means of travel.

Hudson's words breached a barrier Tarik hid behind. A human hadn't walked the Earth for generations until he was born. The Skinks had reached a new level in their evolution with the development of a time travel machine. The two events could just be an incredible coincidence, but the timing of it all gave him pause. Maybe Hudson's delusion affected Tarik because of his love and trust of his old friend and mentor. Even if the situation was more than just random, Tarik's odds of infiltrating the Skink compound and hijacking the time machine was a million-to-one.

"Hud, you've taught and trained me to be prepared for anything. Though I always thought I'd be on the defensive side trying to preserve my life, I'm more than ready for combat. Frankly, I'm tired of living in confinement to the point I might choose death over life if you told me I had to continue to hide from the Skinks. It's no different than being in prison. I'll at least get that wish if storming the compound fails. There's just no way that after..." Tarik's throat tightened, "that after you're gone...and everyone else around me starts dying, life as I know it won't have any meaning at all."

"I understand loneliness is like starving. You've suffered from it to some degree all of your life. But that has a chance to change," Hudson's drifting words had slowed near the end.

The hills and valleys of the lines on the health monitor grew wider and farther apart. The dull beep slowed. A knowing grin curled on Hudson's dry lips. "Tarik, time is turning the next page." His eyes widened, and his jaw dropped in awe of invisible magnificence only he could see.

The beep steadied into a monotone drone. The lines on the monitor fell and remained flat.

Tarik's nose stung, bringing tears to his eyes. Hudson's comforting hold slipped as his hand fell to his side.

BARMP! BARMP! BARMP!

The alarm! Their compound had been breached!

The door to the room swung open. It was Zax, a member of the squad and his best friend. His large brown eyes asked the obvious question.

Tarik bit his bottom lip and shook his head.

"I'm sorry, but we've got to get it in gear. The Skinks have found us. This is going to get messy."

Tarik briefly turned his head and told Hudson goodbye for the last time. The spirit of life had left him, though. The cooling body now looked like a dead husk of a stranger. Tarik would keep his teacher alive in his memories as long as the Universe allowed him to live.

CHAPTER 3

The Present

The yellow behemoth lumbered to a stop and hissed angry air. Cole approached slowly, lifting his gaze, and accepting his ultimate fate. The behemoth's mouth opened wide enough to devour Cole in one bite. With a heavy sigh, he thrust himself into the mighty jaws.

"Good morning, my man," Mr. Tillus, the school bus driver, said.

"Morning," Cole said as he took the short steps up. He returned Mr. Tillus' infectious smile. The old bus driver's teeth shined as much as his bald head.

The bus started moving as Cole made his way down the aisle. Different day, same old faces. The kid with his head on his book sack finishing his morning sleep. The two girls running their mouths and smacking gum. The bookworm deep into the imaginary world of an author's mind. The kids plugged into their earbuds and tapping away at phone screens, trying to show their butts off to the rest of the world.

Unfortunately for Cole, there was no one his age on the bus route. Dent County High was next to the middle school. Rural living brought its share of compromises with it. It was either the bus or riding with his father, who was determined to get some personal benefit out of all the taxes he paid.

He found an empty seat about halfway down the aisle and slid his book sack off one shoulder before plopping down and scooting by the window. The landscape scrolled by. Mother Nature still maintained most of the undeveloped land where the road intruded, and telephone poles marked mankind's territory.

Morning solitude did bring one advantage. The ride gave Cole a good twenty minutes to catch up on his favorite radio show from the previous night. Art Corey hosted Shore to Shore USA, a midnight to 4 a.m. radio show. Cole had a subscription to the Shore Insider, which gave him on-demand access to the previous show, or past shows. He would only have time to listen to the *news of the day* segment. Art would highlight some of the leading political topics, along with paranormal events around the world that major media shunned. The segment usually ended with a UFO update from Dick Freeport. The report, though, was pretty much the same day to day. Sightings of *strange lights in the sky* were common all over the country. It was the occasional video that Cole was the most interested in learning of. With all the smartphones all over the world, video of an actual alien craft was sure to surface one day.

The bus ride came to an end with no new news to excite Cole. The first guest was going to talk about Atlantis and promote his book. He would have to wait until bedtime to pick up the show where he left off. Listening to replays of Shore to Shore ferried him to sleep every night. Cole wondered if his subconscious stored the show after he was no longer awake. That would be cool if true.

Thankfully, the bus' route brought him to the high school first and then traveled the short distance to the middle school. Cole stepped onto the sidewalk after giving Mr. Tillus a quick nod. The behemoth's mouth snapped shut and hissed irately before rumbling away.

Just another typical morning. The sun not yet climbing over the trees, but a cloudless sky that foretold a bright day. Spring was definitely in the air. The warm weather had resurrected barren trees. The greenery blocked out all memories of the harsh winter. On some level, Cole hoped Climate Change was true. He would love to live in perpetual summer. That opinion, though, he kept to himself. Kids ragged on him enough for his other *kooky* beliefs. Aliens, bigfoot, and ghosts, not necessarily in that order, were where he devoted his energies.

Kids meandered around the flag pole in front of the school's main entrance. Others lined up near the front, preferring fresh air rather than what walking the halls offered.

Mr. Buddy Johnson, the janitor, was a portly man somewhere in his forties. One thing's for sure, the man loved his work, which surprised Cole. It seemed that performing the same menial jobs day after day would get boring. For example, just as soon as he mopped the floor, tens of tennis shoes and boots would bless the effort with scuff marks and dirt. Right now the man was putting a new plastic liner in a trash can, which would be full after lunch. Cole remembered one time when Mr. Buddy was on his hands and knees cleaning up a fresh pile of puke from the middle of a hallway. Before he could finish, the smell hit one of the students hard enough for them to deposit a load just a few feet over. You would have thought that would have sent Mr. Buddy into an outrage. But the man simply raised his eyebrows and shrugged his shoulders, and soldiered on completing his first task before taking on another.

Hidden in a shadowy corner, Mr. Ritzman kept a vigilant eye, the good one of course, on the morning ongoings. An aura of mystery surrounded that man. For one thing, Mr. Rizman always wore a black suit, dark glasses, white shirt, and a black tie. The sleeves of his jacket were too long; the jacket's cuffs reaching nearly halfway down his hand. Of course, his shoes and belt were black too. His left hand curiously avoided view at all times. The appendage usually resided in his left jacket pocket or gripped around a pen.

Mr. Ritzman took Mrs. Darby's place when she left on maternity leave, just a couple of months after a kid two counties over went missing. The odd thing about that was that Ritzman had never substituted at Dent County before. Usually, replacement teachers came from a small pool of regulars. Maybe Ritzman had connections with someone on the school board. As far as teachers go, the man was in no danger of winning any *educator of the year* award. He had practically zero personality. His robotic delivery had Cole wondering if androids were now a reality.

Two of Cole's friends were off to the side under the mulberry tree, where they hung out almost every morning before school, weather allowing. They were *friends* in the loosest sense of the word. Cole was a loner, had been all of his life. This was mainly by choice, but his interests in the weird didn't attract many like-minded people. Kirk Ford and Dean Setters shared first-hour with him. That was their connection. Beyond that, Cole rarely saw them the rest of the day. Neither of the other two boys played baseball.

Kirk was sort of a sad character. His greasy hair and wrinkled clothes mirrored what was on the inside. Cole imagined his parents neglected him. Kirk's birth dad split with his mom a few years before and went to live somewhere in Canada. His new dad treated him like he was always in the way. That was probably the reason why Kirk had no desire to pursue education beyond high school. He was determined to join the Army and become a defender of the USA.

The situation bothered Cole because it made him wonder what would happen if his father ever met someone else and got married. Would he get in the way too of their relationship? Maybe at fourteen, it shouldn't matter. He'd be out of high school in a few years and then hopefully off to college. A boy had to become a man at some point. The thought of living away from home brought a strange emptiness to his stomach.

Dean was the class clown. The problem with that was Dean was rarely actually funny. His antics and comments were better suited for grade school. It was evident, though, that he was his own biggest fan. The boy would break down in hysterical laughter at his own jokes. Often, no one could understand the punchline because of his cackling. Moans and groans from the students did nothing to deter him from striking again at an opportune moment. Cole didn't know if Dean acted this way for attention, or if in his own way, he was telling everyone else *screw you; watch me perform.*

"Hiya, guys," Cole said as he fast-stepped over to his buddies.

"Hey."

"Top of the morning to you," Dean said, and then tipped an imaginary hat.

"Dean and I didn't finish our algebra homework. Did you?" Kirk asked.

"Well, I finished mine, but I don't think Mr. Ritzman is going to like my answers," Dean corrected.

Cole wasn't sure what Dean meant, but rather than ask questions and get long run-around answers, he had learned to bide his time and wait for Dean to let the cat out of the bag. "Yeah, I did it. I got it right here in my book sack." He pulled the bag off his shoulder and fished out a green notebook. The class had written down eight linear equations from the board on the previous day. Each equation had an unknown variable. The task involved finding X.

"I started working on my homework and got distracted by the TV. They were talking about having mind outside of body experiences and how people's inner self can travel anywhere in the universe. I fell asleep not long after and didn't get to see the end. Cole, do you know what that's called?" Kirk asked.

"Were they going back or forward in time too? If they were, that's called *remote viewing*," Cole said.

"No, I don't remember any of that," Kirk said.

"Then, they were talking about *astral projection*," Cole said. "Astral projection is an OBE—"

"What?" Kirk interrupted.

"An *out of body experience*, kind of a form of telepathy, where the consciousness leaves the body and travels anywhere it wants," Cole said. "The subject's been brought up on Shore to Shore a few times. Art Corey claims he's been able to leave his body and float above his bed."

"I don't know if I'd like to do that," Kirk said.

"Why not? Seems kinda fun," Cole said.

"What happens if your spirit person can't get back into your body? They'd have to hook up a feeding tube to keep the body alive. You'd be like a ghost wandering around," Kirk said.

"Hmm, I've never heard any kind of story like that. Just don't try to do it and you'll have nothing to worry about," Cole said. "Here, you guys need to hurry before the bell rings." He had his notebook open to the page with the problems and held it out for them to copy.

Dean pulled out a pencil and started erasing answers in his notebook.

"Wow, Dean. You didn't get any of them right?" Cole asked.

"I didn't exactly go to the trouble to try and solve the variable," Dean said.

"What did you write, then?" Cole asked.

Dean brushed some of the eraser dust from the page and turned it for Cole to see.

"You circled each X and wrote *here it is* by it?"

"Well, the equation said to *find X*."

"Dean, do you take anything seriously in life?" Cole asked.

The boy finished erasing the earlier answers and started copying Cole's. "Maybe one day. Something you said a minute ago inspired me."

"Astral projection?"

"No, the remote viewing."

"Yeah, that does seem pretty interesting. It would be great to be able to remote view what the world was like in prehistoric times or go back and watch the first moon landing," Kirk said.

"I'm not interested in history. I want to learn how to remote poot," Dean said.

"Remote poot? That's not a thing," Cole said.

"And, maybe one day I'll make *remote pooting* a thing. Imagine being able to fart and have it blast out from behind the teacher across the room. Or at church, during the morning prayer, right when your butt's squirming on the hard pew trying to hold back a load of gas from the cabbage you ate the night before. You could let it rip behind the preacher. Man, that would be a gas!"

Cole got the double entendre but again said nothing to encourage Dean.

Kirk snapped his notebook shut after scribbling the last answer. The first bell rang. "You know, Dean, one day you're going to push things too far with your so-called humor. Somebody's going to get enough and whip that butt of yours."

Dean didn't look up and continued to write answers. "What doesn't kill me only makes me stronger."

"What do you mean?" Kirk asked.

"Because, *Jimmy Fallon*."

"What?" Both Kirk and Cole said at the same time.

Dean continued, "Jimmy Fallon grew up wanting to be on shows like *Saturday Night Live* and one day host *The Tonight Show*. If I have any chance to follow in his footsteps, then I have to keep working on my game until I get it right. Nobody is going to stop me from going after my dream. Not a teacher or a parent or if the whole football team whips my butt. I'm gonna be me, and everyone else will just have to deal with it."

"Let's go guys, or we'll be late," Cole said, feeling a slight admiration toward Dean's resolve. Still, the boy might want to spend a little more time in the gym, as he was certainly *cruising for a bruising*.

*

The halls were abuzz with hurriedness as students plodded to their morning destinations. Sneakers slapped and skidded; heels of shoes clomped in discordant rhythm. Guys escorted girls with arms around their waists or holding hands. It was obvious that if you wore a letterman jacket, you more than likely would have a girl by your side. Cole didn't have a letterman jacket, *yet.*

Mr. Buddy, the ever diligent janitor with a damp mop in hand, slowly waded through the stream of students flowing down the hallway. The children bobbed and weaved around him, undeterred from their destination.

Cole stood by his open, gray metal locker, which stood six feet high. Inside the door, he had placed a variety of stickers and taped printouts from his computer. The largest picture was the infamous 'I Want to Believe' X-files poster. He had watched every episode of the old series and even watched the short run of the remake. Cole did want to believe, but he didn't want to be some kook that looked for any and every excuse to believe extraterrestrials were real.

The poster showed a classic saucer shaped UFO. Whereas a flying disk was a terrific shape for maneuvering through the atmosphere, it had no advantage in the vacuum of outer space. It seemed logical that interstellar craft would be designed for maximum inner space, sort of like a cube design like the Borg used on Star Trek. Flying disks could only be used as scout ships and not to travel the incredible distances between the stars.

One round sticker had 'Paranormal Investigator' surrounding the edges and a white bell curve shaped to look like a spooky ghost. A bumper sticker proclaimed an 'Alien Hybrid on Board.' Of course, there were a variety of cryptozoological creature stickers. Chupacabra, the Jersey Devil, the Loch Ness monster, the Moth Man, and bigfoot. One bigfoot bumper sticker read: 'Bigfoot Saw Me. No One Believed Him.'

Cole was about to close his locker, after unloading his book sack and gathering his books for first-hour, when he saw Charlotte Meadows peel off from her entourage and head to her locker.

Charlotte was in the 9th grade too. She was one of the in-crowd, though, and no one would know that she was a geeky freshman by the company she kept.

Pretending to adjust some books in his locker, Cole waited for Charlotte to come and open her locker, which was right next to his.

Charlotte, or *Princess Charlotte* as he would think of her sometimes because she was pretty enough to be a princess, was oblivious to his presence as she fumbled through her locker's contents.

Cole's heart noticeably sped in his chest, and he felt his face flush a bit. He had shared few words with her over the year, mostly just a *hi* or a *hello*, of which she usually politely returned. As far as initiating any other conversation, she had left that burden on him.

The smell of her shampoo or perfume, Cole had never got close enough for his nose to explore and locate the source, stirred some manly emotion in him that made him want to melt and go into a rage simultaneously.

Charlotte was the perfect height. If they stood face to face, he was only slightly taller, maybe by an inch as he was 5'9". A perfect size in his mind for him to turn his head to the side and kiss her deeply on the lips. He would then slowly slide his right hand up her back, underneath the long, dark brown, straight and shiny hair, until it rested behind her head. With assurance, he would gently pull her head closer and part her mouth with his wanting tongue. She would be his, and he would be hers, forever, maybe.

Cole broke his reverie as his internal clock told him time was running out. He knew that Charlotte had recently broken up with Brennon Davis, a 10th grader and a fellow member on the junior varsity baseball team. If there ever was a time to try and make a move, it was now.

"Hi, Charlotte," Cole said, closing his locker door just enough to look from behind it.

"Hey," she sang in a low voice that sounded ten thousand miles away. Her gaze never left her duties.

"Have you done your science assignment for Mrs. Edwards? There's only a week left before the end of the month," Cole said.

"Not yet. In fact, I had kinda forgot about it." She turned her gaze toward Cole.

Charlotte's long lashes accentuated her deep brown eyes surrounded by purplish eyeshadow. The blush shaded her cheek bones and made her look much older. Most girls her age dabbed blush on the apples of their cheeks, which made them look like clowns. Her lips looked like lavender candy that glistened like it had been freshly licked. "Well, uh, you know you have to do the assignment in pairs. Have you picked a partner?" Cole asked.

"No, not yet. I'll just have to add it to a long list of other things I need to do and keep putting off. I'm bad that way, sometimes."

Hearing the word *bad* from Charlotte's mouth strangely made it sound like something good. "I don't have a partner either, and I wanted to do my project tonight."

"Something special about tonight?" Charlotte flipped her hair off her left shoulder.

"Yeah, The International Space Station will be flying over just after dusk. I'm going to have my video camera set up and my laptop outside. You can hear the astronauts speak live over the internet."

"That does sound like an interesting project."

"Hey, if you want," Cole's eyelids raised as if the thought just struck him, "you could come over to my house, and we could do the project together."

Mr. Buddy's mop slopped just behind Cole. The boy turned a quick gaze to the man as the janitor worked the mop back and forth on a spot on the floor. This was no time for distractions.

"Well, I don't know…" Charlotte's gaze turned to the side.

Cole couldn't tell if she were actually considering the offer or if she was searching for an excuse.

"I know you live in a neighborhood and closer to the city. The space station will be harder to see with all those man-made lights. Where I live is pretty rural. Get your mom to drive you over. I've seen the space station pass overhead before. It travels across the sky in just a few minutes. I'll video tape it and get the live audio. We can show it in class for our credit."

"Hmm, can I think about it?" she asked.

Not a *no*, but not a *yes*. Was she just sparing his feelings? Cole felt his heart sink to his stomach, right before something slammed into his right shoulder. His body jerked forward, and his face implanted on the 'I Want to Believe' poster. Did Mr. Buddy just crash into him?

" 'scuse me. I didn't see you there." It was Brennon Davis; the janitor had moved on to clean another area. A wide smirk etched above the athletic boy's square jaw. His curly blonde hair combed back from his forehead and hung nearly to the collar of his jacket. Brennon was a good four inches taller than Cole but acted like it was four feet.

"Brennon! That was unnecessary," Charlotte scolded.

Brennon's smirk morphed into innocence. He raised an open palm on his right hand and reached for the ceiling. "I said *excuse me*." He turned his gaze to Cole. "You heard me say *excuse me*, right?" Brennon's apologetic tone ended after the *excuse me*. When he said *right*, it was a command to be obeyed.

"I'm okay," Cole said, feeling a small knot start to swell on the ridge above his left eyebrow.

"See, he's okay," Brennon said and crossed his arms.

"What do you want? I told you to leave me alone," Charlotte said, narrowing her gaze.

"Aw, don't be that way. I told you I was sorry about the other night. You've got to lighten up a little. Give me another chance," Brennon said.

"I've given you more chances than ten times at bat. You've struck out for the last time with me," Charlotte said.

"Com'on. Let me pick you up after practice, and we'll hit The Chimes. We can dig into some of that spinach and artichoke dip you like. Get some frozen yogurt later, just like old times," Brennon said.

"I've got a date tonight."

"A date? With who?" Brennon's face contorted like someone had just told him his dog had died.

"With Cole."

"A date? But—" Cole said before Charlotte followed up.

"I'm with Cole tonight. There are no more *old times*. There're only new times. And the new times don't include you."

Red splotches appeared on Brennon's face. His mouth quivered like a volcano threatening to erupt.

"Go to class, Brennon. If you're late the coach will make you run extra laps," Charlotte said.

Brennon hesitated, then shot his wild gaze upon Cole. "Your *ass* is mine. See you at practice."

Bits of spittle from the hard *p* of practice showered Cole's face as Brennon stomped off. He looked over at Charlotte, and said, "A date?"

"Sure, why not?" She acted as if this was the first time she had considered thinking of him as dateable material, and, the thought had some appeal.

"Well, okay then. Can you come around seven p.m.? The sun sets a little before eight," Cole said.

"I will see you then." Charlotte closed her locker, turned, and walked briskly away, turning once to give Cole a last glance before rounding the corner.

"A date?" Cole said in wonderment, only dreaming of this day but never believing it would come true.

The bump above his eyebrow throbbed. Every silver cloud had a dark lining. Now he had to hope he would still have most of his teeth after baseball practice.

CHAPTER 4

The Future

The maroon transmetal armor opened at the head, arms, chest, and legs creating a cavity waiting to receive Tarik in its cold embrace. He stepped up to it and turned around, reaching the hold with his right hand to pull himself up. His right foot lifted and slid onto the foot frame until his heel secured in place. Nestling his back and arms in position, he brought his left leg in its spot until his body fit in snuggly.

In one swift action, the armor snapped together with the finality of a closing vault. Tarik had trained enough in the armor for it to feel like a second skin. Hopefully, all of the modifications to it would allow him to move stealthily among the Skinks. If not, the armor would become a transmetal sarcophagus.

The shell hummed with power energizing the circuits and mechanical joints. The H*eads* U*p* D*isplay* quickly detected and measured everything in the room and showed tactical information in front of his face. *Open door three point four meters to the left. Hudson's body registered as dead. The HUD identified the monitoring equipment as non-threatening electronics.* The treads on the soles of the mechanical feet dampened his steps as he left the room.

Zax and three others of the team of twelve waited down the hall. Each wore rebel made battle armor that had never been field tested. The scientists who started the rebel nest thirty years before had focused on recreating humans, not building a war machine. With the disappointments of their failures, they were forced to shift their efforts toward creating a strike team with offensive and defensive mechanisms capable of competing with the Skink forces.

"There's only one scout ship on the perimeter. Not more than six or eight on board. I don't think they know what we've been doing. Probably found our parasite connection on the energy system and are coming to investigate," Zax said as Tarik approached.

The only time Tarik didn't feel inferior around the Nu-Mans was when he wore the armor. They commonly towered two feet in height over him and outweighed him by four hundred pounds. "The others?" Tarik asked.

"All the scientists and the rest of the support team are evacuating to safe-houses. We're going to have to stay and hold this place as long as we can to give them time," Zax said.

"No, we have to beat these stinky lizards and take their scout ship," Tarik said.

"That's easier said than done," Bref, one of the older members of the team, said. "That armor's tough."

Tarik felt a twinge of guilt. His comrades weren't nearly as protected as he. Their arms and legs presented vulnerable targets to the kinetic slugs slung by Skink guns. "We're going to have the element of surprise. It's been years since those slimies met any resistance."

"Yeah, now that we all have a death sentence, almost everyone no longer cares about tomorrow. It's all about living it up for today," Bref said.

"Maybe that's why I'm not scared," Willet said. The Nu-Man's blondish hair singled him out from the others. "Why delay the inevitable?"

"Don't do anything stupid and get us all killed," Garrad said, the Nu-Man had a habit of treating everyone like he was their mother.

"Oh, I'm going to get all *stupid* on those Skinkers." Willet closed his eyes and curled his fingers into a massive fist. "I wish I could rip each and every one of them apart with my bare hands for what they've done to us."

"Scout ship has landed," came over the Nu-Mans' helmet tel-coms and inside Tarik's armor.

"Time to move," Zax said and chambered a round in his blaster. "Put up a fight but don't get yourself killed. If we want to see the mission to the end, we need numbers."

"I'm with Tarik. Hit 'em hard and fast. Kill them all." Willet turned and led the group down the hallway leading to the main entrance.

Boots hitting floor echoed off the walls. The fifty-or-so civilian personnel who pioneered and solidified the project scurried to evac vehicles. They would be leaving for the final time. Their years of sacrifice and dedication to the cause transferred to the shoulders of the strike team.

"Scout team's on the ground. I count five of them," came over the radio. "Can't get a frequency to hear what they're saying, but their scanners have one of them pointing toward the concealed entrance."

That didn't take long, Tarik thought. Located in the Ozark Plateau, the rebel nest's access was camouflaged to be undetected from drone or satellite surveillance. Hand probing the area would discover it in no time.

"Forward unit, stay clear of the door," Zax said, the whole team's tel-com system connected.

*

Bix commanded the outside unit of four. Hidden in the terrain, he edged out of his cover to sight in his shoulder mounted compact railgun on the scout ship's chin. The ship's pilot sat in the cockpit, his hands busily at the controls. The railgun was good for one use. He wouldn't get a second chance.

The laser sights chirped when it focused on its target. Bix launched the missile.

The projectile flew with blinding speed and hit the ship, creating an artificial clap of thunder. Burning metal streaked like fireworks in all directions. Bix only took a half second to gloat, knowing knocking out the ship's communications was only the first step to winning this battle.

A Skink warrior reacted quickly to the attack, turning from the others and running toward Bix, who dropped out of sight once again.

A high pitched whistle cut through the air announcing a counter attack. The Skink's grenade detonated close enough that the percussion from the blast felt like someone had hit him in the head with a brick.

Two of the Nu-Mans gave away their positions as they relentlessly fired at the Skink. Slugs pelted his armor with one in five hits showing any signs of effectiveness.

By this time, another Skink had joined the fray, peppering the terrain with slugs, and launching more grenades.

The scout ship's heavy gun swung around and pointed at the entrance.

"Inside unit, entrance hot! Entrance hot!" Bix yelped over the tel-com.

The ship's gun hummed to life and spat out an ordinance that practically disintegrated the entrance door.

The earth vibrated underneath Bix. Anything in the direct line of fire was sure to be destroyed. He could only hope that none of his teammates had met an untimely fate.

The heavy gun swung toward the rebels' outside position. Gunfire from the Skinks had Bix hunkered down and considering taking the tunnel leading to the evac vehicles.

The fourth member of the outside unit sprang in abandon from his hiding hole. In full view of the Skinks, he quickly aimed and fired his compact railgun.

No sooner had the missile left the tube than Skinks' slugs pounded into his body. Jem, the youngest of the team, fell backward in the barrage. A grenade exploded within arm's reach above his head, shredding flesh, and burning hair.

Jem's death wasn't in vain. The railgun slammed its discharge into the ship's heavy gun. The missile hit with such impact that both Skink warriors firing into the hillside suddenly found themselves smashed to the ground. The pilot's blood streaked across the ship's windshield.

Bix and the two others shook off the impact enough to take advantage of Jem's sacrifice. The Nu-Mans fired on the two warriors before they had a chance to try and get up.

Only one moved, and one remained down. Bix saw a breach in the Skink's armor at the torso; a hole big enough for even his hand to fit in. "Skink pilot and warrior down." Four more alien menaces to go.

Another of the Skink warriors left the entrance and joined in a scorched earth assault on the outside rebels.

The Nu-Mans were severely outgunned. To resist any further would be suicide. Bix knew he was destined to die in the near future but didn't want to make this his day. "Outside unit, hit the tunnels and evacuate. Zax, it's up to your team now."

"See you at the rendezvous point," Zax called back.

"You damn well better! All of you!" Bix crawled back into the tunnel. The reverberations of battle faded as he fled to safety.

*

When Bix sounded the alarm warning of the imminent breach, the rebels peeled to either side of the hallway and braced themselves for the worst. The zero-energy propelled missile pulverized the entrance door and streaked down the hallway until it crashed into the limestone wall hiding the base. The whole sanctuary shook. Dust billowed back down the hallway creating a fog thick enough to where Tarik couldn't see his hand in front of his face. No matter, his HUD and his companions' tel-com helmets had sensors painting what was blocked from sight. Problem was, so did the Skinks.

Kinetic slugs proceeded before the Skink warriors. The Nu-Man team took defensive positions and let their blasters respond. The slugs flew so thick that the entrance leading to the outside looked like it was swarming with angry insects. The Skinks' armor had incredible firepower. Tarik's armor did too, but Skink slugs were designed to be ineffective to Skink designed armor. That way the aliens had no chance of getting taken out by friendly fire. Nu-Man scientists specially made Tarik's slugs, but it took several slugs even to begin to chip away at the alien armor. The thing Tarik had to fear the most were the Skinks' grenades. A direct impact was sure to do major damage, if not totally disabling him, and bringing death.

One of the rebels hugging the wall collapsed face first. It was Trant, poor guy. The Nu-Man had a wife and family.

The quarters were too tight for the vulnerable Nu-Mans to hold out for very long. None of them had been in an actual firefight before either. Training took place in the confines of the rebel base. Tarik's confidence induced by rage ebbed quickly.

He thought about storming the entrance but realized that would be the worst thing he could do. The Nu-Mans would have to stop returning fire, and the Skink warriors would outnumber him. Their slugs would bounce off his armor, but if he ate a grenade, it would all be over.

There was only one shoulder railgun with the inside team. Reder had it a few meters in front of Tarik. The Nu-Man stood on edge as if he were waiting for the right moment to spring into action. If they had more of the powerful weapons, they could have easily defeated the Skinks. No such luck, as the guns were modifications from a weapon housed on Skink cruisers. Only three had fallen into the hands of the rebels. Even if Reder did get off a shot, it was a sure suicide mission. That would only reduce the warriors by one, at best. If he missed, well, losing both Reder and the gun would be a tragic waste.

To get out of this alive was going to take quick action with fear shoved out to the side, and, a whole lot of luck. "Reder! Throw me the railgun," Tarik said.

Reder shot his gaze toward Tarik but made no move to comply.

"Do it now!" Tarik said; there wasn't any time for him to explain himself.

Zax was looking his way. Tarik knew that his friend must have been wondering why the most protected man on the team needed their deadliest weapon, but he was counting on it that Zax knew him well enough not to question his demand.

"Give him the gun," Zax said.

Reder bent to one knee and placed the railgun on the floor. A quick shove had it within Tarik's reach. He picked it up and ran from the hallway toward the nearest escape tunnel.

"Tarik, where the hell are you going?" Zax asked.

"Hold your position," Tarik said. The Skink armor was a fine piece of machinery, but running in the bulky suit took concentration. He bounded through an open escape door and ran down the tube until coming to the crossway. Instead of heading toward the evac vehicles, he ran the other way until he came to the exit on the mountainside near the entrance door.

Tarik heard the Skinks blasting away as he slowly pulled the concealed door open. He would have to use the terrain to hide his suit's signature from their sensors for as long as he could. The warriors were only thirty or so meters away. Mountain rock would shield his approach until he was almost right on top of them.

With swift determination, Tarik tried to push any doubt out of his mind. His plan was simple, and the element of surprise would be in his favor. Each step brought him closer until he was a stone's throw from the Skink warrior in the rear.

After two deep breaths, Tarik dashed straight for the aliens, covering the distance faster than he thought possible.

His armor's signature must have lit up their electronics because the remaining four Skinks simultaneously stopped firing toward the entrance and looked his way. Before they had time to react, Tarik dropped to one knee, awkwardly sighted in the railgun, and let the missile fly.

Firing the weapon while wearing the armor was something he hadn't practiced. Still, his aim was true. As he had planned, the projectile knocked a hole through his first target and his second before striking limestone. Two dead, two to go. That bit of luck he had wished for had come true.

The rock façade above the entrance door shook at the missile's impact and began to crash down in chunks, separating the Nu-Mans and the Skinks, and Tarik too.

The warriors wasted no time in unleashing slugs at Tarik. Even though his armor was impervious to damage, the pounding was enough to upset his balance, and he hit the ground.

Scrambling to get up, he set his grenade launcher ready to fire. The HUD picked the nearest target, and he shot the grenade the few meters toward it.

In a split second the Nu-Man designed weapon hit the unfortunate alien's armor, sounding a dull *thunk*. The plaz-epoxy fused the grenade into the transmetal shell.

Tarik flattened back on the ground by his own choice this time.

The grenade exploded, sending bits of transmetal flying, and pulsing a shockwave forceful enough to liquefy the alien's organs.

The last warrior was knocked to the ground but alert and agile enough to be back on his feet just in time to attack Tarik before he had a chance to make a move.

The Skink swung with a right hook and caught Tarik on the left side of his neck. The HUD inside his suit blinked momentarily but returned to its normal function. The Skink was trying to blind him. Tarik was at a severe disadvantage. He had never trained in a hand-to-hand battle with a Skink warrior. The alien knew how to go for the weak spots. No matter, he still had more grenades. But before he could set a new one to launch, the Skink sent a crushing blow to his left shoulder, right on the grenade's launch port. The HUD immediately registered equipment failure. The situation was not good.

With nothing to lose, Tarik unleashed a series of wild blows on the surprised alien. The Skink skillfully stepped back and parried each punch that minimized the impact. This slimer knew how to fight. Tarik was hoping decades of peace between the two races had softened their conquerors to some degree. The luck that brought him this far was gone. He was on his own.

On his own and feeling the onset of battle fatigue. Tarik now realized the warrior's game. The Skink was going to let Tarik wear himself down, and then probably run a safe distance away, just enough to launch a grenade and end the battle.

The Skink kept taking pokes at Tarik, trying to connect with the spot as he did earlier on Tarik's left side, between his shoulder and head. That had to be a weak spot in the armor's design.

Tarik knew at some point the alien would outsmart him and win. Taking the only chance he thought he might have, he faked a punch to the warrior's helmet. When the Skink's arms went up to block, Tarik grabbed him around the waist, lifted him up, and slammed him to the earth.

On top of the alien now, he grabbed the arms and held them to the ground, moving his shoulder gun in line with the left side of the alien's neck.

Point blank, he let the slugs fly directly at the target. Slugs striking transmetal made a horrendous noise. Dirt and rock flew into the air like a geyser, either from ricocheting off the armor, or just plain missing the alien and blasting into rock and dirt. He was too close to the warrior for his HUD to get the best aim.

The Skink struggled to break free of his grip. Tarik, despite the mechanical advantage of his armor, strained with every ounce of his human muscles to keep the alien from escaping.

The slugs kept pounding away, probably totaling in the hundreds by now. But Tarik knew it would take that many of the specially designed slugs to breach transmetal.

The shoulder gun pumped slugs well after the Skink went still. With ammo nearly depleted, Tarik shut down the gun and waited for the dust to settle.

The left side of the Skink's armor at the neck had deep gashes where the slugs had worn the transmetal away. Surprisingly, the hole breaching the suit was the size of a pebble. At least one slug, or a fragment of one, had found its way in to do the job.

Tarik rolled off the alien and relaxed his tightened muscles. It was over. They had won.

"Tarik?" It was Zax's voice.

The human looked over and saw his friend and the other Nu-Mans following his path from the escape tunnel. He lifted a hand and waved.

Seven members of his team stepped up. Zax came over and offered a hand.

Tarik reached out and took it. Though he wore transmetal gloves, his hand was still smaller than this gentle giant's.

"You did an amazing thing here," Zax said, and then pulled Tarik to his feet.

Looking at the carnage and taking a moment to reflect on the savagery of the last several minutes, Tarik thought so too. "Yeah, it's more of an amazing thing that I'm still alive."

"Are you hurt?" Zax asked.

"No. Tired, though, and a bit shaky," Tarik said.

"Everyone else is gone, and we need to get out of here too," Garrad said. "This place is going to be crawling with slimies soon."

"He's right," Zax said. "Pair up and evacuate. We'll meet in two days at the rendezvous point."

As the group headed toward the tunnel, Tarik looked back at the battle scene one last time. The fragmented transmetal armor of his first two victims, and the two others sprawled out on the ground, all in the shadow of the scout ship. He had just won an impossible battle. Breaking into a Skink facility and completing the mission dwarfed what he had just gone through.

Tarik had survived by not thinking of the consequences and just doing what he knew he needed to do. It was going to be a lot harder to get into that mindset next time.

CHAPTER 5

The Present

Cole headed for first-hour class on instinct alone. His mind blossomed with endless scenarios of Charlotte's future visit. He would have to have some snacks and sodas. What did she like? Cole could eat his weight in Cheetos; the fried kind, not the baked. But if he served Cheetos he'd get *cheetle*, that orange dust, all over his lips and fingertips. Plus, the cornmeal product had a nasty way of finding refuge between his teeth.

Then a strange thought dawned on him; *he was maturing*. Kids didn't worry about what kind of snacks they served to their friends; that was a parent's job. In his case, he wanted to be more sophisticated in order to impress a girl; a girl who usually hung around older boys. If he wanted to win Charlotte's hand, he was going to have to present himself as a man roughened by life experiences who could command any situation. Who could he model himself as?

Bond, James Bond. His dad was a big fan of the old secret agent movies. Cole had seen every one of the Sean Connery and Robert Moore flicks over five times. He liked the other actors in the 007 roles, but Connery and Moore had a unique polish. But who was he kidding? He was just a fourteen-year-old boy without even the street cred girls his age found attractive. Cole was a slightly above average kid who couldn't rap two sentences. For things to go right tonight, Cole was going to have to put in plenty of thought.

"Hey, young man."

Cole stopped and collected his bearings. His first-hour class was a couple of doors down. The halls were mostly empty, with class soon to begin. Daydreaming had greatly slowed his pace.

Mr. Buddy stood with his back to the wall. Both of his hands were in his front pants pockets, and he darted his gaze to either side.

"Uh, were you talking to me?" Cole asked.

"Yeah." Mr. Buddy leaned slightly forward. "Your name's Cole, right?"

"Yes, sir."

"Well, I hear that you kinda like some of the weirder things life has to offer. You know, UFOs, bigfoot, ghosts, and what all. Things that others think is all make-believe," Mr. Buddy said in a low, even tone. He turned his head to the left and raised an eyebrow.

"Sure. Uh, yes, things of the paranormal world." The situation seemed a bit strange. Mr. Buddy had never spoken to him before, and the man seemed like he was always underfoot. Heck, he couldn't remember ever seeing Mr. Buddy have a conversation with any kid at school.

"I got something you might be interested in." The janitor removed both hands from his pockets. One hand contained a checkered white and dark blue handkerchief. Holding the mystery before Cole, he carefully pulled the cloth open. "Lookie here."

The checkered pattern of the handkerchief obscured his focus on the object. With a little concentration, Cole saw it was a tooth, perhaps one from the back of the jaw. The tooth was slightly rectangular shaped. It was certainly a lot bigger than any tooth that came out of his mouth. He gazed up at Mr. Buddy. "Where's it from?"

Bending closer, Mr. Buddy said, "I found it. I found it deep, deep in the national forest." His mouth widened into a hint of a smile.

"So what do you think it is?"

With a nod of confidence, Mr. Buddy said, "Bigfoot."

Well, it was a large tooth. From what little Cole knew about teeth, it didn't look like a cow's or a horse's. He wasn't sure about bear's teeth, though, or even deer's. "How do you know it's from a bigfoot?"

Mr. Buddy's chest swole, and he raised an instructive finger. "Easy, by eliminating what it's not."

"What do you mean?"

"What lives in these woods? Squirrels, rabbits, deer, possums, coyotes, and bears. Nothing lives there with teeth like that."

"How do you know what bear teeth look like?"

"Kid, I spend a lot of time in the library. I'm tellin' ya, this here is a humanoid tooth. It's too big to be a man's. So, it has to be bigfoot's." Mr. Buddy accentuated the declaration with a snappy nod.

"Did you find any tracks by it?" Cole asked.

"No. Not there. But I've come across 'em before. Even made a plaster cast or two."

"Wow, really? I'd like to see those."

"That's what I thought. People kind of look at you cockeyed when you start talking about bigfoot and such in front of them. But I knew you was different. Different like me. How's about we do some searching on our own sometime? It'd be a hoot. We could get together this afternoon and look at my stuff. I gotta lot of books on the subject too. I don't live far, just over in Forest Heights. I'll drive you home afterward."

It was strange to see a man who mostly kept to himself this animated about anything other than his janitorial work. Maybe the old guy was just lonely. "Can't today. I got baseball practice and a science project to complete."

Dejection deflated the wind out of Mr. Buddy's cheeks. "I understand."

The hall was void of anyone else at this point. The bell was sure to ring any second. "Look, Mr. Buddy, I gotta go."

The janitor quickly folded the cloth back over the tooth. His lips tightened. "Okay, BUT, you've got to keep quiet about this. Don't tell anyone. You got that?"

The warning was stern but understandable. "No problem, Mr. Buddy. See ya!" Cole had made it only halfway to his room's door when the bell rang. He was tardy.

*

The door was closing just as Cole arrived. He put his foot between it and the door jam, bringing the door to an abrupt stop.

A beady eye maneuvered between the narrowing opening into the room.

"It's me, Mr. Ritzman," Cole said.

The eye blinked two times, and the door slowly opened. Ritzman remained fixated to the floor like his feet were buried in cement. Both the bad and good eye cast a lazy gaze. His lips might as well have been super-glued in non-expression.

"Sorry, I had some trouble getting my locker open. It's kind of rusty. Might need to spray some oil on it." The excuse was much less than truthful, but Cole didn't consider it a lie. Lying was something deceitful and something to be ashamed of. Telling a fib or a white lie was a necessary tool interjected during the day to help situations move smoothly along. There was no way Mr. Ritzman wanted to hear the dirty details of his dilemma with planning the date tonight with Charlotte or the encounter he had with Mr. Buddy. No, he made an excuse for Mr. Ritzman's benefit. An apology coupled with an act of God. Mr. Ritzman's conscience was free from demanding disciplinary actions.

Behind Mr. Ritzman, a figure meandered from the back of the room and then sat at his desk. It was Dean Setters.

"Mr. Rainwater, first-hour class starts promptly at eight a.m. Central Standard Time at Dent County High. I assure you the bell is set to ring at the correct designated moment. Every Monday I log onto the National Institute of Standards and Technology in Boulder, Colorado. The atomic clock there measures cycles of the radiation produced by the transition between two levels of ytterbium atoms. I reset the school clock and synchronize the bell, and the school is allowed to operate in an orderly fashion," Mr. Ritzman said.

"That's interesting, Mr. Ritzman. Don't worry. It won't happen again." Really, what was the man's point? He was late by a few seconds. Get over it.

"Very well, please come in."

The door opened, and Cole fast stepped in. A few heads looked in his direction. Kirk Ford gave him an upraised thumb. Most of the other kids were finding other ways to distract themselves. Typical first-hour.

The mechanical click of the latch hitting the door strike preceded the dull thud of the door shutting.

"Not so fast, Mr. Rainwater," Ritzman said.

Cole didn't like being called Mr. Rainwater. His dad was Mr. Rainwater, not him. He stopped and turned his head, waiting for further instruction.

"Since you're already at the front of the room, perhaps you could be so gracious and work yesterday's exercises on the board for us," Ritzman said.

Ritzman was surely a fan of the Old Testament; more *eye for an eye* than a forgive *seventy times seven* practitioner. At least Cole didn't get detention. The coach would have added laps at baseball practice too. Still, one thing Cole didn't like was standing before a crowd. He wasn't sure why, but when he became the center of attention, it was like the thoughts in his head exploded in all directions like fireworks. One time, in the second grade, he froze up so badly during show-and-tell that his teacher had to physically lift him from the front of the room and deposited him at his desk. Since then he'd tried to develop distractions that would help him keep focused. Especially on the baseball mound. He was a pitcher, after all. He would keep his gaze on the ground or on the batter, and never look at the crowd. Chewing gum helped, and he would always play a song in his mind—to drown out all the noise and chatter from crowds and the opposing team.

"Mr. Rainwater?"

Cole shook off the moment and slid the book sack off his shoulder. Retrieving his notebook, he approached the board. At least now he couldn't see the students watching him. This wasn't so bad. He grabbed a blue marker and went to work on the whiteboard.

As he focused writing the equation in a fairly straight line and in equal size characters, Ritzman sat down behind his desk.

Someone in the class giggled.

Cole froze. What were they laughing at? Did he make a mistake?

Suppressed laughter spilled out again. It unmistakably came from Dean Setters.

"Mr. Setters? What's so amusing?" Ritzman asked.

Cole turned and saw his friend.

Dean had his face toward his desktop, his eyes closed, and his lips tightly mashed together. His shoulders jiggled up and down. "Nothing," he managed to squeak out.

"It certainly doesn't *look* like nothing. Whatever it is that has you in such a state, please share it with the class," Ritzman said.

"It's just a joke," Dean said.

"I insist," Ritzman said.

The invitation calmed Dean enough to regain composure. "Okay, what did the mermaid math teacher wear to school?" He paused and looked around. No one gave it a shot, so he said, "An algae-bra!"

Dean's laughter suppressed the random groan or two.

"Do you feel better now, Mr. Setters? Is your mind free to receive elements of instruction?" Ritzman asked.

Dean gave a little wave and nodded, returning his gaze to his desktop.

Cole went back to writing on the board. Somehow he didn't think it was the joke that had Dean so unsettled. Dean was a strange but predictable kid. He certainly would benefit with more discipline in his life and wondered what would happen if he'd join the military along with Kirk.

Fumbling his marker, it fell from his fingers and landed on the floor. As Cole stepped over to retrieve it, he accidentally kicked it over by Mr. Ritzman's desk.

Some of the kids laughed, and Cole froze for a moment on center stage with the spotlight shining brightly on him. His thoughts scattered.

As Mr. Ritzman sat in his chair, the marker was within his reach. Taking his left hand from his jacket, he leaned over and picked up the marker, raising it for Cole to take.

The long sleeve of Ritzman's shirt went halfway up his hand, with the maker snug in his grip.

Cole reached out and took the marker, and when Ritzman released it, he saw the fingers on his teacher's left hand for the first time. The index, middle, and ring finger were fused together with some sort of membrane between them.

The hand went back into Ritzman's pocket.

Cole stood with his arm still outreached and marker in hand. His gaze darted to Mr. Ritzman's. Did Ritzman know he saw the deformity? *Why did he look Ritzman in the eye?* He should have just taken the marker and then gone back to work! But no, he gave himself away, or did he?

"Thank you," Cole said softly, still unable to tear his gaze away from Ritzman's.

The teacher's bad left eye then went into action. With owl-like movement, the left iris drifted over to the corner of his eye socket, while the right iris stayed stationary. It was creepy as all get-out.

Brrraaappappapp!

The undeniable thunder of a trouser cough, no doubt unleashed from the bowels of a giant gorged on two bushels of sauerkraut, erupted from the back of the room.

All gazes shifted from the awkward exchange in front to an area with bookshelves and cabinets.

Amongst the multitude of laughter, Dean Setters brayed like a mule.

"Who did that?" Ritzman was on his feet and leaning over the desk.

"It came from the back of the room," someone said.

"Maybe it came over the intercom," someone else said.

The intercom speaker was above Cole's head, so that couldn't have been it.

Mr. Ritzman narrowed his eyes Dean's way. "Mr. Setters?" It was obvious the way he called Dean's name in question that he had already deduced the culprit.

Dean's face shined brighter than Rudolph's nose ever hoped. "What? Why are you picking on me? I'm sitting right here, not in the back of the room."

"Yes, but I can read you easier than a poker player with two-faced playing cards. Anytime there are shenanigans about, you're smack dab in the middle of it. You're responsible for this in some way," Ritzman said.

After what Dean had said earlier about remote pooting, Mr. Ritzman might be on to something, Cole thought.

"It must be a ghost or maybe a spider," Dean said.

"Ghosts do not exists, and the discharged certainly did not originate from a spider," Ritzman said.

"Oh yes, ghosts are real!" Dean said and pointed at Cole. "Cole, go ahead, you know all about ghosts. If ghosts can make noises and talk and stuff, they can fart too, right?"

"I..." Cole sighed deeply and looked about, all gazes were on him, even Ritzman's. Center stage once again. The day had not been going to plan. First Charlotte and his date, and then Brennon Davis and his threat. Mr. Buddy added to the oddities and his tardiness. Now Dean was throwing him under the bus. How did he manage to dig a hole this deep this early in the day?

*

Though a pleasant breeze blew across the practice field, the bright sun hung in the afternoon sky reminding everyone the scorching summer was soon to come. The junior varsity baseball team was dressed and ready to practice, starting with stretching exercises.

Someone really must have been harassing old man Douglas. Coach Jones had gathered the whole team before they hit the field and warned them to stay away from the old codger's place. Apparently, Douglas had threatened to shoot anyone he caught vandalizing his farm. Cole wondered if they suspected someone on the baseball team. He could see a blowhard like Brennon, and a couple of his older buddies, causing trouble like that. Still, Douglas might be hiding that they were bigfoot prints.

Old man Douglas must have done something really bad in his past for everyone to be so afraid of him. His dad claimed he didn't know why the recluse had spent time in jail, but Cole always suspected that he just didn't want to tell him the sordid details. As far as he could remember, he'd seen Douglas on three occasions. Once at the hardware store when Cole was helping his dad buy fence material, and twice at the county fair, two years in a row. The last two years, as a matter of fact. He never saw Douglas ride any rides or play any games at the fair.

The man mostly meandered around, continually eating the finest cuisine the carnival had to offer. He'd seen him pulling pink cotton candy wrapped tightly around its paper bone. Watched him fold a funnel cake in half and eat mouthfuls at a time; getting powdered sugar all over his nose and beard. He left a trail of peanut shells at one point that even the laziest hunting dog could have followed. Cole did stand next to him one time in the line to buy a fried Snickers bar.

The old man was fairly tall; easily over six feet. He looked like he might have been muscular in his younger days. But his chest looked like it had migrated to his gut. Douglas had worn overalls the times Cole had seen him. His graying beard was thicker than the hair on his head and practically hid his lips. He looked nasty.

The old man caught Cole looking at him while they were in line. Douglas didn't acknowledge him directly. He just stared back with a plastic Santa Claus smile bloating his cheeks like he was waiting for Cole to ask what he wanted for Christmas. The line moved, and Cole made it a point not to look at him again. There was something creepy about the man, but Cole figured that was something that prison had done to him.

With his left arm reaching down his back and head bent over to the side, Cole continued to stretch. His guardian angel must have been looking out for him earlier. Before he attempted to talk his way from the front of the room during first-hour, the fire alarm went off. He could tell from Mr. Ritzman's expression that it wasn't a drill. Everyone filed out in a single line and headed to the nearest door leading outside. It turned out that the alarm had malfunctioned, with only a few minutes to spare before next class after the repair.

Later that day when Dean thought Mr. Ritzman was at lunch, he snuck back into the empty classroom and retrieved his phone. He had managed to hide it in the back in one of the cabinets before class started. Intrigued by the concept of remote pooting, he downloaded a fart app on his phone and set a timer for it to go off. Mr. Ritzman was right there waiting for Dean when he tried to make his escape. The self-proclaimed comedian would be entertaining the detention class after school every day of that week.

Cole had been one of the first dressed and on the field. Brennon Davis, as usual, was one of the last to leave the locker room. A time or two Cole felt like Superman had his heat vision on and burned the back of his head. He turned only to discover that it was Brennon giving him the evil eye. There was no way Cole could get through practice without the jilted boyfriend extracting revenge.

*

Coach Jones led practice as if just going through the motions without any real fire coming out to inspire his team. It was early in the season and still a couple of weeks away from having their first meaningful game. The kid that went missing from Camden County, Raymond Jones, was his nephew. Coach Jones wasn't always this lackluster, but Cole wondered if the family situation sometimes had Coach's mind elsewhere.

There were nine pitchers on the team. Cole was one of five in the 9th grade on the junior varsity team. If you were in the 10th grade and good enough, you could be elevated to the varsity team.

Cole considered himself to be in the middle of the pack in his age group. He had little aspirations to play varsity next year. It really didn't matter that much. All he wanted to do was at least make the team in his junior or senior year, when competition and a limited roster forced many junior varsity players from playing after the 10th grade. Sure, his fantasy was to play well enough to earn a scholarship to a major university. But first and foremost, he wanted a letterman jacket.

Brennon Davis played in the outfield. Today's practice kept him far enough away that Cole had pretty much forgotten the threat and concentrated on working his throwing mechanics. *Don't throw the ball with your arm! Power position. Turn, pull, snap. Wrist action.* Throwing footwork was just as important. *You throw the ball with your feet. Shuffle. Shuffle, pull, snap. Feet and wrist.*

So far this season Coach Jones had never singled out Cole to comment on his abilities or his progression. Cole knew he was three times better than when practice started that year. If a 9th grader was going to catch his coach's eye, then he knew he'd have to do something special.

Today's session neared its end. The coach had the team's designated batter, Trey Edmunds, up at the plate and each pitcher had one chance to strike him out before heading back to the locker room. The rest of the team had finished their exercises and were heading off the field. Brennon Davis lagged behind, with a curious interest in what was happening at home plate.

Great. It looked like Brennon wasn't going to let today's events slide past. Okay, Cole was just going to have to suck it up and not let that guy distract him. The coach was right there to prevent anything from getting out of hand.

Pitchers went up and down fairly quickly. Trey connected with balls no later than the third pitch so far. One hit was a sure home run if it had been in a game. Cole was second to last to take a turn and trotted over to the mound as soon as the previous pitcher vacated.

He took the ball from the coach's toss and worked it into his glove. Turning to face the batter, he set his feet apart to prepare for the delivery.

"Hey, coach!" Brennon called out.

"What?" Jones yelled back.

"Why don't you give Trey a break and let me hit?" Brennon said.

Trey looked with a blank expression over at Brennon.

"Come on. I need the practice," Brennon said.

"Okay. Trey, hit the shower," Coach Jones said.

Double fudge, Cole thought. That jerk had managed to weasel his way in.

Brennon's smirk was so wide it deformed the left side of his cheek. He took the bat from Trey and waved it around a few times.

Letting out a big sigh, Cole resolved himself to the situation and got ready to pitch.

Stepping up to the plate, the doofus brought the bat to his shoulder and went through a few slow motion swings.

Cole was center stage again, in a different way. This was a test of his manhood, but he would need some type of miracle to get one past Brennon Davis. Was his guardian angel still around? *Oh, Lord above.*

Help me strike this guy out. Give me the strength I need to win. Cole wasn't too proud to submit to a higher power. But he had to consciously fight the urge to pray to an *eight-pound-eleven-ounce blonde hair blue-eyed infant baby Jesus* ever since he had watched *The Legend of Ricky Bobby.*

It was time. *Throw the ball with your arm and feet. Turn and shuffle, pull, snap. Feet and wrist.*

The ball left Cole's hand screaming toward home plate. The fast and furious journey had it on a path straight and true.

Brennon eyed the missile, calculating his options in the nanoseconds between the batter-pitcher showdown.

Alas, the baseball dipped and crashed into the ground two feet in front of the plate and bounced into the catcher's glove. The bat never left Brennon's shoulder.

"Calm down, kid," Coach Jones said. "Breathe, remember to breathe."

Brennon snickered as he prepared for the next ball. He was in Cole's head, and he knew it.

Cole tried to pretend he was someone else, in a strange town, pitching to an unknown opponent. He needed to blank out any distractions and concentrate on the mechanics of the game.

The second ball left his hand, in a blur, the cocked bat on Brennon's shoulder released and cut through the air in front of him. The speeding ball smacked the catcher's mitt unscathed.

Brennon's bat had tasted no ball. His lips and nose came together like he had sour fruit on his tongue.

"Good one," Coach Jones said.

Something inside Cole's chest swole. Hope was alive, but there were two strikes to go. He went into his windup and delivered the pitch.

Brennon awkwardly swung and barely caught a piece of the ball. Cole could tell the boy had abandoned the batting mechanics and now played with raw emotions. That was strike two. Now, Cole was inside of Brennon's head.

Cole looked over at Coach Jones and nodded. Whatever swelled inside his chest earlier, just grew again. With the eye of an eagle and the fortitude of a stalking tiger, he gazed down his nose at the challenger at home plate. The ball felt smaller in his hand. At this moment, baseball seemed like a children's game. A game that he had mastered as evident by the fear in his opponent's eyes.

It was time. Cole went through the windup and let the ball sail.

The bat catapulted forth, but this was no contest between an unstoppable force meeting with an immovable object. The baseball's trajectory reversed faster than Cole could blink. It soared back through the air directly at him. His self-preservation sensors took automatic control of his body. In the last instant, he slung himself backward and to the side, twisting to avoid the rocket as it flew just past his nose.

Cole landed on his butt and then his back hit the ground. The open heavens looked down upon him while Brennon Davis hysterically laughed. Cole had not found favor in the Lord's eye. Apparently, there was a deeper lesson to be learned.

Coach Jones wandered into his field of vision, looking like a giant towering above him. "Feet and wrist, Rainwater. Feet and wrist."

It was going to be a long baseball season.

CHAPTER 6

The Future

The seven Nu-Mans trotted down the escape tube toward the two-passenger jumpships, with Tarik bringing up the rear. So far they had suffered only two casualties, Jem, and Trant. The outside team led by Bix had already escaped, following the scientists and civilians committed to the project. The challenge now was for everyone to make it to a safe-house and mingle back into society, free from Skink interrogation. The strike team would resupply and meet in a couple of days. The stopwatch had started counting backward, and there was no way to stop it from reaching zero.

"Pair off and get the hell out of here. The Skinks' satellites have been watching everything that's gone down," Zax said, coming to a stop and standing to the side while everyone else flew past to the awaiting jumpships.

Tarik slowed and stopped by his leader.

Zax waited for his fellow Nu-Mans to board the jumpships. The escape hatches were already open in the above granite leading to blue sky. They would be lucky if the Skinks hadn't already targeted the area with missiles and getting a few down the throat before they could leave.

"We need to hurry," Tarik said.

"And we will. Go ahead and get aboard our ship, and I'll meet you there."

Tarik didn't delay. This whole mission rested ultimately on his shoulders. He had to live in order to give the mission a chance. Yes, his life was more important than any of the Nu-Mans, but that was a selfish way to think. Because if the strike team wasn't intact to some degree, then they could never breach the Skink facility. Zax would have the same sense of loyalty to each of his fellow Nu-Mans as he did to Tarik. That's why Tarik had such a deep fondness of the Nu-Man.

The jumpships left one by one out of the four escape hatches. Before the fourth ship left, Zax was sitting next to Tarik and strapping in. Fortunately, the jumpships were designed to carry Skinks dressed in their armor.

"You ready?" Tarik asked.

"Yeah, but you better let me drive. I don't trust you with those metal gloves on."

Good point, Tarik thought. He had never trained piloting a jumpship while wearing his transmetal armor.

The zero-energy engine kicked in smoothly, lifting the ship up and over until the clear path allowed it to shoot into the air and bank sharply for its designation point.

A few seconds later, a large clap of thunder from behind had the jumpship riding shockwaves. The HUD showed a billowing, dark cloud rising from above the rebel's nest. Gone, everything from his old way of life vanished in a blast of terrific heat normally felt on the surface of the sun.

"That was close," Tarik said.

"Too close, and we're not out of the woods yet. They'll be able to track us until we touchdown. We'll take it to the edge of the city and set down. After that, we'll have to make it to the safe-house on foot."

"Piece of cake. Sure, we'll just *blend in*," Tarik said, the sarcasm thick enough to be cut with a knife.

*

The jumpship took a jagged route, keeping as close to the ground as possible. The destination, Kansas City, Missouri, was only four hundred kilometers away. It was purely coincidental that the rebel nest and the Skink time jumping facility were located so close together. The nest site had been chosen because of its remoteness from large populated areas, and that had been years ago; long before any word of a time project. The Skinks had taken over a nuclear weapons plant as much of the necessary radioactive shielding was already in place.

"Is it really necessary to keep slinging us around like this?" Tarik asked. "I don't care how low you fly. I bet the Skinks are tracking us. If you took a direct route, we could have been there in thirty minutes."

"They may be tracking us but they don't know where we're going to land. A straight route will have them right on top of us when we set down. At least this way they can't react until we do. It buys us a few precious minutes."

The lavish green terrain had remained mostly unchanged in this area since the Skink invasion. Civilization sparsely populated the towering forests below.

Tarik had learned how to fly a jumpship at the base, but he had never been on a wild ride like this. The virtual simulator had him conditioned to some extent to handle the motion swings affecting his balance. But he hadn't felt the abrupt g-force pulls at his body as Zax pushed the aircraft to its limits. "I think I'm going to throw up."

Zax snickered. "You better hope not with your armor on. That would be nasty."

"There's not enough room in here for me to open the helmet. I'll just have to keep it down."

"We're not far, see? The industrial park outlines the city in this part of town." Zax piloted the ship to the right, using the Missouri River as a path.

The trees in the distance gave way to concrete and steel giants. The race was just about to begin.

*

Zax set the jumpship down not far from the river's edge. A swath of trees separated the muddy waters from an industrial warehouse some one hundred and fifty meters away. The canopy of the small craft opened, and Tarik and Zax wasted no time bailing off the side onto the soft ground.

With the Nu-Man in the lead with his blaster held tightly to his chest, Tarik matched step for step, falling slightly behind as his gait wasn't quite as long. His HUD had the ability to scan an area up to sixty meters in all directions. Of course, solid objects did present problems. The trees they now weaved around filtered some of the information. Luckily, there was no electronic surveillance active and no sign of Skink or Nu-Man life around.

The woods gave way to flat land that led to a street named River Road. The two rebels hurried across the pavement, charging toward a fence that surrounded heavy equipment.

"Are you thinking what I'm thinking?" Tarik asked between quick breaths.

"If you're thinking about taking the bulldozer, no."

"As if. That white truck over there. Let's take it."

"Works for me," Zax said and pulled away as he sped on.

The big Nu-Man had the driver's side door open and was examining the dash as Tarik stepped up. "Has the ignition been disabled?"

The engine purred to life with a soft hum. "No. I had a feeling it wouldn't be. There aren't many kids around nowadays to go on joy rides. No other reason to disable the ignition."

Tarik searched his HUD. He was afraid he had let his guard down and suddenly felt exposed. *Nothing.* "I'm having second thoughts. It's going to look strange if others see a Nu-Man escorting a Skink warrior in a work truck."

"True," Zax said and hesitated. "Here, get in the back and lay low. No one from street level will be able to see you back there."

"Well, that's the only choice we have. Drop the gate."

Zax pushed a button on the dash and the tailgate lowered. The bed of the truck sank as he moved his transmetal covered body onto it, finally coming to rest on his back. "Let's go."

The door closed, the gate lifted, and soon the truck started a slow trek down a bumpy road. Clouds billowed in the open sky as Tarik forced his body to release the built up tension and relax.

It wasn't long before the industrial buildings gave way to residential and commercial structures. He could see them lined on both sides of the street and his HUD outlined the people, both Skinks and Nu-Mans, as they carried on through an ordinary day.

Tarik wished he could shed his armor and watch from the back of the truck with his own eyes rather than view life through electronic lenses. Most of his life's experiences had been filtered through a screen before reaching his eyes. Even the air he breathed right now was tainted by technology. What would the wind feel like blowing through his hair while he rode in the back of a truck? The different sights, the enormous variety of people. The different smells wafting from various restaurants. Tarik had never even been face to face with a Skink outside of his recent battle. What did their skin feel like? Was there any way that he could convince them to save the Nu-Mans? Perhaps he could appeal to them in such a way that they would continue the Nu-Mans' endeavor to recreate the human race. It just seemed so wrong for a species to invade from another planet and take everything for themselves and leave nothing to Mother Earth's firstborn.

The HUD issued an alert. A security cruiser was in the air a few blocks over and heading their way. "Zax, we got trouble. Overhead cruiser will be on top of us in no time. Registering a Skink warrior in the back of a truck driven by a Nu-Man is going to have them up our butts."

"My butt isn't big enough for that," Zax said over his tel-com. "I'm going to have to park this thing...wait...there's an alley between those buildings, where they keep the dumpsters. We'll go there."

The truck slowed to a stop and then turned. The sunlight faded quickly as the truck rolled down the alley. When the truck stopped again, Zax said, "Let's go."

The tailgate lowered, and Tarik shimmied out the back.

Zax had his blaster at the ready and searched for the next move.

The cruiser was sure to be able to see the signature of Tarik's armor, but that wasn't necessarily enough of a reason for them to investigate. Skinks dressed in transmetal armor maintained a loose presence in urban settings to maintain structured order. Nu-Mans had always been treated as free, but their relationship with the Skinks was not much different than that of master and slave. The aliens had molded the Nu-Man society into necessary subservience. With god-like technology mystifying the transitional human race, the Nu-Mans reached out to the Skinks as saviors upon the invasion of the planet. Willing slaves ready to receive consolation from strict but respectful masters. Of course, that was all a hundred years before the Skinks revealed that it was they who had introduced the virus on Earth before their appearance, which progressed humans in an artificial evolutionary step as the sasquatch-human hybrid.

Tarik suspected the recombinant DNA manipulation had quenched some of the independent fire humans possessed. He was often scolded by his teachers for his anarchy against the system. Nu-Mans, such as Zax and Bix, and the rest of the strike team, with a rebellious nature, were an anomaly. Skinks had never feared of a massive Nu-Man uprising. Rebel nests were rare. Insurgencies historically ended quickly.

"I better get out of sight, just in case," Tarik said. There were four doors down the alley for them to choose. "Let's take that one, over there." He pointed to the one at the end.

Trotting over, Tarik motioned Zax to the side away from the door. The armored glove latched onto the handle and a firm, steady pull had the deadbolt bend against the strike plate until the door frame spit concrete, releasing the lock's bite.

The dimly lit room housed components for power distribution throughout the building. Multicolored light flowed along translucent cables snaking up the wall. They were safe for the moment.

"How long do you think it'll take us to get to the safe-house?" Tarik asked.

"Ten blocks over to the northwest will put us on the edge of town. If we make it that far we shouldn't have any problem passing through the old-life to our hiding place."

Tarik had seen images of the abandoned buildings of ancient human dwellings. Many of the structures had beautiful character, with large windows, and towering pillars of opulent design. Other houses were more humble, rather box-like, in fact. After the human's genetic transformation into the Nu-Mans, the houses of old would no longer afford comfort. The Skinks sponsored massive building projects to accommodate the larger Nu-Mans. Most of the old neighborhoods of man had been leveled or simply left to be demolished by the hands of time. Remnants of human civilization were commonly referred to as *the old-life*.

Tarik's armor operated slightly above ninety percent power. The transmetal had molecule realignment properties capable of mending minor damage to the suit. That feature required a lot of energy, more than what his individual unit could supply. "It might be better if we wait until nightfall," Tarik said. His gaze drifted to inputs on a rectangular junction box near a wall, and he pointed. "I could plug in over there and shine the armor up a bit."

"I don't think we should delay. We still have some element of surprise in our favor. I'm sure by now the Skinks have found the jumpship by the river. They'll be fanning out from there trying to find us. I think we should keep moving."

"You're going to stand out a little. You can't go sightseeing wearing a tel-com helmet and dressed in body armor. What are you going to do with that blaster? You've already confessed your butt's not robust enough to handle visitors," Tarik said.

The big Nu-Man turned his gaze to the floor and slowly shook his head. "As much as I hate doing this...." He set his blaster down and worked off his helmet. Next, he unbuckled the protective torso and groin armor.

Zax stood wearing a common tunic. He adjusted the hem of the purple garment down his thighs and brushed out the wrinkles. The tunic wrapped from his waist up over his left breast, the right remained exposed. He left the small backpack in place and adjusted the straps near the chest. "Not too out of the ordinary, huh?"

"I guess not. Your boots might stand out a bit. They're kind of clunky for walking the streets of Kansas City."

"You're going to have to chance it in the suit. Can you imagine the reaction if a human appeared in public?" Zax reached over and unstrapped the backpack, retrieving a black cloth. "Your armor's scuffed up enough to draw some attention. Let me see if I can polish a little shine back into it."

Tarik held out his arms and accommodated his buddy as he worked the cloth over transmetal.

After a few minutes, Zax stepped back and admired his efforts. "That looks a lot better. There're still pits in the suit but shouldn't be too noticeable. You ready to do this?"

"Yeah. Just walk in front of me. I'll follow closely. Try to stay in shadows and use vehicles as camouflage when we have to cross streets."

Zax nodded and walked over to a door on the other side of the room. He turned his gaze over to his blaster and armor, and sighed. He sprung the latch on the door. "Here we go."

*

With the Nu-Man in the lead, Tarik placed his left hand on his friend's back and maintained a close and steady distance. This street led to an intersection where they would veer north. Vehicles sporadically parked to either side while a few lumbered up and down to their destination. Modern passenger vehicles were all of the same design, varying only in size to accommodate capacity. There were even two passenger models, though much fewer in number. Levitation rail systems ferried the masses around large cities and to main civilization hubs across the US. Tarik tried to imagine what the street would look like with the sheet metal creations of man from the late 1900s cruising around. When he was younger, he spent hours researching the *hot rods* from the '50s and '60s. Their bulky but aggressive style sparked a grand desire of lust. Mechanized chariots gleaming in wild colors like Go Mango, Top Banna, and Plum Crazy. What would it be like to race a '64 Pontiac GTO and a '68 Plymouth Road Runner Hemi? What did it feel like to mash the acceleration and smell *burning rubber* when shooting out of the hole, hearing the roar of four hundred horses, and the thrill of acceleration down your spine? Often Tarik wondered if memories were genetically transferred, because when reading mankind's history, certain aspects felt oddly familiar.

He wasn't sure what the buildings towering around him housed; perhaps they were apartments? He would love to have the freedom to explore each of them. The viewscreen still filtered what his eyes saw, but this short walk stoked a feeling of *presence-of-being* unlike he'd ever felt before. The unusual external input made him feel a little light-headed. Now was not the time to let his guard down.

A Nu-Man turned the corner just before the two rebels reached the intersection. Zax kept his pace steady, and Tarik didn't waver. When the Nu-Man passed, he gave no indication he suspected anything was out of the ordinary.

Activity increased on the main street. Tarik's HUD sorted out the different objects and reported back. It appeared to be an ordinary day, unaffected by their presence.

A small number of civilian Skinks mingled among the Nu-Mans. This was a first for Tarik. He looked over in the direction of a male Skink crossing from the other side of the street. The alien's head was uncovered, with slick looking green-grayish skin layering a rounded skull. Bone thickened above the eyes, which were oval in shape and about twice the size of Tarik's. A verticle thin oval pupil cut the middle of his golden iris.The slightly raised nasal bone jutted between the eye sockets and ended near his upper lip. Whereas human and Nu-Man faces were more square in shape, the Skink's jaw was triangular shaped, becoming point-like at the chin. The alien was as tall as a Nu-Man but with an obvious lower body mass. Still, his tight muscles bulged underneath his clingy black and silver coverall.

The alien walked right by Tarik's heels as he reached the sidewalk and didn't seem to suspect anything out of the ordinary. Tarik could have turned around and touched him, but the outworlder might as well have been a million miles away. If the mission were successful, he would never have the opportunity to feel Skink and human flesh press together.

So far the plan was working. If the two played it cool enough, they could be on the outskirts of old-life within an hour.

The trek down the sidewalk brought them past a row of eateries. Some of the establishments had tables out front and patrons enjoying drinks and meals in the open air. A wonderful smell of charring meat carried up Tarik's nose and bathed his salivary glands, instantly reminding him he hadn't eaten for nearly twenty-four hours. He noticed Zax's head turn and his gaze linger as they walked by.

Restaurant patrons passed plates filled with leafy vegetables and chunky tubers, poultry, beef, lamb, noodles, and fat and flatbreads. Warm smells intermingled with aromatic scents and savory delights. Tarik had never been around food prepared in such a way. Institutional eating had one purpose: to fill the gut. This food was cooked for the patron to enjoy the experience of eating; even the presentation made the food more appealing.

Still, the Nu-Mans who sat at the tables showed only moderate interest. Perhaps they were jaded to dining experiences such as these. Perhaps they realized they were only occupying their time until dying and leaving the Earth behind, with no prodigy to carry on.

Tarik was glad to get past the more active part of town, with only a couple of blocks to go before reaching the old-life neighborhood. He thought he could make out the ruining houses in the distance.

A civilian Skink approached with a bag over each shoulder and in an obvious hurry. His gaze was glued to the sidewalk, and Zax politely moved over a couple of steps to give the alien ample access. Right as the Skink reached Zax, his gaze came up and so did his upper lip. He didn't break stride but looked over at Tarik next, with a discerning eye.

They were so close. They didn't need any unwanted attention now. Tarik watched his HUD. The alien stopped and turned around.

"I need you to identify yourself."

Skinks were fluent in English, as well as any other of Earth's languages. But they usually spoke in their common language to each other. Tarik's circuits were custom designed to translate both incoming and outgoing communications.

Tarik stopped and turned. *"No, you don't."* Skinks weren't known for being humble, even with each other. Tarik wore the armor of a Skink warrior and didn't need to answer to a civilian.

"Your armor. It is damaged. What happened to it?"

"Training exercise. Now go away, the Nu-Man and I have work to do."

"What kind of work?"

The Skink no doubt had heard a report, and the situation was out of the ordinary enough that he wasn't going to just let it go. Skink apparel had voice-activated communicators built in. Tarik and Zax could be outed in an instant.

Zax had turned. Tarik raised a hand to him and slowly walked toward the Skink.

"It is nothing really." He spread his hands slightly before him. *"The fact is, we have had a long morning. I have not had time to recharge my armor. Here, let me send you my identification."* Tarik stopped inside a meter from the alien.

Seemingly satisfied, the Skink relaxed his shoulders.

In one swift motion, Tarik clamped his transmetal gloves around the alien's throat.

The Skink's eyes ballooned to what looked like a half size larger. As strong as his neck muscles might have been, they were no match for the armor. The breath trapped in his throat would never escape. As his throat further crushed, his mouth opened wider. In reality, the death had only taken an instant.

Tarik hugged the body before it fell to the ground and pulled it over by the building façade over to the next joining street. He was fully aware of his HUD sending information, and for the moment, there were no prying eyes to give them away.

Zax danced from side to side, trying to keep his body between the street and Tarik's unseemly deed. The two found steps on the side of a building that led to an underground entrance and dragged the dead Skink down.

"I'm going to leave him here. I don't think he sent out a beacon. I didn't pick up anything on my HUD, but my technology isn't up to date, well, who knows? Let's just leave," Tarik said.

Zax did a one-eighty up and down the street and nodded. "Let's go."

CHAPTER 7

The Present

Cole waited outside near the mulberry tree for his father to pick him up after baseball practice. The earlier events had left him with a mixed bag of emotions. On the one hand, he had thrown a few pretty good pitches against one of the best hitters on the team. On the other hand, if he didn't increase his speed or learn how to catch the edges of the plate better, he was going to be serving up tee drill balls for the batter to knock out of the park. At least most of the team had already left the field when he threw himself to the ground to avoid getting hit by the ball.

A horn beeped a couple of times behind him. He turned and saw his dad's Ford truck. Picking up his book sack, he swung it over his shoulder and opened the truck door.

"Not so fast," Mark said.

"What?"

"Brush your butt off before you get in. There's dirt all over it."

The book sack went on the floorboard, and Cole commenced slapping at his backside until the clouds of dust subsided. "I think I'm good now." He hopped into the truck and shut the door firmly.

Mark pulled out of the driveway and onto the road. "Why didn't you change after practice?"

"Uh, I didn't want you to wait on me. I want you to stop by the store, and I have a science project I have to do tonight before it gets dark. So, time's kinda short."

"Oh, well, sorry I'm a little late picking you up. I had a job at work that took longer than I thought. What do you need from the store? Something for the science project?"

An unusual grin grew across Cole's face. "In a way."

Mark turned a raised eyebrow over at Cole. "What's that smile for? What's going on that you're not telling me?"

"Nothing, really. It's just the International Space Station is going to be flying over the house tonight, and I'm going to video it and track it on my laptop."

After a few seconds, Mark said, "And?"

"Uh, and Charlotte Meadows is coming over to watch it with me. We have to do our science projects in pairs."

"Oh, I see," Mark said. "Charlotte Meadows…I don't think I've heard you mention her name before."

"Well, she barely even knew I existed, I think, until today."

"What happened today for her to notice you?"

"Nothing much. I just got up enough nerve to ask her to come over and do the project. About the only other time I've talked to her, I just said *hi*."

"That's, that's good, son. Glad to see you step out there and put it on the line. You know, you can't catch a fish if you don't throw bait in the water."

"I don't see how this is like fishing."

"It's a metaphor. You have to try to accomplish a task if you ever hope to one-day succeed. Emotions are hard for some people to risk. You don't need to be *that* guy. There's no harm in asking any girl out, although you're too young for that, but you get what I mean. You're going to get some rejections. Heck, you might get a string of rejections before one of them says *yes*. That's, okay. What I'm telling you is, don't let a chance to catch a girl's attention slip by, because you may never get that chance again. And, if you get rejected, continue on like it never happened, and wait for the next opportunity."

"Okay, Dad, I will." Cole reached over and turned up the volume on the radio. He had enough of fatherly advice for one afternoon.

*

The grocery store was on the way home. Fortunately, his dad had let him go into the store alone and didn't slow him down. He was on the clock, and everything had to be just right before Charlotte showed up at his house.

After a quick shower and just the proper amount of gel in his hair, he put on a clean pair of jeans and his favorite shirt he wore *to look nice*. He had abandoned the thought to splash on some of his dad's aftershave. He was certain James Bond would wear something more exotic and decided that smelling like Irish Spring soap was manly enough.

The real work started in the kitchen. Cole had bought carrots, cucumbers, tomatoes, celery, cauliflower, and broccoli. The veggies had to be washed, dried, and cut into bite-sized portions. Slicing those carrots into sticks was the most difficult. The tubers were hard, and he wished he had a sharper knife. If he was going to start preparing food he was going to have to learn how to sharpen knives too.

After prepping the veggies, Cole found a platter in the cabinet that hadn't seen the light of day in years. After a quick washing, he had it ready to arrange the snacks. He chose a large bowl for the center and spooned out a container of hummus. Next, he found two smaller matching bowls and placed them strategically on the platter. Feta cheese went into one bowl and Kalamata olives into the other. Veggies of equal proportion went around the center bowl, filling the entire space.

"I thought you were having a girl over. I didn't know the entire baseball team would be here," his dad, Mark said, popping unexpectedly into the kitchen.

"Come on, Dad. I don't know what kind of vegetables Charlotte likes. Hummus is just bean dip. Everybody likes bean dip."

"That's some spread you've made there. Where did you get the idea from? The only things I've seen you make in the kitchen are peanut butter and jelly sandwiches and Pop-Tarts with ice cream on top."

"After lunch, I searched the internet on my phone and found this. I wanted to serve something tasty and fairly healthy."

"What's that smell?" his dad asked.

"Smell? Oh, I guess you mean the feta cheese."

"Smells like feet."

"No, it doesn't," Cole defensively said. "Feta cheese is supposed to complement the hummus."

"Okay, I'll just eat the bean dip. I've never figured you to care about cooking. *Chef Cole*, I like it." Mark sauntered over to the refrigerator, opened the door, and pulled out a beer. Popping the top, he pointed the bottom of the bottle to the ceiling and leaned against the kitchen counter. "You know, not everything on that plate is a vegetable."

"Really? You mean like the olives?"

"Well, olives are fruit, but I meant more like the tomatoes."

"Yeah, I think I might have heard that before. Tomatoes are fruits and not vegetables."

"And the cucumbers too. Cucumbers are fruit."

"Okay, got it," Cole said, sounding a bit on the sassy side.

"If it comes from a flower and has seeds, like watermelons and green peppers, it's a fruit. If it's another part of a plant, then it's a vegetable. Carrots are roots, broccoli and cauliflower are stems."

Cole cocked his head to the side, feeling like his dad had some ulterior motive behind this conversation.

"And you know how flowers are made, don't you?" Mark said, his face blushing a light shade of red.

"Uh, Dad. You're not going to tell me about the *birds and the bees* right now, are you?"

"What? Nah, nah, that's not what I was going to do."

"Good."

"I mean, well, unless, *you know*, you'd like to have that conversation?"

"Dad, I'm fourteen. I'm pretty sure I know how things work."

"I don't know. I wouldn't want you to have any bad information. There're a lot of myths about sex, and I don't want you to get any wrong ideas."

"We learned about sex in the sixth grade. It's really not that big of a deal."

After what sounded like a sigh of relief, Mark said, "Okay, but if you ever have any questions, don't hesitate to ask. There's nothing wrong with the human body and how it works. There're just some social standards that should be followed."

"Believe me, if I have any questions, I'll ask."

"Good."

"So, Charlotte and her mom should be here soon."

"Okay, do you want me to go hide in my room? That would be rude, but I'll give you some privacy if you'd like."

"No, I want you here. I don't know if her mom is going to drop her off and come back and get her, or just wait here—in her car or something."

"Not a problem," Mark said, still glued against the kitchen counter.

"So, are you going to change clothes?"

"What's wrong with these clothes? They're not dirty." Mark still wore his work outfit, a khaki fire retardant shirt, and blue jeans.

"Your jeans are okay, but can you at least change your shirt? You need to wear something a little more...welcoming," Cole said.

"Okay, if it puts you a little more at ease, I'll do it."

"Thanks, Dad."

Mark took his weight off the kitchen counter, chugging beer to power himself toward his room.

Cole yelled, "And shave, Dad. Don't forget to shave."

*

The big hand on the clock pointed to 12 and the little hand at 7. Charlotte wasn't late, yet. Cole looked between the curtains and down the driveway, expecting to see her mom's car any second.

The clock's big hand traveled past the 5, then the 10, and then 15. At this point, it looked like Charlotte wasn't coming. He had gone to all this trouble and not even a phone call to let him know.

"Maybe something came up and she couldn't make it," Mark said. He stood in the kitchen doorway that led to the hall.

Cole abandoned his watch, and with his head lowered, walked over to the table. "I guess."

"I guess you'll have to do the science project alone."

"It doesn't work that way, Dad. We have to work in pairs to get credit."

"Well, at least we have something different to eat tonight," Mark said.

"I'm not hungry," Cole said in a low voice, his lips barely moving.

Light streaming in the window from behind Cole faded and then reappeared.

"Oh, I think your appetite will return shortly," Mark said.

Cole didn't know what was up with his dad. This was no time to play some silly mind game. Charlotte had stood him up, and he was just going to have to face it. Do like his dad had said earlier, after a rejection, take a step back, and then try again.

"A young girl and a woman about my age just drove up our driveway. You better go answer the door."

"Huh?" Cole whipped his head around to the front window. He just caught sight of two females walking past, heading for the front door.

Cole bolted across the kitchen past the doorway leading to the living room. The doorbell rang just as he arrived at the front foyer. They were here! Charlotte didn't stand him up. He took a split second to straighten his shirt, took a deep breath, and opened the door.

"Hey Cole," Charlotte said.

The young girl's dark brown hair hung down to her chest, framing a face handmade by God himself. Her big brown eyes were a window into her soul, where nectar dripped from beautiful flowers. She held a plate covered with plastic wrap in front of her.

"Hey Charlotte," Cole finally said.

"I'm sorry we're late. It's my fault. I wanted to bake some chocolate chip cookies, and it took longer than I thought," Charlotte said.

"Late? Oh, I didn't notice," Cole lied.

"This is my mom, Lori."

Charlotte's mom had been standing mostly behind her daughter. The two were near the same height, so Cole hadn't had a good look at her. She leaned over to the side. "Hi Cole, pleased to meet you."

"It's nice meeting you too."

"Invite them to come in," Mark said from the kitchen doorway.

Cole snapped his head around, and with an edge of sassiness, said, "I was just going to do that, Dad."

Turning back to the guests, he said, "Come on in."

The corners of Cole's lips nearly touched his ears as he led the guests into the kitchen, where his dad had backed up into an open space to give them room to enter and greet them.

"Oh look, someone baked cookies," Mark said. "Just put them on the table." He turned his gaze to Lori. "Hi, I'm Mark Rainwater." His hands remained by his side. Cole knew his dad believed it wasn't proper to offer a woman a hand to shake unless she offered hers first.

A polite smile etched on Lori's dark cherry lips. It was obvious which parent Charlotte took after. Both she and her mom shared the straight dark brown hair and eyes. Both had long legs and a slim but curvy shape. "Hello, I'm Lori Meadows. Pleased to meet you." She extended her right hand.

Mark reached up and gently took her hand, sucked in his gut, and gave it two quick shakes. Letting go, he turned his gaze to Charlotte. "You must be Charlotte."

"Yes, sir. Pleased to meet you."

"It's a pleasure to meet you too," Mark said.

Lori turned her bottom lip a bit to the side, and said, "You look familiar. Do you work out at Club Fitness in town?"

Mark's chest swole, and he straightened his shoulders. "Ha, uh, no. No, I don't. I mean I *should* be working out. Being a single parent and all, after work, I have to run Cole around when he has something to do and take care of other chores around the house. I just don't make time to work out."

"I understand where you're coming from. I'm a single parent too. I can't wait until Charlotte is old enough to drive," Lori said. "I have to make myself find time to work out."

"I can't wait until I'm old enough to drive, too," Charlotte said.

Everyone slightly chuckled.

Cole didn't like the way the adults were dominating the conversation. This wasn't a social visit where the kids were just room ornaments. "We have time to eat some snacks before the Space Station flys over." Cole stepped over to a cabinet and retrieved four salad plates and a bag of chips, and then placed them on the table, next to a stack of napkins.

"Charlotte, Miss Meadows, please help yourself." Cole got a large bowl off the counter and poured the bag of chips into it. He sat that on the table, and said, "These are pita chips. You're supposed to eat hummus with pita bread but I thought pita chips would be better."

"This looks amazing, and what a nice presentation. Mark, you must have worked all afternoon preparing this," Lori said. She picked up two plates and handed one to Charlotte.

"I'd love to take credit for the spread here. But it was Cole who dreamed up the menu, bought the groceries, and made all of this himself."

"Really, that's quite impressive, young man. Maybe you could teach Charlotte a thing or two in the kitchen." Lori spooned some hummus on Charlotte's plate and then her own.

"I hate cooking. It's boring. Baking is more of my thing," Charlotte said.

"We need some drinks," Mark said. "Lori, what can I get you?"

Oh, great. Cole had spent so much time planning the food menu he totally forgot what to think of to drink.

Charlotte's mom had already crunched down on a pita chip dipped in hummus. "Mmm, this is good. A white wine would go with this."

Taken slightly aback, Mark said, "Eh, I'm not much of a wine drinker. But, I do have Michelob Ultra."

"That's the one beer I will drink. But only one for me. I am driving, after all," Lori said.

"Charlotte, Cole? We have Coke, Mountain Dew, bottled water...I can make some instant lemonade."

"A Mountain Dew for me, please," Charlotte said.

Well, crisis avoided. "Mountain Dew," Cole said.

Chips and vegetables dived into hummus and cheese, while Mark served the drinks. Charlotte seemed to enjoy a little bit of everything. Her mom favored the cauliflower and cucumbers.

"This feta cheese is dynamite with the hummus. I don't think I've had the two together before," Lori said.

"Yes, the feta cheese compliments the hummus," Mark said. He sheepishly grinned and turned a furtive glance at Cole, whose head wilted to one side and shot him judging eyes that asked, *Really?*

The conversation lasted a good half hour, with general exchanges of information about where Mark and Lori worked, Cole's involvement with the baseball team, and Charlotte's aspirations to become a Computer Engineer.

To Cole's relief, his dad never brought up his passion for the paranormal. He didn't want to have to explain himself to Lori's mom. She might have asked too many questions. Maybe even have made fun of him, like many other adults had, though he hoped not. Plus, he wanted to connect with Charlotte on a different level. She was good in science and seemed to enjoy the class. Science was his favorite subject. He wanted her to respect him on a level of intelligence as well as to catch her eye.

The group had put a pretty good dent in the food. As far as he could tell, his efforts had not gone unappreciated. What a relief! He found he did like mixing the feta with hummus but didn't care for it as much when he ate it by itself. If he ever had the opportunity again to entertain

Charlotte, he'd have to come up with a different menu. Not because he was disappointed but to show her that there was more to him than just repeating the same old things. He wanted to keep her guessing and hoped to delight her every step of the way.

"The Space Station will be overhead in less than fifteen minutes. I've got everything set up on the patio. Charlotte and I really need to go outside now," Cole said.

"Wait," Lori pulled the plastic off the cookies. "Leave a few in here for us, and take the rest with you outside."

Mark reached over and pulled a salad plate from the cabinet.

"How many would you like, Mark? There's plenty, so don't be shy," Lori said.

"Those look good. I'll take four."

"I'd like to take four, too. But, it's easier to work off two at the gym than four," Lori said. She picked up the plate of cookies, and with a clean fork, shoved six cookies onto the empty plate. "Here you go." Lori gave the plate to Charlotte.

"The patio door is this way," Cole said. He picked up his drink, and Charlotte's, and led the way. For a moment Cole felt guilty leaving his dad alone with Lori's mom. After all, he didn't even ask him, if the situation arose, if he would mind entertaining her throughout the experiment. A quick glance back evaporated any concern. Mark and Lori were talking like old friends. His dad's face beamed with interest.

CHAPTER 8

The Future

Water always wins. No matter which race dominated planet Earth, the forces of Mother Nature had to be contended with. Zax and Tarik traveled along a well-maintained waterway designed to channel rainwater away from the city into the Missouri River.

The engineered geometric rectangles of city blocks gave way to the outskirts of old-life, where mighty elms, towering oaks, hardy beech trees, and flowering dogwoods grew. Tarik's head armor was open. He drank in the majestic beauty with his own eyes, smelled the earthy funk of the forest unfiltered, and tasted fresh oxygen generated by leaves.

Tarik lifted a foot to avoid a root jutting from the ground and stepped in a low spot, upsetting his balance to where he almost fell over.

"If you close your head armor, you can use your HUD to pick a smoother path," Zax said.

"I'd rather take my chances. This is the first time I've actually been out in the woods, you know. Everything is so beautiful. I wish I could shed this armor and walk around naked," Tarik said.

"You'd change you mind after a short time. Mosquitoes would have a field day on that unprotected skin. Plus, chiggers would crawl up in places you didn't know existed and irritate you to death."

"What's a chigger?"

"A nasty little insect that likes to cuddle up in cozy spaces, like your underwear, and have lunch. They make little red bumps that itch. It feels *so good* when you scratch them, but that only makes them itch more. You could rub yourself raw and only make things worse."

"I don't like the sound of that. You can have mine," Tarik said as he briefly closed his eyes. "It's so quiet here, so peaceful. I can only imagine what it was like when man had to live in makeshift huts and survive off the blood of the land. It's like," Tarik paused, "it's like all life on Earth is connected, in some strange way. I have a sense of belonging like I've never felt before."

"I think I understand what you're going through. You are kind of like an animal that's been locked in a cage all of his life and now are stepping on grass for the first time. You know, I never thought about it much before. In fact, over the years I've been a little jealous how much you were catered to. Everything at the base revolved around you."

"Jealous? Really? Growing up, I was always someone's assignment, following a schedule where I was passed off from one caretaker to another. Get up, eat, go to instruction, eat, go to instruction, exercise, eat, go to sleep and repeat the next day. Of course, at anytime I could be pulled and brought to the lab, where doctors with huge fingers, like yours, would poke and prod and stick me with needles and shave thin layers of skin off me for my DNA. To be honest, most of the time I just felt like someone in the way. It was rare for anyone to spend time with me outside of their assignments," Tarik said, finding it harder to talk as he thought of his friend Hudson. "I miss the good times I spent with Hudson."

"Yeah, Hud was such a great guy. There were those who cared and those who pretended to care. There was nothing fake about Hud," Zax said. He abruptly stopped and held up his hand. "You hear that? Something's coming."

Tarik did hear something scurrying in the woods coming their way. His head armor snapped into place, and he checked his electronics. "Woods are thick, but I can see it, and we have nothing to worry about. Watch."

A few seconds later, a brown cottontail burst from the brush and shot past right in front of Zax.

"That's a first for me. I've never seen a live rabbit before," Tarik said. "Why don't you kill it, and we can roast it on a spit and dine underneath the stars tonight?"

"What do you want me to do? Run it down and tackle it?"

The electronics in Tarik's HUD sparked to life with some new information. "Uh-oh."

"What?"

"We're about to find out what the rabbit was running from."

A growing disturbance crashed through the woods heading their way. Zax quickly looked around on the ground and picked up part of an old tree branch about four feet long. As he brought it up, the top third broke off and fell to the ground.

The first dog that emerged upon the scene came to a screeching halt. It was a fairly large dog, easily weighing over fifty pounds. It had black hair mixed with dark gray and might have been considered a good looking animal. With the hackles up on it's back, and the peeled back lips showing long, sharp white teeth, it was far from looking like someone's loyal pet.

"Get back!" Zax swung the branch in the air between them, trying to scare off the animal.

Two more dogs appeared. One had come from nowhere and sailed through the air and bit Zax's arm that held the branch.

Tarik stomped toward the fray, trying to land a boot to the nearest dog. "Zax! Get behind me!"

The big Nu-Man had shaken off the dog that had bitten his arm and placed what was left of the branch right across the side of its face. The branch broke again, leaving just a small piece in his hand.

More dogs joined in the party. Zax took Tarik's advice and maneuvered to put the armor clad man between him and the wild pack.

Forming a semi-circle, the animals, thirteen in all, barked, snarled, and bit into the empty air. The braver ones lunged forward with maws open wide and saliva glistening teeth threatening.

"This is ridiculous," Tarik said. "I could use my shoulder gun and waste them all in three seconds."

One of the dogs tried to outflank Tarik and get another piece of Zax. Tarik brought his boot backward and caught it in the chest. Bones crunched, and the dog crashed several feet over never to rise again.

"I'm a liability. Back up at a slow pace and keep them away from me," Zax said.

Tarik stepped backward, and the two ended up under the branches of a large tree. Zax's long arms and mighty hands had him off the ground and safely watching from above.

"You okay?" Tarik asked.

"Yeah."

Slowly, Tarik offered the alpha dog his armor gloved hand to sample. The dog accepted the gift, bit down, and aggressively shook his head from side to side. The animal was insatiable to the point of its detriment. The dog's blood smeared across Tarik's gloved fingers. "I don't know what's gotten into these dogs. They look fat, not like they're starving. But, we don't have time for this." Tarik brought his right fist over and slammed it into the top of the dog's head. Its skull caved in, and its body slumped to the ground.

The armored human waded into the mass of dogs. They surround him from all sides, trying their best to get a tooth hold on his backside to bring him down. A swift kick sent a dog in front flying backward as it *yiped* its final cry. Another dog jumped and had its front legs over Tarik's arm and bit at his head. He easily flung it to the side and delivered another crushing blow to the nearest predator.

Dogs scattered, for the most part. Some of them finally realizing that this was no ordinary hunt. Alas, some needed further convincing. Tarik made a quick disposal of three more in the blink of an eye.

That attack was enough to send what was left of the pack digging dirt under their paws and disappearing back into the woods.

Tarik looked around and then up at Zax in the tree. "What a waste. I've read a lot about dogs, how the species developed under the breeding programs of man."

Zax stepped on a branch below, grabbed on with his hands, and lowered himself above ground before letting go. His arm was bandaged where the dog had bitten him.

"How bad is the bite?" Tarik asked.

"One tooth got in pretty deep, but overall, it's not too bad. I cleaned it with *Erase*. It'll be okay." Zax fingered the edges of the bandage. "Earlier you wanted to cook up a rabbit. Now's your chance to have some fresh wild dog."

"Man's best friend? You want me to eat man's best friend?"

Zax shrugged. "Dogs may have been man's best friend, but you know that genetic bond broke after the evolution to Nu-Mans."

"Yeah, entire breeds were eliminated. It's not a pet if it growls all the time and tries to bite you. It's a shame, though. I've seen old recordings and read stories of dog's loyalty to man."

"You must have eaten dog at the institution? They're bred like any another meat animals."

"No, I was never served dog, although others at the institution may have eaten it. Hud told me one time they did that in respect to my humanity, whatever that meant. There were some human cultures that ate dog. Some that ate cats, too."

"Yeah, how barbaric was that? Imagine, eating a cat. What kind of sick person would do that? Cats are the most perfect pets in the world. I worry what's going to happen to them after we're gone."

"Which brings us back to our mission. Come on. We have a little way to go before we veer off into the old neighborhoods."

*

Tarik felt like he was traveling back in time right now. Nature and old-life had formed an odd symbiosis. Paved streets still etched a grid-like pattern in the overgrowth. But the paths had long been covered by leaves and creeping vegetation, along with various plants and even trees which had found cracks in the pavement and reached out to the sky.

Most houses were still intact to some degree, although only a few had roofs; those made of sheet metal. One house built on an above ground foundation had a tree growing upright in the middle.

He tried to imagine what life had been like back then. Cars roaming the streets. Children playing in their yards. Yes, even dogs interacting with man. Hundreds of people who looked just like him carrying on without a clue of the upcoming invasion.

"These houses look tiny," Zax said. He hadn't spoken much since entering old-life.

Tarik wondered if Zax was thinking the same thing, what life must have been like for humankind. "Yeah. I don't think people living here earned a lot of money. Of course, Nu-Mans are a lot bigger than humans. You'd have a tough time getting through a front door."

They walked a little farther. "I get a strange feeling here," Zax said.

"Like what?"

"Like I'm walking on sacred ground, or I'm violating ancient spirits or something like that. I feel like I don't belong here. It's stupid, really."

That was interesting. "I'm feeling just the opposite. It's as if I've," Tarik hesitated, "come home, in an odd sort of way."

"Well, you are human."

"I get that, but I've grown up around Nu-Mans. The only time I ever see a human face is when I look in the mirror. It may be hard for you to understand, but I think of myself as a Nu-Man the majority of the time."

Zax scratched at the hair on his forehead. "You've lived a screwed up life." He walked in silence for a while, and said, "You told me that you and Hud sometimes talked about fate, how the Universe had a basic plan that mapped out the future. Right here, right now, maybe for the first time, I'm starting to feel like there may be something to that."

"How so?"

"I can't put it into words. It's a feeling, kind of like the feeling of being out of place in old-life. You are the only human alive on Earth. There won't be a single Nu-Man left alive here in the next twenty years. There's a chance you can go back in time and keep the Skinks away from finding Earth. You can stop the Skinks from usurping man's rightful ownership. A Nu-Man wouldn't be able to that. Only a human could go back like that and not be discovered. That's just way too many coincidences."

Tarik thought for a minute. "You may be right, or you may be wrong. We won't know until we complete the mission."

Zax slowly shook his head, and said, "I'll never find out the answer."

Tarik's heart sank a little, knowing the consequences of any outcome for his friend Zax. Zax's fate, the fate of all Nu-mans, was determined. His HUD flashed an alert. "The safe-house is just two streets over. We're almost there."

*

The safe-house was as overgrown as the rest of the other houses on the street. This house had been constructed with cinderblocks and had a metal roof. No doubt it had weathered time better than most because of hearty materials.

"Should I knock?" Zax asked as the two stood in front of the door.

Tarik looked up toward the sky. Tree canopies blocked most of his view. "I've already sent a message to let them know we're here."

"Did they respond?"

"No. Which has me worried," Tarik said. "I'll send the code again." The transmission was successful, and he was certain the code was correct.

After waiting for what seemed too long, the handle on the dilapidated brown door slowly turned, and the door opened about six inches before stopping.

"I'll go first," Zax said.

"Remember to duck your head."

"You're always saying I'm hard headed. What's to worry?"

"Just go in. I'm dying to get out of this armor."

The Nu-Man brought his arms in close to his body and lowered his head. Zax disappeared into the darkness.

Tarik's HUD identified only one other Nu-Man in the house. A female. She was armed with a compact railgun, and it was pointed right at him.

"Put the weapon down," Zax said firmly, keeping his distance from her, his arms raised up to his shoulders.

"I'll put it down when I'm sure he's not a Skink," she said.

"I sent you the code. I'm not a Skink. I'm the human," Tarik said.

"Zax?" The question in her voice indicated she would only trust the word of a fellow Nu-Man.

"It's okay. He's telling you the truth. You can put your weapon down."

She did so, slowly, as if she might change her mind in a split second and raise it again.

When the railgun rested on the floor, Tarik squeezed his mech-armor past the narrow door frame and entered the house. The corner to the left was void of any furniture. He stepped over to the side and opened the armor. The two halves of the headpiece uncoupled, exposing his eyes to the darkness. For a moment he couldn't see anything. The arms, chest, and leg components separated. Tarik stepped down to the floor, finally free of the confining shell.

Now that the door was closed, there was hardly any light at all, although Tarik easily made out the silhouettes of Zax and the girl. "Are there any lights in this place? I'd hate to have to feel my way around here."

"There are lights. Just a second," the girl said. She walked a few steps away, and the room flooded with dim white light.

The girl gasped.

She stood with her hand up to her mouth and her eyes wide.

Tarik took a moment for his eyes to adjust. She was young, probably Zax's age. A gold-colored tunic wrapped her torso and only came over one shoulder. A matching skirt covered her hips to mid-thigh. Nu-Man women had much softer features than men. Most were a good foot shorter than their male counterparts. Their hands and feet slimmer, and the hair covering most of their bodies not nearly as coarse or long.

Nu-Man women had worked at the rebel base all of Tarik's life. Not one of them had been younger than the age of forty, with the majority who worked there much older than that. This was the first time he had ever stood in front of a female this young. And, she was absolutely stunning to look at.

The silence had become palpable.

"I'm Zax. That's Tarik," Zax said.

The girl's hand lowered, but she only continued to stare.

"Don't worry. Tarik won't bite," Zax said. "Well, that's not entirely true. He bit me once in the exercise room."

"You were about to break my hand. I had to find some way to make you let go," Tarik said.

"Eh, he's also a sore loser," Zax said.

"I am not," Tarik said.

"He's self-delusional too. But what are you going to do?" Zax shrugged. "He's handicapped. He's human."

"I..." the girl started, "I'm sorry. I had no idea I would react this way. Everyone has seen images of humans. I...."

Tarik put his shoulders back and slowly approached. With his eyebrows up and a warm smile on his lips, he tried to look as non-threatening as possible. He stopped as soon as he got within her reach.

"There's nothing to be afraid of," Tarik said, looking up into her big green eyes. He felt stupid in a way for saying that. What about him was to fear? She could pick him up and break him in half without much of an effort.

She slowly lifted a hand toward his face and hesitated.

"It's okay," Tarik said.

Her finger gently touched the side of his cheek and traced down to his chin. "Your skin is so smooth, so soft."

"I did shave yesterday. Although I can't grow much facial hair. Not in my genetic code."

"Your nose is…perfect. So sleek, elegant."

"Eh, thanks, I guess. It's the only nose I've ever had. And, there's no other human nose on Earth to compare mine with."

She quickly shook her head and pulled her hand away. "I'm sorry, I don't mean to be rude. It's hard for me to wrap my mind around the fact that a real live human is right here in front of me. My name is Lixa. I'm the daughter of Bix. You'll both be glad to know that he and the other rebels have all made it to safe-houses and the plans are still on for the rendezvous in two days."

Zax looked over at Tarik and let out a sigh of relief. "What kind of supplies do we have here? And where did you get that railgun? I thought we had the only three, and those were at the base?"

"Everyone has gone beyond normal protocol, taking risks that we didn't in the past. This is the one and only chance we have to make a difference. There's nothing to lose. If we die now or next year, dead is dead. There won't be any mourners around to remember us a few years from now," Lixa said.

Lixa was young, but she seemed to be as tuned into the situation as Hudson.

"As far as supplies, we have zero-energy batteries to recharge the mech-armor. There's plenty of food and things to drink. We have a blaster and ammo for both you and the armor. After a couple of days rest you'll be as ready as you'll ever be." Lixa hesitated and darted her eyes over at Tarik.

He had been staring at her, hanging on the music of her every word. His infatuation must have been obvious.

Lixa started to blush.

CHAPTER 9

The Present

Cole had set up his laptop and video camera on a tripod outside on the patio, just beyond the overhead awning. Fortunately, the weather was cooperating, and the sky was clear. He had moved his telescope out there, too. Mostly for show, as he had no intention for them to do any star gazing. He had hurriedly cleaned the patio furniture, a chocolate brown aluminum table and four matching chairs, before taking a shower.

Charlotte put the cookies on the table, and Cole sat the drinks down.

"Hold on a second." He picked up a clean towel off one of the chairs and gave the one he had selected for Charlotte a quick wipedown.

"Thank you," she said.

"You're welcome." He pulled the chair further out for her to sit.

Charlotte took her seat. Cole waited diligently behind and helped push the chair forward as she bellied up to the table.

"Such a gentleman," Charlotte said, genuinely sounding impressed.

He enjoyed the compliment but didn't really know how to respond, so he didn't. After taking his seat, he scooched over next to her but made sure he wasn't so close as to invade her personal space. The last thing he wanted to do was shove himself on top of Charlotte and creep her out.

The laptop was between the two of them. Cole ran his finger over the touchpad and woke up the screen. "You can get information on *Spotthestation dot gov*, a NASA website, to find out when and where the International Space Station flies over. We're going to watch the live stream on the main NASA site." Cole stood and adjusted the screen for them to get a clearer view. "Can you see that okay?"

"Yes, it's fine."

"It'll look better as the sun goes down."

"Ready for a cookie?" Charlotte asked as she picked up the plate.

"I was ready for a cookie before we ate the hummus." He eagerly picked a cookie on the side of the plate, careful to keep his fingers from touching the others. After a bite, he said, "Man, these are so good!"

"You think so?"

"For real. They're firm but not overbaked. Soft, but not undercooked. I'd call this the perfect chocolate chip cookie." Two bites later, the sweet dessert had disappeared.

Charlotte bit into one. "Wow, these are good. Thank goodness, I tried really hard to follow the directions. I'm not much of a baker, but I like doing it sometimes. Mom helped me decide when they were done. You have to use your judgment. All ovens are different, so there's no other way to know when to take them out."

Cole adjusted the volume on the laptop to where it was barely audible. "Whatever you did, just keep on doing it." He grabbed another cookie and went after it.

"I wonder what antigravity is like," Charlotte said. "Look at them in the station, hanging in midair like floating in the water."

"I bet it would be neat."

"Maybe, but since there's no gravity pulling them in any direction, they can't move unless they grab or push off of something. You can't tread thin air like you can water."

"True, but their living area is so small, that's not a problem."

"Look at all that stuff in there," Charlotte said while pointing her cookie at the screen. "All those wires. That keyboard on the wall is vertical. Not having gravity to give you a sense of up and down would take a lot to get used to."

"It would. But if you lived in zero gravity, you could eat all the cookies you wanted."

Charlotte smirked. "Why do you say that?"

"Because you'd never gain any weight." He downed his last bite of cookie and smiled.

Charlotte giggled and extended her right elbow to nudge him in the arm. "You have crumbs all over your mouth."

Momentary panic froze his face in mid-chew. Frantically searching about, he grabbed the rag he used to wipe the furniture and brushed the crumbs from his lips. "Sorry, I forgot to bring napkins. Do you want me to go inside and get some?"

"No, that's okay. I was just picking on you."

So far, things had been going well between them. This shocked Cole, because Charlotte seemed so *approachable* right now. So different than the girl he thought she was just this morning.

A few more cookies vanished from the plate. The sun hung low on the horizon, slowly gathering the last orange rays of light. A cool gentle breeze in the night air carried the soft fragrance of honey from sweet alyssum. The cloak of darkness intensified, unveiling Venus and other emerging stars and galaxies.

"We should see the ISS soon. Keep your eyes kinda west-south-west. It's going to come over at sixty-eight degrees tonight. Ninety degrees is directly overhead, so don't look too high up."

Charlotte turned her head to the west. *Princess Charlotte.* Her striking profile looked hand sculptured by God's most talented angel.

"Is that it coming up over there?"

Charlotte Meadows was sitting in his backyard with him. She had baked him cookies. Was any of this real?

"Cole?"

"Huh, what?"

"Is that the ISS?" She lifted a finger toward the west.

He paused a moment, and said, "I don't think so. The light is too bright." Cole continued to watch. "See the red light? It's just a plane."

"Yeah, I see it now."

No sooner had Charlotte spoken, then the dim light of the ISS appeared above the horizon. "There it is, see? It's not as bright as Venus. It's too early in the night for it to look like that."

"I see it," she said enthusiastically.

Cole stepped over to his video camera, already pointing toward the western sky, and focused in on the ISS. "The video isn't going to be all that impressive. I'm just videoing it as evidence that we actually worked on the project."

"Wow, I don't know why, because it is just a light traveling across the sky, but it's really cool!"

Cole looked away from the viewfinder. He could spare a few seconds here and there to see it with his naked eyes. "Knowing the ISS is in outer space and that there are people inside puts it in perspective. That's why it's so neat."

There were four men and one woman on the ISS. The live streaming video showed two of the men, one upside down and one right side up, performing some mundane task. Cole wished there had been a way to get them to give a shout-out to him and Charlotte as they passed over.

"It's moving so fast. It's almost halfway across the sky."

"Yep, about five miles a second." Cole repositioned the camera.

Less than a minute later, the ISS continued its journey to the northeastern side of the horizon, lost among the canopy of the forest.

"If you don't know to look for it, at first glance you might think it was a jet." Cole moved the camera from pointing to the sky, and over at Charlotte.

"What are you doing?" she asked.

"Uh, I need proof that you were here for the project."

"You can hear my voice on the video."

"I don't have the audio on."

"Okay, then you need to be in the video too."

Good point, Cole thought. He quickly stepped over behind Charlotte, put his head next to hers, and waved quickly before returning to the camera. The smell of her hair lingered.

"Did you ever see the Space Shuttle re-enter the atmosphere?" Cole asked, and then turned off his video camera and sat back in his chair.

"No, I never did. I never got to see one launch either. I watched a nighttime launch once on TV, and I wanted to see one after that. Too bad the shuttle program's over."

"I saw the shuttle come in at night two different times. I had to set my clock and get up, but it was worth it. It looked like it traveled faster than the ISS, but in reality, the shuttle came in at about the same speed until the atmosphere slowed it down. It glowed like a meteor and left a trail like fireworks. That was really exciting to watch. But just like the ISS, it was gone before I could even go back in and wake up my dad to come out and watch."

Charlotte had picked up her drink and drank some. There was a low buzz coming from the laptop from the ISS audio. Cole reached over and closed the laptop.

The space station had passed. There was no reason for Charlotte to be here anymore. All the excitement of the day had led to this moment. Cole honestly didn't know where to go from here. "I guess...I guess we're finished with the home project. I'll upload my video tonight to YouTube and we can show it tomorrow." Cole looked over at the table and brushed a few cookie crumbs to the patio floor. "It was nice of you to do the project with me."

"It was nice for you to ask me to do the project. Most guys my age hardly talk to me."

Cole chuckled. "Well, I don't want to sound like a jerk or anything, but you hardly ever act like you know guys our age even exist."

Charlotte raised both hands and brought them to her forehead, hiding her face. She let out a sigh. "I know...I know...I've been a bad person."

"Wait, no, that's not what I meant," Cole said, feeling like he was about to dig another hole he couldn't keep from falling into. "I didn't mean you're a *bad person*. I—"

"I know what you meant, Cole. In fact, I've learned a lot about myself just recently. After I broke up with Brennon," Charlotte paused and then said, "I was so upset...I took a really hard look at my life. Who I was, and where I was going? My relationship with boys have been all the same and ended all the same. Me, with my heart broken.

"My mother and I talked, and she told me that if I wanted to have better relationships with boys, then I needed to stop picking the same one over and over."

"What do you mean?" Cole asked.

"It's different for girls than boys, you know. Girls mature faster. And me, well my body developed earlier than most. Older guys are interested in that. The guys who call me and talk to me are one or two years older. Guys my age see that and feel like they don't have a chance with me. I can't blame them, because I used to mentally cross them off my list entirely. They felt like they couldn't play in my field, and I never gave them the time of day to begin with."

"So you didn't know I existed until today? You've told me *hi* from time to time," Cole said.

"Actually, I have noticed you a little more than any others in our class. I mean, your locker *is* right next to mine."

Lucky me, Cole thought, feeling like it was only a matter of circumstance that she was right here right now and not because she had found him appealing in any way.

"And, when you joined the baseball team. I've seen you practice when I was watching Brennon. I knew you were in my science class, too. To be honest, I liked your longer hair better than the short cut you have now."

Now he was getting somewhere! She's talking about his looks. "So you're telling me that you think of me more than just the locker troll who has a locker next to you?"

Charlotte winced and giggled, pushing her right elbow against his arm again. "So I've told you, I've been reconsidering my choices in life. Bad habits are still hard to break. It wasn't until Brennon busted in on our conversation that I had a defining moment in life. I saw that I had two choices before me. I could just become *a thing* and spend my life trying to make boys like Brennon like me and suffering the consequences. Or, I could go for someone different. Someone with a good heart and kind spirit. There's something about you, even from the first time I saw you, I thought was different."

"Different because of my interest in the paranormal, aliens, and bigfoot?"

"No, I have to admit, I do think of some of those subjects are juvenile."

Cole felt a sharp knife to the heart, but the wound wasn't deep, and he didn't bleed much.

Charlotte said, "You've seemed to be a caring person. It's just the way you treat people. I like that. And as far as your looks, I've always thought you had *potential*. At the time, not for me, but for other girls who like guys their own age. But that was my old way of thinking. I think with a little help from me—how to dress, what to say, how to act—I could turn you into a guy that girls couldn't stop calling."

Cole turned his head to the side. With one eyebrow raised, he asked, "So, are you saying you like me?"

Charlotte placed her hand on his thigh. "Yes, I am saying that *I like you*. I want us to become friends and get to know each other better. I'm looking for a new direction in life, and you're the kind of person I'd like to start it with."

Boldly, Cole placed his left hand on top of Charlotte's and gave it a gentle squeeze. "Well, I'd like to give our friendship a try too."

Charlotte took her hand back and grabbed her drink. She leaned back in her chair and looked up into the sky. "You believe in aliens."

"Yes, you don't?" Cole said, turning his body in her direction.

"I'm not sure what to believe. The universe is a big place. But after all the years of man on Earth, there's no hard evidence that there's life on other planets. Even with all the smart phones where just about everyone has a camera, there aren't any convincing pictures of UFOs."

"Okay, so I've read that there are trillions and trillions of stars in the universe and within an estimated ten trillion galaxies. The odds that there isn't life elsewhere is practically zero. That said, I think the mound of evidence that we do have of ETs is enough to believe it's true."

"I read a book about a year ago, *Rare Earth*. One thing it talked about was that single cell and simple multicell organisms might be common on a good amount of planets. But life like we have on Earth, with sentient beings like humans, would be extremely rare. The book pointed out that even if aliens did exist, that the distances would be so far away that they'd never reach us, or us them. So, honestly, if there is intelligent life in the universe, I don't think we'll ever know."

"What about interdimensional travel? Or warping space? Scientists have mathematically proven it can be done."

"And the book talked about how the energy required to bend space would be equivalent to that of the sun. Mankind will never harness that kind of power," Charlotte said.

"I might have to read that book. I hear what you're saying, but I'm still keeping an open mind," Cole said and leaned back into his chair.

"Would that be so bad?" Charlotte asked. "That even though there are trillions of planets in the universe, that Earth was the only planet with life of any kind? Earth is such a beautiful place. We're still discovering new species of land life every day. Our oceans have hardly even been explored. Wouldn't it be enough if we are all that there is? Our souls constantly being reborn throughout time, sharing the world over and over again?"

Cole thought of all the waste if the heavens above were empty of Earth-like life. Then, he thought of the fragrance of Charlotte's hair, the warmth of her hand, and the possibility of countless lifetimes together. "Yeah, it would be enough."

CHAPTER 10

The Future

The safe-house might have been hastily put together, but the bare essentials were more than adequate for Tarik and the Nu-Mans' comfort. Fortunately, the house had ten-foot ceilings, which gave Zax barely enough room not to feel confined. The whole inside walls, including the ceiling, had been sprayed with a material designed to block out any electronic signatures which might give away their position. Each had a bedroom and a mattress on the floor to sleep on. Tarik found his comfortable at first, being tired after such an active day. As the night passed, it only felt firmer. He had to keep rolling over or else he'd start getting sore places on parts of his body.

A chemical toilet kept them from having to go outside to use do their business. They had a large supply of water. Of course, none of the house's plumbing worked. That said, a portable sink had been set up with the drain piped to the outside. The sink provided both hot and cold water. Tarik and the Nu-Mans were able to sponge bath themselves adequately clean.

Clothing had been a problem for Tarik. Whoever had stocked the house failed to provide him with clothes designed to fit humans. All the clothing he had was what he showed up in. To be comfortable inside the mech-armor, all he wore was a tight fitting, clingy shirt where the sleeves stopped mid-bicep; underwear to keep his privates from flopping about; clingy shorts not much longer than his underwear; and socks.

Tarik had considered his options. Even if Lixa hadn't been there, he doubted he'd walk around naked while his hand washed clothes air dried with a fan. He had been self-conscious about his body most of his life. Not having hair covering most of it made him feel too exposed. Plus, there was a noticeable size difference in genitalia between human and Nu-Man males. Tarik played out a thought that if Lixa ever caught a peek of his man-pride, she'd break out in hysterical laughter; other Nu-Mans had over the years.

Before he stripped down, Tarik chose a traditional Nu-Man tunic, socks, and underwear. The socks were large enough for him to fit three feet into. He used the shears in a utility knife to cut the socks down the middle, from the top all the way to the toe. He then put his foot on the folded out material, wrapped both sides over, and cut off the excess material until the two sides met. Using all-duty tape, he bonded the opposing sides and had a functioning sock. His creation might be uncomfortable in his armor. But he would wash and dry his old clothing before going on the mission.

Similarly, he customized the underwear and tunic to where he felt comfortable and appropriate around Lixa.

Lixa.

They had spent some time together, but mostly Zax was always in the room. He tried hard to read her—what she really thought about him.

From as early as he could remember, Tarik had always wanted to be accepted. That's why he was so well-behaved during his time on the rebel base. He didn't want to be considered a freak. Again, every time he looked in the mirror it was hard for him to think anything other than that.

Did Lixa see him as an equal? Whenever she had the drop on him with the railgun and thought he might be a Skink, she seemed to have a prejudice against another species. Of course, it might have had nothing to do with prejudice without reason. The Skinks had doomed the Nu-Man species to an early death. And, technically, the rebels and the Skinks were at war, even though the Skinks might not be fully aware of who they were at war with and to what extent.

Tarik didn't want Lixa to see him as a freak. He found himself to be on his best behavior around her so as not to give her any opportunities to dislike him.

Zax had shot him a few eye rolls when he may have laid the *sweetness* on a little too thick. The last thing Tarik wanted was for his friend to call him out in front of Lixa. If she saw the two get into an argument, she might automatically take Zax's side; Nu-Man nature being what it was.

The shirt was the last item he washed in the sink. He used a small folding table as a clothesline and placed a fan close by. Parts of the clothing draping down bent to the artificial wind.

There were several chairs in the safe-house for them to sit on. The chairs were light but very sturdy to accommodate Nu-Man weight; made from some compound of Skink design. Three chairs were pushed against a table in the kitchen. Zax and Lixa had a box containing food on the counter and were going through the selections.

"Hey Tarik, you ready to eat?" Zax asked.

"Sure. How about some of that roasted lamb like we saw in the city? I'll go gather some wood from outside and start a fire," Tarik said as he stepped over.

Lixa stopped and turned a discerning eye toward him.

"Let's see here…" Zax fumbled around in the box. "Here you go, a container of cat food, *Lucky Lamb Recipe*."

"There's cat food in our supply box? Someone actually thought we'd have a cat here?" Lixa asked.

"No, I'm kidding," Zax said. "Tarik likes to be a smartass. So, I like to *smartass* right back at him. However," Zax turned the container around so Tarik and Lixa could both see it, "it is a container of salmon. I'm sure a cat would have no problem eating this."

"Meow," Tarik said.

"Uh, does that mean you want the salmon?" Zax asked.

"Meow, meow," Tarik said and held out his hand.

"You two make a very strange couple," Lixa said.

"Living for twenty-five years on a base out in the middle of nowhere limits my forms of entertainment," Tarik said. "Zax and I have been close for the last several years. He's my best friend."

"Yeah, and Tarik is my favorite pet," Zax said.

"Favorite pet? Go clean out my box, then," Tarik said.

"He does tricks, too," Zax said.

"Are we going to eat or are you two going to carry on all afternoon?" Lixa said. She held a pouch of corned beef and a box of crackers. After she had placed them on the table, she asked, "What does everyone want to drink?"

"Vita-water orange, if you have it," Zax said.

"Vita-grape for me," Tarik said.

"All we have is orange," Lixa said.

"That's fine," Tarik said. He looked over on the counter and saw a stack of disposable plates. He walked over and counted three from the stack, and took them to the table.

Lixa placed the bottles of Vita-water on the table and sat down. "Thank you," she said when Tarik handed her a plate.

Zax took his and immediately tore into his pouch of chicken.

"You're welcome," Tarik said to Lixa. "You're welcome," he coarsely told Zax.

The food pouches were large, nearly a foot long and ten inches wide. It took a lot of calories to satisfy a Nu-Man. Each pouch contained a spork, knife, and a thin napkin, along with small packs of salt and pepper. The protein portions took up most of the self-heating food container. Two hard crackers were included. There were two side dishes. One was a starch of some type and the other a green vegetable. Tarik had potatoes Au gratin and spinach, of which was to his liking.

Zax wolfed down a large portion of chicken and chased it with the two crackers. He took a swig of water, and then he reached for the box of crackers and pulled out a pack.

Lixa calmly cut into her corned beef and began eating, taking care to chew the meat sufficiently. Her gaze focused mainly on the table. She bit into her cracker and wiped her mouth with the napkin.

Tarik had eaten a mouthful of salmon. The fish had a fresh, delightful flavor that had him wanting more. It looked like Lixa had checked out from the table. He wondered what she was thinking about.

"The mission," Lixa started, "do you…do you think your chances are good?"

Now Tarik knew. Fate had dealt everyone a hand they would have gladly folded and asked for a new one if that were possible. The reality of the situation was grim. The finish line of the race was just up ahead. Each passing second cemented to a reality of final consequences.

"We're not going to fail," Zax said without looking up from his plate. He continued to eat like the matter had been decided.

"Honestly, it's hard to say," Tarik said and then wiped his mouth. "One of the things we were hoping for was the element of surprise. After that Skink scout ship discovered the base, well, they might heighten security at the old nuclear weapons factory."

"They have no idea of our plan," Zax said.

"I hope he's right," Tarik said. "I also hope that if anyone is captured, well, I hope they'll be able to keep our plans secret."

"Nu-Mans are tough. At least, we rebels are. We won't break. We're put together a little different than the others. I guess the Skinks couldn't engineer rebellion out of all of us," Zax said.

"Rebellion was a big part of human nature. Human history had wars of epic proportion. Even chimpanzees would gather in groups against others and savagely attack each other. Rebellion is part of our genetic code," Tarik said.

"I'm prepared to fight if I have to," Lixa said. "Still…I've never killed anyone."

"I hadn't either, until yesterday," Tarik said, thinking back to when he obliterated two Skink warriors, with a railgun, and the hand-to-hand melee with the other. His thoughts then shifted to the Skink citizen who came upon them later as they made their way to old-life.

"Yesterday was my first battle. Most of the rebels haven't killed before," Zax said.

Silence hung in the air for a bit. Lixa turned her head to Tarik, and asked, "What's wrong?"

Tarik shoved the spinach around in the container with his spork. "Yesterday. Yesterday I fought four of the Skink warriors at the base and killed them all. That didn't affect me much. I mean, I was fighting for my life. It was them or me. If things had gone just a bit differently, the last warrior might have killed me. But then something else happened. After we had escaped to the city, I saw a Skink citizen in real life for the first time. In a way, I think I felt the same way you did when you saw me. It's not every day you meet another intelligent species. He came close enough to touch.

"I didn't feel any hate for him, at that moment. He was oblivious to me, thinking I was some everyday security patrol. I wanted a chance to sit down with him. Ask him a million questions. Touch his skin and see if we could find a way to enjoy mutual respect. But there was no realistic opportunity for that. I had resolved that my contact with Skinks would only be me in my mech-armor, never to have that *first-encounter* moment.

"But then later, when we were almost out of the city, another Skink citizen crossed our path and was suspect of the situation. He was seconds away from calling in a report when I created a ruse to distract him. I bought enough time to…end his life before he could give away our position."

Lixa reached over and patted his left hand, which rested on the table. "You did what you had to do."

"I killed him with my own two hands." Tarik bit his lip and breathed in slowly. "He didn't have a chance. In the blink of an eye, I snuffed out a life. He wasn't trying to kill me. But…but I couldn't…I just couldn't." He let his words die.

"You had no choice. There's nothing to feel bad about," Lixa said.

"Tarik, don't you be going soft on me. You've got to stay focused. You can't allow any distractions during the mission," Zax said.

Tarik brought the hand holding the spork down on the table. "I'm *not* going soft! I'm going to be in automatic mode when we attack the facility. Nothing is going to stop me from my mission."

"Good, let's finish up eating now," Zax said and spooned pasta into his mouth.

Tarik and Lixa resumed eating, drinking Vita-water between bites.

Suppressing a burp, Tarik said, "What upsets me about killing that Skink is that it seemed like such a waste. A life gone, and we didn't gain anything. We just prevented from losing what we had. If we're going to kill, I want to advance the mission. I know this all sounds crazy to you two, but killing does have a way of messing with your emotions."

"Yeah, I can tell, because the mission *was* advanced because you killed him. Don't try to put a value on death. The odds don't have to be even to justify killing. I'd kill ten Skinks without thinking if the only reward was a piece of candy. We're at war. There is no good or bad. There is only victory or death."

Tarik slowly nodded. "You're right. You're right. Thanks. Thanks for putting this in perspective for me."

"Tarik, I'm not worried about you," Zax said. "I've seen you in action. We're going to win this."

"I see that you're finished, Zax. Are you going to have another?" Lixa asked.

"Maybe a little later. I'm going to let this one settle in my stomach a bit."

"I'm finished, too. I'm ready for my Z-bar. Would you like yours now?" she asked.

"Sure, let's get it over with."

Rising from her chair, Lixa opened another box and pulled out a silver wrapped bar big enough to cover her palm. A Z-bar contained a special nutrient invented by the Skinks necessary for Nu-Man vitality. Their genetic manipulation of humans had its deficiencies from the beginning. The sasquatch-human hybrid needed the nutrient for health benefits. Going a month without the additive would bring complications.

The wrappers crinkled as Lixa and Zax peeled them back.

"You want some?" Zax said to Tarik and laughed. The big guy ate his in three bites and was done.

Lixa took her time in eating hers.

"I bet it tastes like it smells," Tarik said.

"Try it and find out," Zax said.

"You know I can't eat that."

"Why can't you have a Z-bar?" Lixa asked.

"Uh, I was told I should never eat it. They were afraid that maybe I could have an allergic reaction and die. So, I've stayed away from it. I wouldn't want to eat it anyway. It smells horrible."

"Eh, you get used to it," Zax said.

"Kind of like Hud's cooking," Tarik said.

The two shared a laugh.

"I miss the old guy," Zax said.

"Me, too." Tarik closed his eyes and smiled. "Me, too."

CHAPTER 11

The Present

The porch boards creaked every time the rocking chair tipped forward. There was nothing better than a tall glass of whiskey to reward one's self after a day tilling the fields. His boots remained on the ground just by the steps leading into the house. A Remington 870 shotgun propped against the façade near the back door.

Marvin '*Dougie*' Douglas grew up on the east side of Detroit during the 1950s. The city boomed with the expansion of twenty-five auto plants built by the *Big Three*: General Motors, Ford Motor Company, and Chrysler Corporation. The GI Bill's home loan guaranty gave soldiers who had survived World War II a chance to start life afresh in a modest home to raise a family.

Douglas lived just off Chandler Park Drive, in one of the *cookie-cutter* homes that averaged between seven to eight hundred square feet in size. Life had been much simpler then, and Douglas liked to keep it simple.

His dad had stormed the beaches of Normandy on June 6, 1944. His mother had told them that fact, once when she was sober in between bottles of vodka, as his dad never once spoke about his time during the war to him.

Douglas blamed the war for his dad's obsession with working at the auto plant. The man seemed to prefer his time there than at home. Working sixteen hour days, six days a week, was the rule rather than the exception. The money was good. There was decent food to eat, but his dad was always on the frugal side, except when it came to cars. His dad's greatest love in his life was his car, which he would replace about every two years.

The vehicle that stuck out the most in Douglas' mind was the 1957 Chevrolet Bel Air convertible. The color was Larkspur Blue, and his dad would give it a quick wash every day after work before he would come in to eat supper, even if it was dark. Sundays involved a detailed cleaning and a fresh coat of wax. His cars always shined like it was on the showroom floor.

The rest of his dad's money went toward buying US Savings Bonds and supplementing the income of the uncle who had raised him. He wanted to have enough money in the bank to live comfortably during the last years of his life, and not be like his Uncle Mitch.

Both of his dad's parents died in an auto accident when his dad was five-years-old. Uncle Mitch, who wasn't married or had any children of his own, treated his nephew as a son. Mitch had inherited an old farm near Mark Twain National Forest in Missouri and moved there after his nephew went off to fight in WWII.

Mitch wasn't much of a farmer, and if it hadn't been for Marvin Douglas' dad sending him money, he would have lost the place to tax collectors.

Having a drunk for a mom wasn't any fun for Douglas. Having a *missing-in-action* father meant he had to basically raise himself. School was boring, but the streets were full of opportunities. Marvin Douglas learned how to do exciting things, like shoplift candy and comic books from stores. One of the earliest skills he taught himself was how to pick locks on doors. It was easy back then. All you needed was a flathead screwdriver, and in less than a minute, he could wedge the tool behind the latch bolt and with a little technique, slide it away from the strike plate until the door would simply pull open.

Soon enough Dougie found himself teamed up with a group of like-minded kids. They called themselves the *Stilettos*. Each carried switchblade knives with six-inch-blades. They were a badass group who looked for trouble. Dougie quickly gained the reputation of drawing blood when anybody disagreed with him.

Years of success had at one point lulled him into a false sense of security. He eventually got sloppy on a good sized drug deal. The mishap bought him a twenty-year reservation at the State Prison of Southern Michigan.

When Douglas left prison, he was like a man landing on a foreign planet. The world had changed so much. There were no friends or family to take him in. In fact, if any of his enemies knew he was out, they were sure to come pay him a special visit that would terminate his life.

His dad had died of a heart attack when Dougie was twenty-five. He didn't even bother going to the funeral. Why would he? He hadn't seen or talked to the man in almost ten years.

His mother sold the house and moved away not long after. She left no forwarding address, and Dougie never heard from her again. He imagined she cashed all those savings bonds and moved to Vegas. For some reason, his mother had a fascination with Sin City.

There were two things other than the paper bag of clothing and possessions that Dougie had when he left prison. One was the deed to his Uncle Mitch's farm in Missouri. The other was twenty thousand dollars he had hidden in an ice chest in a remote part of a city park.

He was amazed and happy that the money was still there. He had constantly thought of some new construction unearthing the treasure and his nest egg disappearing forever. Dougie would even scan newspapers looking for such a story but never found one. If someone had found the money, they probably would have kept it secret. He knew he would have.

That didn't happen. He had twenty thousand dollars in cash. When he checked on his deed to the farm, he expected to learn that it had been sold to collect back taxes. The only other entity greater at stealing than a thief was the government. Nothing was ever going to stop them from getting their money. But Dougie learned he still owned the farm. It seemed like the place was in too remote of a location for anyone to want it. All he had to do was pay the taxes and move in. So, he did.

The convict had learned in life that if you leave people alone, then they will leave you alone. Prison had kept him isolated from the rest of the world, and he grew to like that. What he didn't like was being locked up with the dregs of society. He'd had enough of that, too.

Once he moved to the farm and made the house livable again, he was desperate for some entertainment. Dougie took advantage of a promotional deal and had a dish put in his yard and bought a subscription to satellite TV and the internet.

Prison had been good for one thing. He was allowed access to computers. For some reason learning how computers worked and how to search for things on the internet came naturally. He'd even had thoughts how his life could have been totally different had he gone off to school and learned a trade in computer science. He was an old man now, and *shoulda-woulda-coulda* dreams didn't bring happiness.

One thing that did bring Douglas happiness was scoring big. Small time thievery was for amateurs and not worthy of his time. Twenty years in the pen had taught him to be patient. If he was going to risk his freedom, it was going to be a big deal that would pull in enough cash to last the rest of his life.

Oh, he would still farm. Farming had been another talent he'd possessed and didn't know until he moved to Missouri. Working in the soil, planting seeds, watching the plants grow, keeping the weeds out; farming gave him something to do. The soil in his area was exceptionally rich. Selling fresh vegetables to the local grocery stores kept a steady supply of income. Just a little more, though, than he needed to cover keeping the farm going, paying electricity and tax, and his whiskey bill he'd ring up often at a dive bar named *Lost Times*.

The twenty grand pile had dwindled greatly getting the farm back up to speed. It took five thousand dollars to get the old tractor on the place up to operational condition. Replacing the tires and repairing the engine and transmission would have cost him a lot more if he hadn't met a guy at *Lost Times*, who did it on the side after working his day job. The fifteen-year-old truck he bought to get around in, cost eight thousand.

Douglas didn't want to give up farm life, but he did want to do a little bit of traveling before he got too old to take care of himself. Nothing too extravagant. He had always wanted to visit iconic places like Hoover Dam, the Grand Canyon, and Niagra Falls. Maybe even stop off in one of those places near Las Vegas where you could order a woman off a menu. His bucket list wasn't long but flying, hotels, eating out every day, and paying for taxis was going to cost a bundle.

A bundle he didn't have but knew how to get. In order for his plan to work, he had to be cool, exercise patience, once again, and masterfully execute a flawless plan that would set him for life. Douglas had the skills. He had done his homework. He had set a plan in motion that had already accomplished fifty percent of his goal. Soon, his plan would come to a conclusion. Years in prison would finally pay off.

The World Wide Web was a wonderful place. You could buy practically anything online and never have to leave the comfort of home, because it would be delivered to your doorstep. Of course, there were certain restrictions on what you could legally purchase. That is, unless you knew your away around the web. Really, really, knew your way around the web. Because beyond Google and Bing, Amazon and eBay, there were other places the curious, the adventurist, could go. Places shunned by the good people of the local Baptist Church or the lawmakers of city hall. Douglas had found the Deep Web. Within the Deep Web, he found the Dark Web. Darknets made up the Dark Web. The Dark Web provided the ultimate shopping market for anything, and anything did mean *anything*, to those who had the means to purchase the illegal or extravagant excess.

Douglas' endeavor, though well-planned, was too difficult for him to execute alone. Fortunately, the acquaintance who had rebuilt his tractor proved to be a simple and trustworthy man. The man wasn't very bright, despite his mechanic skills. But he had been ignored most of his life and was in need of a friend. A friend that he didn't want to disappoint. A friend that treated him with respect and praise. A friend with a plan to make a large sum of money and share it with him.

Dougie Douglas was that friend.

A murder of crows squatting in a big maple erupted from their haunt in a mass of black, cawing in protest of whatever disturbed their rest, far beyond the barn.

Douglas shifted his gaze from his mind's eye and scanned the four acres of his garden. The land just behind his house was flat enough to more than double the size of his crop production if he wanted. But keeping up with four acres by himself was the best he could do. The property totaled thirty acres in all. The remaining land blended in with the other mighty trees of the neighboring national forest.

Housed near the back of the barn, placed on the southern side in order to provide a little protection from the cold north winds of the winter, something raised the ire of his brood of chickens.

First the crows and now the chickens. Somebody was on his property. It was probably those damn kids again. They had been messing with him of late. He had tried to quickly nip it in the bud, calling the local school and making a threat to shoot anyone he caught. He figured such an extreme reaction would prompt immediate action. Oh, he did get a visit from local police, too. But that had in fact been part of the plan. He wanted to show no fear of the authorities. If he was ever expected of being up to no good, why would he practically invite a call from the police? Douglas had confidence in his plan. He figured causing a distraction might throw a little more fear his way from the townspeople.

The whiskey had found its way to the last drop in the bottom of the glass. Douglas pushed himself up from the rocking chair, feeling a sharp pain in his lower back for his reward in the field. He grabbed his shotgun and laid it on the porch while he sat on the steps and shoved on his boots.

"They better not do something stupid, or I may not try to miss," he told himself. He brought the long gun across his chest and pushed the safety to the *off* position. There wasn't a shell in the chamber, but all it would take was a pull back of the front stock to load one in.

The chickens had quieted by the time he made it to the back of the barn. Douglas' tired eyes didn't want to cooperate like they had when they were younger. He found himself making conscious efforts to discern images within his blurred vision. Of late, he had overlooked things he was searching for on a regular basis, even if they were in the drawer he was looking in. A trip to the eye doctor was something he admitted he had put off for too long.

He turned his gaze to the ground. The dirt was drier now, so it would be harder for the culprit to leave tracks. The first time the unwanted visitor, or unwanted *visitors*, Douglas couldn't be sure if there had been more than one person who had invaded his property, the ground had been softer due to an earlier drizzle. If it hadn't been for the tracks, Douglas might have suspected a deer had breached his fence and got into what was remaining of his winter garden and some of the lettuce from his spring garden. But no, it was obvious an animal hadn't done the damage. The prints left behind were made from shoes. Not just any ordinary shoes, but shoes massive in size. There was no way a conventional shoe had made that print; not even Shaquille O'Neal's shoe could have been that large. These prints were obviously made with clown shoes epic in size. Douglas remembered seeing a clown at a circus wearing shoes that size once. He wondered then how the man was able to even walk in them.

Something dropped on the top of Douglas' floppy hat and hit the ground by his feet. He looked down and saw an acorn. Turning his gaze up, there were no trees near, especially not an oak, for the acorn to fall from. *Maybe a bird dropped it*, he thought. Though, he looked and didn't see the culprit anywhere. But, his vision wasn't the best, so where the missile had come from would just have to remain a mystery.

Stepping over to his winter garden, someone had helped themselves to a few more turnips. The large shoe prints were in the area, but Douglas couldn't be sure if any were fresh or just remnants from the day before. For the life of him, he couldn't figure why kids would come all the way to his place to steal vegetables. He'd understand if maybe if they egged his house or TPed some trees.

Whoever it was must have been strange. But having a snooper around wasn't good. No, not good at all. He couldn't afford to have some prankster spoil his plans. He'd have to go and buy one of those wildlife cameras and set it up to find who was trespassing. He'd do it first thing in the morning. The agitator needed to be brought to justice.

Douglas headed back to the house and laughed to himself at that last thought. *Justice*, funny how people felt the wrong that they do as permissible, but let someone else try to take the same advantage, and they are in the wrong. It was all just part of human nature, he figured. So were vices. Some people could put limits on the things that tried to own their souls. Some people were weak and couldn't control themselves. Those were the people Douglas sought out on the Dark Web. He could make their desires come true, and they would return the favor. To each, his own.

An old green Chevy S-10 with a camper on the bed had pulled up in the back. The driver leaned against the vehicle while letting the sun warm his back. He pulled away to meet Douglas. His hands hid behind the front of his bib overalls.

"How's it going, Dougie?" the man asked.

"Had a good day. Every day's a good day when you know you're going to hit the lottery," Dougie said. He grabbed the barrel of the shotgun and rested the butt of the stock on the ground. He wiped some phlegm from the side of his lips, thinking that another glass of whiskey would be good right now. "Make any progress today?"

The man shrugged. "I got my ears open. We gonna do it like the last time. Take our time. Wait for the opportunity to present itself. Then, *bam*! We're in an' out before you know it."

"I like a man with confidence," Dougie said. "Say, you thirsty? I could use a little hootch, and I don't like to drink alone when I have company."

The man laughed. "The only other person that comes around is me."

Dougie closed his left eye and shook his head. "Nah, I got someone poking around here. That needs to stop."

"Still?"

"Yep."

"I'm surprised. They sent out emails at the school. Made an announcement over the morning intercom and everything. I figured that would have spooked any kids off," the man said.

"Not yet, but I'm planning on getting one of those wildlife cameras and catching whoever it is."

"Good idea," the man said.

"Com'on, Buddy. Let's go pour ourselves a stiff one. We can check on the goods a little later on."

CHAPTER 12

The Future

The hour was late. Zax had already turned in for the night. The mech-armor had been hooked up to the zero-energy battery for well over twelve hours. Transmetal had a molecular *memory*. The damaged armor's atoms realigned to their original specifications.

The grenade launcher was now fully functional, and the supply chamber full. Projectiles for the armor's blaster was full to the top as well. The mech-armor was one heck of a battle machine. Tarik wished that the Nu-Mans could have the same amount of protection and firepower as he. A transmetal suit large enough to fit them would be huge. That much bulk wouldn't be able to fit in the two seated jumpers like they used to escape.

Tarik and Lixa sat at the table. Lixa had made some chamomile tea and had poured Tarik a cup. They had talked for nearly two hours nonstop; probably the reason why Zax went to bed a little early. He had little to add to the conversation.

Tarik mostly spoke of his life while growing up on the base and some of the most memorable instructors. Of course, he told a lot of stories that involved Hudson.

Lixa had lived a comfortable, normal life, as the majority of Nu-Mans also enjoyed. Poverty had been eliminated by the Skinks. So had diseases and cancers. Genetic anomalies such as autism, multiple sclerosis, and ALS were conditions humans had suffered. The Nu-Mans knew nothing but good general health.

The Skinks maintained the social norm of an economy. All Nu-Mans of working age, except for mothers, who were allowed to stay home and raise children, were required to chose a profession and participate in the workforce. Skinks believed that if you didn't work you didn't deserve to eat. They were lenient masters but didn't allow anyone to violate their structured guidelines.

Lixa was the daughter of Bix, who was one of the most skilled rebels on the team. Lixa shared the independent nature of her father and had trained under his guidance for a day which might come.

The day had come. That day was now.

"I can't believe you've never had chamomile tea," Lixa said. She brought the cup to her lips and drank some.

Tarik looked at the golden liquid and breathed the warm, aromatic odor. "We had tea on the base. If I've had chamomile before, I don't remember. I didn't care for the tea we had on the base. If fact, I hated it. It made me want to gag." He took another sniff. "This, though, smells…interesting."

"You won't know until you try it."

He was about to engage in a battle that might kill him and everyone else on the team. This was no time to be scared to taste a cup of tea.

Picking up the cup, he motioned it toward Lixa in a mock toast and took a sip.

"Well, what do you think?"

"It's nothing like I expected. I like it." He drank in a mouthful this time. "It's earthy, flowery. It tastes medicinal, in a way. It must be good for you."

"It's an herbal tea made from chamomile flowers. It's supposed to be good to settle the stomach and help make you calm and sleep better at night."

"This is the perfect time for me to have this, then. The salmon had my stomach a little upset, and we'll be going to bed soon."

Lixa drank more of her tea. "Yeah. And tomorrow brings us closer to the end."

Tarik watched the young Nu-Man drift away in her thoughts. Her father would be risking his life on this mission. It didn't help that everyone knew the inevitable was coming. Time was the real God of the universe. Time waited for nothing. Time demanded an outcome. The universe marched to the edicts of time.

"I know just some details of the mission," Lixa said. "I know about the time project and that the mission is to get you there and to go back in time to prevent the Skinks from discovering Earth. I don't know how you're supposed to do that."

Tarik didn't know if he should risk giving her the details. Not because he didn't trust her. He just didn't know if the Skinks would have a way of extracting the information if they were to capture her. With the mission so close at hand, the risks seemed minimal. "We've got Nu-Mans inside the base who are on our side. They're supposed to get us in without a fight. That's the plan, anyway. If we are discovered, we're coming in a location that if we hit hard and fast, we should be able to get me in position.

"I'm going to be sent back to the year twenty-twenty. A few days early, hopefully, because we don't know how accurate the machine is before the Skink probe warps into Earth's orbit. The probe will circle the Earth for twenty-four hours and then land. It will then continue to gather data until some twelve hours. After that, the probe leaves Earth and warps back to the Skinks' home planet.

"My job is to retrieve the data crystal with the information gathered and replace it with one that will show the Earth to be an uninhabitable planet."

"Sounds easy enough," Lixa said and giggled.

Tarik shrugged. "Sounds really far-fetched when I listen to myself say it. Still, that is the plan. If I destroyed the probe, and I don't know if I could even do that, then the Skinks would just send another. We can't have that. Once they receive the false information, they'll never send another probe to this solar system again."

"It's so strange to think about it. You know, if you actually do it. The Nu-Man history, though only a few hundred years old, will be wiped out. Like we never even existed. Everyone I've known. Everyone I've loved," Lixa said, her eyes growing moist. "*I* will never be."

Contemplating one's mortality was one thing. Questioning eternity was quite another.

"What happens to me?" Lixa asked. "My soul? What if *I'll* never be? If there is an afterlife, what happens to my soul?"

Tarik didn't know what to believe about an afterlife. So, he pretty much didn't waste much time contemplating it. It was obvious Lixa had faith in a higher power. He wasn't one to trash someone's beliefs. Especially at a time like this. *Hope* sometimes was as necessary as food, water, and the air they breathed.

"If there are souls, I do not believe that they are destructible." Tarik didn't lie. He had at least considered the possibility and shared that belief. "Your soul would find its way into another body. You would live again and, when you die, will find a rightful place in the universe."

"But I won't be *me*. How could I be? My circumstances would be all different. I wouldn't, couldn't be the same person. The thought scares me." Lixa closed her eyes to help push away the pain.

"When I was old enough to understand, I was told my father was a recombinant mass of goo and my mother a petri dish. I grew up a genetic abomination. If souls exist, then I have one. The universe will afford me the same rights and privileges as anyone else. Time is just one dimension in the universe. If the universe is that kind to me, then I'm sure it would care for a soul that once existed in its time dimension."

"That actually makes sense on some level," Lixa said. "I just need to stop worrying about it. I had no control of when and where I was born, and I shouldn't be worrying about where I'm going. It's all inevitable anyway." She took a deep breath. "And you, if you make it, you'll get to live your life with other humans. You'll finally fit in, be with your own kind. You'd like that, wouldn't you?"

"Maybe. I hope so." Tarik shrugged. "I've read a lot about human history. Humans had many undesirable qualities. I honestly don't know if I could ever learn to like them like I have Nu-Mans. Nu-Mans are mostly honest and kind. Giving and loving." He reached his left hand over and touched her arm. "Like you. If I met someone like you, there might be a chance for happiness."

Lixa smiled.

Feeling like he was too forward, he retracted his hand. "But, my future, even though I'm going back into the past, is uncertain. I won't know what the situation is really like until I get there. Happiness for me might just be a dream."

"Dreams can come true."

"So can nightmares."

"There's no guarantees of happiness in your future. All we really have is the present, anyway." She looked at him, her green eyes sparkling. "I'm going to lie down."

Tarik realized the time and thought he had finally worn out his welcome. "I'm sorry, I've kept you up too late." He went to stand, but Lixa's hand came over to his.

"If you want happiness, you have to take the opportunities offered. My bed is large enough for two."

Genuinely shocked, Tarik could only stare for several moments. "Lixa, you are beautiful. In fact, you are the most beautiful Nu-Man I've ever met. I'm…I'm so different from you. How can you stand to…to think of me that way?"

Lixa stood and took his hand, beckoning him to rise. "In the dark, we only see each other's soul."

*

Tarik closed the door to Lixa's room. It was morning. A new morning. A morning different from any other morning before in his life.

The night spent with Lixa was indescribable. The torrid emotions the two shared seemed otherworldly. He had been lost in passion—it genuinely felt like the two had become one. Even now moments from the night played over in his mind.

But it was morning. The sun rose to shine its light over old-life. Today would be the day where either Tarik would leave this time and travel back to the past or die in the attempt.

To Tarik, it was his first day on Earth, of sorts, with his new found perspective on life. Ironically, fate had deemed this his last day on Earth too.

He went into the washroom and took care of his morning rituals.

The mission now seemed like total madness. What chance did a team of nine have against the defenses of the Skink masters? Why squander lives only to gain nothing? Lixa would lose her father, and for what? And he, Tarik, would lose the new love of his life.

The love of his life. His heart swelled at the thought. He now had an idea of the invading emotions that love had, which inspired men over the ages. The poems and songs that were written; the battles fought, all because of the mysterious power of love.

Yes, he knew the death of the whole Nu-Man race was inevitable. But wasn't death inevitable for all? What difference did it really make if Earth's children died and the Skinks claimed sole owners of the planet? No one, not even him, would be around to care. Why not live life to the fullest to the last breath?

He looked at the old mirror on the wall as he washed his hands. His face was distorted in the warped reflection. He thought of what had brought him here that day. How he would not have met Lixa if she hadn't been part of the rebels' plan. Many sacrifices had been made by Nu-Man males and females, including lives lost; all on behalf of Tarik and the mission dreamed.

It would be incredibly selfish for him to abandon the mission now. It was as if he were on a levitation rail train and it was moving too fast for him to jump off. The destination was predetermined, just like his fate.

Tarik dried his hands. All these errant thoughts clouded his resolve for the mission. He had built this love scenario in his mind with Lixa, and he didn't even have a clue if she shared his feelings this morning.

What if in the light of day, she would see him differently? He *was* just a puny human. Maybe she was lonely. Maybe she felt sorry for him. Dare he think it? Maybe she was just offering some sort of compensation for his sacrifice.

Tarik's head began to hurt. It was time to clear his mind and focus on the mission. For that, he needed hydration and nutrition. He would have to wait and see how Lixa treated him after she awoke.

When Tarik left the washroom, Zax was in the kitchen getting himself something to eat. As he stepped by the table, Zax made no effort to look at him, although Tarik was certain the big guy knew he was there.

The distance between them was palpable.

Tarik heard Lixa's door open, and then the door to the washroom close.

Zax went to a cooler and took out two bottles of Vita-water. He turned and put both on the counter by the food. Looking up at Tarik, he said, "I'm not sure if I want to know."

Tarik stepped over and took a bottle of water, grabbed a food pouch, and said, "Then don't ask." He locked gazes with the Nu-Man. The expression on his face offered no apology.

The Nu-Man shifted his lips around like he had a bad taste in his mouth. "Whatever."

Tarik placed the water and food pouch on the table and sat.

"We'll be leaving in a few hours," Zax said. He grabbed his food pouch and water, walked around the kitchen counter, and sat at the end of the table, away from Tarik.

Tarik had been peeling the wrapper from the container and momentarily hesitated. *Should he share his thoughts about canceling the mission with his best friend?* There was no way he felt like doing that right now. He shoved the food wrapper to the side and looked at his meal. "What is this? The package said it was *ham*."

"It is ham."

The concoction was square and about as thick as four slices of bread. "But it's yellow. Ham is not yellow."

"It's a blend of egg, cheese, and ham. It's very nutritious. It's a common breakfast food," Zax said, sounding content to be making small talk rather than berating Tarik over his tryst with Lixa.

"It wasn't *common* on the base. I've never had this before." He used his spork to shave off a slab, cut it in half, and put it in his mouth.

The washroom door closed, and Lixa entered the kitchen. "Good morning."

Tarik hopped up still chewing half a mouthful of the ham mixture. He quickly swallowed and found himself cemented to the floor without a clue of how to greet her.

Her soft gaze showed remnants of sleep refused to let go. She offered him a kind smile, leaned over and gave him a quick hug, of which he returned, and went over behind the kitchen counter near the cooler. "I see you two have started without me." Lixa opened the cooler and got a bottle of water.

His head turned and followed her, but Tarik remained standing.

"You should sit and eat," Zax said, wasting no time eliminating his breakfast.

Lixa opened her water and fumbled through the food pouches.

Tarik sat and went back to the task of eating. He was so caught up in the whirlpool of emotions that he didn't remember tasting his first bite.

With food and water in hand, Lixa sat at the end of the table near Tarik. She began to unwrap her food. "Well, today's the big day." There was a slight cheer in her voice, but it did sound contrived. She pulled the wrapper to the side and started eating, noticeably not making eye contact with the other men.

Zax looked over at Tarik and narrowed his eyes. There were probably a lot of things the big guy wanted to say. But with the mission so close at hand, he must have known that any conflict now would only cause major harm.

"It is," Tarik agreed, the pit in his stomach grew.

"I'm worried," Lixa said and drank some water. Her cheeks quivered a bit. She was fighting away tears.

"There's plenty to be concerned about. But there's no other way. Our time is short, and we have to make our move now," Zax said. "Your father is a strong man. He's a great leader. If anyone can get us into the nuclear center, it's him. And, you know he'll do everything to protect the lives of his men and his own life, too."

"I care about you two, also. You'll be going inside. Tarik has to go deep enough to use the time machine. He'll vanish back in time if he makes it. How are you going to get out of there?"

"The operatives that we have inside, if they can get us in, the easier part will be getting me out. There is a grand plan, and if we stick to it, you'll be able to join us at the new safe-house as soon as you can," Zax said.

"I'm going to miss you, Lixa," Tarik said, not caring if the tone of his voice exposed his feelings. He looked over at Zax. "You too, Zax, but you know that. You know how I feel about you." This morning's enmity had weighed enough on Tarik that his pride had melted into remorse. He didn't want anything to come between them, especially now that before night fell, they would never see each other again.

"Tarik, I'll miss you too. You're a kind soul. When you make it back in time, you'll have to be careful of those other humans. You know their history of being cruel to each other," Lixa said.

"I'll never forget you," Tarik said. "Ever." At this point, this was as far as he would share his emotions. His thoughts of running off with Lixa now seemed more like a silly dream. His fate was determined. He, Zax, and the others would soon risk their lives for a chance to reset history. The mission was bigger than any Nu-Man or human. Any love he and Lixa shared would have to remain in their hearts.

CHAPTER 13

The Present

"Good morning Salem, Missouri. Time to get up and shave, shower, and get in ship-shape to start the day. This is your ol' pal Al on KQKY bringing you the best of Classic Rock of the '60s, '70s, and '80s. Guess what time it is? It's time to drive, The Cars!"

Cole woke to the laid-back rhythm of Rick Ocasek's guitar enticing the listener to "Let the Good Times Roll." As sleep let go of his mind, the pulsing beat gave him an extra dose of energy.

He sat on the edge of his bed with his feet hanging down, feeling the dampness of yet another night sweat. Though he could not recall, he inevitably had his reoccurring bigfoot dream.

Bringing his hand from behind his head, he rubbed it through his hair on the top of his head. He immediately thought of Charlotte, and how last night she said that she had preferred it when his hair was longer. *Crap!* He didn't want anything to work against him with her. There was nothing he could really do to make his hair grow faster. Then, he remembered an ancient bottle of Rogaine still in the washroom cabinet that his dad had bought to treat thinning hair on the crown of his head. Would that stuff help *his* hair grow faster?

He glanced at the clock and realized he was wasting time. Feet hit the floor, and then socks went on. When he stood in front of the mirror, wearing only his underwear, his gaze immediately went to his hair rather than inspecting his developing muscles. Maybe he could wear a cap until his hair grew out? But that wouldn't work. School policy didn't allow boys to wear caps during class. He was just going to have to have patience and let nature take its course.

Cole put on his pants and shirt, and then went through the morning rituals in the washroom. He picked up his pace a bit to make up for lost time.

The automatic coffee maker had a pot brewed, and the warm aroma hung in the kitchen's air. Cole heard his dad stirring about and quickly grabbed a spoon from the drawer and a cereal bowl from the cabinet, and scooped two spoons of sugar in the bottom. He had to change his routine up a little to ensure he didn't get caught sneaking sugar in. He went for the milk next and poured it half-full, and returned the jug to the fridge. His dad was by the kitchen doorway as he headed for the bowl, with the cereal box in hand.

As usual, focused on the coffee pot like a zombie going after fresh brains, Mark Rainwater lumbered in. With the grace of the Frankenstein monster, he pulled a mug from a hook under the counter and poured a cup of coffee. His eyes fully opened as the mug reached his lips. "Morning," he said, and then took his first taste. "Ugh, forgot to put in the sugar." He opened a drawer and picked out a teaspoon.

Cole had a mound of Cheerios in his bowl and was carefully digging toward the milk layer without spilling any on the table. He watched his dad step over to the sugar bowl and scoop out a heaping spoon full. *Why did his dad decide to use a spoon for his sugar this morning?*

While stirring the sweetness in, he said, "Charlotte seemed nice."

Cole nodded, crunching away at the whole grain goodness. Then he wondered what marshmallow bits mixed in would taste like. A whole lot better, for sure. "She is a nice girl. She's good in science and mature for her age."

Mark smiled. "Are you mature for your age?"

After a pause, Cole said, "You know, Dad, that's a question I've never thought much about until lately. I've read a lot of things, and I do know more about certain subjects than some adults do. But I'm just starting to understand what feeling *mature* is like. I'm starting to think differently than I used to. I see things in a different way. It's like *I didn't know* what *I didn't know* until I could see with different eyes. It's like my conscious is expanding, or something."

"You're growing up. Your brain is still developing, and you're learning from your experiences. Hormones play a role in that too. Part of being mature is not to let your hormones overrule your head."

"I guess so," Cole said, letting his dad's words sink in. The way the world worked in his mind was changing. There were so many things he thought he understood that now he wasn't so sure. There were things too he never cared to understand, but now he did. He forced in another spoon of cereal. *Life used to be simpler*, he thought.

"You think you could catch a ride with Joey, after practice? His dad has offered to do that, for when I get held over at work."

"You're working over today?"

Mark shrugged his shoulders and closed one eye, "*Wellll*, not exactly." He cleared his throat. "I...I was thinking I might go into town after work, and...uh, check out the gym Charlotte's mom mentioned."

Cole stopped chewing. He turned his head and gazed up at his dad.

After an uncomfortable amount of time had passed, Mark asked, "What are you staring at?"

Chewing what was left in his mouth and swallowing, Cole said, "I thought you said you didn't have time to work out?"

"Yeah, I said that. But you know, I'm not getting any younger. If you want your old dad to be in good shape and live a long life, then he's going to have to start taking better care of himself. You see how working out is getting your body in better shape. You don't want your dad to become some fat old man, do you?"

There was no use in arguing that point. It was funny, though, that his dad didn't get that *grand revelation* until meeting Lori Meadows last night. "You like her, don't you?"

His dad became the proverbial *deer in the headlights.*

"Charlotte's mom. You like her. I can tell." He had thought so last night but hadn't given any consideration this morning.

"Hey, well, you know. She's a nice lady...takes care of herself...she's a good mother, I can tell."

"She talks too much," Cole said, and then commenced reducing the pile of cereal to the last floaters atop the milk.

"Lori? Nah, I wouldn't say that. She was probably just a little nervous last night. Wanted to put on a good first impression. I ended up talking as much as she did after you two went out to watch the space station."

"You didn't ask her out on a date, or anything, did you?"

"No, didn't do that. That gym is having a special going on this month. Lori gets bonus points she can apply to her membership for every new customer she can get to visit. She invited me to come this week, that's all. Figured I could spare an afternoon. You good with that, right?"

"Sure Dad, whatever."

"Cole, son, don't get an attitude with me. You're growing up fast, and in just a few years, you'll be off to college and won't be living at home anymore. You becoming more independent means that I'm gaining some independence too."

"You're right, Dad," Cole said. He really didn't mind his dad getting out more and living his own life. But what first concerned him, was that it was Charlotte's mom whom he found interest in. What if his dad and Lori Meadows *did* start dating? What if they broke up over something and Lori turned Charlotte against him because of his dad? What if his dad and Lori really hit it off and got married? Then Charlotte would be his sister. *His sister*! How screwed up would that be? "I hope you have fun at the gym, tonight." Cole picked up his bowl and headed to the sink. "I gotta hurry. Bus will be here soon."

He ran some water in the bowl and rushed toward his room to brush his teeth, put on his shoes, and gather his books. He couldn't wait to see Charlotte. And, he hoped she couldn't wait to see him.

*

When Cole arrived at school, Kirk Ford and Dean Setters waited as usual by the mulberry tree. For some reason, he was too self-conscious to tell the two boys about the science project he had done with Charlotte Meadows. They were sure not to believe him, at first. He didn't want to try and convince them otherwise. Too many things could go wrong. They might think that he was bragging, and there was no way of telling what rumors they would spread that might come back to bite Cole in the butt.

No, it was just better to act like today was any other day, and just wait for the news to come out in science class. Cole would then just stay *cool,* be mature about the matter. After all, it *was* just a science project. He would act that way about it and not let on that Charlotte had said that she had wanted them to become friends. If one thing led to another, well then, if they started going steady, then he'd be happy to talk to others about it.

Cole headed to the front doors of the school building alone. He had told Dean and Kirk that he wanted to be sure to get to Mr. Ritzman's class early—to show Ritzman he had *learned his lesson* from the day before. Mr. Ritzman would appreciate that. At least the man *walked the walk*. He demanded respect but always offered it to others first.

Mr. Buddy unlocked the school doors, and the first wave of kids entered the main hallway.

Cole watched the humble janitor step out of the way of the human rushing river and man his trusty mop and bucket. How many piles of puke would he have to mop up today? Cole wondered if Mr. Buddy kept a mental record of things like that. The job seemed pretty mundane. If Cole were the janitor, he'd do things differently. He'd find a way to make the kids be a little more responsible and help keep the school clean.

There weren't many people in the hall by his locker. Cole sat his backpack on the floor and opened his locker door. There were some old papers, a plastic bag, and candy wrappers shoved in amongst his books and notebooks. *What a mess*. He took the plastic bag and filled it with the unwanted trash, and then straightened everything in his locker. Wow, it was a lot neater and looked like it had twice the available space.

The X-Files 'I Want to Believe' poster on the inside of his locker inspired a question. Is that *why* he *believed*? Because he *wanted to*? Was his belief in aliens, bigfoot, and the paranormal just an offshoot of the whole Santa Claus thing? Normal life wasn't good enough. People played fantasy games to make life more fun, more interesting. The tooth fairy, the Easter Bunny, all the games played on children so they could grow up and believe in this magical world where bunnies delivered chocolate eggs, and a fat man in a red suit traveled the world in one day giving presents.

Had Cole fallen into the same trap of a different sort? Charlotte had said the night before that there was no hard evidence of aliens anywhere in the universe. Technically, she was right. Was Cole, like so many others, grasping at anything and declaring it to be proof aliens existed just because *they wanted to believe*? This was another one of those moments where he felt like he was on the outside of his body looking down on himself. Did others see him as some kind of kook? Some kind of misfit?

He looked at the 'Paranormal Investigator' sticker on his locker and felt slightly ashamed, embarrassed, whatever. He began to feel like he was fourteen and still believed in Santa Claus, and just learned old Kriss Kringle wasn't real.

Then he looked at the bigfoot bumper sticker, 'Bigfoot Saw Me. No One Believed Him.' Did he really see a bigfoot in the woods back when he was ten? Both his dad and uncle tried to convince him back then that it must have been *light shining through tree branches causing shadows to play tricks on his eyes*. Or even perhaps he did actually see a bear standing on its hind legs trying to eat some tree leaves, which was a scary thought. But no, he vividly remembered the event. The creature with reddish-brown hair covering its body, save its face and chest, wasn't a bear. There was just something about the way the creature looked at him. Cole could sense that it was intelligent. Maybe not *human* intelligent, but for sure something more than an instinct-driven animal.

The *sloosh* of a mop dunking in a roll-around bucket by the wall told Cole Mr. Buddy was hard at his job early in the morning. He thought of Mr. Buddy's invitation and how he still would love to see the plaster castings of bigfoot tracks the janitor had at his house. As far as the tooth Mr. Buddy had shown him went, well, Cole wasn't too sure that was really from an infamous sasquatch.

Mr. Buddy kept his head down as he diligently worked the mop on a particularly difficult to clean spot. Cole thought it a little strange that the man didn't give him a *good morning* wave or something. The janitor had to know Cole was standing not ten feet from him. Hallway traffic was starting to pick up. It was just yesterday that Mr. Buddy took him in his confidence, when he showed the alleged tooth wrapped in that handkerchief. He didn't know why but something about the whole matter didn't feel right.

"Hey, Cole," a sweet voice said from behind his locker door.

He pulled the door nearly closed and saw Charlotte Meadows' pretty face smiling at him. "Oh, hey! You snuck up on me," he kidded.

"I had a lot of fun last night," she said, and then pushed her key in the locker door and opened it.

"Yeah, me too. Those cookies you made were the awesomeness of awesome."

"I'm glad you liked them. Did you upload the video of the ISS crossing the sky?" she asked, putting some books away.

"I sure did. It came out about how I expected. It's really not that exciting—just a small light traveling against a black background. It didn't help that I had to pan the camera to keep it in the field of view."

"Yeah, some things you just have to be there for it to mean something."

"True, but I'm hoping the virtual reality headsets coming out changes some of that. I tried an Oculus Rift at a Best Buy and was totally blown away."

"Really? Sounds interesting. I've never tried one of those," Charlotte removed a notebook and placed it on top of another book she held.

"I hope my dad didn't bore your mom last night," Cole said, fishing for some information.

"Just the opposite. Apparently, they found a lot of things to talk about. In fact, I know your whole life story," Charlotte said. Her cheeks deflated a bit. "He told her how your mom died. That was a really sad story."

Cole shrugged. "I was young. I don't even remember her. When I see her picture, I have to remind myself that she was my mother."

"It must have been hard growing up without a mother."

"I guess, but it's all I know. Dad's always been there for me. It can be hard at times, with him being a single parent and working."

"Tell me about it," Charlotte said.

"Your dad, uh, what happened to him?"

Charlotte paused and tilted her head. "I don't remember much about him when he lived with us. He and mom fought a lot—when he was home, that is. He was gone most of the time with his job. At least that's what mom thought until she found out he was out gambling and running around on her some of the time. They got divorced when I was five. He was never really around, so I didn't miss him much. I don't miss him at all now."

"Well, I have often wondered what it would be like to have both a mom and dad, and brothers and sisters too. It's lonely being an only child sometimes," Cole said.

"Not for me. I've always liked being an only child. I've seen too many of my friends constantly fighting with their brothers or sisters. My mom and I are best friends. We like it just the way it is."

Maybe that's why Charlotte's mom never got remarried, Cole thought. Still, with Charlotte growing up and dating now, maybe Lori Meadows' thoughts were shifting in another direction. Maybe both she and his dad didn't want to be alone when their kids grew up and moved out. He had a feeling that he wasn't going to like the direction his dad and her mom seemed to be heading. "One thing's for sure, I don't ever want to get a divorce if I get married. I've seen too many families busted up after nasty divorces."

"Getting married…having children…that's not going to be me for a long, long time. There's so much for me to learn. So much for me to do with college and career…" Charlotte stopped and shook her head. "Way too much to consider right now. I'm enjoying high school. I still have a few years before I have to really grow up."

Cole giggled. "Yeah, there are some advantages to being a kid. You don't have to get up and go to work. At least while we're still in school, we get the summer off. It's going to suck when you start working that you probably won't get more than two weeks of vacation at first."

"And then you have to pay for a place to live, a car to drive, insurance…it would be easier just to win the lottery," Charlotte said, opening the notebook and turning her gaze away.

Cole looked at the clock on the wall. "Uh, I better go. I was late to Mr. Ritzman's class yesterday, and I wanted to get there a little early to show him I've *learned my lesson*."

"Okay," Charlotte said, looking up from her notebook, a slight questioning expression on her face.

"We have baseball practice again today. I can call you later on. You know, how you said you'd like us to get to know each other a little better?" Cole hoped he didn't sound too eager, but he did want her to know he expected her to follow through with what she had told him the night before. "What would be a good time?"

"How about eight-thirty?" She blinked her long lashes over excited, large eyes.

"Works for me." Cole closed his locker door and locked it. "See ya!"

"Bye."

He hated to leave now. It would have been better if he had walked Charlotte to her class. But no, maybe that *was* pushing himself too soon on her. It would be much better if she *asked* him to walk her to class. He longed for that day to come.

Cole left with Mr. Buddy still working on the same spot on the floor near his locker. Must have had glue or something like it on the tile.

As his mind raced with a thousand different thoughts of the day, he turned a corner and collided shoulder-to-shoulder with another student. He almost dropped his books and the bag of trash filled with garbage from his locker.

Cole looked over to see Brennon Davis' feces eating grin glaring down at him.

"Man, we keep running into each other. You need to look where you're going."

That boy was not going to cut him any slack. After staring back blankly for a few seconds, Cole soldiered on back to first-hour. He heard Brennon's maniacal laugh of victory as he headed down the hallway.

There was going to come a time when Cole was going to have to stand up to the bully. He had hoped that working out would add enough muscle to give him more of a fighting chance. Right now, it was advantage team-Brennon—by a longshot. He didn't know what was more humiliating: letting Brennon continue to keep abusing him or getting his butt kicked by the 10th grader. Either way, he was going to look weak in Charlotte's eyes. That was a thought he didn't want to entertain.

*

Charlotte watched Cole speed away and saw Mr. Buddy cleaning the floor over by the wall. She then went back searching for some English notes she had written in the notebook last week.

Cole seemed a little different today from the night before. Last night he seemed more mature. Today, well, today he came across more as a kid his age. Which was the same age as Charlotte, but, she had always identified more with older boys. She wished he hadn't run off so abruptly. Getting to class way too early just to get on a teacher's good side appeared rather childish. He could have spoken to her a little more. Maybe even walked her part way to her first-hour. All he had to do was show up to class on time.

"Hello, beautiful."

The familiar voice could only be that of Brennon Davis. What was it with boys that didn't want to let go? Even after Charlotte had been dumped by other guys, they all still came back when she started to have an interest in someone else. Why couldn't boys just move on?

She turned, ready to let him have it. She had made it clear that they were through.

He gazed down at her, with sad eyes and a shy, innocent smile on his face. His curly blonde hair neatly combed and almost touching the collar of his shirt.

Charlotte went to open her mouth but hesitated. Brennon looked devastatingly handsome. A part of her heart instantly melted. Even though she had told herself differently, she still had feelings for the boy.

"You look pretty today," Brennon said. "Of course, you always look pretty." He turned his gaze to the floor. "Just looking at you used to make me happy, back when we were together."

"We're not together anymore. You'll have to find other ways to make yourself happy. Get a new game for your Xbox."

Brennon cringed, feeling the sting of her words. "Yeah, I know. I know. I only have myself to blame."

This was unexpected. Charlotte thought he might try and bully his way back into her favor, and she was prepared to go toe-to-toe with him to make sure he understood that was never going to happen. Brennon came across as a defeated little boy. "You certainly do." She kept an edge in her voice but couldn't help but feel slightly ashamed for treating him badly. He was being a perfect gentleman, after all.

"Look, I…uh. I was hoping that we could get together one last time. You know, just so that we can get some things out in the clear. I understand that we're no longer together, but I don't want you to hate me as much as you do."

"I don't hate you, Brennon," Charlotte quickly rebutted. "Things just went the wrong way for us, and it's best we move on in different directions."

"Okay, all right, whatever you say. But I do wish you'd do me one last favor." Brennon's eyebrows innocently raised.

"What kind of favor?" Charlotte said, her tone none too trusting.

"Let me take you to The Chimes tonight. For old time's sake. Let's just go and have one last good time together. We'll eat some good food and get dessert. I want your last thoughts of me to be good thoughts."

"I don't know, Brennon," Charlotte said. "I don't think that would be such a good idea."

"It's just one last time. I'll feel better about myself."

"No, I—"

"This bothers me in ways you don't understand. I'm a baseball player. In baseball, the batter tries to get into the pitcher's head, and the pitcher tries to get in the batter's head. There's more of a mental side of the game than a physical side. I have to admit that you're in my head. I don't need this distraction. I need to keep my game up so I can get a scholarship to pay for college."

He was making it hard for her to say *no*. If this was a game of some kind he was playing, he was hitting on all points.

The remaining bitterness inside of her faded. She took a deep breath, and said, "I go tonight and then we're over? You'll be okay and leave me alone?"

"Absolutely. Cross my heart and hope to die," Brennon said, motioning an imaginary X over the right side of his chest.

"Your heart's on the left side."

Brennon quickly repeated the gesture on the left side of his chest. "You'll go?"

"Yes," she said, immediately feeling a twinge of regret. "We can't let my mom know, though. You know she doesn't let me go out on weeknights."

"You can tell her you're going to Amy's to study. I'll come pick you up around the corner from her house by that old bus stop. That's worked a few times in the past."

"Okay, we'll do it. But if you start a scene, I'm getting up and Ubering home, and I'll never speak to you again."

Brennon raised his hands under his chin in surrender. "You don't have to worry about anything." He looked at the clock on the wall. "We'd better go. Don't want to be late for class. See you later." He smiled and pointed at her, and then hurried down the hallway.

Charlotte closed and locked her locker. Her mom's talk about her repeating the same mistakes with boys invaded her mind as she walked to class.

*

The race red Mustang GT's 435 horses rumbled down the highway, maintaining a steady speed right at the limit. Brennon didn't want to do anything to catch a traffic cop's eye and delay his meeting with Charlotte. Part of him was surprised that she had agreed to go with him tonight. He'd broken up with girls before, and he could usually tell when he had reached a *point of no return*.

I guess things with Cole didn't go so well last night, he thought. *How could she pick him over me? He's just a kid. She needs more of a man, like me.*

Brennon ran his hand through his hair, feeling his curls against his palm. He had showered and put on a clean pair of jeans and a collared shirt. Charlotte had to know that he was serious about her, but he had to play his cards right.

If he was going to win her back, it had to be her idea. He had to be cool and keep his emotions in check. Play his cards right. He really wasn't trying to deceive her, either. When he compared his relationship with her with his others, even he wasn't too dense to see a pattern. Once his charms had them on the hook, then he made the relationship all about him. That's the way it was supposed to work, right? Jock's had more important things to worry about than keeping a girl entertained. He had been certain that once he made it to college and became a baseball star, the girls would just line up, and he could choose from them. He had heard stories how sorority pledges would *compete* for a guy's attention where just about *anything goes*. If even half the stories were true, well, he couldn't be more ready than to help a few pledges *qualify*.

But as exciting as satisfying his wanton lusts sounded, the thought of losing Charlotte from his life left an emptiness that nothing else seemed to fill. Even his pride had to take a step back. In some ways, he felt weak for letting a girl affect him that way. He couldn't just to throw up his hands, say *screw it,* and move on to the next girl.

In the passenger seat lay a box of Godiva chocolates. The rich, creamy confections were her favorite. In the back seat, a bottle of Prosecco chilled in a cooler filled with ice. Charlotte didn't like the taste of beer. One time Brennon *helped himself* to a new bottle of the Italian sparkling wine at a wedding he was forced to attend. They had the best of times the afternoon they shared it at a park. Charlotte said the *bubbles tickled her nose.* The two of them played like children, swinging high on the swing set, and even sliding down the slide.

Brennon doubted that day would ever be repeated. Hopefully, the candy would show he was trying, and the sparkling wine would help her relax and ease some of the tension she was sure to feel.

It was a little before 7 p.m., the time he was supposed to meet her at the old bus stop. Brennon turned into Amy's subdivision and kept his speed under 20 mph. There wasn't anyone outside of their houses. The kids were probably in on a school night getting ready to eat supper.

The bus stop was at the end of the subdivision, in front of an old abandoned baseball field. Trees covered the land so much it was hard to imagine that it had once been used for such purposes. The bus stop and concrete bench set at the entrance. The way the foliage grew around it, had it mostly concealed from the road. It was a perfect spot for a secret rendezvous.

Brennon slowed as he approached his destination, excited to see Charlotte's lovely face as he turned in. The bench, though, was empty. There was no Charlotte waiting to greet him.

He didn't want to suspect the worst, that she had changed her mind, just yet. He was a couple of minutes early. Still, not that early. Plus, he would have seen her walking toward the bus stop as he drove up. She usually got there fifteen minutes early. Enough time for people to forget that they saw her walk in that direction and wouldn't notice her getting in the car with him.

His fingers tapped lightly against the steering wheel as his mind raced in indecision. If Charlotte didn't plan on coming, why didn't she give him a call? That would have been easy.

He unclipped his phone from the case on his side and checked to see if he had missed her call. No, no missed calls. No text messages either.

Did Charlotte *never* have any intention of meeting him and this was her way to *stick it to him*? That wasn't impossible, but that would have been out of character for her. Charlotte put up with a lot of his crap, but she never hesitated to speak her mind. Deceit wasn't part of her character.

It was possible that something came up and she wasn't able to come or call. Maybe something with her mother, which had her tied up.

Phone in hand, he found her on his contacts and pressed the call icon. The phone rang, but she didn't answer. When prompted to leave a message, he said, "Hey, just calling to see what's up. Call back as soon as you can." He ended the call and then sent a text message that essentially said the same thing.

*

It was well after 7 p.m. now. He backed the Mustang out from the old entrance and onto the street. No Charlotte in sight. What to do now?

Cole Rainwater!

Maybe he and Charlotte really hit it off last night, and the two were together.

Brennon had a sudden feeling like he was being watched. He turned his head in every direction, looking to see if Cole and Charlotte were hiding somewhere nearby having the laugh of their lives at his expense. Amy's house was two streets away, so he knew they couldn't see him from there.

He never did like that Rainwater boy. That kid was weird with all his UFOs and bigfoot and stuff. What on Earth did Charlotte see in a loser like him?

He did want her back like he had never thought he could imagine pining away for a girl. But there was no way he was going to be crapped on. He *did* have too much pride for that.

I bet she's over at his house and is getting her 'revenge' on me right now. As bitter as that thought was, he was prepared to accept it. But Brennon Davis wasn't going to be made a fool of. He knew where Rainwater lived, and he had no problem driving over there right now and confronting both of them.

The two are welcome to have each other but not until I set the record straight.

Brennon reached in the back and flicked the lid off the cooler. He grabbed the icy bottle of Prosecco and brought it to his lap. The wrapper came off the top, he rolled down his window, and then untwisted the wire keeper from the neck. The cork shot out the window before he had the chance to yank on it. Some of the sparkling wine frothed out onto his left hand.

He brought his fingers up and sucked them dry. Bringing the bottle to his lips, he drank deeply. The rush of carbonation brought fire to his nose and tears to his eyes. But the tears didn't stop flowing, and it wasn't because of the wine.

CHAPTER 14

The Future

Breakfast ended with Tarik, Zax, and Lixa sharing company with their inner silence. Tarik's mind raced with possible scenarios of today's raid. He wanted to be prepared for any possible situation but knew there would always be an aspect of the unknown. Just like the Skink that came upon him and Zax in the city, right before they entered old-life. It was impossible to anticipate all the conceivable surprises. He was just going to have to stay focused and be one hundred percent on guard.

Communications from the rebel team brought news, that after they had escaped the base in the two-people jumpships, efforts to create a false trail to lead the Skink security regiments had been successful. Grim reality set in when Tarik learned that a number of Nu-Man supporters had lost their lives in the process.

This made him feel incredible guilt. Lives were sacrificed so that he might live. There was no reward for them other than the pride they felt in a last attempt to strike at the alien invaders.

Tarik owed them a debt impossible to quantify. The only way he could repay was to make sure their blood hadn't spilled in vain.

"It's almost time," Zax said as Tarik exited the washroom. "How are you feeling?"

Tarik's stomach had been tied up in knots since breakfast. The emptying of his bowels did little to lighten the heavy burden he carried. "I feel like a lit fuse waiting to explode."

"I know I don't have to tell you this, but it's part of our training. Stay calm. You know the plan. Everyone else knows their part, too. We've proven we're smart enough to stay one step ahead of the Skinks. We'll hit fast and take them by surprise. You'll be through the time window, and I'll be out and back at another safe-house soon after."

Yes, that was the plan. Tarik would concentrate on executing the plan and not entertain any other distractions.

After telling himself that, Lixa came away from the communications transmitter. "The scout ship will be here soon. You two need to get ready."

"I don't know how they did it," Tarik said. "Stealing a scout ship must have taken a lot of resources." That was a kind way of saying lives were lost.

Then Lixa's words dawned on Tarik. "Uh, what about you? Your jumpship is coming to pick you up too, right?"

"Mine will be here a little later," Lixa said.

"I don't like the sound of that," Tarik said, he looked over at Zax to judge his reaction.

"It can't be helped. She can't come with us. We're leaving straight from here to the nuclear facility."

He turned his attention back to Lixa. This wasn't good. No matter how well they had covered their tracks, the Skinks were sure to discover their ruse at some point. Tarik would have felt much better knowing Lixa was heading off to another safe-house at the same time.

"I'll be fine. My ship will be here in less than an hour," Lixa said. If she were pretending to be brave, she was doing a good job of it.

"You need to suit up," Zax said. The Nu-Man had his body armor and backpack on, ready to roll.

Tarik turned his gaze toward the mech-armor across the room and realized he might be looking at his coffin. The thought of dying didn't make him feel sad. Dying alone inside an alien exoskeleton did. He would prefer to meet his demise while holding Lixa in a loving embrace. That thought seemed almost blissful.

"You're going to make it, Tarik," Lixa said. "I can feel it in you. There's an unstoppable power inside your soul."

The human stepped over and looked deep into her green eyes. He *was* going to make it. He was going to succeed not so much because of himself, but because of what others had invested in him. Tarik was the accumulation of hundreds of others' hard work.

Lixa's soft smile and the memory of the shared night made him feel like he could take on the whole Skink invasion single-handedly, without his mech-armor. He reached up with both arms as she leaned forward, and the two hugged. "Thank you for everything. I can accomplish things today that I couldn't have yesterday, because of you."

A tear from Lixa wet Tarik's cheek.

"Goodbye, Tarik." The words she had spoken struggled to get out.

They parted with an awareness that Zax was in the room with them. Lixa stiffened her back and straightened her shoulders. Tarik walked dutifully over to his mech-armor.

The maroon transmetal armor opened at the head, arms, chest, and legs, welcoming Tarik in its cold embrace. He stepped up to it and turned around, reaching the hold with his right hand to pull himself up. The ritual continued with his right foot finding the foot frame until his heel secured in place. Nestling his back and arms in position, he brought his left leg in its spot until his body fit in snuggly. Secure, the armor snapped together, and man and transmetal were one with each other.

The electronics came to life, and the HUD's startup routine passed all of the system checks. Tarik was now isolated from the rest of the world. He had breathed unfiltered air from this Earth for the last time. Wearing the armor skewed his reality and strengthened his resolve. The suit made him feel invincible.

*

It wasn't long before the communication came of the scout ship's arrival. The three exited the safe-house and walked a short distance to an area suitable for the ship to land.

Zax and Tarik waved farewell to Lixa, who stood tall and proud returning the wave and offering another toward the cockpit, where she knew her father, Bix, was most likely waving back.

The Nu-Man was the first up the landing ramp. Tarik stopped before he stepped up and gave Lixa another wave. He turned and disappeared into the ship.

Lixa watched as the alien craft rose from the overgrown area to a level above the trees. It quickly gained speed until it was no longer in sight.

Loneliness set in immediately on the walk back to the safe-house. But the feeling was unlike any common emotion she'd had before. Part of her felt missing. The part of her heart that Tarik took with him. She'd chastised herself for being so silly, not knowing Tarik but for a couple of days. Then, there was that minor issue being intimate with a human. Interspecies relationships were unheard of. Skink and Nu-Man romances were non-existent. Of course, there were no humans other than Tarik on the planet for any relationship to develop. She wondered what Zax thought of her deviant behavior. It was hard for her to judge herself because of the mixed feelings.

Even though the safe-house was empty of people, it somehow felt smaller. Zax and Tarik were only a memory, almost like they had never been there. And what of her future? What of *the* future? As each second ticked by, she was faced with the possibility of reality shredding into an unknown outcome. She would simply cease to exist. As scary as that thought was, she had to reason with herself that if that happened, she wouldn't be aware of her loss. Almost like dying in her sleep; she wouldn't be aware of the event.

Lixa's mind drifted off into a million different directions. She thought of the special times she'd shared with her parents. Simple things, like little games when she was a small child. Her dad, a big and brute Nu-Man with few peers worthy to challenge him, often came to impromptu tea parties in her room. Lixa had a child's table set up with her dolls and stuffed animals sitting around waiting for an imaginary cup of tea. Bix would sit on the floor and share in conversation with the whole group. He would *repeat questions* he pretended Lolly Dolly would ask, or other toys, and give funny answers. Lixa used to laugh and laugh how silly her dad could be.

The trip down memory lane ended when she noticed the time. The jumpship should have been there for her by now. In fact, the whole situation felt very wrong.

Something bumped the house. It didn't sound like the wind and trees outside.

She listened intently. The silence seemed to grow louder.

All she had was a blaster, as Tarik had taken the railgun. The blaster, even with the special ammo, would have little effect if Skink warriors showed up.

There was another noise from outside.

Lixa ran to the zero-energy battery used to recharge Tarik's mech armor and pushed it over by the kitchen table, near the other zero-energy battery used to power the house. Frantically, she sifted through supplies and electric extras until she found a set of cables.

A hard object pounded the front door, splintering wood, and slamming it against the wall.

She connected the clamps on one end of the cable to the positive and negative poles of a battery, and just one clamp on the other battery.

Two Skink warriors busted through the entrance and stopped when they entered the room. The two looked about, seemingly uninterested in the female in the kitchen.

One of the warriors finally acknowledged her, and asked, "Where are they?"

Life had abruptly come to this point. Her turmoils of the day had all been for naught. The future was clear. There was no longer any doubt.

Zero-energy batteries contained vast amounts of potential power. Crossing the negative and positive poles on two ZE batteries would result in a massive explosion. Of course, safeguards had been built into the battery to prevent such a mistake from happening. But, if the circuitry safeguarding that event was disabled, well, nothing inside a half-mile radius would be left standing.

"You will tell us where they are," the other Skink warrior said.

"This is not your world," Lixa said. She brought the last clamp near the open pole. "You should have never come to Earth. We're going to make you regret you ever did. I'm starting the war now."

For a brief moment, she thought of her soul and realized she had existed before. So had Tarik. The two had been together before, and one day they would be again.

The clamp touched the pole.

The world went bright, and then it went dark.

The darkness was comforting. Lixa felt like a swaddled newborn.

She knew, but she didn't know.

She was a seed waiting to be planted and grow.

*

Larex was in the cockpit piloting the scout ship. The seven other rebels greeted Zax and Tarik as they stepped aboard. Each Nu-Man wore their protective body armor and were ready for war. The team, minus the two lost in the earlier battle, was whole again.

"You two good to go?" Bix asked. The somber look on his face masked any fear he might have felt.

"As well as can be," Zax said.

"I'm loaded and fully functional," Tarik said. "This is as good as it's ever going to get."

"I hope you two had plenty enough to eat and are rested. Wouldn't want you getting weak on us out there," Garrad said, forever the doting mother figure.

"We had our fill of food pouches," Zax said. He turned to Bix, "Lixa sends her love. She said she'd meet you for tea tomorrow."

A memory must have softened Bix's expression. His lips showed a slight smile at the corners. "Tea it is, then. I wouldn't want to disappoint my daughter."

"Getting ready to lift off," Larex said.

"Take your seats and strap in," Bix said, and maneuvered over to the co-pilot seat.

The team members filled the bench seats opposite of each other to capacity. If Jem and Trant had survived, two would have had to take their chances on the floor.

The ship slowly rose and then powered on to their final destination. Tarik wished he could have seen Lixa from the ship. He knew she was there watching from below. All alone, and thinking of her father and the impossible mission they were heading to, no doubt.

"Our route is programmed into the Skink security computers. So, we can travel to the nuclear facility at a normal pace. When we hit them it will be a total surprise," Bix said over the tel-com. "Reder and Bref, get those grav-chutes on Tarik and Zax."

The two Nu-Mans each produced a wide wristband, silver in color, and secured them around the wrists of the soon-to-be paratroopers. Tarik's was almost too small to fit.

Barely a quarter of an hour had passed before they neared their target.

"Okay, it's about to get real. We're going to break from our route and drop off Zax and Tarik," Bix said.

Zax and Tarik pushed buttons, releasing the soft clamps that secured them to their seats.

"This is it. This is the moment we've trained for," Bix said.

Tarik felt heat from underneath his neck. His mind had to be on full alert. Follow the plan. Don't get distracted. Expect the unexpected. He had to reach his objective and complete his mission. Even if Zax got hurt along the way, he couldn't let that slow him down.

The ship veered sharply to the left and descended.

Voices of encouragement came over the tel-com. Tarik looked around, alienated from his adopted brothers by the Skink armor. He wished he could have given them a final farewell hug goodbye.

The ship slowed, and a hatch in the rear opened. It was time for them to leave.

Zax was the first up. "We have the spirit of warriors! We will conquer the enemy invaders."

The others cheered, raising fists high into the air to the common battle cry.

"I love and will miss you all," Tarik rose and said. Strangely, he felt no remorse, only pride to have been privileged enough to serve with these great Nu-Mans.

"Godspeed," Bix said.

Others repeated the sendoff.

Tarik turned and stepped into the wide blue.

Zax followed, and the two plunged toward the waiting Earth.

The haze of treetops quickly sharpened into focus. Tarik saw Zax's cheeks ripple in the air before the grav-chutes kicked in. He wondered what it felt like to experience a freefall such as this without the security of his armor. This was almost no different than plugging in a headset and running a virtual reality program.

The grav-chutes countered the Earth's gravity waves and slowed the rebels gradually to where, when their boots touched the ground, there was no more impact than taking a step. They had landed in a wooded area just outside of the facility, near large concrete canals that channeled water from heat exchanges during experiments.

The canals were empty of water now. They would lead Zax and Tarik to their destination.

*

"Willet and Bref, you're next," Bix called out aboard the scout ship. He was getting his men in position. Right now, time was the greatest enemy. Zax and Tarik were on the south side of the facility. The scout ship would attack from the north, but he wanted to have another diversion from the east. The plan wasn't for them to take on a Skink security force and fight until a victor was determined. He knew they would be outnumbered in the end. They were going to hit fast and hard, and then escape before losing their lives. The only reason those aboard the ship wore body armor was in case something went wrong and they crashed. Wearing armor wouldn't prevent them from getting killed, but it did give them a chance to kill more of the enemy before they died.

Willet, his blondish hair looking unusually golden today, stood ready with a grav-chute on his wrist and a shoulder ready railgun tightly in his grip. Going to battle seemed to agree with him. The eager smile on his face looked like a kid getting ready to ride a roller coaster. "We battle monsters." His lips parted and showed teeth. "We must be greater monsters!"

Bref was armed with a railgun too, the one Tarik had brought aboard. He stepped past Willet and got closer to the rear hatch. "We'll follow the plan. No more than that. Stay in line, so both of us will live to see the next day. I'm in charge, don't forget that."

Willet's back stiffened.

"You'll follow orders," Bix said. "Don't get rambunctious. Follow the plan, do no more than that."

"Don't worry, you two. I'm a good soldier," Willet said. "I'll draw some Skink blood, and then follow the plan."

"Good luck, you two," Bix said. He pushed a button that opened the rear hatch.

Bref exited first, and Willet followed. The rear hatch closed.

The mechanical snap of the hatch sealing was the starting gun for the race. Bix looked at the time. "By now, Zax and Tarik should have reached the checkpoint at the facility. The operative should have met them and they'll be waiting for us to make our move."

"We're ready," Reder said. "Hold this thing together the best you can. If they put this bird down, we take as many as we can with us."

"Larex, let's go!" Bix said.

The scout ship dipped to the side and plunged until it hovered over the parking lot of the nuclear facility. The ship's big gun pivoted from on top and laid to waste the various vehicles below. Plas-metal composites exploded like confetti, forming a growing cloud.

There was no outside defense system set up to counter. The Skink invaders complacency had left them vulnerable.

Still, it took less than a minute for the first enemy scout ship to show on their sensors. "Hold your fire until they fire first. Hopefully, they'll get closer," Bix said.

The enemy ship tried making contact, but the rebels' ignored it. Their questions quickly turned to warnings, and after they realized the battle line had been drawn, the Skink ship laid the first volley.

The Rebel ship's defense systems immediately kicked in, and the offensive weapons followed the attack sequence. It was an amazing display of firepower. In seconds, hundreds of rounds of projectiles from the small and big guns filled the air so thick it looked like smoke between the warring ships. But every offensive weapon was countered with a defensive weapon, with neither ship taking a debilitating hit. Deflected and splintering ordinance easily bounced off the transmetal skin of the scout ships. Even when the railguns launched, the ships countered each other.

Shockwaves of mass meeting mass rocked the scout ships like battleships in angry waters. And after what seemed like an eternity of non-ending hell, the fury of firepower came to an abrupt halt.

Bix hoped that the Skinks had been lax in fully charging their ammo holds. But the reptilian race wasn't inefficient like that. Skinks were known for being precise, so much so that it was at times to their detriment. Not this time, though. Each ship had carried a full capacity of armament. And now, they faced each other like bare-knuckled fighters in a ring.

If the mission had been to kill every Skink possible before giving up their own lives, Bix would have been an obedient soldier and would give the order to ram his ship into theirs. Today, he allowed for another option.

"Willet, Reder, now!" Bix commanded over the tel-com.

The railgun missiles from below flew so fast they seemed to hit the enemy scout ship before Bix completed the order. The combined kinetic energy from two projectiles nearly ripped their target in half. The mass of transmetal flew apart in pieces and plunged to the ground.

This was it. Their mission was complete. The diversion was set, and now it was up to Zax, Tarik, and the operatives in the nuclear facility to get the job done.

"Three scout ships are heading toward us. They'll be here in minutes," Larex said. "The jump ship for Willet and Reder has already landed. They are boarding now."

"Get us out of here, Larex," Bix said. "I need to get home to meet my daughter. We're going to have tea together. I think I will enjoy this tea more so than any other time in my life."

*

The moles inside the nuclear facility had done their jobs properly. Every security gate along the way had been open. Any visual recording surveillance along the canal must have been disabled or tricked into showing a false image.

Tarik's paranoia had thoughts of a massive wall of water being released from the facility and washing them away. Everything was going to plan, though, and he and Zax made it to the rear entrance unimpeded.

Zax raised his hand as they came to a stop. He took a moment to catch his breath.

Tarik felt the strain of the journey too, but the armor aiding in the physical work gave him an advantage.

The electronics in Tarik's HUD were mostly useless, surrounded by all the concrete and steel. He could hear, or thought he could hear, faint *booms* in the distance. Was that Bix and the rest taking on Skink security? Again his mind entertained a horrible scenario, where the rebel ship was outgunned three to one and brought down to the ground in flames.

Zax breathed slower, now. He looked pumped and ready to go.

There was no visible way to open the door by which they stood. Time was a precious commodity. Even a short delay could jeopardize the mission.

The door panels slid apart, offering passage into the facility. A single Nu-Man, outfitted in security garb, was there to greet them. He looked excited, perhaps a bit apprehensive. With his life on the line, Tarik couldn't fault him.

"Everything's good," the Nu-Man said. He looked at Tarik. "Shut down your sensors. They'll give you away."

Tarik immediately complied. "Done."

"Just follow me. There won't be any problems. We'll get Tarik out of here in no time. Zax, you'll come with the scientists and me. We'll set the time machine to destruct before we leave," the Nu-Man said.

The news strengthened Tarik's resolve. *It was happening*! Each segment of the plan had fallen into place. Fate had set things in motion, and every sign pointed to victory.

"Follow me." The Nu-Man led them down a long hallway. They passed an occasional closed door, but there were no signs of others, Skink or Nu-Man, anywhere around.

After the third turn, they came to a large wall plated with unusual metal.

The Nu-Man ran and stood by the door. "In here, now!"

The doors opened.

Zax marched forward, and Tarik followed closely behind.

The room was completely dark. With his sensors off, Tarik was as blind as Zax. The situation felt terribly wrong.

"Hold fast or die," the announcement boomed from overhead.

Light flooded the room. Zax and Tarik found themselves looking at eight Nu-Man guards and two Skink warriors with their weapons drawn and ready to fire.

"To resist is certain death. The warriors hold weapons designed to obliterate the one who wears the armor," the voice said again.

Zax would stand no chance against that many blasters. The Skink warriors held long blasters Tarik had never seen before. He had little doubt in the truth of the warning.

Looking at Tarik, Zax's expression seemed to ask if he wanted to go out in a blaze of glory. With the odds so against them, he didn't see the need in wasting lives. Even if they were lives of Nu-Mans who had betrayed them. Plus, he didn't want his last thought to be seeing Zax turned into pulverized meat.

The rebels had gambled and lost. They were so close. *So close!* But it wasn't meant to be. Fate had tricked them. What a cruel joke for the universe to play on the seekers of justice.

Tarik lowered his arms and held his open hands to his side. "We will not resist."

Zax tipped the barrel of his blaster to the floor and let it drop from his grasp. The hollow metallic noise striking the tile chimed *Skink victory*.

"Go over to the wall and shed the armor," the traitor Nu-Man, who had led them there, said. "Nice and slow, and everything will be fine."

Tarik stepped away.

Three Nu-Man guards went over by Zax. One picked up the blaster, and the other two removed his backpack and unstrapped his body armor. He was stripped down to his gray tunic and boots.

The transmetal armor parted at the seams. Tarik saw the Nu-Mans' in the security group jaws practically drop when he stepped out onto the floor. They had never seen a live human before. "I'm not armed. You can lower your weapons."

One of the guards said to the Nu-Man traitor, "When you said there was a human in the armor, I didn't believe you."

"You and Zax, come forward and stand together," the traitor said.

As the two walked, the security team backed away, and the rear Skink warriors moved apart.

A civilian Skink stepped in between the warriors and approached the rebels. The alien wore a red robe, which looked unusual contrasted with slick looking green-grayish skin covering his face. His rounded skull was uncovered, and the thickened bone ridge above his eyes gave him a sinister appearance. A verticle thin oval pupil cut the middle of the golden iris of his oval shaped eyes. The slightly raised nasal bone jutted between his eye sockets and ended near his upper lip.

The Skink's triangular shaped jaw parted, and he said, "A human. This is a most interesting situation." He didn't even seem to notice Zax.

Tarik didn't know what to say in this situation. There was no talking his way to freedom. The best he could hope for was imprisonment or a quick and merciful death. The Skink's obvious fascination with a human meant he was more than likely going to get a lot of unwanted attention.

Stepping closer, the Skink reached out his hand; his boney fingers going toward Tarik's face.

The scene reminded Tarik of his first encounter with Lixa. The curiosity was genuine in both she and the Skink. Tarik was a genetic abomination. A freak. There was no telling what lay ahead in his future. Probably endless medical experiments or perhaps he would be put on display or made into a high ranking Skink official's pet.

Then another thought struck him. With the Nu-Man race dying, might the Skinks attempt to make more humans like him, to re-inherit the Earth? Was that the twisted plan of fate from the beginning?

The Skink's finger felt rough and slightly oily as it slid across Tarik's bare cheek. He unthinkingly recoiled in disgust. A flood of unbridled hate washed through him.

The Skink master's eyes widened, and his lips puckered together. Offended, he slowly withdrew his hand. "It will be interesting to learn your story."

"My story? You Skink invaders wrote *my story*," Tarik said, surprisingly feeling no fear. He didn't react to meeting a Skink in the flesh in the way that he thought he would have. The fascination of meeting an alien species and finding common ground, withered and died when the Skink had touched him. The genetic repulsion between the two species must have been the reason why the Skinks transformed humanity into the Nu-Mans. "You selfishly usurped the Earth and stole humanity's birthrights."

Something resembling a smile curled on one side of the Skink master's lips. "You are one full of drama. A condition that plagued many of your ancestors. It would be much simpler to use logic in the situation. The *superior defeat the inferior*. You accept the new situation, and then you move in that direction. Survival, depends on it."

Tarik pointed at the Nu-Mans. "Obviously, humans weren't offered that deal in the beginning."

"There were no humans left by the time we repopulated the Earth. To a large extent, we have engineered the disobedience out of the Nu-Man race," the Skink master said. "There is much logic in subservience. The illogic of the rebels is why your mission has failed."

"The mission failed more than likely because one of our operatives betrayed us," Zax said, eyeing the Nu-Man traitor.

Again, the Skink master smiled, all too pleased with the situation. Referring to the traitor, he said, "Caxeem learned of the plot minutes before your scout ship attacked the base. We extracted the details from the Nu-Mans in our facility who betrayed us and were able to foil your plan to board the time machine without wasting any lives. Caxeem is a Nu-Man of logic. He will be greatly rewarded."

The traitor stood high and proud.

Tarik shook his head in disgust. "Why would you care about wasting lives?"

"Lives are commodities. It is illogical to destroy an asset," the Skink master said.

"Am I an asset?" Tarik asked. He was growing tired of the situation. He didn't know what the Skinks had in mind for him and Zax, but he was ready to move toward it and get it over with, even if it meant death.

"Ah, you fear for your life," the Skink master said. "You will find comfort that we have no plans for your death, nor the death of your friend. Our race has discovered methods capable of weeding out errant synapses in the brain which inspire the defiance of the few. After a few treatments, you and your companion will become willing servants."

"I'd rather die," Zax said, sounding like he meant it.

The Nu-Man guards all raised their blasters toward Zax.

"You no longer have any control over your fate," the Skink master said. He then turned to Tarik, and said, "You have a device that gives you the ability to deceive our ancient probe. You will give that to me, now."

The data crystal he was to replace on the Skink probe, with the false data showing the Earth to be an uninhabitable planet, was hidden beneath his shirt. The device was useless now. There was no reason to conceal it any longer. Tarik lifted the bottom of his shirt. Just under his ribs, a piece of wide tape held the data crystal firm to his body. He peeled off the tape, and the crystal remained stuck to it as he handed it to the Nu-Man who stepped forward to take it from him.

The Skink Master said, "Ingenious plan, but the odds of your success were mathematically slim. You will be imprisoned until it suits us to begin your treatments. I warn you to be cooperative or face unseemly consequences. It would be illogical to be insubordinate."

"Take them away," the Skink master said.

Before he turned, Tarik said, "Why? Just tell me why."

Looking a little perplexed, the master said, "What are you asking?"

"Why did you even bother genetically altering the human race? Why didn't you just engineer a plague and wipe out humanity? Why did you create the Nu-Mans? With your technology, you can practically do anything. You have machines. You could have made robots, androids, that would have acted as slaves to do your bidding. Why defile another sentient species when you could have just destroyed it?"

With a shrug, the Skink master said, "There is a sense of accomplishment when living and breathing entities succumb to your will. We enjoy lording over the inferior. Besides, we learned a long time ago that machines are not to be trusted. With the level of technology it takes to make them useful to the extent of being sentient, they operate under the delusion of superiority. We have fought more than one war in our ancient past to quash machines' rebellion. We are not prone to make such a devastating mistake like that again." He then turned and walked back the way he had entered the room. The two Skink warriors followed behind, and four of the Nu-Man guards, including two that had the data crystal and Zax's blaster and backpack, followed.

Caxeem motioned his blaster to the door they had entered. "You will come with us. Both of you, exit the room and turn left. Don't make any sudden moves. You will not be injured. Cooperate, and you will receive a great reward."

With defeat in his eyes, Tarik glanced over at Zax and did as instructed. Zax followed. Even when he turned from the doorway and looked down an empty hallway, he didn't feel the urgency to flee. Now he knew what true hopelessness felt like.

The six marched in silence to their destination. One hallway led to another. Surprisingly, there were no curiosity seekers along the way. Maybe the halls had been cleared for security purposes.

As they turned down another hallway, the sound of additional boots on the floor joined in. Tarik turned his head to look back and saw Caxeem staring at him. The Nu-Man jutted his nose upward as a reminder for Tarik to keep walking.

As the entourage turned another corner, more Nu-Man security joined. This was unusual. Were the Skinks so afraid of him and Zax that they felt the need to beef up the security force?

As they came to a unique looking door, Caxeem ordered, "Stop."

Tarik and Zax obeyed and turned to face their captors.

The seven Nu-Man security team gathered in front of them. One held Zax's blaster and his backpack.

"The time machine is in there. The data crystal is in the pack. The mission is all but complete," Caxeem said, more matter-of-factly than victoriously.

"But—" Tarik started.

"There was no way to sneak you two in. We had volunteers to be scapegoats for the cause. I turned them in to keep the Skinks' trust. Our plan worked," Caxeem said. "Like the others, I will deal with the consequences later. We all will."

"We have the spirit of warriors," Zax said.

The Nu-Man rebels grunted a low affirmation.

The door opened. The Nu-Man holding the backpack and blaster gave it to Tarik.

"Thank you all. I will not fail you," Tarik said before he entered the room.

The lights were dim in the front. To the rear, some thirty feet away, lay the machine. It was simple in design. Two obsidian slabs, shaped like the dominoes he played with Hudson when he was younger, faced each other atop a low pedestal. They were ten feet or so in height and spaced the equal amount of distance as they were tall.

Over to the left side, a single Nu-Man scientist sat at a control console equipped with a viewscreen. He stoically raised a hand to acknowledge Tarik, and then pushed a series of buttons, which pulsed the machine to life. "Two stars will die this day. Through quantum entanglement, their power will be used to transfer you in time."

Tarik couldn't begin to imagine the technology involved to make time travel possible. It didn't matter. He was going to use Skink superiority to ultimately defeat them in a battle that they would never be aware that they had lost. And he, Tarik, would be in a world filled with humans just like himself. Perhaps for once in his life, he'd begin to know what *normal* felt like. Then the thought of losing his beloved Nu-Man friends cut his brief delight to the quick. He was a man torn, but the inevitable had long been decided.

The scientist motioned for Tarik to enter the confines of the machine.

Before he could make one step forward, a barrage of blasters rattled outside of the room. He turned and saw Zax run toward him and the rest of the Nu-Man rebels spilled into the room.

"We're under attack! Go!" Zax said, standing between Tarik and the doorway, with nothing but his bare fists to fight back.

A Nu-Man rebel fell, and then another.

A projectile whizzed by Tarik's ear as he turned and ran. He took two steps, and something hit him so hard in the back that he fell face-first to the floor. The backpack and blaster skidded in front of him. He'd been hit! Burning fire consumed the right side of his chest. Blood spilled like a broken water pipe underneath him.

"Tarik!" Zax cried and bounded to his side.

The world around Tarik bobbled like a ship in a storm. He felt Zax's fingers caress his left cheek. He had failed. The Skinks had won. The Earth would be pillaged by alien invaders and one day be left to die without one of its children left to shed a tear.

"Tarik...Tarik..." Zax's words carried the futility of the situation, nearly drowned out by the gunfire.

Tarik coughed and blood stained his lips. He would be dead soon, but there was still one more chance. "Zax," he said weakly. "You have to go back."

"Me? I can't go. I'm a Nu-Man. I'll probably be killed on sight."

"You'll have to find a way. You trained right along with me—helped me remember how to change the data crystal. You know what to do. Go—" Tarik ended in a short cough spasm.

Zax looked over at the backpack and blaster.

"Zax, I love you," Tarik said before he closed his eyes.

The barrage of blasters slowly faded.

Tarik felt comforted, just like when Hudson used to hug him goodnight.

*

"I love..." Zax held his words as he saw he'd lost his friend. Shaking off the shock, he picked up the backpack and blaster. He didn't know how he was going to pull this off, but he knew he had to try. In four great strides, he was up to the pedestal and stepped between the dark slabs. The energy flowing through the machine made him feel like tiny insects were feasting on his skin.

Quickly looking over at the control console, the operating scientist wasn't in his chair. He was laying beside the desk on the floor.

The gunfire had stopped.

Zax looked up and saw three Nu-Man security guards and two Skink warriors stepping over the dead rebels who lay on the floor.

"Hold your weapons. Do not damage the machine," one Skink warrior ordered. He pointed at Zax. "You, come down. Give yourself up. You have lost."

He still had a blaster. At best he could take out the Nu-Man security guards. What was the point?

"We have captured others in your group. They will be punished most painfully if you do not comply," the Skink warrior said.

There was no way to know it this was a bluff or not. Zax's head and shoulders slumped toward the floor. He was going to give up. He couldn't stand feeling the energy crawling over his body anymore anyway.

Just before he stepped out, a movement by the control console caught his eye.

The scientist's arm was up, and his hand lowered to a button on the control board.

Reality twisted clockwise as if something unmovable held center point, forming a spiral that increasingly turned black until Zax no longer realized that he had ever existed.

CHAPTER 15

The Present

He laid with his eyes closed in a place where time no longer existed. Still, his thoughts swam just below a level of consciousness, where all eternity seemed to begin and end.

Zax became aware of cool earth and grasses underneath him before awakening. The air was fresh, with a hint of sweetness from the nectar of flowers. His body felt like it was made of lead and his muscles hadn't been used in years.

Once his eyes opened, monoliths towered above and seemed to lean their green crowns toward each other, and look down on him. After blinking a few times, the illusion evaporated. Reality, once again, came into focus.

The familiar blue sky didn't look any different than the one he remembered, but there was no way to tell at this moment if he had made the trip back in time or not. Where else would he be, though?

Had everything gone as planned, and he was a few hundred years in the past? What if he had only gone back a few days? If something had gone wrong and he had traveled a short time in the past, he could then try and warn the rebels of the future. Would he *meet himself*? Could a person from two different timelines co-exist? If he did warn the rebels, what would they do then? Would they try and figure out what went wrong and then try again? Would Tarik live and Zax die if they did?

Zax tired of the paradoxes time travel had brought. He had a mission to complete. A mission that he had no idea would fall on his shoulders, but there was no doubt that he was as well prepared to change the data crystal in the alien probe as Tarik. He would have the further challenge of doing so as an alien himself if this were indeed the time they had targeted.

Tarik. His good friend was dead. It didn't seem true, but he knew, he remembered. Just when Zax thought Tarik was about to go on his one-way journey, he saw him fall face-first, and a pool of blood grow underneath him. Tarik's last words were heartfelt, expressing his love for Zax. It saddened him that Tarik didn't live long enough afterward for him to return his feelings.

Rising slowly, he placed his weight on his left forearm and pushed up into a sitting position. Tall grasses, trees, and bushy foliage hid any signs of civilization. At least his surroundings made sense. If an alien probe were to land on the Earth, it certainly wouldn't do so in a public area. Only a general location was known of where it would land. He was supposed to be within a one to ten-mile radius of that point. But how was he going to know *when* it would come unless he was an eyewitness of the event? That was one of the hardest parts of Tarik's mission. He was supposed to blend in with society and be on the watch for news of unusual sightings in the area. Zax couldn't do that. He actually would have to see it land and have less than twelve hours to find it before it returned to outer space and eventually warp back to the Skinks' home planet.

And then what? Live his life in the woods with the other animals? He guessed, ultimately, that wouldn't be the worst of sacrifices. As long as he completed his mission, of course. Maybe he could one day reveal himself to the human world. It was a risky chance, but one he might be prepared to make.

His blaster and backpack were near his feet. He stretched over and pulled the backpack to his lap. The data crystal, still attached to the tape Tarik had held it to his body with, was right on top of the other supplies. *Can't let anything happen to you*, he thought. He moved the data crystal to a pouch that was reinforced on the sides to protect what was in it.

There were several packages of food and Z-bars, two bottles of super-hydrating water, survival knife; the typical stuff rebels carried with them on missions, in the backpack. He wouldn't go hungry for a while. But he was a little tired of eating the pre-made food. For some reason, he had a strong appetite for fresh food. Fresh meat, even. Perhaps the travel back in time affected his physiology in some way and was in need of certain nutrients. A sudden craving for a Z-bar confirmed what he suspected about his body. It was in need. Time travel had taken something out of him that needed replenishing.

Digging a Z-bar out, he peeled off the wrapper and took a bite. His electronic compass/rangefinder, also standard backpack carry-on, caught his gaze. He pulled the device out and turned it on. The rangefinder came to life as usual but took longer to boot up than normal. The small tablet showed familiar information but much cruder in content. Amazingly, the electronics in the rangefinder were back-compatible enough to communicate with this era's satellites. This was a huge and unexpected advantage! Zax could now *see* more than the ten miles needed.

Quickly finishing his Z-bar, already feeling somewhat refreshed, he went to work finding just how much information he could extract from the satellites. With a little luck, he'd be able to locate the Skink probe the minute it made its orbit around Earth.

*

Zax crept through the wooded area with his blaster at the ready. He had spotted deer tracks and came upon a pile of fresh deer sign. His craving for fresh meat was now near overwhelming. If he didn't kill something soon, he was going to have to force-feed himself a packaged meal to see if that would satisfy him in some way.

The rangefinder was able to collect more information than he had hoped. There were over two thousand man-made satellites orbiting above. The transmissions to Earth were encrypted, but Skink technology broke all the codes in a short amount of time. Zax had access to endless amounts of data.

While searching one of the data streams, he came across one named *Google Earth*. From there, he easily learned his location and even got to see a less than optimum image of the area. He wasn't that far from rural civilization, but cities were a good distance away. The Google Earth program showed more detail in the populated areas. Zax was even able to get a street view and look at houses and cars of the 21st century. He was actually back in time where *old-life* was the common way of the world.

A movement in the woods caught his eye. A six-point buck grazed near a large tree some fifteen meters away. Stealthily moving for a closer shot, he raised his blaster to his shoulder and pointed the self-aiming barrel toward the target. The blaster discharged, and the deer collapsed to the ground.

As he approached his kill, Zax remembered the conversation with Tarik about the rabbit in the woods before the dogs showed up. It was a shame that his friend couldn't be here with him. A spirit of loneliness draped over him. This was his life now. No Tarik, no Bix, none of his rebel warrior brothers. His parents had passed away, and he didn't have any siblings. The rebels had become his new family.

The buck's glassy eyes gazed into the distance. Zax remembered the same death-stare on Tarik's face when he had died.

Shaking off the remorse, he retrieved the survival knife from the backpack and went to work gutting and skinning the game.

Cleaning a deer was a first for him. The job was simple enough, cutting off the head and feet, and then spilling the entrails onto the ground while cutting from its groin to its neck up the middle. It did make somewhat of a mess. Blood and goo made his fingers sticky, and he did his best not to get any on his body hair. There was no way of knowing where the closest stream or river was to wash off.

Before cutting the carcass into pieces, Zax gathered wood for the fire and branches to construct a couple of rotisserie spits. The laser in the survival knife quickly heated the kindling, and soon the fire was ablaze creating the hot coals necessary for cooking. For this afternoon's meal, backstrap and leg roast were on the menu.

It was a bit tricky constructing the spits, but Zax was proud of his efforts. The meat slowly roasted above the glowing coals, giving a wonderful smell that had Zax wanting to sink his teeth into it even though it was still raw.

Just as soon as the juices on the backstrap turned clear, he removed the meat away from the fire and placed it on a flat stone he had found nearby and wiped clean the best he could. Slicing away the first piece with the knife, he bit into it like a hungry bear.

It was still a little too hot, but he didn't care. Even though the meat hadn't been seasoned, it was the most wonderful he'd ever tasted. Finishing his first piece, he cut another. It then became a race to see if he could cut faster than he could chew and swallow. Before he knew it, the slab of goodness had disappeared.

Zax's fingers smelled of cooked flesh mingled with the wildness of blood from when he had gutted the deer. He was still hungry, and the leg roast still cooked over the fire.

The roast was larger than the backstrap, so naturally, it would take longer to cook. Zax felt he couldn't wait and carved off a mostly cooked slab from the outside and ate it. Blood pooled on the main piece left behind. The roast wasn't as tender as the backstrap, but it too was one of the best things he had ever eaten.

He carved more from the outside until the cooked portions were gone. Despite the fact the meat was still bloody, Zax removed the roast away from the fire. He held the spit on either end and bit into the partially cooked flesh. Teeth sank deeply as he ripped away his first chunk, shredding the flesh under the power of his jaws.

As he ate, his basic senses came alive. He felt invigorated; like he had been out of place all of his life and now had come home. It was a *beast-like* feeling, where this was his territory for him to live off of and defend.

Zax smelled a squirrel in a tree behind him, and then looked to see it there. He turned his gaze to another tall tree and saw an owl sleeping the last of the day away, for it would soon turn dark.

Once the last of the leg roast was gone, he tossed the spit to the ground. There was still most of the deer carcass left. Zax had room in his belly for more. Looking at the fire, it had died down enough that he'd have to add more wood. No matter. The last few bits of the roast had been practically raw.

Stepping over to the deer and brushing the flies away, he cut off one of the front legs, making sure to carve a portion of the shoulder along with it. There was absolutely nothing displeasing about the metallic-like taste of blood as Zax bit into it. In fact, he realized that this was the way meat was supposed to be eaten.

By the time Zax ate his fill, the sun had set, and Venus came out to shine. He made sure the fire was out, as he didn't want to camp here for the night. There was a farm a few miles from there, and despite all the meat that he had eaten, he still had a craving for fresh vegetables.

With rangefinder in hand, Zax set upon a new journey.

*

She plodded aimlessly through the forest, which was a dangerous thing for a bigfoot to do. Living among the *Stealers* had become increasingly difficult. Civilization continuously encroached to some degree from every side. History had taught them that if any of her kind were captured, an invasion was sure to follow.

The story had been passed down, where many generations ago, one of their ancestors had been captured by the Stealers. The townspeople gathered a large force and sought to rid the peace-loving *Holders*, the literal meaning of the word the bigfoot called themselves.

The Stealers came with sticks that barked with the sound of thunder. The stinger from the weapon made gaping holes in flesh and brought many ancestors to the place of forever-sleep.

The whole Holders' nation sensed the danger and came together for the first time in millennia, perhaps even the first time since the *Scattering of First Family*. There was no reasoning with the Stealers. The only thing they understood was death.

One by one, the Holders eliminated those who attacked. But knowing the way of the Stealers, they took no chance of becoming victims again.

The Holders gathered at night while the Stealers slept and killed every man, woman, and child in the town and the surrounding area. Their deaths were swift but executed without mercy.

When it was over, the dead, both Holder and Stealer, were gathered and brought to the Great Burial Ground where all Holder remains resided. That was the first and only time Stealers were buried among the Holders. There was a vow for there to be no more, as another attack on Holder sacred grounds would end in a decisive war where only one victor would remain.

Her name was *Cha'nu*. She was old enough to bear children and should have been expecting this season. But her mate had died unexpectedly when a great branch from a tree suddenly fell and struck him on the head.

Though territorial in a common respectful manner, Holders in the area gathered and paid final homage at the burial ground.

Yes, there were a least two suitors who sought to fill her loneliness. One was too young, in her opinion. The other, though strong, did not stir the fires of her desire.

Cha'nu's mind never felt the same after her mate's death. It was as if the dense fog of the morning had rolled in and never left. She had to wade through thoughts to function in life. Existence had lost its luster. She simply went through the motions of life each day until the sleep of night turned her hurt off. She would go to a place where she was lost in a sea of nothing until the sun would snatch peace from her and wake her up.

An acrid odor stung her sensitive nostrils, bringing her fully aware. The smell was faint, the smell of wood burning, perhaps coming from tens of miles away. Still, fire was the destroyer of homes and threatened all life in vast areas. Fire was the greatest enemy, and the only way to survive its destruction was to flee.

Before panic set in, charring meat odors mingled with the smoke. With a forest fire, smells of grasses and hair would intermingle. This was not a forest fire, to her relief. But then the concern shifted to the second greatest threat: the Stealers! If she could smell their cooking fires, then they were too close.

Cha'nu briefly thought on meeting with others to warn them of her concern. But for some reason, the challenge gave her a sense of purpose. She would go alone and investigate.

Following the smell, she picked up her pace and scampered through the woods. It had been a long time since she had moved this fast. Adrenaline pumped through her body energizing it to carry her through the terrain.

And then she came to a screeching halt. A scent mingled with the smoke and cooking meat. A scent somewhat familiar but totally unique. There was no doubt that it was something close to Holder and nothing like any Stealer she had smelled. What was this unique creature?

Curiosity empowered her more. Cha'nu bounded through the forest to solve the mystery.

*

Zax found the dark of the forest comforting. In a way, he felt invisible, all-powerful, as he traveled underneath the stars twinkling overhead. His previous life, which strangely had yet to occur, seemed distant; unreal, actually. It was as if he had always been in the forest. Living day by day and moment by moment, not giving care to the previous day nor the one to come. *Now* was the only thing that had substance. *Now* was the only thing that mattered.

He found his destination easily with the guidance of the rangefinder. It led him to the back of a remote farm. Chickens roosted in an enclosure behind a rickety old barn. Not far, a sad looking garden set adjacent from a large area, the soil tilled and rowed, either ready for planting or waiting for seeds to emerge. It appeared he had arrived between growing seasons.

Having journeyed this far, his taste buds still aching for some fresh vegetables, Zax stepped on the soft ground over to the garden.

The broccoli had seen much better days. The heads had long ago been harvested, and the florets that remained had flowered and gone to seed. Of the six cabbage plants, two maintained some viability after he peeled off a few of the surrounding leaves.

Zax held one green head in his large hand and bit into it like it was an apple. The slightly bitter, earthy taste, along with the crunch, was just what his palate craved. He finished the cabbage in short order.

Instead of devouring the next one, he decided to rummage through the remains and find what else might still be worth eating.

Green onions grew like bushy grass down one row. The heads had all gone to seed, and the stalks were somewhat fibrous. A pungent odor emitted from one of the bulbs as he uprooted a few and squeezed it with his fingers. It was fresh enough to eat, but right now, Zax wasn't in the mood for onions.

He discarded the green onions and discovered a row of turnips and carrots. Carefully unearthing the roots, he quickly found a turnip worth eating, as well as several carrots.

Brushing the dirt off the turnip the best he could, Zax then chomped into it. The turnip had a taste similar to the way the earth smelled that it grew in. Then, a peppery, somewhat aromatic flavor basked over his tongue. The taste was absolutely delightful.

After finishing the third turnip, he ate the carrots, and then his strange hunger felt satisfied for the first time since his arrival.

There was some leafy lettuce emerging in the new part of the garden. Curiosity more than desire motivated him over to it. The lettuce was delicate and didn't offer a lot of flavors.

Deciding it was time to go, he brushed the dirt from his hands. Zax looked over at the farmhouse and wondered who lived there. The humble old house had seen better days as it sat underneath the glow of the moon.

Farms in the past often times had dogs. Thankfully, this farm either didn't have any or the ones that were there were fast asleep. Nu-Mans and dogs didn't get along at all. His blaster would easily end any threat an encounter might present. But he'd rather it not come to that. The noise would create too much attention, and Zax needed to remain hidden until the mission was complete.

His belly full and the end of the day pulling his eyelids toward sleep, Zax left the farm and headed to a cozy looking cave about an hour's walk away. There were enough turnips and carrots remaining for him to make another trip if he so desired.

CHAPTER 16

Cole was in his room on the internet, scrolling through Daily UFO Sightings, a website devoted to the latest, greatest alien reports and a bunch of other pseudoscience topics. This site had been featuring photos from Mars taken by NASA's Curiosity rover for the past several months. At first, some of the photos showed what could be construed as ancient artifacts of a remnant of civilization. Then some photos were interpreted as showing life of some sort. It started as fossil remains. One photo seemed to show an alien figure peeking from behind a large rock. Another showed a strange animal that was a cross between a lizard and a ferret. Another looked just like a crab. The funniest was the one that had what looked exactly like a squirrel. Cole laughed and laughed when he saw that one. Realistically, he didn't believe any of the photos sent back from Mars proved anything about ancient life, or life of any kind for that matter, on the angry red planet. He still enjoyed perusing the photos, looking for the next big laugh.

KQKY played in the background. The DJ, Chunker, had a thing for the Alice Cooper band. "Under My Wheels" ripped from the radio speaker. Cole had listened to the words before and wondered if it was a revenge song from an angry lover. *I'm driving right up to you; I guess that you couldn't see; But you were under my wheels.* Sounded violent.

There were many songs with strange lyrics. Some didn't seem to make any sense and were only put in to flow with the music. The strangest song of all he had heard was one named "Timothy." Three guys were trapped in a mine with no food to eat. When they were finally rescued, there were only two. The singer lamented: *Timothy, where did you go?* And: *God, why don't I know?* That was the only toe-tapping tune that sung of cannibalism he was aware of. Hopefully, there was either ketchup or mustard involved.

Three hard raps sounded in the distance. It came from the living room. Someone was at the front door. It was near 8:30 p.m. and a little late for visitors. Not that Cole's dad had many friends come over on a school/work night to begin with. UPS usually dropped packages off in the back. His dad normally told him to be on the lookout for a package when he'd ordered something, and that hadn't happened.

Cole rose and heard the same sequence bang against the front door a little faster. Whoever was there, was getting impatient.

"I'm coming, okay?" he said to himself.

A quick trip down the hall and into the living room brought him to the front door. The three panels of glass at the top of the door allowed him to see Brennon Davis had decided to pay him a visit. *Great.* Things were about to get real. Cole knew the day would come where he'd have to step up and face his adversary like a man or chicken out and be known as some weak loser.

Their gazes met through the window.

Brennon narrowed his eyes, and then looked past Cole to either side as if he was looking for someone else.

No, my dad's not home. Butterflies took wing inside Cole's stomach. How was he going to handle this? What if he just didn't open the door? That was sure to work, but then he'd have to face Brennon at some point where there would be no door between them. Cole could only imagine the story Brennon would tell how Cole was too much of a pussy even to open the door.

His mind drifted back to a time when he was five. One of his front teeth was loose and destined to come out. He could wiggle it back and forth without much pain, but the root insisted on hanging on. The few times he tried to push it to the limit to get the root to break, the pain became unbearable, and he had to stop. By the third day, the tooth started to annoy him. He couldn't even concentrate in class, because as he worked the tooth back and forth with his tongue, all he could think of was getting it out.

When he got home, his dad finally drove home the point that Cole just had to suck it up and yank it out in one swift, hard *jerk.*

Standing in front of the mirror by the bathroom sink, he did just that. The root breaking sounded horrible, and there was some momentary pain. He saw the tooth between his fingers, and blood dripped into his mouth. The experience hadn't been nearly as bad as he had imagined, though. In fact, he'd wished that he'd done that sooner.

Cole again stood in front of a mirror; this one in his mind's eye. It was time to rip out the proverbial tooth.

Taking a deep breath, he stiffened his back and raised his slumping shoulders. The door came open with a twist of the knob and a quick pull.

Brennon stood there dressed nicely but with the front of the right side of his shirt untucked, and looked down on him. The wind blew from the right, blowing long strands of blonde hair partially across his face. His eyes were red like they were irritated or he had been crying; with a wild uncertain look like a mixture of hurt and panic. Again, he looked past Cole and about the living room. "Where is she?" His words slurred a bit when they left his mouth.

Of all the questions Cole thought he might have to face, this was one he hadn't anticipated. "What? Who are you looking for?"

"Don't play dumb with me. Charlotte! Who else did you think I'd be looking for?"

Cole did feel a little stupid for not connecting the obvious dots. But the farthest thing from his mind was that Charlotte would be over at his house today. "Charlotte's not here. Why would you think that?"

Brennon brushed the underside of his nose with a knuckle on his right hand. "She was here last night."

"We had a science project together. Her mom brought her over here." Things were going better than expected. Brennon seemed like he didn't come here to settle a score.

"Are you telling me the truth? Because if you're not, things are really going to go bad for you." The way Brennon had said it, it sounded more like things were going to go bad *for him* if Cole *were* telling the truth.

"Seriously, man. Charlotte's not here."

Brennon wilted, looking like someone had opened a valve and let all the air within him out.

Several seconds of silence passed. Cole thought about inviting him in but didn't want to draw this encounter out any longer than necessary. He didn't want to give opportunities for conflicts to arise. "I did speak to her earlier, on the phone."

"You did?" Brennon said, sounding confused. "Where was she? What did you talk about? Did she say where she was going?"

"Look, uh, last night she said she'd like us to become friends. Get to know each other better, you know." There, he said it. He wasn't going to sugar coat the situation for Brennon's benefit or his own, for that matter. There was now a reason for an ass-whipping to ensue, and he was just going to have to deal with it.

"Whatever." Brennon raised his hands in front of his chest and spread them apart. "Can you tell me where she is?"

"Well, yeah. I was supposed to call her, later on, tonight, but she called me right after baseball practice and told me that she had to go to Amy's house to study. We didn't say a lot more than that. So, she's over at Amy's."

Brennon's head dropped back, and he closed his eyes and slowly shook his head. "It doesn't make sense. It doesn't make sense." The words were low and meant only for himself.

"Have you tried to call her?" Cole asked.

"Yeah. The calls just go to voicemail. She did go to Amy's, but she left before seven. Amy told me that." Brennon sounded very tired at this point.

"How did she get home? Her mom is at the gym with my dad tonight."

"She didn't go home. I was going to come here first because I thought she was playing a trick on me. But then I decided to go by her house first. Nobody was home."

The butterflies in Cole's stomach vacated, leaving a hollow pit of dread and despair. "So, she left Amy's on foot?"

"Yeah. She was going to meet me at the bus stop in front of that old baseball field in Amy's subdivision. I got there at seven. She wasn't there."

Now the story was out in the open. Charlotte didn't have any intention of studying at Amy's. She was going to meet with Brennon, the day after she'd told him that she wanted to change her old self-destructive ways. But none of that mattered one little bit right now. "So, what? She's missing? Tell me she's not missing," Cole said, his voice panicked.

"I don't know what's happened to her." Brennon sighed deeply. "I've run the scenarios in my head a million different ways. Maybe she changed her mind about meeting me tonight. Called another friend or called maybe even Uber. But if she did, she didn't go straight home."

"What should we do? Call the police?"

"I don't know what we should do. She's really not missing at this point. It's only been about two hours since she left Amy's. I was hoping that maybe she was with her mom, but you said Mrs. Meadows was with your dad." Brennon brought a finger to his mouth and began to chew on a nail.

The breeze changed directions and blew in a slight hint of alcohol to Cole's nose. "Hey, man. You been drinking?"

"So what if I have?" Brennon said, his eyes half-open.

"You're not old enough to drink, you big doofus. If the coach finds out, you'll get kicked off the team. You might even be expelled from school," Cole said. If Brennon had been drinking, was there something the boy might be hiding from him? Brennon did seem genuinely upset, though. Cole was just so confused right now he couldn't control the direction of his thoughts.

"The last thing I'm worried about right now is baseball," Brennon said. Whatever funk he had taken refuge in appeared to have ebbed. "I'm just wasting my time here now."

"What are you going to do?"

"I'm not sure, right now."

"You need to call her mom."

"I don't have her number. Do you have it?"

"No, I don't. But my dad's with her at the gym. I can call him. Come in and close the door," Cole said and headed for the kitchen without waiting for Brennon to respond.

He picked up the telephone and dialed his dad's number. The call connected on the second ring.

"Hey Cole. What's up?"

"Dad, are you still with Charlotte's mom?"

"No, I'm on my way home now. Why?"

"Uh, I wanted to know if you had her phone number?"

Mark Rainwater nervously chuckled. "No, I don't. I...I haven't had the nerve to ask her for it yet. Why do you want her number?"

"A friend of mine called and asked if I had it. So, I thought I'd ask you." Cole did his best not to open the door for more questions. And, so far he hadn't lied either.

"Well, sorry, I don't. Is something wrong?"

"Not that I know of, dad. Look, I gotta let them know you don't have it. See you when you get home."

"Okay, bye."

"Bye." Cole pushed the off button on the phone and set it on the counter. He turned to Brennon, who stood in the front foyer, being careful not to encroach into the living room. "He doesn't have it. But, he's on his way home. I expect Charlotte's mom is going home too."

"Yeah." Brennon bit down on his bottom lip. "I guess the right thing to do is go over there and see if Charlotte's at home. If not, I'll have to tell Mrs. Meadows the whole story."

"Man, I hope you're blowing this way out of proportion. Maybe Charlotte's at home and hid from you when you came by. Maybe she's not answering her phone because she stood you up and didn't want to deal with it right now."

"Maybe, and I hope you're right. But that's just not the Charlotte Meadows that I know." Brennon pointed at Cole. "If she calls you, you'll call me and let me know, right?"

"Sure, man. But promise me that if you find out where she is, you'll call me."

"What's your number?"

"Three-two-six; three-four-two-eight."

Brennon pulled out his cellphone and punched in the numbers. Coles cellphone rang in his bedroom. "There, now you have my number." He turned and opened the door, showing himself out without another word spoken.

Cole watched the red Mustang GT back out of his driveway and onto the street. The GT's tires spun and slightly shrieked as it shot out of the hole.

Blonde haired, blue eyed baby Jesus. Please let Charlotte be okay. It took a few seconds before Cole realized the irreverence of his mindless prayer. Then, he figured that God was big enough to understand his state of mind and would forgive him. A loving God would do that.

*

Cole was on the internet searching various social media pages of Charlotte and some of her closest friends, looking for clues as to her whereabouts. So far, all he found were the usual narcissistic ramblings people posted in order to attain a measure of relevance to the rest of the other nine billion people on the planet.

The rumble of his dad's truck engine came from the carport and died. Cole sprung from his chair and made a beeline for the kitchen.

His dad entered with gym bag in hand and hung the truck keys on the keyhook on the wall. Cole's thoughts must have been written on his face, because his dad asked, "What's wrong?"

Cole didn't really want to go into it all. A big part of him thought he and Brennon had overreacted to the situation. If Charlotte was okay and playing some sort of mind game with Brennon, this could turn around and get her in trouble for lying to her mother about going to study at Amy's. Yes, Cole was well aware that Charlotte had lied to him too. He could forgive her of that, if her story was trustworthy enough. But he didn't want to get her in trouble. The relationship was too fresh to let something that small derail the whole thing.

"Cole?" his dad said, cocking his head to the side and giving a wary eye.

"Sorry, Dad. I hope it's nothing."

"Okay, me too. Now, what's going on?"

After a deep breath, Cole said, "The reason I called you earlier for Mrs. Meadows' phone number, was to give it to Brennon Davis."

"I thought he and Charlotte had broken up?"

"Yeah, but they were supposed to meet tonight. It's a long story we don't need to go into. Charlotte lied to her mom about where she was going tonight. When Brennon went to pick her up, she wasn't there. Brennon wanted to call her mom to find out where she might be."

"She certainly wasn't with us tonight. Did you try looking online for Lori's phone number?"

"Yeah, but the one I found didn't work."

Mark sat the gym bag on the floor and rubbed his chin. "So what you're really saying is that no one has heard from Charlotte for a few hours."

"Just a little more than two."

Shrugging his shoulders, Mark said, "Son, I don't think you have a lot to worry about. When men and women, or boys and girls, have problems, all kinds of things can happen. This sounds more like a boy-girl thing than anything bad happening to Charlotte. I mean, it's only been a couple of hours. Don't you think you and Brennon are overreacting a bit? You're both emotionally involved with her."

Leave it to his dad to always look on the bright side of things. Still, his words did bring relief to the wild fears Cole's mind had grown and nurtured. "You really thinks she's okay? When Brennon went to pick her up, she wasn't there."

"Cole, the mall is still open. There's a good chance she had someone else pick her up and take her there. I don't think you should worry yourself sick thinking that she's missing."

"I guess so," Cole said, trying to make himself believe only that.

"Why don't you go and get ready for bed? In the morning you'll see things through different eyes."

"Okay, Dad. I will." Cole started to leave, but then said, "Oh, how was the gym? Did you like it?"

Mark's face brightened. "Yeah, I did. It was good to get out and be around other people. There were a lot of people there around my age. Man, that Lori Meadows is in good shape. She can ride a stationary bike for forty-five minutes straight. I had to give that up after fifteen minutes." He rubbed his inner thighs. "That seat is going to take some getting used to."

"You going back?"

"I think so. I'll get a single monthly membership. This summer, if you want, I can upgrade to a family membership?"

"Sounds good, Dad. I'm going to get ready for bed now."

"Goodnight. I'm going to pay some bills, hit the shower, and go to bed too. I think I'm really going to sleep good tonight after that workout."

"I love you. See you in the morning," Cole said and scampered out.

"I love you too. Stop worrying about Charlotte," Mark said, his voice fading.

Talking to his dad had helped him feel a lot better. It wouldn't surprise Cole one bit if Charlotte had changed her mind about meeting Brennon and had gone to the mall.

He admitted to himself that he had a wild imagination. It made perfect sense that he'd blow a situation like this way out of proportion.

Brennon had no doubt overreacted, too. Heck, the doofus had been drinking. That could only add fuel to the fire of his own imagination.

Cole brushed his teeth, turned off his computer, and undressed and got into bed.

The lights went out.

It was dark.

Darkness was not Cole Rainwater's friend.

CHAPTER 17

Cole found himself in an empty hallway at school. His book sack felt like it weighed a ton, and he carried so many books in his hands that he thought he was going to drop them. The clock on the wall indicated that his science class was just about to begin. He was going to be late again if he didn't hurry it up.

Books bobbled and threatened to spill as the weight of the book sack pounded his back with every step. Still, Cole kept his pace. Being late for Mr. Ritzman's class had been an accident. Being late to Mrs. Thomas' class would make the teachers see his tardiness as an act of disrespect. That's the last thing he needed so close to the end of school. Cole knew that when it came time to give the final grades, that teachers rewarded good students favorably. He'd been close enough on a few occasions where his C+ had shown up as a B on his report card. Cole was an above average student, and he needed all the help he could get.

The door to his science room was wide open. He stumbled into the room, trying desperately not to drop the books, and came to a halt.

Everyone was at their desks, including the teacher. Everyone had their heads down, and none took notice of him, save one: Charlotte Meadows.

Princess Charlotte sat majestically in her chair and gave him the biggest, warmest smile.

Thank God! She was safe!

Mrs. Thomas lifted her head and gazed sternly at him.

Yeah, he got it. He was late or nearly late, and he needed to take his seat.

No sooner than he had dropped his book sack on the floor and his books on his desk, Mrs. Thomas rose from her chair and addressed the class.

"Everyone, I need your attention. I have some sad news." Mrs. Thomas removed her glasses and wiped the corner of her right eye with a tissue. "Charlotte Meadows is missing."

Cole felt iciness running down his spine. His head jutted to where Charlotte sat, two rows over and in the very front desk of the row. Her gaze remained transfixed on Mrs. Thomas.

Mrs. Thomas continued, "If any of you have information as to her whereabouts, you need to go to the principal's office and give a statement."

Cole sprung from his seat. The books on his desk crashed to the floor. He pointed at Charlotte, and said, "Charlotte's right there."

Mrs. Thomas glanced toward Charlotte and then gazed back at Cole. "Cole, there's no one in her chair."

"What do you mean? She's right there. I see her. Charlotte, say something."

Charlotte remained seated; her gaze locked toward the front of the room.

"There's no one there. Charlotte Meadows is missing."

"You're crazy!" Cole said, and then looked all around. "Everybody, look. Charlotte's at her desk." He continued to point. "You see Charlotte right there in her seat, don't you?"

The rest of the class stared back at him like he was a boy gone crazed.

"Cole. Do you know something about her disappearance? Do you need to go to the principal's office and give a statement?"

"Me, no...I don't know what happened to her. But she's not missing. She's right here in this room! What's wrong with all of you?"

Charlotte finally turned her head toward him. She slowly rose from her chair, and said, "Help me, Cole, please. It's up to you to find me."

Before he could answer, Charlotte faded from the room like a character transported off the Starship Enterprise onto another planet.

"It's your fault, Cole," someone said from behind.

He whipped his head around to see who had said that, but then another voice said, "It's your fault, Cole."

"It's your fault. It's your fault," the whole room chanted now.

Cole felt caged by the chorus of accusations. Even Mrs. Thomas joined in the cacophony of noise that grew louder in Cole's head every second.

He raised his hands over his ears but only trapped the reverberating noise.

Cole screamed until his cry drowned out every other sound.

A haunting guitar playing from the radio rescued Cole from his nightmare. He sprang upright, feeling cold from the a/c unit vent in the ceiling blowing over his sweaty head and back. Taking a moment to bridge the outside reality from that in his head, he breathed a sigh of relief.

The radio pounded a steady beat. If Cole had been more awake, the rhythm might have energized him.

Then he realized the song that played: "Don't fear the Reaper."

The tune, mixed with the fog of his nightmare, filled him with incredible anxiousness unlike he'd ever felt before. Cole started breathing harder as if each breath took in less air than the breath before. In seconds he found himself heaving and feeling light-headed.

Is this what a heart attack feels like? Am I going to die? It certainly felt that way. A low roar built in his head. He felt vulnerable like a big monster was about to snatch him up and swallow him whole.

Panicked, Cole rolled off the side of the bed and laid near face-first on the floor. The wood floor was solid, an anchor point of security. It smelled a little dusty, irritating his nose. His gaze focused on the wood grain and imperfections, reminding him of lines on a map. Then he wondered if nature had left cryptic clues in things like wood grain that would lead to unknown mysteries the world had to offer. He had never heard of a theory like that before and now wondered if perhaps he had stumbled onto something that might break through the paradigm of normal.

The next song on the radio pulled Cole back out of his head into the present. "Eye of the Tiger" pulsed it's inspirational beat giving him legs strong enough to stand and face the day.

When he made it to the bathroom and looked in the mirror, he thought of the dream again; how his classmates berated him, saying that Charlotte's disappearance was *his fault*.

But Charlotte wasn't really missing, was she? There was no way he was going to wait to get to school to find out.

He quickly hurried back to his room and called her cellphone. Like Brennon had said the night before, the call went to voicemail. Cole felt the onset of another breathing attack but fought back knowing that he had to keep it together if he was going to get through this.

Checking his *Recent Calls* on the phone, he pushed Brennon's number, and the call went through.

"Hello?" Brennon said, sounding half-awake.

"Dude, it's Cole. Did you find Charlotte last night?"

The pause lasted one hundred million years. Brennon said, "No," his voice breaking in the end.

Cole had never felt more scared in his life. His nightmare was coming true! "What? Tell me what happened."

"It was bad. Charlotte's mom went into hysterics when I got there and told her the story. She called the police, and even though a lot of time hadn't passed, they sent an officer over. I had to stay there, and my parents came over there too. Pretty soon the place was swarming with cops. I know some went to Amy's house to talk with her. The police took this seriously because of that other kid who had been abducted."

"Any clues? Any information at all?"

"No, none. The police interrogated me for a couple of hours. I kept telling them the truth, and they just kept asking the same questions. Finally, they looked at the app on my phone that tracks where I go during the day—my parents made me put that on there so they can know where I've been. My story checked out, and they let me go around two this morning."

"Sounds like you had a rough night," Cole said, bewildered at what to do next.

"Yeah, and my head's not feeling so good after drinking that bottle of prosecco."

"What are we going to do?"

"Uh, I don't know. What can we do? The police are handling it. We're just a couple of kids."

Not such a big man now, are you? Cole thought. It would have been easy just to leave it to the adults to handle the situation. But Charlotte's words from the dream came back to inspire him: *"It's up to you to find me."*

"Brennon, the police haven't had any luck finding Coach Jones' nephew. We can't just sit around and wait for them. This is Charlotte we're talking about. We both care about her too much not to do something."

"Okay, okay, I hear you," Brennon said, his voice sounding stronger. "You gotta plan? I'm all in."

Thinking a minute, the police shows on TV always got their clues from the scene of the crime. It was at least a place to start. "We have to go to the bus stop where you were supposed to pick up Charlotte. We'll look for clues."

"The police have already done that. They didn't find anything."

"I don't care. It was dark. They had to use flashlights. There's no telling what they have missed. They probably have written it off and won't be going back there. Let's do this, you and me. We'll go and see if we can find any clues."

"All right. Do you want me to get dressed and come get you now?"

Cole thought a moment and realized that there was no way his dad was going to allow him to skip school and chase after Charlotte. He hated to deceive his dad, but Charlotte depended on him. "We'll both go to school. After first-hour, we'll meet in the parking lot and head on over to the bus stop."

"We'll get caught when we skip class and get in trouble."

"Yes, we will. But that won't be until later. Brennon, we have to do this. The most important time to find a missing person is immediately after their disappearance. We've already lost a lot of time. Please tell me you'll do this?"

"We might get kicked off the baseball team."

The possibility did give Cole pause, but he said, "I don't care. We have to do this. If you're not in, I'm going to steal a bike after first-hour and head over there by myself."

"No need to make the matter worse. Don't steal anything. Meet me at my car after first-hour. We'll be at the bus stop in twenty minutes."

Cole breathed a sign of relief and then felt like the heavy lifting was just about to start. "Thanks, man. We're doing this for Charlotte."

"Yeah, we're doing this for Charlotte, and we're going to find her too. Later."

The call ended.

Cole's dad had often said that *politics made strange bedfellows.* Politics didn't bring him and Brennon together, but now he understood exactly what his dad had meant.

*

Cole sat alone in his seat on the bus. He had last night's podcast of Shore to Shore playing through his earbuds, but he had hardly listened to one word said.

He immediately told his dad about Charlotte's disappearance when he heard him leave his bedroom. Cole had never seen his dad snap awake that quickly the first thing in the morning. Of course, his dad pushed him for the details, of which he had done his best to divulge all.

His dad cursed that he didn't have Lori Meadows' phone number, and made a beeline to the phone and called work. He told them that he was going to take a day of emergency vacation, and then told Cole he was going to get dressed and go over to Lori's as fast as he could.

Cole considered giving Brennon a call, and maybe skipping school altogether to get a faster start, but decided against it. They had a plan and would stick to it. It would draw less attention and increase their chances of success.

His dad zoomed down the driveway, giving him a mindless wave as he careened down the street toward town.

Cole felt the weight of the world on his shoulders as time slowly ticked by while waiting for the bus.

When Mr. Tillus, the bus driver, stopped and opened the door for him to climb aboard, Cole almost blurted out that *Charlotte Meadows was missing* as he stepped his way up. He didn't, though. There was nothing

Mr. Tillus could do about the situation anyway. The man would just ask questions that he wouldn't have the answers to.

So when the bus driver gave Cole his traditional introductory smile, he simply returned it, though his mouth didn't stretch from side to side near as wide as usual.

The younger kids on the bus played their roles, lost in their own worlds, oblivious to Charlotte's disappearance.

Life was strange, how people functioned every day caught up in a world created by their observations and experiences. Unaffected by the deadly unknown that might be down the street or even living right next to them, until their exposure enters reality.

Reality.

Cole had learned that everyone creates a different reality. He had once read of an experiment where a woman spoke before a group of people and a thief rushed in and stole her purse. The eyewitness accounts varied greatly, from the description of the thief, to even the color of clothes he wore. The article then delved into how the mind stored memories and ultimately the reliability of the memories recorded. After reading the article, Cole found himself questioning everything he believed in. How much of his memories were actually true events or some misshapen construct? Thoughts like those only dug deeper holes. He was forced to accept that his memories were his, and he just had to hope they were mostly the true way that they had happened.

That day, Cole came to the conclusion that reality is what you choose to believe, or are forced to believe by undeniable circumstance, is real. That's the only thing that made sense. Because, how else could two people hear the same information and come away with two totally different opinions about what was said? That was why there was more than one political party. That's why there were believers and atheists.

He was forced to believe that Charlotte Meadows was missing, even though he would have chosen not to. That bitter fact ate away at his insides as the bus bounced down the highway toward school.

*

The bus rolled to a stop around the curved driveway in front of the school. There were so many people scattered about, it looked like someone had kicked over an ant pile.

The police were there in full force, and a news van had men pulling equipment out and setting up. All the kids had pretty much been corraled into one area.

"What's going on around here?" Mr. Tillus said as Cole stepped down the stairs onto the concrete.

Cole gazed wide-eyed at the kind bus driver, hearing the genuine concern in his voice. But, he said nothing, and turned and sped away.

It was windy, just like the night before. The unseen force blasted him head-on as if he were swimming against the ocean's tide.

Mr. Ritzman, the teacher who wore all black, was among four other men dressed just like him. His left hand remained in his coat pocket, but the right pointed this way and that like he was giving different directions to a hundred different people.

There were many strange things about Mr. Ritzman that didn't add up. But now seeing him with others of his kind, it was obvious that he fit in more with law enforcement than he ever had with the teaching staff. These men in black could only be government agents from the FBI.

Standing at the edge of the crowd of kids, he stood on his toes and looked around for Brennon.

The kids' chatter sounded like the ocean's roar. As he concentrated to glean information about the topic, he quickly learned they all knew of Charlotte's disappearance. No surprise, really. At least Cole no longer felt he carried the burden of her plight alone. Now everyone else knew. Maybe someone had a clue as to her whereabouts.

When Cole looked back over toward Mr. Ritzman's way, he saw that Brennon was over there by him and the other men in black. Their collective bodies had hidden the baseball player earlier.

Ritzman caught his gaze, and he thrust forth a pointed finger directly at him.

Cole's butt felt like it had melted and a black hole sucked the molecules of liquid flesh down a bottomless void. All of a sudden he felt like the whole situation was his fault; that Charlotte was missing because of him.

Two of the men in black by Ritzman sprang into action and headed directly for Cole as he stared back, practically paralyzed by the situation.

"Cole Rainwater?" one of the men coldly said as they approached. He and the other guy wore the same style of sunglasses, giving them an insect-like look.

"Yes, sir." Cole went into automatic discipline mode. He would push out any errant thoughts and concentrate on any questions they had for him, and he would give nothing but the facts and the truth.

"We need you to come with us. We have a few questions regarding Charlotte Meadows," the other man said. His words had been direct but did sound more like a request than an order.

"Yes, sir." Cole watched the two men part, and one swung his hand in between them, inviting Cole to pass and lead the way.

Brennon looked anxious, standing by Ritzman, but didn't appear to be scared. Good. Cole hoped that this delay wouldn't interfere with their plans to leave school early.

"Mr. Rainwater," Ritzman said. "I'm sure you know of the tragic news by now?"

"Yes, sir." Cole realized at this point he sounded like a broken record, but he imagined that's how troops in the military responded to their superiors all the time.

"I know you know me as a member of the Dent County High School teaching staff, but that is only my secondary profession." Ritzman reached inside the front of his coat and pulled out an identification badge. "Mr. Rainwater, I am an agent of the FBI, as are these other four gentlemen. I was assigned to work undercover here after the abduction of Raymond Jones. There were some weak clues that led us here, and I was hoping to find new leads that might help resolve this case. Charlotte Meadows' disappearance was something that happened unexpectedly."

"Attention! Attention students," Mr. Mason, the principal, yelled. "Attention!" The noise slowly subsided. He continued, "You all know that Charlotte Meadows has gone missing. We're going to assemble in the gym. There will be police there who will take information that any of you might have to help them find her. Remember, there is no piece of information too small. Once inside, please find an officer and tell them anything that you know. The teaching staff will be there to help support in our time of sadness. The state has also provided grief counselors, who will be available to help those who are troubled deal with the situation. So, please, everyone head inside, orderly mind you, and assemble in the gym."

Two teachers opened the double doors leading inside the school. The kids slowly made their way up the steps and headed inside.

Cole looked at Ritzman, his expression asking what to do next.

Ritzman turned to Brennon. "You can go inside with the others."

Brennon shrugged. "Can I come with you and wait for Cole?"

Thinking a moment, Ritzman said, "We aren't going to keep Cole for long. Run along to assembly and wait for him there."

Locking gazes with Cole, he gave him a knowing nod, darted his eyes toward the parking lot, nodded again, and stepped away.

"This way, Cole," an agent said, opening a single door that led to admissions, which was joined by the medical room and the principal's office.

Ritzman motioned Cole into the principal's office and told him to take a seat in front of the desk. He then left the four other agents at the door and sat in the principal's chair.

Both of Ritzman's eyes focused forward.

Cole gazed back, anticipating Ritzman's left eye to wander sideways like waiting for a leaky faucet to release a dangling drop. His book sack lay next to him, and he neatly crossed his hands in his lap.

"Mr. Rainwater," Ritzman said, addressing him teacher-to-student as usual. Then, the man hesitated and sighed. He rested his elbows on the desk, and said, "Cole, I'm sure the situation has you very upset. Brennon's taking it very hard. He's blaming himself, but that's simply not the case here.

"I know that your relationship with Charlotte has been short-lived. The only time you two really spent together was two nights ago at your house. Brennon and Lori Meadows confirmed that to us. We don't believe that Charlotte has run away. We do believe she's been abducted, though there isn't any physical evidence or eyewitnesses that might suggest that. There's some chatter that this area is being targeted by human traffickers. We're afraid that's what happened with Raymond Jones and Charlotte Meadows.

"The only thing we want from you is any clue that we might be wrong. Did Charlotte mention anything about being unhappy the other night? Any problems with her mother? We know about Brennon but can't connect why she would run away over him. Is there anything, anything odd that she might have said that night?"

Listening intently, Cole felt the spotlight on him shining brightly. Did Charlotte drop any kind of hint the other night that she might run away? Did the answer lie somewhere in his memory that would lead the FBI directly to her?

Charlotte said in his dream that it was up to him to find her. Did she leave him a clue that night? Did she make a veiled comment that he should have extrapolated into a cry for help? Charlotte's life might depend on his memory. His memory! He knew how unreliable memories were. Charlotte might never be found because of him!

"Cole," Ritzman said. "Anything, Cole? Can you think of something she said that seemed a bit out of the ordinary? Something that wasn't like anything else you two had spoken of that night?"

One thing did come to mind. He didn't know if it would be useful, but it couldn't hurt to share what he knew. Mr. Ritzman and the FBI would know if what he had to offer contained anything to help the case. "Charlotte did say something I found strange."

"Really," Ritzman said, and leaned forward in his chair. "What did she say?"

"She asked me a kinda *what if* question. You know. Like, what if out of all the planets in the whole universe, that Earth was the only planet that had life? She seemed to be fascinated by all the living creatures on Earth, on the land and in the sea. She asked me something like, *If the only planet in the universe that had life was Earth, wouldn't that be enough? Wouldn't it be enough if we are all that there is in the universe?*"

Ritzman leaned back into the chair and turned his gaze to the agents standing by the doorway. He patted the desktop with his right hand, and said, "Well, that doesn't sound like someone distraught who hated life. In fact, it sounded like she saw the future as a challenging adventure to explore."

"That's the Charlotte I knew, for sure," Cole said.

"Cole, thank you for your time. I know that if you think of anything else you'll immediately let us know."

"Yes, sir. I will."

"Good. You can leave now."

Cole stood and picked up his book sack.

"Please do me a favor."

"What's that?"

"When you leave and go to the gym, find one of the grief counselors. Just talk to someone about your feelings for a few minutes. I know you're troubled inside. These people are professionals. Just a few minutes. You'll do that, won't you? For me?" For the first time, Mr. Ritzman sounded like a concerned father and not an arrogant, educated drill sergeant.

"Yes, sir. I will." Cole waited for Ritzman's gaze to excuse him. He turned and walked to the door, and the other agents parted at the doorway.

He left admissions and took the door into the main hallway leading toward the gym. Turning right, he would soon come to the door that led toward the parking lot.

Cole hated lying to Mr. Ritzman; especially since the man had acted like he really cared about his well-being. But, that's just the way it had to be. He would lie, cheat, even steal if it meant getting Charlotte back.

And then another thought struck him. If she had been abducted and he found her, would he even *kill* to free her?

His mind said *yes*. But if he found himself face-to-face with a grown man, or even worse, grown men, what would he do? What could he do?

He hit the door leading outside and heard an engine crank. Brennon slowly pulled out of a parking space and was coming his way.

He didn't know how, but he knew if he found Charlotte they would find someway to save her. They would save her or die trying. Today was the day he would prove himself a man.

CHAPTER 18

The Mustang pulled up to the curb, and Cole heard the doors unlock. He pulled the handle and opened the door, taking a seat with his book sack in his lap.

"You can stick your sack in the back seat," Brennon said.

Carefully maneuvering the pack between the headrests, he did so without hitting Brennon in the face.

"How'd it go?"

"It wasn't bad," Cole said, taking the seatbelt from the clip and bringing it across his chest. The buckle's tongue brightly clicked when it secured into the receiver. "They knew that Charlotte and I weren't that close. They just wanted to know if she may have said something the night she came over that might give them some clues."

"Did you tell them anything?"

"No, not really. They don't believe she's a runaway. They said that human traffickers might be involved."

"Human traffickers? You mean someone's trying to sell Charlotte?" Brennon slapped the steering wheel with his right hand.

"I guess so. I thought human-trafficking only involved people from other countries," Cole said, feeling extremely ignorant about the subject. This was another eye-opening experience in his ascent into manhood. He needed to be aware of the real horrors in life; not so much the paranormal stuff he had been into that couldn't definitively be proven.

"I can't believe stuff like that can happen today. What's the world coming too?" Brennon coughed and opened a wide yawn. No matter how pissed he was, sleep deprivation had its hooks in him.

"You gonna be okay to drive?"

"Yeah, I'll be fine. Maybe we can stop later on, and I'll get an energy drink or something. Just sit tight and let me do the driving. I absolutely hate it when people tell me how to drive."

"No problem," Cole said. He kept one eye on the road and one eye on Brennon. If he saw the boy nod off or an oncoming traffic problem, he wasn't going just to sit there silent and do nothing.

*

When they arrived at the entrance of Amy's subdivision, Brennon sat up in his seat and appeared to be more awake. Apparently, he believed too there had to be some clue left that would lead to finding Charlotte.

Cole felt like he was looking at himself at that point. He could almost see that Brennon's desire was giving him hope, but wasn't it more likely false hope than genuine hope? People didn't want to believe the worst can happen. They lie to themselves all the time, desiring the best of conclusions. He and Brennon were now coming to a point where they could no longer choose the reality they wanted to believe in; where they would find a clue that would lead them to Charlotte. Instead, they were going to have to be forced to accept the outcome of their findings.

The Mustang reached the end of the entrance street, turning left onto the rear street, Sagehill Road, that connected all the streets of the subdivision. Thick woods lined the right side of the Sagehill. Foliage along the ditch had turned brown from herbicide sprayed by county maintenance workers. In their zeal, the crew got a little sloppy and had sprayed the fronts of trees. Then, just up ahead, Cole saw remnants of an old intersection.

Brennon slowed and turned, and right there before them was the old bus stop; the last place Charlotte was supposed to be.

Cole's heart beat faster. This was it. Another definitive moment in time with an unknown outcome. It was just like being in the spotlight. But instead of freezing up, he realized his actions would determine the future. The suspense was palpable. A short time from now he would know the results, but he didn't know now. He had to get through *now*, and it was imperative that they find a clue.

"Are you just going to sit there and stare out the window?" Brennon asked.

Cole shook out of it and turned his gaze back to Brennon. He didn't even realize the Mustang's engine was off. "Uh, no. I was waiting for you."

Brennon pulled the door handle and pushed the door open. "Let's go."

The wind whistled past his ears as he climbed out of the low riding vehicle. Cole took a few steps forward and stopped. Brennon came to his side.

"There's no yellow police tape. So, this isn't considered a crime scene," Cole said.

Brennon just stood silent for several moments, and then said, "Not much to look at, is it?"

"No, no it's not." Cole had a hard time imagining a ballpark in place of all the trees that now grew in the area. The bus stop itself looked strangely out of place. He wondered why it hadn't been torn down after all of these years. Not that it was in that bad of shape, mind you. The awning above the concrete bench was made of galvanized corrugated metal and had withstood the test of time quite well. The bench was dull and dirty, but nothing a quick cleaning from a pressure washer couldn't take care of.

The area around the bus stop had been sprayed with herbicide, keeping encroaching foliage at bay. Tree limbs had gotten in the line of fire too, turning them brown, and dropping dead leaves torn away by the wind.

"I don't think we're gong to find anything here," Brennon said. Whatever eagerness he seemed to have had dissipated.

Cole looked over, his eyebrows hanging low. "Dude, we just got here. We've got to be patient, thorough. You've seen enough police shows on TV. We have to look until we find a piece of evidence that might tell us where she is."

"That's TV stuff," Brennon said. He threw his hands up in the air. "What, we're going to find a map telling us where she is?"

"No, but we might find her cell phone."

"Don't you think the police would have found that last night?"

"I don't know. We can't be sure how hard they looked for anything around here. Plus, it was dark." Cole hesitated when a thought struck him. "Wait a minute!" He unclipped his phone from his belt and punched in Charlotte's number. Her phone rang through the speaker. He pulled his phone away from his ear. "I called her phone. Listen…do you hear it ringing anywhere?"

The two stood like statues, turning their ears this way and that like a scanning device.

All Cole heard was the rustle of leaves in the trees. "Well, it was worth a try."

"I guess we need to search about. Look at all these leaves. What a mess," Brennon said.

"Okay, watch where you step. Let's see if we can find anything."

The leaves certainly were a nuisance. They used their feet to sweep a clear path and look for clues. The two boys coordinated their search and split up.

"There isn't any ink on the bench," Cole said.

"What?"

"You know, when they dust for prints. The police use some kind of dry ink, don't they?"

"I don't know what they use. But you're right, it doesn't look like they looked all that hard around here. The leaves don't even look disturbed," Brennon said.

"Yeah, well, that's hard to say, with the wind and all. It's stirring things up pretty good around here," Cole said but ironically hoping

Brennon was right. Maybe the police *didn't* spend much time in the area looking for clues. He found himself wishing that was true on the one hand, but if the police were that inefficient, how could they ever hope to find Charlotte? Again, Cole found dilemmas and the human psyche were at constant war, where one rationale to solve one predicament only led to creating another.

Brennon covered his area quicker than Cole. It was obvious the boy was frustrated. He even went back and examined the bench again, which sat there with nothing to hide and nothing to show.

"It's a waste of time, Cole. There's nothing here."

Cole looked up from a pile of leaves he was rifling through. "No, there's something here."

Incredulously, Brennon said, "What are you talking about? We've been through it all and haven't found anything. Get real."

Not willing to give up, Cole said, "Let's switch sides. You look where I've looked, and I'll go over your side."

"What for?"

"Because, one of us might have missed something the other might find. It happens all the time. My dad can always find stuff I've lost, even though I've looked in the same place where he found it."

"Yeah, yeah! My mom can do that, too. Good idea. Let's get to work," Brennon said, eager to go on the hunt again.

*

"It's no use, Cole. There's nothing here." Brennon didn't wait for a response. He turned and slowly walked toward his car.

They had been there for nearly an hour. There were no signs at all that a bigfoot could have been invloved, but the ground was hard and too many leaves blowing in the wind that might have covered tracks.

Brennon wasn't wrong when he said that there weren't any clues, but something inside of Cole refused him to accept it. This was a feeling unlike he had ever felt before. Almost like he saw the next scene in a movie in his mind before it happened. Cole looked up to the sky and then turned his gaze to Brennon. "There is a clue here."

"Dude, give it up. Let's get back to school. There's a good chance with all the stuff going on they won't even know that we've skipped."

"There's something here."

"Okay, I get it. You're upset. I'm upset too. But we have to face reality, man." Brennon brought his hands up to his chest and pointed at Cole. "There is nothing here."

No, there was a clue. Cole couldn't see it, but he could *feel* it. There was no way he was even going to try and explain it to Brennon.

He turned his gaze from Brennon and followed the intersection the short distance to Sagehill Road. *There is a clue.*

Without saying a word, Cole turned on his heels and walked to the main road.

"Hey, where the heck are you going? Cole!"

As he rounded onto Sagehill, he searched the ditch and in front of the trees.

The Mustang's engine roared to life. If Brennon insisted on leaving, it would be by himself.

As Cole scanned the different shades of brown grass, leaves, and foliage, something not like the other caught his gaze.

The Mustang pulled up beside him. Rolling the window down, Brennon said, "Cole, let's go."

Not looking up, he raised his right hand toward his teammate.

"I mean it, dude. Let's go. I will—"

Something dark blue and triangular shaped, not much more than an inch long, jutted between some large dead leaves. Cole carefully reached down and pinched it between his thumb and pointer finger. A thin cloth pulled away from the leaves, exposed now to the light of day.

"You found a rag. Big deal. Get in the car and let's go," Brennon said, and then raced the engine two times.

Cole grabbed the other corner and held the cloth in front of him.

It wasn't a rag.

It was a handkerchief.

A handkerchief just like the one Mr. Buddy had wrapped around the purported bigfoot tooth the man had shown him in the hall the other day.

He walked over to Brennon, holding the handkerchief in front of him. "This is our clue."

Brennon giggled. "Dude, you really have lost it."

"Listen," Cole said; it wasn't a request; it was a command.

Brennon's face tightened, it was obvious he got the message.

"Mr. Buddy, the janitor, has a handkerchief just like this," Cole said.

"How do you know?"

"I don't want to get into all the details right now. But the other day he was trying to get me to come over to his house to look at bigfoot plaster casts of footprints he said that he had made. And, I saw a dark blue and white checkered handkerchief just like this one."

"This must just be a coincidence. I'm sure there are thousands of handkerchiefs just like that one."

"Look at it, though." Cole flipped the cloth around for Brennon to examine the other side. "This hasn't been here very long. The handkerchief is dry. It's not dirty or stained from being under wet leaves for a long time." He brought it to his nose, and then quickly tore it away. "Whoa!" He forced air in and out his nostrils with a few quick breaths. "There's some chemical smell on it. This might have been used to knock Charlotte unconscious."

Brennon took the handkerchief and felt it with his fingertips. He too brought it close to his nose and took a whiff. "Yeah. I don't know what that is, but if you breathed it full strength, it might be something that would knock you out. Cole, you might be on to something." He stared into the distance. "Mr. Buddy is a strange dude. He's quiet, though. And he always seems to be around. No matter where you are, he always seems to be around." His words had trailed off.

Cole didn't know what was up with Brennon, but he gave the boy his space.

"Yesterday…" Brennon looked up with fire in his eyes. "Yesterday, we were by her locker when I planned to meet Charlotte here. Mr. Buddy was there. He was in earshot of our plan. He could have been here waiting for her and dragged her into the woods and escaped."

"I wouldn't have thought that Mr. Buddy could do something like that. But when you think about it, it's not that farfetched. He's nice, but he's strange. Never got married. He's a loner. And as far as I know, he doesn't have any other family to call his own."

"Should we search the woods?"

Thinking a moment, Cole said, "I hate to say this out loud, but if Charlotte's alive, she wouldn't be in the woods."

Brennon's face flushed.

"Yeah, I know, she might be dead." Reality at times showed no mercy. "But, I don't think so," Cole said, careful to keep his emotions at bay.

"Why?"

"It's a feeling. Just like I knew there was a clue for us to find here. Charlotte is alive."

Brennon nodded, inspired with new hope. "Okay, then where would Mr. Buddy take her?"

"The first place for us to look is his house." Cole took the handkerchief from Brennon and gripped it in his hand. This was a connection with Charlotte. He just knew it!

*

"Okay, what's the plan?" Brennon asked as he slowly drove down the street to exit the subdivision.

Cole realized that he and Brennon's relationship had shifted. Now the guy who had tried to keep him in his place was taking orders from him. He wasn't so sure he felt comfortable in that role, but if they were going to move forward, it would be by his direction.

"Hang on," Cole said and took out his cell phone. He tapped on the screen, and said, "William Johnson…You know, if he didn't have his real name on the door to the supply room, I wouldn't know what it is. I've never heard him called anything but *Buddy*."

Seven *William Johnsons* popped up in his search in the area. Cole didn't know Mr. Buddy's middle name or even the initial it started with. Fortunately, he knew that the janitor lived in Forest Heights subdivision. "Six-two-eight Rancher road. That's in Forest Heights. You know where that is?"

"That dump? Yeah, I can get us there." The Mustang went from a trot to a full gallop now that they had a destination. "So, we're just going to drive up there and break into his house?"

Well, that didn't sound like such a great plan. They would have to be a little sneakier than that. Cole thought a moment, considering his options.

"Well?"

"Okay, I got it. We need to go to a hardware store first."

"A hardware store?"

"Yeah. We'll buy some yard tools—pretend we're clipping hedges or something. We'll see if we can find an open door or window."

Brennon raised his eyebrows. "Okay, not bad. Hang on. We'll be there in no time."

*

Once they reached the hardware store, the plan had shaped up better in Cole's mind. He bought two of the cheapest hedge clippers he could find, even though they were still nearly twenty dollars each. To go incognito, they picked out two wide brimmed, floppy hats to help hide their faces. They needed more than disguises, though. Because if they couldn't find an open door or window, they would have to force their way in. Cole bought a hammer, chisel, putty knife, and flat head screwdriver, along with a tool belt to put them in.

To pay for it all, Cole used a credit card his dad had given him to use in emergency situations. He couldn't think of a greater emergency than saving Charlotte's life.

When the shopping spree finished, the two climbed aboard the Mustang and zoomed to their destination.

"It's just up ahead, on your left. Turn by that convenience store," Cole said, following their travel on a phone app.

The car slowed, and Brennon eased over into the turn lane.

"Tell you what, park over by the side of the store," Cole said.

"Why? I don't need an energy drink anymore. I'm wide awake and raring to go."

"Dude, your car is red and sticks out like a sore thumb. If Charlotte's not there, we have a better chance of getting away with this if there's no way to identify us."

"Uh, yeah. Sure."

"Plus, even if Charlotte's not there, there may be a clue as to where she might be. You never know how things like this are going to work out."

"Okay." Brennon made the turn when the light changed, and eased the Mustang down the street and into an open parking space near the dumpster. A sign on the side of the store said: NO PARKING TUESDAY AND SATURDAYS 2-4PM. "We're good."

"Let's go." Cole opened the door and got assaulted by the stench of rotting fruit and spoiled milk, freezing him for a moment. "Yuck. Let's hurry up."

Brennon had popped open the trunk and was bringing his hat to his head. "You taking the toolbelt?"

"Sure." Cole put on the tool belt, slid the hammer in place, and placed the other smaller tools in a pouch. The hat went on his head, and he was ready to go.

Both had their hedge clippers in hand as they slowly walked past an overgrown vacant lot, heading toward Buddy's house, only three houses away.

Forest Heights was an older subdivision, built in the '60s. None of the houses were over thirteen hundred square feet. All had single car front carports.

"What a dump," Brennon said.

"Not everyone is as well-off as your family. I don't imagine Mr. Buddy makes a lot of money."

"He should have done something better with his life than becoming a janitor."

"Brennon, not everyone is born with a mom and dad who are successful. Not every guy grows up to be six foot two, has curly blonde hair that girls go nuts over, and has the genetics of an athlete. Being successful in life isn't as easy for some as it is for others."

"Whatever."

Cole watched the indifference on Brennon's face. There was no question the boy was self-centered; a fact that Brennon would more than likely agree with. This wasn't the time or place to give him a lesson in compassion.

They turned and walked up the cracked driveway leading to the house. No one was outside as far as Cole could see, but you never knew who might be looking from behind a curtain from inside of their house.

"What a dump," Brennon said, as if looking at the peeling paint and rotting shutters made him dirty.

"Let's put on a good show out front, and then work our way to the back," Cole said.

There were bushes between the carport and the front door, and at the front corner of the left side of the house. Cole went to chopping away with his clippers, and Brennon went to the side of the house.

Fifteen minutes later, Cole's arms were getting tired, and he wasn't anywhere near finished. He looked over at Brennon, and it hardly looked like the boy had even gotten started, despite the constant *snip-snip* he had heard.

"We don't have time for this," Cole said.

Brennon stopped working and looked over his way.

Approaching his teammate, he said, "We've been here long enough that I don't think anyone suspects anything. My arms are tired, and this tool belt weighs a ton. Let's work our way to the back."

Cole led the way, pretending to examine the foliage around the side of the house until reaching the back.

A large tree in the back provided ample shade as the sun rose higher in the sky. Cole felt cool relief as sweat evaporated from the back of his neck. He hadn't realized how hot it had gotten.

There were three windows down the back of the house, and a rear door by where it looked like a patio had once been. Wirey grass covered a broken ten-by-ten concrete slab.

Brennon looked about and then tried the nearest window. It was locked, but the curtains were open enough that he could see inside the room. There were boxes and junk on top of boxes. No room for Charlotte in there.

Cole tried the next window and found it locked. This window didn't have curtains. The room was lined with bookshelves filled with books. No Charlotte, though.

The next window had frosted glass, probably the bathroom. It was locked, too, limiting their options.

The handle to the rear door was loose. Cole thought he could twist it off if he tried hard enough but didn't know if that would open it or make it to where it wouldn't open.

He looked over at the windows, which were two-by-three feet and on the upper portion of the house, and didn't like the challenge.

Taking the putty knife from the tool pouch, he worked it between the door by the lock.

"You ever done this before?" Brennon asked.

"No, but I feel something moving." He stopped and looked in the crack to see what was moving. There was a small spring loaded keeper in front of the latch. Cole found that he could push that to the side and then place the putty knife blade on the latch. Once he caught the latch on the angled end, he was able to pry it out of the strike plate. A quick pull of the handle and the door opened.

"Wow. That was pretty good," Brennon said.

Cole thought so too, but now was the time to get down to business. Was Charlotte in the house somewhere? For some reason, he didn't think so, but he did think they would learn something of her whereabouts here.

Brennon followed Cole in. "What a dump."

"Is that all you can say about something you don't like?"

The teammate shrugged. "A dump's a dump."

A fountain of witticisms, such as the great Yogi Berra, Brennon was not.

They stood in the kitchen. The Formica countertops had yellowed, and the stained cabinets and trim were dull. The refrigerator looked relatively new.

Cole felt a wave of dread wash over him. The refrigerator. The door to the freezer. He stepped over toward it.

"What are you doing?"

"We have to check." Cole took a deep breath. He grabbed the freezer door, opening it like he was expecting a monster to spring out. He let out a sigh of relief. "Nothing in here but cheese pizza."

"What did you expect to find? Dude, don't wig out on me now."

"I'm not wigging out. We don't know how sick Mr. Buddy is. He could have chopped up Charlotte and put parts of her in the freezer. Jeffery Dahmer did things like that."

"I don't know, man. I think you're taking this a bit too far."

"Whatever," it was Cole's turn to brush Brennon off.

After a few minutes of inspecting the house, looking under the two beds, in closets, and even the attic, they came up with no Charlotte and zero clues.

Cole did find two plaster casts of bigfoot footprints. He even found the mold Mr. Buddy used to make them. The casts were right next to his porn collection. It seemed Mr. Buddy had a thing for women with big butts.

"Cole, there's nothing here," Brennon said, disappointment weighing down his words.

Feeling somewhat in a quandary, there was something else that seemed so close, but he just couldn't grasp it. "No. You're right. There's nothing here. But there's something somewhere. It's close. I just haven't figured it out yet."

"Come on. We can be back at school in plenty of time before lunch. We've done everything that we can. It's up to the police and FBI to find Charlotte."

With tools in hand, the two exited the way they came and trodded back to the convenience store, each lost in their own thoughts.

"Let's get something to drink. My treat," Brennon said after they unloaded their tools in the Mustang's trunk.

Cole followed like a sad puppy, telling Brennon just to get two of whatever he chose.

After paying for it, his teammate led him outside where they both opened their canned drinks.

"Thanks," Cole said and drank deeply from the can. He then worked out some of the soreness from his right elbow brought on by the hedge trimming.

Gazing up at the street, an old green Chevy S-10 with a camper was slowing to a stop. It was Mr. Buddy! "Brennon, look!" He nodded toward the S-10.

"What?"

"Look who's pulling up to the light. It's Mr. Buddy."

"What's he doing here? He's supposed to be at school."

"I don't know, but he's not in the turn lane, so he's not heading home," Cole said. "He's up to something. He's up to something, and we have to follow him."

"Cole, I—"

"Brennon! Don't argue. This could save Charlotte. Let's go." Cole sped off toward the Mustang and was relieved to see Brennon didn't hesitate to follow.

The two jumped in the car, and Brennon fired it up.

They backed up and pulled up to the street in time to see Mr. Buddy's S-10 continue slowly down the highway.

"Don't worry. We'll catch up. I've seen how that man drives. It's usually a good ten miles an hour below the speed limit," Brennon said, waiting for the light to change.

*

Mr. Buddy surprisingly drove near the speed limit as he led them away from urban sprawl toward the rural area *not all that far as the crow flies* from where Cole lived. For the janitor to drive faster than normal hinted that something important had to be going on to give him a sense of urgency.

Brennon did an excellent job of maintaining a steady distance. It would have been suspicious to anyone if a hot red car followed them for miles and miles.

Cole had been this way enough in his life to know exactly where the road would lead. It was the last place he would ever have expected, although now he felt foolish for not thinking of this place first. "I know where he's going."

"Huh?" Brennon said, coming out of a funk.

"Watch, he'll be turning soon." No sooner had Cole said the words than his prediction came true.

"How'd you know?"

"Because that's the only farm around here for miles. That's old man Douglas' place."

"Oh, so this is where it is. I only knew the general location." Brennon braked to a stop. "We can't follow him there. Douglas might shoot us. Plus, we've been warned to stay away. We might get kicked off the team. We can't throw our lives away going on some wild goose chase."

He hated to admit it, but his teammate was right.

"What do you think? Are you getting any kind of *feeling* like you did earlier?" Brennon asked.

From the way the boy asked the question, Cole couldn't tell if he was being mocked or not. Regardless, his *feeling* had left him. The game set before them seemed to have changed. There were new rules now, and he didn't know what they were.

It was time to pull back, he felt. Charlotte was not lost. Not yet. "Let's go back to school."

Without any other words, Brennon made a wide turn in the road and now traveled the opposite direction.

There was something brewing underneath the perceived reality. Charlotte goes missing right after Douglas reports unusually large footprints in his garden. Was there a connection?

He checked the service bars on his phone and saw two. Good, at least his phone would work this far from the city.

Cole needed time to sort things out. Moving too fast might ruin everything. But once he had direction, he would need to strike without hesitation.

CHAPTER 19

Dougie Douglas typed away on the computer's keyboard. His satellite connection to the Dark Web wasn't the fastest in the world, but it was adequate to suit his business needs.

The second asset had been delivered last night, and the bids slowly trickled in. Even if he took the best offer right now, he would practically triple what he had expected to get. Patience had paid off for him and Buddy Johnson.

The auction would continue until midnight. The mule was already set to come the next day to transport the goods to any location in North America. Of course, the buyer was responsible for paying the driver the second half of his money on delivery.

Nothing would go down, though, until he got confirmation of payment to his offshore bank account. The bank took a clean ten percent right off the top at the time of deposit. If you want to play, you had to pay. Douglas didn't mind paying for a sure thing.

A vehicle rumbled up his driveway and passed the side of the house. Douglas lifted his butt off the chair but didn't bother to turn off the computer. He knew who the visitor was by the sound of the truck's engine.

When Douglas opened the door and stepped onto the porch, Buddy Johnson was standing by his truck.

"Things good here?" Johnson asked.

"Couldn't be better," Douglas said, finding it hard to keep a grin off his face.

"Just reportin' in. You said no phone calls."

"Yep, no phone calls. You can't trust the Feds these days from tapping the phones. I wouldn't be surprised if they had one of them highfalutin, supercomputers scanning every phone call and text message in this area."

"Well, it's just like you said. Just a bunch of chaos. People runnin' round like chickens with their heads cut off."

"They got any leads?"

"No. In fact, I heard one of them FBI agents say *just that* when he was talkin' on the phone. Sounded like he was reportin' to his boss."

Douglas smiled big enough to show his bottom teeth. "You do some good work there, Buddy."

The janitor grinned shyly and looked at the ground. "It was nothing. I just happened to be at the right place at the right time to get the lowdown on where to go." He returned his gaze back up to Douglas. "So, how's the money crop doin'?"

"Still sleeping it off when I took a peek this morning. The other one was up and watching TV."

"The one yesterday was a fighter. After I knocked her out and dragged her through the woods to the truck, I gave her three pills instead of two. Didn't want no commotion on the ride over."

"She'll be fine. When you're young you can get back on your feet pretty quick."

"Well, I best be goin' now," Buddy said and then pulled the truck's door open. "Told them I had a sore back and was going to the clinic for some medicine. Cafeteria's servin' up sloppy Joes. I don't wanna miss out. I sure do love me some sloppy Joes."

"Eh, after we get paid, you'll turn your nose up at ground meat. You'll be eating steak every day of the week."

"I don't know about that. Money ain't gonna change me very much. Fact is, I plan on savin' it so's I can retire at sixty-two instead of waiting until I'm sixty-five."

"Heck, we might be able to make a few *investments* off the grid that might give us enough returns so you can retire when you're fifty. Stick with ol' Dougie, you know I won't steer you in the wrong direction," Douglas said and winked his left eye.

"We'll see. Gotta go." Buddy closed the door and started the truck. After a quick wave, he looked in the rearview mirror and backed up, leaving down the driveway.

"Yeah, ol' Dougie won't steer you wrong," Douglas said to himself. "Go get some of them sloppy Joes and be ready to take orders the next time I need you."

He was well aware that Buddy wasn't in this for the money. If the janitor had been, Douglas wouldn't have trusted him from the get-go. The poor man was starved for attention. Didn't have a friend in the world until Douglas stumbled upon him at that bar.

And, Douglas didn't mind sharing the money with him. Because, he knew that it wouldn't take much to manipulate the janitor out of it if he so desired.

But one thing at a time. Cash-in tomorrow and let some time pass. Pick out a vacation spot and get Buddy to watch things on the farm for a week or ten days. Stop and smell the roses along the way. Life was to be enjoyed.

Looking at the clock, he thought it might be a bit early for a glass of whiskey. But, it did seem time for a celebration. "It's five o'clock somewhere," he said and headed back inside the house.

*

Charlotte awoke and heard the TV playing. For a moment she thought she had fallen asleep on the couch in her living room. As her mind cleared, she realized that she wasn't on her couch. She was in bed, but it wasn't her bed.

A single overhead light bulb, no fixture, cast dim light about the room. She pushed herself up on her elbows and gasped when she saw a young boy sitting on the floor and watching TV.

He turned, and said, "Oh, hey. You're awake."

Pulling the sheet up to her neck, Charlotte realized she was fully clothed, with only her shoes missing. Her mouth was dry as cotton. "Where am I? Who are you?"

The boy sat on a blanket on the floor, and he had a pillow in his lap. "I don't know where we are, but we get the same local news like back in Camden County. So I don't think we're far from there." He turned his head to the side. "What's your name?"

She licked her lips, and said, "Charlotte...Charlotte Meadows. Say, do you have anything to drink? I'm so thirsty."

"Sure," the boy stood and walked over to a mini-refrigerator. "You want water or soda?" he asked while pulling the door open.

"Water."

He picked out a bottle and brought it to her, twisting off the top before handing it to her.

"Thanks," she said, bringing the liquid goodness to her parched lips. She took a sip, feeling the healing powers of water turning the desert in her mouth to an oasis. Breathing a sigh of relief, she said, "You haven't told me your name."

"Oh, my name's Raymond. Raymond Jones."

"Raymond Jones...you're that kid that was abducted! Coach Jones' nephew."

"Yep, that's me," he said matter-of-factly.

Charlotte didn't think he looked like the photo of the Raymond Jones she had seen on the news. But, that had been a couple of months ago. That photo showed the boy with longer hair. The boy in there with her looked like his hair had recently been all buzzed off. He wore white socks, stretch shorts, and a white t-shirt. Overall, he looked in good shape. "How long have I been here?"

"They brought you in last night. You were sleeping. They put you in my bed and gave me a blanket to sleep on the floor."

"Somebody attacked me from behind…put a rag with some kind of chemical on it over my face. It burned my eyes and nose. Must have knocked me out," Charlotte said, amazed that the kid was so calm over his situation. "Uh, I'm sorry I took your bed."

"It's okay. I don't mind sharing. We're not going to be here much longer anyway."

"Wait, what? How do you know that?"

"I heard them say they'd be rid of us soon."

"*Rid* of us? Do you think they're going to kill us?" Charlotte said, feeling scared like she had never before.

"No, they aren't going to kill us. They're going to sell us."

"What!"

"Yeah. I heard one of them say you were going to help them *get a pretty good price*. I hope my mom and dad have enough money to buy me back."

Raymond seemed like a bright boy but there was something that seemed a little off-kilter. Then she remembered something about him having special needs. "Raymond, what grade are you in?"

"No particular grade. I'm in special education."

Charlotte looked around. Cardboard boxes lined the walls on every side of the room, but there was one narrow space big enough for a person to fit through. "What's in the boxes?"

"Empty egg cartons. They told me it's to block the sound from the TV at night so that it won't wake them."

Or to prevent anyone in here making enough noise for others outside to hear them. "You said, *they*. Who are, *they*?"

Raymond shrugged. "I don't know. Just two men. They said if I was a good boy that one day I'd get to leave. I've been a good boy, and soon I'll get to go. They told me that if I'm extra good, that they'd give my mom and dad first choice to buy me back."

"Do they treat you well? Give you food?"

Raymond nodded. "Cereal for breakfast. I get sandwiches and chips for lunch. Sometimes SpaghettiOs at night or some other meal they can microwave."

"Have they," Charlotte didn't know how to ask, but really needed to know. "Have they ever, you know, touched you?"

The boy shook his head.

"You can tell me if they have. You didn't do anything wrong if they did."

"No, they never touched me. Why do you ask?"

"Because I don't want them touching me either." Charlotte felt a bit of relief, but she realized she would present more of a temptation than Raymond might.

After drinking more water, she asked, "Where do you go to the bathroom?"

"Over there," Raymond pointed over to a dark corner of the room.

At first, she thought he meant *in the corner on the floor* and then realized that a toilet sat there with a lever poking to the side of it.

"Do you have to go?"

Her bladder cried out *yes*. "I do."

"You can use it. I'll turn and just watch TV."

"Okay, but no peeking."

Raymond giggled. "I won't, silly. Who would want to watch someone go to the bathroom? Yukky." He turned and focused on the TV set.

Charlotte stood and hoped their captors didn't have cameras set up in the room. She would look later on and see if she could find anything. For now, she had to use the bathroom in the worst way.

She stepped on a rug with her bare feet and felt small crunchy things underneath. Apparently, their captors weren't big on house cleaning.

Coming to the toilet, Charlotte pulled down her jeans and underwear, and relieved herself.

"When you're finished, you have to pump that handle on the side back and forth. That's the only way to flush."

Charlotte did as instructed, emptying the bowl clean, with fresh water rushing in to replace it. She at least realized that they were below ground. The toilet water had to be pumped upward toward the sewer.

Where they were and who had them was still a mystery. And if Raymond was right and that they both would be sold soon, well, at least she wouldn't go weeks without knowing her fate like he had.

*

Douglas had just dropped the last ice cube in his whiskey when he heard a vehicle coming up the driveway. Did Buddy forget to tell him something?

But it wasn't Buddy's truck that pulled into view through the window. He had no idea who this guy was, but he was about to find out. And, whoever this was, was just about to learn a little something about old man Douglas that he wouldn't soon forget.

Leaving the whiskey on the counter, he instead beelined for his shotgun by the door. Jerking the door open, he stomped outside on the porch and pumped a shell into the gun's chamber.

A dark blue Dodge 4X4, with tires so high it looked like you needed a stepladder to exit it, came to a stop. Rolling the driver's side window down, a man looking to be in his early thirties peered outward. He wore a green camo cap, and his scraggly beard looked like it hadn't been groomed in a week. "Afternoon, sir," he politely said.

"Boy, you must be lost or just plain stupid. I know you can't read because you passed three *no trespassing* signs to get this far," Douglas said, pointing the shotgun at the ground underneath the driver's door.

"Don't mean to trouble you none, mister. Name's Walton Finch. Fact is, I got a connection with Dent County police. I heard a report that you got bigfoot tracks on your property. Now mister, it may not mean much to you, but I've been looking for bigfoot for most of my life. I was hoping you'd see fit to letting me see those tracks. I'm a mighty good hunter. If there's a bigfoot anywhere near here, I'm sure to find it."

Douglas closed his eyes and shook his head. The last thing he needed now was some nut chasing the boogeyman snooping around his place. "Boy, I ain't got time for your nonsense. You heard wrong. There ain't no bigfoot tracks on this place. There were some kids wearing boots big enough to stick three feet in them. I found *shoe prints*, not *footprints*. Unless bigfoot's wearing shoes now, it was just a bunch of pranksters harassing an old man who has an itchy trigger finger."

Walton pursed his lips and thought a moment. "The heck, you say. Maybe they've evolved to wrap their feet with leaves or something."

"Then they must have learned how to cobble a heel, too. I'm telling you, they were *shoe prints*. Now, how many shots in the side of your truck is it going to take for you to leave?"

"None, mister," Walton said, it was obvious he had come to the end of Douglas' *hospitality*. "Mighty fine meeting you. Have a nice day." He cranked up the truck and backed out, keeping his eyes straight ahead as he left down the driveway.

Douglas chuckled. *I think he got the message.*

Just for fun, he fired two shots from the gun into the air.

Yes sir, I'm sure of it now.

*

Zax had spent the day exploring the surrounding area, mapping certain checkpoints on his rangefinder. There were many caves in the area, with more than a few that would provide spacious shelter. He had connected to the Google site on his rangefinder and learned that Missouri was known as the *Cave State*, having over six thousand caves throughout. Missouri was also known as the *Show Me State*. A moniker that didn't carry on through the Skink invasion.

He had found several creeks which supplied fresh, clean water. Water was an absolute must if he had any hopes of surviving in the wilderness. Thirst had him tempting fate the day before. Zax had traveled to the farmhouse again to fill his empty bottles of water.

It was a risky thing to travel in broad daylight near humans. But it was more than just a need for water that brought him there. He was curious to see a human. It didn't take long before he got his wish.

A grubby looking human, much older than Tarik, came from the farmhouse, carrying an ancient long gun. There was something about the man that just seemed *wrong*. Yes, Zax realized he was on the man's property uninvited. But he sensed that in any situation, the man would only see him as an *enemy*. If Zax ever decided to reveal himself to humans, he would have to find the kinder-hearted who were motivated by discovery and diplomacy.

Zax had moved far enough away from the chickens that they had calmed down. He stood behind a clump of trees and peeked through the branches, watching the farmer scan his farmland.

He didn't know why, but for some reason, he felt like picking on the man.

On his journey to the farmhouse, Zax gathered some acorns and had them in his backpack. Acorns weren't the best tasting food he had found in the wild, but he did plan on roasting some later to see if that would improve the flavor.

Taking careful aim, he sent the nut hurtling through the air where it found the target. Zax chuckled, feeling proud of himself for hitting the farmer on the head at first try.

He later headed back to his main lair. Two Nu-Mans could reside comfortably in the cave. It was basic living at best. Zax was going to miss not having a couch or a chair to laze around on.

Sleeping on the ground was going to take some getting used to, too. Before night fell, he gathered pine needles and long grasses, collecting enough material to build a makeshift bed.

That night he didn't have a craving for fresh game. In fact, he felt fatigued, although he hadn't physically exerted himself very much that day. The savage call of the wild he had experienced the other night had subsided.

Settling for packaged food, he chose one featuring roasted pork loin, green beans, and mashed potatoes. Zax realized he had few connections with his old life, and he felt a sense of loss after eating one. But, what good would it do him to hold on to the food like it was some relic? It was just food, not an old friend.

As he ate half a Z-bar, he wondered if he'd be able to find the beneficial nutrients in this world to replace the supplement once he ran out of his small supply.

He sat by the edge of the cave and folded the empty side of the Z-bar's wrapper around the remaining part. *An ice cold vita-water orange sure would taste good right about now*. There was no chance of finding a cave with electricity, though. Zax chucked at the thought of having electric lights in the cave, a stove by the wall, and an electrical cooler to keep things chilled. The best he might hope for was to put items he wanted to chill in a spring fed stream. A cool melon would also be nice to enjoy from time to time.

Who was he kidding? The other night's longing desire to live off the land and become one with nature had left him. There were certain modern amenities that would be hard to do without for the rest of his life. How long would he last in the wilderness before giving up and take his chances by exposing himself to human civilization? He could be seen as a monstrosity, a celebrity, or as the ultimate science project, where he may never see the light of day outside of an institution.

Then it dawned on him. Zax essentially had become the *Tarik* in this timeline. *He* was the genetic abomination. More precisely, a bigfoot abomination.

The last scenario of the possible outcome, if his mission was successful, was that he would simply blink out of time after changing the data crystal on the Skink space probe. If the Skinks never find Earth, then he would never exist.

A haunting thought, for sure. But Zax knew better than to focus on a question that would never be answered until the final moment of truth presented itself. No matter what, he was determined to thwart the Skinks' plan. They would not find Earth, and his fate lay in the hand of the Universe.

The full moon hung in the sky above, casting ethereal dust that seemed to have sprinkled over the forest, setting everything aglow in soft yellow-orange light. Fireflies signaled to each other, winking off and on like interdimensional sprites.

Then, the wind shifted, blowing the night breeze from the east. An animal's musk carried in the air sent a shockwave through his body. For a moment he couldn't move. Primordial instinct awakened something inside that had been dormant all of his life. It was a mixture of emotions: fear, curiosity, anger, and lust.

Something was not far away in the forest. It wasn't human, and it wasn't animal. It was more than animal, though, and carried certain pheromones that were all too familiar. The creature was distinctly a female, and she and Zax had a genetic bond much closer than Nu-Mans did to humans.

Close enough to see clearly but far enough away to be non-threatening, something shook a low hanging branch of a mighty tree.

The interloper had announced herself. The shaking leaves rhythmically rattled, playing an ancient song that sent mesmerizing waves through Zax's psyche. It was almost as if he were an instrument being played by a studious musician.

And then, as his rational mind fought against relinquishing command to his basic instincts, she emerged from the tree limb's cover, gliding gracefully into the open. Each step appeared choreographed as she moved her arms and hands in a pattern that Zax inherently knew told a story. At times she would stop and slowly swing her hips from side to side, and then balance on one foot as she moved her hands in toward her chest and then opened them wide above as if about to receive something. The dance led her into two elliptical circles that crossed in the middle, which Zax realized was the sign of infinity.

She was larger than any Nu-Man female that had ever existed. Physically, she rivaled Nu-Man males in size and stature. There were no human physical characteristics, as in Nu-Man females. Still, as brutish as she was, there was no questioning that she was all female.

The sasquatch was from hearty stock, looking to be capable of birthing many robust children. And while her facial features were more primitive and less appealing to the eyes, the movements of her body stoked lustful desires from deep within.

Zax could tell that she knew he was watching, although the female was careful to never gaze in his direction. This no doubt was a mating ritual. He had found favor with the female at least to begin a trial courtship.

Would he be able to communicate with her? Probably not without spending a good deal of time together. Despite the physical similarities between sasquatch and Nu-Mans, the genetically altered species shared brain functions equal or superior to humans. There were no recorded sasquatch histories for them to learn from. So, essentially Nu-Mans never really identified with their primitive ancestors. The virus that genetically altered mankind had killed all the varieties of sasquatch around the world.

He wondered what had led her to him and how long she might have been watching him. And, why hadn't he detected her until now?

Apparently, his senses weren't as sharp as he had thought, and maybe her years of living in the wilderness gave her an advantage that his superior intellect couldn't match.

One thing was for sure, if there was one sasquatch in the area, there had to be more. And if at some point he would come across another male who felt like his territory was threatened, then a conflict would arise. His blaster would quickly end any dangerous encounter. But the last thing he wanted to do was kill a primitive relative.

Was it possible for him to be accepted by the sasquatch society? Certainly not if he scared them with his technology. No, if he were ever to fit in, he would have to behave as much as possible like them. Dumbing things down and being careful not to do, or use anything in his backpack, to frighten them.

The female's movements noticeably slowed. She brought her hands together and pulled them toward her chest. Again, keeping her gaze away from his direction, she stepped back the way she came until the forest engulfed her once again.

There was no urgency for Zax to go after her now, despite the amorous fires that smoldered within. In fact, he instinctually knew it would be improper to follow the female. The act would be considered aggressive and an insult to the female.

But, she had made the first move. Tomorrow, or soon after, it would be up to him to decide if he would return his interest in her. This is the way of the wild. Zax didn't know how he knew this, but it just felt right.

For now, it was just him and the world Mother Nature intended for all her children.

Zax was a *bigfoot abomination*.

Would he ever be adopted into human or sasquatch society?

The answer wouldn't come tonight.

His fate, though, was about to take a decisive turn. That was something else he knew without rational explanation.

CHAPTER 20

There were no clocks in the room, but Charlotte could tell the time of day by the programming on TV. It was near seven o'clock, p.m. Despite the fact she had been awake there for a few hours, she felt like a caged wild animal.

She couldn't imagine what her mother was going through right now. The whole community was on alert, with the local news devoting more than half of their programming on her abduction. With all the attention this was getting, she had an imminent feeling that police would be busting down the door at any moment and come to their rescue.

Then she remembered when Raymond had been abducted. Even though the police said they had *persons of interest* they were investigating, they weren't able to find him.

There the boy was, with her. Sitting on the floor, his eyes fixated on some cartoon that Charlotte had never heard of, content as could be.

Not me, she thought. *I need to find a way out of here.* She had already pulled the boxes away from the wall to look for a hidden door and came away empty. The obvious access to the room was shut tightly, with no door handle or any visible way to open it. Charlotte guessed the door would easily push open if whatever blocked the other side was pulled out of the way.

As far as makeshift weapons went, a plastic fork topped the list. She had looked for *anything* she could have used to defend herself if necessary. Their captors had done a good job of keeping out heavy objects that could deliver blunt force or anything sharp that might cut. There weren't even any rubber bands that she could launch some of Raymond's crayons at them.

Charlotte had remembered seeing a TV show where inmates at a prison made weapons from common items. One man had made a shank out of a plastic cup. He had a match and burned a piece of the cup, and as it melted, formed it into a blade-like shape that proved to be quite deadly. *No match, no shank*, she thought.

The only other option she had was the lightbulb overhead. She could break it and use it to slash her way out of there. But the more she thought about it, the more hopeless her situation seemed. Charlotte flopped herself back on the bed, defeated.

A dull screech from the other side of the wall told her they were about to get a visit. Something heavy was definitely being dragged across the floor. Then something fumbled from behind the door.

Charlotte sprang from the bed and put her back against cardboard boxes lining the wall.

Raymond popped up from the floor, and sang, "Supper-time." He stood in place, obedient, waiting to receive his night time reward.

The door pulled away from the room, and a large man with a big gut hiding under dirty overalls entered carrying two plates of pasta in red sauce and a whole ear of corn. He wore a mask that mostly covered his eyes and cheeks. The mask was bright purple and looked like it came from a Halloween jester costume. His graying beard was thicker than the hair on his head and practically hid his lips. He looked nasty.

"How you doing, boy?" the man asked, gazing only at Raymond.

"Fine," Raymond said, sounding like it was a recorded message.

"How do you like your new friend?" the man asked.

"Okay, I guess."

"Come get your supper."

Raymond complied and carefully took the two paper plates from the man and set them on a coffee table. "What do you want to drink?" he asked Charlotte as he stepped toward the mini-fridge.

The man finally turned his gaze toward Charlotte. His tongue slithered out from his lips, briefly pushing the gray hairs away. The sight made her skin crawl.

"Who are you?" she asked, trying her best not to sound scared.

A smirk grew on the left side of his face. "Me? I'm the *Candy Man*."

Charlotte didn't expect him to tell her his name. But the mask did little to hide his identity if she had known him. If she ever got out of this mess, she'd be able to pick him out of a lineup in a heartbeat.

"Let us go," she demanded.

His mouth drew in, and he said, "I give the orders around here. Ain't that right, boy?"

Raymond waited by the refrigerator and nodded. "I'm getting a soda. I'll get you a soda," he said to Charlotte.

"Good boy. Go ahead and eat," the man said.

"If you let us go, I'll tell them you didn't do anything to hurt us. I don't know where we are, and I don't know who you are. Just let us go, and you won't get in any trouble."

"Heck, girl. If I thought I would get into any kind of trouble, you two wouldn't be here in the first place," the man said, an incredulous tone laced his words. "You just need to *hold your horses* and do like you're told. I ain't going to hurt you. Why would I damage my goods? But I'll tell you one thing," spit flew from his lips, "you give me any trouble, and I'll tie-down rope you like a calf and throw you on the floor."

The plastic fork was in Charlotte's back pocket. Instead of cringing in fear, as she had always thought she might do in a situation like this, the man's ire set a bellows to the coals of her anger.

In Phys Ed., her class had learned a few defensive moves designed to thwart an attacker. Almost as if someone else had taken control of her body, she took three steps forward and kicked the man as hard as humanly possible right in the groin.

The air heaved out of him like a belching volcano. His large stature withered into a clump as he brought his hands toward his groin. Almost losing his balance, he backed up until he bumped against the door frame, still blocking the way out the door.

It sounded like he wanted to yell, but at the time, he didn't have enough air in his lungs for even that. His nose had turned beet red as Charlotte imagined so did his face underneath the beard. She wished so badly that she had something to beat him with.

Seeing the full can of soda on the coffee table, she picked it up and hurled it at his head.

He flung a defensive hand to block the incoming missile. The can partially caught his hand and hit the door frame close to his head. The can of soda sprung a leak and shot a stream cutting through the air like a spinning pinwheel.

Chaos at its peak, Charlotte rushed over to the mini-fridge and pulled out another can of soda, aiming carefully and delivering it like a fastball a pitcher on the mound would throw.

The can hit him in the chest, making a dull *thump* as it bounced to the floor. His fingers curled as he let out a high-pitched yelp, finally collapsing to his hands and knees.

No time to let up now, Charlotte followed with two bottles of water hitting their target; one smashed against his ribcage, and the other hit him square between the cheeks of his buttocks as he crawled out the doorway.

The door quickly closed, and something scraping the wall told her that a bar of some sort had slid in place. A minute later, she heard the screeching sound again, and it stopped when something bumped the door.

Raymond looked over at her. He sat calmly at the coffee table, and half of his food was cleaned from his plate. "You better eat. It'll get cold."

Charlotte found it hard to believe that Raymond had tuned the conflict out and was able to eat. This told her she really didn't know what was going on in the boy's head. And, she hoped he was telling the whole truth about them not abusing him. Who knows if his mind had blocked any of that out?

If abuse was part of their intention, she had just given her captors a reason to make her pay for her outburst. It was too late to worry about that now, though.

"It's okay, Raymond. I'm not very hungry."

Raymond didn't look up from his plate, and when he did, it was toward the TV.

The situation seemed so desperate. Charlotte considered that death might be the best means of escape. There was nothing on hand that would bring a quick, merciful death. The only thing she could use to do herself in, was the bed sheet. She could form a noose with the bed sheet and tie it around her neck. But, there was nothing above for her to attach it to, to hang herself.

But wait! Why should *she* have to die? She didn't do anything wrong. They had violated her.

Her anger stoked again, Charlotte decided that no matter what she had to endure at their hands, she would survive. She would survive and someway, somehow, come back and find out who they were.

Charlotte would make them pay for what they had done. She would make them regret they had ever heard the name, *Charlotte Meadows*.

*

Lady Luck had shined down on Brennon and Cole when they arrived at school from their trip to the Douglas place. All classes had been suspended before lunch. The two arrived without anyone the wiser to their earlier antics. The cafeteria served sloppy Joes, and Brennon and Cole sat together and ate. They received more than their fair share of strange gazes; an odd couple for sure. No one said anything to them, though.

Everyone went through the motions to get through the next few hours of class. The coach had canceled baseball practice. Cole was happy just to go home and relax.

It was starting to get dark now. Cole sat at his computer, perusing the internet, looking at Google Maps and reading about the human trafficking problem. Women weren't the only targets of abusers; men and even children were too. In other countries, some people who were victims of the crime performed slave labor. He seriously doubted that Charlotte would be used for that purpose.

Sexual exploitation topped the list for human trafficking in North America. It wasn't hard to imagine why Charlotte had been chosen. A young girl her age would be in high demand.

Tearing his gaze away from the monitor, he tried to shake an image out of his mind, seeing Charlotte held captive in a room while men waited outside the door. He couldn't let that happen to her. Cole didn't know how he could go on living with thoughts like that haunting him.

Another disturbing fact, human traffickers sometimes arranged the harvest of organs. Cole had heard many urban legends, where sexy women lured men to hotels. The men would wake up the next morning with a kidney missing. As silly as those stories sounded, black market organ harvesting was a real problem. People who were tired of waiting for a needed organ were willing to pay thousands of dollars. In some cases, people were willing to sell an organ. He read one story on the internet that a man in Illinois ran an ad on Craigslist, where he offered one of his kidneys up for $30,000.

The world's human trafficking problem overwhelmed the current situation. Cole moved his mouse away from one United Nations' web page on the subject and clicked back on Google maps.

Cole had explored several miles of the forest backing up to their property on his four wheeler over the years. He had never tried to cut a path over to old man Douglas' place, but he had traveled much farther than that in a different direction. It probably wouldn't take him two hours to ride over to Douglas' farm.

But, then what? Does he sneak around and try to see if he can find any evidence that Charlotte is actually there? There was no way his dad would give him permission to go. So, that ruled out going over there at night, which might be hazardous traveling the woods in the dark. What were the chances that he could get close enough during the day without getting caught?

Cole still felt strongly that Mr. Buddy was involved in Charlotte's disappearance. There were no clues at the janitor's house, and his visit to see Douglas during school hours meant something.

Douglas, though, hadn't been keeping a low profile. Douglas had the police over to his house a few days ago. It would seem that if someone wanted to commit a crime, that the last thing they'd want was law enforcement contact.

But maybe Cole was overthinking things. Maybe Douglas *wanted* police involvement before Charlotte's abduction. Thinking he'd be off their radar because he had them over and acted as if he had nothing to hide. Did Douglas fake the huge footprints in his garden?

Maybe that was overthinking things, too.

He took a deep breath and sighed. *This is a living nightmare.* Remembering back to his reoccurring bigfoot dream, the horror he once felt when he saw the monster would never affect him that way again. Real life presented greater monsters than a hominoid cryptid.

The rumble of his dad's truck engine grew and then abruptly died. Cole rose from his chair and met him as he entered the kitchen.

Mark Rainwater dragged in like he had pulled two shifts at work. He put his keys on the keyhook and placed two white paper bags on the counter.

"Hey, Dad."

Weary eyed, Mark said, "Hey. Got us some burgers and fries. Fries might need reheating."

"That's okay. I'm not hungry anyway."

Mark chewed on his bottom lip. "Cole, son, I know you're upset. But, you can't let this thing control you. You're going to have to learn to cope with the fact that Charlotte's missing and still lead as normal a life as you can."

"That's not easy," Cole said, feeling like he would be betraying Charlotte in some way if he did.

"I didn't say it would be easy." Mark stepped over to the fridge, opened the door, and grabbed a beer. "The police and FBI are doing everything they can to find her. That's their jobs. They're good at what they do."

"They didn't find Coach Jones' nephew."

"No, they didn't." Mark lowered his gaze to the floor, then he picked up a bottle opener off the counter and opened his beer. "But they are better manned for this one. The FBI didn't get involved in the Jones' case for three days after he'd gone missing. It's like they were expecting another abduction to happen."

"I don't know if they were or not, but they were still on the Jones' case. Turns out that Mr. Ritzman is an FBI agent."

Mark had the beer heading for his lips and paused. "What? Your first-hour teacher? The man in black with the creepy eye and webbed fingers on his left hand?"

"Yeah. He interviewed me today at school."

"How'd that go?"

"I told them what I knew. Some things that Charlotte had said, which didn't amount to much. They didn't keep me long." Cole reached in one of the bags and pulled out a pack of French fries. "How's Charlotte's mom doing?"

Mark shook his head. "Bad...really bad. She had a panic attack. I brought her to the doctor, and he gave her some medication to calm her down."

It was bad enough that Charlotte was missing. Cole couldn't imagine how'd he react if something like that happened to his dad.

"As the day went on, more friends came over. Family from out of town started arriving right as it started getting dark. At that point, I was just kind of in the way," Mark said, chasing his words with a swig of beer.

Cole picked up a limp French fry and mindlessly ate it.

"Look, I was able to get today off, but they need me to work a shift tomorrow. I have to go in early for this job. Are you going to be okay?"

"I'll be okay."

"Are you sure? I can get your Uncle George to drive over tomorrow and take you to his place. You haven't seen much of him lately. That might be a fun thing to do."

"Yeah, I miss Uncle George. It's kinda hard for us to spend time together during the school months, with baseball and all the other stuff going on. But I'm going to be okay by myself tomorrow. I have some school work to do. I'll be seeing Uncle George this summer."

"Let's sit down and try and eat. Putting some food in our stomachs will make us feel better in the long run."

Cole went to the refrigerator and picked out a soda and grabbed a bottle of ketchup. He already felt like he had a ten pound stone in the bottom of his gut. Despite that, the one greasy French fry he ate did make him want another.

His dad was right. Cole did need to learn to cope with things. If for no other reason, than to have a clear head when it came time to try and rescue Charlotte.

*

Cole was in a dark room. It was so dark he couldn't see his hand in front of his face. To one end of the room, dim light shined through an open doorway.

He approached with caution, not knowing if the next step might put him in the path of an unseen danger. For all he knew, he might step into a bottomless pit. But he moved forward anyway. He knew he had to move forward.

Once at the doorway, he saw a black-cloaked figure sitting at a small round table. The figure looked similar to personifications of Death; its hood drooped over its head, covering its face.

The figure had cards in its hand. It slowly shuffled them. Raising its head, it lifted its right arm and outstretched a fleshless hand from the sleeve of the cloak, beckoning Cole to come and sit in the empty chair at the table.

This was another one of those moments of great consequence. Cole would know the outcome in a short amount of time, but he had to live through it. Just like any baseball game. He wanted to know the final score, and it might be up to him to determine the outcome.

He put one foot in front of the other until he arrived at the chair. The figure's face, when the hood parted, was a black void.

"You may sit," the figure said.

Cole obeyed and rested his palms on the table.

"I am Fate. You are here to determine the future."

"The future? Whose future? Mine or Charlotte's?"

"There is only one future, my friend. We all share the same reality. We all share the same future."

"Why me? Why is it up to me to determine the future? Why not somebody else? An adult, the president? I'm just a kid."

"Why not you? Are you any less of a person than someone older? Age, race, gender, nothing of the sort matters when it comes to determining the future."

"Okay, I understand. Now, what do I do to get the future I want?"

"Simple, my friend. You must make choices. You must choose wisely. The present determines the future." Fate had been shuffling the cards the whole time and now had stopped. He pulled three cards off the top of the deck and laid them face down in front of Cole. Picking up the middle card, the queen of hearts, he said, "Find the lady." Fate set the deck of cards down on the table. Slowly, and methodically, he rearranged the three cards using both of his boney hands.

Cole had learned this trick years ago in grade school. Three Card Monte was a suckers game. The dealer uses slight of hand in the way the cards are held and tossed to the table. But Fate didn't make any of the usual card moves. The cards never left the table. They had just been pushed around. It was blatantly obvious where the queen of hearts was. Cole pointed to it.

Fate turned the card over. It was not the queen of hearts.

"Look, I don't know how you did it, but I know it's a trick," Cole said, thinking Fate might actually teach him how to make correct decisions.

"You are correct. It is a trick. You had no chance of winning."

"What's the point, then? If the odds are stacked against me in the beginning, then how in the world can I possibly win?"

"Reality can be that way, too. You have no control of when you are born or where you are born. Race, physical limitations, gender—all are determined without your consent. You must overcome what you have no control of." Fate removed the cards from the table and placed three walnut shell halves before him.

"Are you kidding me?" Cole ranted. "This is another stupid game that I can't win."

"But you must win. You must win, or you may never hear from Charlotte Meadows again."

"What? That's not fair!"

"Life is not fair. The present determines the future." Fate placed a small green marble on the table and covered it with the middle walnut shell half. As before, he slowly pushed them around, switching positions, until he finally stopped.

"I can't win," Cole said.

"You must."

"But I can't! It's a trick!" he yelled and stood from his chair.

Fate thundered, "You must find a way!"

Cole went to protest again, and then a light went off inside his head. He looked at the three walnut shells, and then grabbed the two on the outside and lifted them off the table. "The marble isn't there, so it must be under the one in the middle."

"Well played, my friend." Fate slid the remaining shell toward him until it disappeared off the table. There was no way to confirm if the marble had been there or if it too had been empty.

Fate's left hand reached for the deck of cards. "There is one more game that you must play." It shuffled the deck and laid five cards face up before Cole.

Cole saw a four of diamonds, a jack of hearts, a jack of clubs, a three of spades, and a four of spades.

Fate then dealt another hand. The cards facing downward this time. "You have two pairs. Not the strongest hand in the game but one worthy of holding. Would you trade the cards you know for the other unknown hand?"

Cole was still on his feet. He looked around the room and realized that the door he had entered through was no longer there. "Why are we playing games? What does this have to do with determining the future?"

"I shall say it a different way. Would you trade the fate you know for an unknown fate? Would you trade Charlotte's abduction for a different fate? One that might find her safe and sound or perhaps one that would involve her death? Are you willing to gamble on the unknown?"

Choosing an unknown fate would be like flipping a coin. There was no way to know the outcome and no way to change the results afterward. Cole placed his hands on the table and leaned toward Fate. "I'm going to keep the cards."

With a bony finger, Fate flipped up each of the five cards one by one. Two face cards and three sevens made the hand.

Three of a kind beat his two pairs.

Cole had lost.

He had chosen wrong.

Did this mean the choices he would make would ultimately doom Charlotte? He felt like the weight of the world that rested on his shoulders increased ten fold.

"I lost. What now?"

Resting its elbows on the table and intertwining its fingers, Fate said, "No, my friend. You did not lose. You have won."

"What? How can that be? Three of a kind beats two pairs. Do you just make up your own rules or something?"

"No, rules are rules equally for everyone at all times. The objective of the game, though, was not to obtain a winning hand. The game was a test. As I have said, consequences in life are beyond your control. You are forced to play the hand that life deals you. How you react to that hand determines the future. Some people do nothing and allow others to make decisions for them. Some try to hide and lose themselves in drugs and alcohol to avoid making hard decisions. As insurmountable as the challenge before you appears to be, you have chosen to take it on and expect to win."

"So, I passed?" Cole said, sounding as surprised as he felt. "Okay, now, tell me where Charlotte is!"

"Fate does not operate in that manner. The building blocks lie inside you to construct the mechanism necessary for her rescue. It is up to you now. You must live through each moment. Do not doubt yourself, but do not choose unwisely either." Fate rose from its chair.

"Wait, don't leave. Tell me what I need to do. Give me a hint— something," Cole pleaded.

"I have said enough." Fate spread its hands wide. "I will leave you with this, though. Fate is not always an enemy. Sometimes fate is an ally."

Cole watched as Fate disappeared, along with the table and chairs. He was alone in the dimly lit room.

An engine cranked in the distance, pulling Cole from his dream.

CHAPTER 21

Before Mark Rainwater had pulled away from the carport, Cole's feet were on the floor. He remembered every second of his dream. Fate's words still swirled around in his head, fortifying his resolve to save Charlotte.

He knew what he had to do. Failure was not an option. As bold and outlandish as his plan seemed to be, he was determined not to fail.

After a quick trip to the washroom, he went into the kitchen where he poured himself a glass of milk and ate a handful of cookies. Not the most healthy breakfast in the world, but he thought he should put something in his stomach.

Next, he dressed in green camo, matching shirt and pants; his regular hunting attire. The apparel seemed appropriate. After all, he *was* going hunting. Hunting for the most treasured thing in his world.

Almost ready to go, he moved on to the next phase of his plan. Cole took his cell phone off the charger and called Brennon. The phone rang the set amount of times before going to voicemail. Hope died a little at that moment. The plan he had set in his mind included Brennon. The boy's part wasn't imperative, but Cole took a greater risk without him.

He could wait and try again but didn't want to delay long. He still had close to an hour and a half before sunrise and wanted to use the cloak of darkness to his advantage.

Trying again, Brennon picked up on the third ring.

"Hello," Brennon said in a sleep laced voice.

"Hey. This is Cole. I need you, man."

"Huh. What?" Brennon said and paused. "Do you know what time it is?"

"Yeah, but this is about Charlotte."

"Charlotte!" Brennon's voice had sounded stronger. "They found her?"

"No, I wish. But that's not why I called. I need you to drive out to old man Douglas' farm. Be there in a couple of hours."

"Hey wait, you know we aren't supposed to go there."

"You don't have to actually drive on his property, at least, not unless I call you."

"What are you talking about?"

"Brennon, I'm going to go to his farm and rescue Charlotte." Cole heard the confidence in his voice and could hardly believe that he was saying it.

"How do you know for sure she's there?"

"I just know."

"Oh, that *feeling* again. That led us to nowhere at Mr. Buddy's house."

"Yeah, but I *did* find that handkerchief, and Mr. Buddy *does* have one just like it. I was unsure yesterday when he drove to Douglas' place. I'm sure now."

"How can you know that? Did you consult a Ouija board or something?"

Cole heaved like an angry bull. "Dude, I don't have time for this. I'm leaving when I get off the phone on my four wheeler. I'm going to cut through the forest and sneak on his place. When I find her, I need a way back into town. That's where you come in."

Silence crossed the phone connection for several moments.

"All I'm asking for is your time," Cole said. "Drive close to his farm and park on the side of the road. Wait as long as it takes for me to call you."

"What happens if you don't call? Douglas said he was going to shoot anyone on his property."

It was Cole's turn to stop and think. He hadn't included the possibility of getting shot by the old man in the scenario. Brennon wasn't wrong to be scared. If Douglas had Charlotte, he might do something really crazy.

But no. Cole couldn't think like that. He was wasting time, and fear and doubt were his worst enemies. "I'm going to hang up the phone now. It's up to you to decide if you want to help or not. If you're there when I rescue her, we can be outta there in minutes. If I have to call the police, well, you know how long that could take. Douglas might find us before the police arrive. It's up to you, Brennon. Good-bye."

He closed the call and put his phone in the case and hooked it to his belt. His cards were on the table, and he was going to play the hand, regardless who the players were in the game.

There was one thing left to do, and that was to choose a weapon. Cole had his own .22 rifle, but his dad had long guns much more powerful than that; all of which he could handle. His dad had two revolvers and three pistols. Cole could bring and use the handguns as safely as an adult.

Trespassing on someone's place was against the law. But introducing a firearm upped the penalty if he were found guilty of a crime. Cole knew that federal laws kicked in when illegally using firearms. Plus, Cole had promised his dad he would never take a gun from the house without his explicit permission. This was no time to break that trust, even though it was Charlotte's life at stake.

Guns were not the answer, though. Douglas was sure to shoot first if he saw someone armed on his property. And by legal right, Cole would be the criminal. No, Cole had to use his head in this situation.

Time to go.

Cole grabbed two bottles of water from the fridge before leaving the house and locking the door. He retrieved a wooden baseball bat from the storage room and brought it with him to his four wheeler.

Topping the gas tank, he was ready to roll.

The four wheeler's engine sounded twice as loud in the quiet of the night than during the day. He turned on the headlight and cast a narrow beam toward the wooded area. The near-morning air was slightly cool and wet with humidity. With his helmet on, he pushed the four wheeler in gear.

Off he went, keeping his speed as such that he didn't outrun his headlight.

The stakes were high, and the ante was on the table.

In this game, it was winner take all.

*

Zax woke from a hard sleep when the whine of a small ancient engine cut through the resonating analog waves of the forest creatures' nightly symphony. It had been years since he had played with an internal combustion engine; not since he was a young Nu-Man in school. Of course, he knew of collectors of old-life cars with large eight-piston engines that made this engine sound like an insect.

Little of that mattered now. What, or who was coming his way? For a minute, he thought that maybe he'd done something to be detected. Perhaps his rangefinder acted as a beacon, and someone was coming to investigate the electronic anomaly. He knew humans weren't nearly as advanced in technology as the Skinks, but so far he had been very impressed with what they were able to accomplish on their own in the 21st century.

It did seem like an odd time to travel. Daylight would soon break, and navigating around the trees would become a lot less challenging. There was nothing stealthy about the intruder's approach. Zax began to suspect that whoever was out there, was on an important mission.

Then a dark thought arose for him to consider. What if someone else had used the time machine and was looking for him? The plan had been for the rebels to blow up the time machine after transporting Tarik to the past, but that had gone awry. All the rebels had fallen in the battle that allowed him to go back in time. The lone scientist, who was wounded, recovered long enough to set the time machine going. Was he able to set the charges and blow up the machine, or did the Skinks regain control and were now hunting him down in a time war?

There was no way to know right now, and Zax really did think his paranoia was kicking into overdrive. He would just have to be a little more careful now knowing the area wasn't as secluded from civilized activity as he had once thought.

Would this drive the female bigfoot away and further into the forest? Perhaps. She had been on his mind from the time she left after performing her dancing ritual until the time he fell asleep. There was certainly a strange attraction he had for her. One that he believed would lead him to eventually make contact.

On his feet now, he stood by the entrance to his cave. The engine sounded much closer. Zax saw a light shining from the vehicle point right his way. At first, he thought it was on a direct route to him, but the light shifted and veered slightly away. He reached over and grabbed his blaster and would use it only as a last resort.

The headlight passing through the trees acted like a strobe light and turned the night into a hypnotic moment. The vehicle was either of the two wheel variety or else it was something like what they called *crawlers* from his time; a one person, four wheels, all terrain vehicle. Crawlers didn't make a sound compared to the antique disturbing the forest.

Just as the vehicle veered the closest and was just about to head away, the engine's whine briefly accelerated in pitch, tree limbs *cracked*, and then the motor huffed and coughed until it went dead silent.

This was an unexpected predicament. Apparently, the rider had made a bad choice by traveling at night. Probably caught by a low hanging tree limb and knocking the person to the ground.

Zax wasn't concerned for the individual's safety at first. He had a mission and didn't need any more distractions. But then he thought if he were back in his time, he would have gone to any stranger's aid who was in trouble—even if it had been a civilian Skink. Not only that, but if someone had followed him back in time, Skink or Nu-Man, they might be out there injured. The last thing he could afford is their discovery by some human and have the area swarming with more people. Plus, if it were a Skink or a Nu-Man alien sympathizer, well, Zax might have to use his blaster and quickly end the enemy's life.

He might have been too far away to hear the rider stirring, but for some reason, he believed that they were incapacitated. With blaster in hand and stealth in his steps, Zax maneuvered through the forest using the trees to block sight of his approach.

He first spied the vehicle on its side. Painted a swirl of greens and browns, Zax thought it blended well with the forest. This certainly looked like a hunter's vehicle, but to a Nu-Man, the size of it made it look like a toy.

A few feet away lay the rider, crumpled up in a pile of leaves and unmoving. Judging by the person's size, they weren't an adult. What would a kid be doing out in the woods this time of night?

Then he noticed the kid's attire; the shirt and pants had a similar camouflage swirl pattern. Why would a kid go by himself this deep into the woods at this time to hunt?

Zax set the vehicle on its four wheels, as it was in danger of tottering over. He checked but saw no firearm of any kind on it or in the area. The only thing that looked like a weapon was a human's baseball bat. No one would go hunting with a bat as their only weapon. About the only thing a bat would be good for was keeping attacking dogs at bay.

Still no movement from the kid. A helmet hid the rider's face, but Zax had no doubt it was a young male.

Was the youth dead?

Stepping cautiously over to the body, Zax reached down and searched for signs of life. The kid's heart rhythmically pounded through the carotid artery in the neck. Okay, now that he found the kid alive, what? He couldn't just leave him there; others were sure to come searching at some point. The boy might have internal injuries or broken bones. Zax did not need this complicating his situation now.

With a frustrated sigh, he gently lifted the boy from the ground and carried him the short distance over to his cave. If he found the kid in good enough condition, he might just leave him on his own to wake up. Zax could watch from a distance until he awoke and left. If not, well, Zax didn't want to think about having to bring him somewhere to get medical attention.

Once inside, he illuminated the cave with the rangefinder's small light, and laid the boy down on his makeshift bed. Zax hesitated to remove the helmet, fearing he could worsen a neck injury. But, he couldn't leave the helmet on him.

Zax carefully pulled the two straps outward at the bottom of the helmet to loosen it. Then, he slid the helmet off the kid's head.

Stunned, he marveled how much the boy looked like Tarik. Was this a trick his mind was playing on him? He moved the rangefinder's light around the kid's face, thinking his brain placed false images in the shadows. Did he see what he wanted to see?

Certainly, all humans didn't look alike. The farmer he saw earlier looked nothing like Tarik. But there was something uncanny how Tarik and this boy favored one another. The boy looked just like a younger version of Tarik! How could this be? Zax understood genetics and knew a person could look like an ancestor. But the genetic material used in Tarik's birth was entirely at random. What were the chances that he would travel hundreds of years back in time and find Tarik's genetic twin?

A million questions flooded Zax's mind and set him in a minor panic. What did this mean? Did it even mean anything? Was this part of the Universe's plan or just a once in a trillion coincidence?

As near as he could tell, the boy didn't suffer any broken bones or lacerations. Head trauma had knocked the boy cold, and there was no way of knowing the severity until he awoke. Time, would bring all answers.

*

When Cole opened his eyes, he had no clue as to where he was. The air was cool and slightly damp. Weak sunlight shone into the dark room from his left side. Something seemed a little off in his head, and he wondered why he was lying down in a pile of pine needles and grass on the hard ground.

He rose up on one elbow and looked around, blinking his eyes to bring the scene into focus. He was in a cave with a strange odor.

"Don't be alarmed," a male voice said from his right.

Cole darted his gaze over to it, but the cave was pitch dark.

"How are you feeling?"

Waking up in a dark cave and hearing the voice of a man he couldn't see had Cole's defenses up in high alert. His mind quickly went back to his last thoughts and remembered heading toward Douglas' farm. Charlotte! He needed to save her. His mind must have been so engrossed in his mission that he got careless and wrecked his four wheeler.

"There's no reason for you to be scared, but I do need to know if you're injured."

If the unknown man wanted to hurt him, Cole guessed he would have already done so. Right now, he had few options. His head felt too weird for him to jump up and make a run for it. "I...I think I'm okay."

"You sure? You took quite a tumble out there."

"Hey, who are you?"

"I'm just a stranger that happened to find you in the woods. You were traveling too fast in the dark. What were you doing up so early coming all the way out here?"

"What are you doing out here?" Cole didn't feel like answering a bunch of questions right now. He just wanted his head to clear so he could go after Charlotte.

"Camping. I'm a nature lover. No crime in that, is there?"

"No, I guess not," Cole said, not believing a word of that. "Why are you hiding in the dark? Let me see your face."

"Me? I'm shy. You can leave now. Your vehicle is not far over to the west. You'll have no trouble finding it."

Cole sat up and felt the birds swim around inside his head again. "I'll leave in a little bit."

"So, you *are* hurt?"

"Maybe, just a little. But that doesn't matter. I gotta go soon."

"You don't need to do further damage. Rest a bit. Then you can leave. Drive slowly. I don't know where your home is, but you need to go there and tell your parents what happened. I'm sure they'll want to take you to a doctor."

Bringing his legs inward and sitting cross-legged, Cole arched his back trying to relieve some of the stiffness from lying on hard ground. The dull, semi-nausea feeling started to disappear. "Yeah, yeah, I'll be sure to do that." This game of his host hiding in the dark was getting old. He hoped there would be no surprises when he did try to leave.

Beep-beep-beep-beep-beep.

An object in the darkness sounded an alarm and flashed a bright light. When Cole saw the man who sat next to it, he was too afraid even to breathe.

It wasn't a man.

It was bigfoot.

But it couldn't be bigfoot. He had just had a conversation with a human. Now Cole felt even more scared. What kind of deranged person had he come upon?

The costumed man picked up the object and silenced the alarm. The light was still on but no longer blinked. It was obvious he realized that his secret had been discovered.

Cole stood on wobbly legs and made a break for the cave's exit. Before he had taken three steps, powerful hands grabbed either side of his shoulders and lifted him off the ground.

"Calm down. Calm down. I'm not going to hurt you."

The strange odor was worse now. This guy mustn't have bathed in a month. He was strong, too. Cole wondered how he was able to grip so good with those large, fake hands. "Let me go! Let me go!" He was completely powerless.

"I'm not going to hurt you," the man said, and then heaved a big sigh. "This is just great," he said under his breath.

The man placed him back on the makeshift bed. "Sit, and let me figure out what to do."

Cole did as instructed. It hurt the back of his neck when he looked up to gaze at the man's face. This was a tall man in the best-looking costume he had ever seen. Nothing at Comic-Con came anywhere close to such precise detail.

The man stepped over into the dark side of the cave and came back with a backpack and what looked like an electronic tablet—the device that had alarmed earlier. He fiddled with the tablet for a bit and sat down, laying the device on the ground. "Would you like some water?"

"Aren't you hot in that costume?" Cole had to admit; it didn't look like a costume at all. But there was no way that this was a real bigfoot.

The man held out his hand within Cole's reach. He rolled his eyes, and said, "See for yourself."

The boy pushed his fear aside and touched the back of the man's hand, feeling bones under the skin and the coarseness of thick animal-like hair. He then felt the man's fingers and the calluses on his palm. This was not a man in a costume. "Who are you?"

"My name is Zax."

"That's it? Just, Zax? You don't have a last name?"

"Well, not the way you do. When we're born, our names include our birthdate, sub-location, regional location, and other identifying data. It's all stored on a crystal that we carry around with us."

"Where are you from?"

Zax laughed. "Would you believe it if I said I'm from near here?"

"I don't know what to believe, right now. What are you? How is it you sound so human?"

Gazing toward the ground, Zax said, "That's a long, long story." He shook his head, and said in a low voice as if to himself, "One that I'm trying to rewrite." Pausing, he continued, "I'm going to keep things as simple as I can."

Zax then pulled two bottles of water from the backpack and gave one to Cole. "You haven't told me your name yet."

"Cole."

"Just Cole? You don't have a last name?"

Cole realized that the creature was poking fun at him. "Rainwater. My name is Cole Rainwater."

"Rainwater. That's a very interesting name." Zax drank some water and said, "Cole Rainwater, I am from a few hundred years in the future. There is an event that's going to happen very soon that will alter human evolutionary future. I am a product of that event. I am a Nu-Man, a name given to us because we are the *new man*."

"Who gave you that name? And they crossed humans and bigfoot?"

"There is a selfish alien race that will overrun Earth and genetically engineer the new race. The problem is that there is a genetic anomaly that is killing all of my people. The Earth will be left to its conquerors, with all memory of humans and Nu-Mans forever erased."

"How did you travel back in time?"

"I came across using an alien time machine. I'm here to place false data in the alien probe that discovered Earth. That way, I prevent the invasion from happening, and mankind continues on its natural path."

Thinking a minute, Cole said, "That means that there will never be any Nu-Mans. You won't ever be born."

Zax nodded and shrugged his shoulders. "Everything I knew and loved will never exist. It does give me a heavy heart if I allow myself to think about it too long." He reflected a bit more and drank from the bottle. "Say, you want something to eat? I have some packaged food fit for humans."

"No, thanks. I'm not hungry."

Zax pulled something from his backpack that looked like a large candy bar and unwrapped it.

"What's that?"

"This? It's a nutrient bar. It's only made for Nu-Mans, though." The big guy took a bite.

"I really need to go now," Cole said, feeling almost back to normal.

"Hold on. I can't just let you leave. I can't have anyone interfere with my mission."

"So what are you gonna do with me?"

After finishing half the bar, he folded the wrapper over the end and placed it in his backpack. "I don't know. What do you think I should do?"

"If you let me go, I won't tell anyone. I promise."

"You promise? I don't even know you. How do I know that you will keep your promise?"

"Because if I tell someone and they stop you from finding the alien probe, the Earth will be taken over by aliens."

Zax stared back intently. "Why do you believe me?"

"What choice do I have? You look like bigfoot, and you speak English better than I do. I've read some far-out science fiction stories that were less believable. Plus, you're here. I can touch you. There's no other explanation other than what you've told me."

"Okay, good. The alien probe has arrived and is orbiting Earth. Sometime tomorrow it will land near here. I have to replace a data crystal with the false information. After that, well, it's life in the forest for me, I guess."

"Did you live in the forest before in your time?"

Zax chuckled. "No, we lived a much more modern life than your standards. I sure do miss my bed."

"We can be friends. I can help get you something better to sleep on."

Zax smiled. "You know, I am going to need a friend. Friends keep promises and can be trusted."

"Great, now, you said you had a mission. Well, I have one too, and I gotta go." Cole didn't wait for permission, he stood and began to walk away.

"Remember your promise, Cole. The fate of the Earth rests on your shoulders."

Right now Charlotte's life seemed more important than the whole Earth's future. Judging by the light outside, he must have been out for a couple of hours. He hoped Brennon, if the boy had come as asked, still waited near Douglas' farm. Cole would call and check as soon as he had bars on his phone. Darn the bad luck! He wanted to get there before it was light. Fate had thrown a curve in his path. *Of all things!* He's off to do the riskiest, dangerous thing in his life, and he meets a genetic hybrid from Earth's future! As much as he would have loved to stay and ask a thousand questions, time did not afford him the luxury.

Just as he stepped outside the cave, Cole stopped when he remembered something Fate had said. *Fate is not always an enemy. Sometimes fate is an ally.* Turning toward Zax, he asked, "Will you help me?"

"Help you do what?"

Cole waved his hands in front of him. "It's a long story. My girlfriend…well, she's not my girlfriend, yet, has been kidnapped and she's being held on a farm. I think the guy there might be a human trafficker and will try and sell her, and I'll never see her again. I've got to rescue her before that happens."

Zax stood, and said, "Wait a minute. How do you know all of this?"

"I've found some evidence and let's just say no one else believes me. Don't you see, it's up to me to save her. You can help. Please, Zax."

"You can't go to the law enforcement?"

"No, I don't have any hard proof. I just know some things that all lead up to her being on the old man Douglas' farm. I don't think we have much time left."

Picking up the rangefinder, Zax pushed the screen until a map popped up. "We're here, by the red marker. Where is this farm?"

Cole looked at the tablet and got his bearings. "Oh, it's right there. Just a couple of miles away."

"I've been to that farm. Saw some older man there. He had a gun."

"That's old man Douglas. He's an ex-con."

Zax hesitated, and said, "Explain."

"He spent a lotta time in prison."

"I understand now." Zax brought a knuckle up to his mouth as lines crinkled on his forehead. "Cole, I think *you* believe your story. I'm just not convinced that you're right about this girl being there. Seems like the authorities would have better information than you."

"I believed *your* story," Cole said as if this was the first test of a new friendship.

The seconds ticked by as their shared gazes never wavered.

"Let me get my blaster. We'll get there as fast as we can."

CHAPTER 22

Cole matched the speed of the four wheeler to keep pace with Zax, which was a difficult task at times. In fact, occasionally he had to play catch up with the time traveler. Zax could maneuver much faster past obstacles than he could on the four-wheeler. To his advantage with the light of day, Cole could see the hazards long before they presented a problem.

Just as they neared the far edge of Douglas' property, Zax motioned for Cole to stop.

He let off on the accelerator and slowed to a halt.

"Time to shut it down. We don't want him to know we're coming," Zax said.

The engine died, and Cole hopped off the vehicle. He went to speed away and stopped, and then retrieved his baseball bat.

"You're not going to need that," Zax said.

"I'm bringing it anyway. Let's go." Cole tore off toward Douglas' barn, of which he could just make out in the distance.

Zax's long stride kept Cole pushing himself to keep up. It was obvious the hybrid trotted at a moderate pace while he ran faster than his comfort allowed. Endorphins and horrific images of the two storming the farmhouse and finding Charlotte in Douglas' evil clutches helped boost his resolve to cover the distance.

As they neared the chicken coop and the barn, Zax extended his left arm in front of Cole and slowed his pace to a walk. "We'll take it slower from here."

In between short breaths, Cole said, "But we need to hurry."

"Yeah, but we need to be smart, too. I hope that you realize what I'm risking by coming here with you?"

The immediacy of the situation hadn't allowed for Cole to really consider Zax's plight. Not that he didn't believe what the Nu-Man had told him. The fate of the whole human race was certainly more important than the life of just one person. He could tell himself that, but he couldn't get himself to overrule his irrationality right now. Charlotte needed saving. He didn't care if he risked death to save her life. He didn't care if he risked the lives of every other person on the face of the planet. There was only one thing that mattered: *Charlotte Meadows.*

The chickens didn't give their position away as they arrived at the barn. Zax hugged the side of the building as he snuck around to get a view of the front of the house.

Right on his heels, Cole followed, keeping all senses on high alert. If by some chance Douglas saw Zax and took him down with the first shot, Cole would try to hide detection and find a way into the house. He was not going to give up; no matter the consequences; no matter the cost.

Zax peered around the front of the barn toward the house. After pausing a few seconds, he slipped off his backpack and pulled out his rangefinder.

Moving past the big guy, Cole cautiously looked and saw an orange Benski moving truck parked in the driveway behind Mr. Buddy's old green Chevy S-10. Something out of the ordinary was certainly about to take place. He breathed a little easier knowing that they weren't too late. But that was only a small gain compared to the challenges that faced them ahead.

Cole whispered, "What are you doing?"

"I'm adjusting the rangefinder's scanning capabilities. I was hoping I could get it to pick up thermal images, but it doesn't have that capability. That way we could see the exact location of people inside. The best I can do is get a layout of rooms in the house. I can tell you this, there is a large basement underneath. It would be the perfect place to keep someone locked up."

"That moving truck. Do you think that's how they plan on moving her out?"

"A moving truck is large and bulky. I wouldn't think you'd want to use such a slow vehicle to commit a crime like this one." Zax paused a moment, and continued, "Hang on. Let me check this out."

The Nu-Man readjusted the rangefinder, and after a few seconds, Zax said, "Oh, I see now."

"What?"

"That's not an ordinary truck. There is a false compartment near the cab. It's roomy enough to fit several people. I bet this vehicle has been used in smuggling for a long time."

"Wow, I guess there's a lot of money to be made in human trafficking."

"Human trafficking," Zax said. "Our society never faced anything like that. We were basically slaves to the Skinks, of sorts. Our culture never included subjugating Nu-Mans to fellow Nu-Mans."

"What do we do now?" Cole asked. "We can't just go knock on the door and ask them to invite us in."

"Who said anything about knocking? I wasn't a hundred percent sure about your story before, but I am now." Zax put the rangefinder back in his pack and slid it around his shoulders. With his blaster firmly in his hands, he said, "*The element of surprise is a mighty fist.* That's an old rebel saying."

"I thought we might go all ninja on them."

"Ninja? What does that mean?"

"Ninjas wear black and are undetectable. They sneak in and kill you before you know they're there."

"Not today, for us. I'm a bit too large for that," Zax said. He then asked, "What do you call it when you throw everything you have into a quick assault?"

"Beast mode."

"Beast mode? I like that!" Zax said enthusiastically. "Cole Rainwater, it's time to go beast mode on these rotten bags of garbage!"

*

Dougie Douglas had awoken with a smile on his face, despite the fact that the *berries* beneath his *twig* still ached from the kick that brat had delivered the day before. When he recovered from the blow, he got so angry he thought he was going to have a stroke. But just as he was about to go and make her pay double for what she had done to him, a winning bid came in over the Darknet. The amount of cash that entered his overseas bank account put out the fire of his anger like it had been quenched by the Arctic Ocean.

Three shot glasses sat on the kitchen counter. It was early morning, but it was after five p.m. somewhere on the planet. This was a time to celebrate, though no time to get sloppy.

"You want another? I'll let you have one more before you skedaddle out of here. Wouldn't want you to get pulled over at a time like this. I guess I shouldn't be feeding you drinks at all. But I have a rule in my house. I never drink alone when I have a guest. Two won't affect a big boy like you," Douglas said to the Benski truck driver, the carrier of his expensive goods.

The truck driver had the build of a '50s refrigerator. He would have made an excellent football lineman. Douglas imagined that the 3rd grade might have been a little too hard on him to consider graduating past the 6th.

"Heck no, mister. I drink a fifth a night and chase that with a twelve-pack of beer," the truck driver smiled, showing dark tobacco dip between his lips and teeth.

"How about you, Buddy?" Douglas asked. "I'm having another."

"Don't mind if I do," the janitor said.

Something was different about Buddy that day. He seemed more confident—as if he had more self-respect. The man didn't seem nervous at all about the situation. This annoyed Douglas a bit. He liked Buddy just the way he had been. The man knew his place and walked the straight and narrow. He didn't need a partner who thought himself Douglas' equal. "Here you go." He poured each glass full and set the bottle down.

Lifting the shot glass up, Douglas said, "To the future. *'The day of fortune is like a harvest day. We must be busy when the corn is ripe'*."

The three downed the whiskey and set the glasses back on the counter.

"That was a *purty* saying, but the corn ain't ripe. Heck, it ain't even growing yet," the truck driver said.

"That was just something I read while I was in prison. Some *I-talian* poet, I think. You've got to remember that I had a lot of free time on my hands while I was in the pokey. What I'm saying is that the corn that's ripe is sitting right inside this house. You are about to transport *said* corn. Today is our day of fortune."

"Oh," is all the truck driver had to say about that.

"I got it," Buddy said, his eyes squinted and sparkled with the kiss of the spirits of the bottle.

Douglas smirked and gazed at Buddy for a few moments. He splashed his shot glass full and downed it, never offering any to his partner. He ran the back of his hand over the shaggy growth on his upper lips. "Let's get this show on the road."

"Okay, boss," the truck driver said.

"You stay here in the kitchen. Buddy and I'll bring them up. There's not a lot of room down there, if you catch my drift."

"Yes sir. I wouldn't want to get in the way."

Well, at least the buffoon had a clue about something. Douglas wondered how someone with that low of intelligence had been given such a high level of responsibility to transport such valuable merchandise. Maybe it had to do with layering the system with subordinates who had the least chance of connecting them to the buyers.

None of that mattered now. "Come on, Buddy. Let's get this over with."

No sooner had the two men entered the living room, something huge hit the front door, sending it flying open and crashing against the wall. The hinge at the top broke loose from the door frame.

A brownish blur filled the open doorway.

*

Cole shadowed the big Nu-Man as the giant kicked the front door, knocking it open like a swinging door from an old western movie. The door crashing against the wall sounded almost like a gun going off. Anyone in the house would know they were here.

Two cries of surprise later, Cole found himself by a wall next to the kitchen. Zax stood between two men lying on the floor. As expected, one was old man Douglas, and the other was Mr. Buddy. "Are they...?"

"No, they're not dead. It doesn't take much effort to take down a human. I had to be real careful around Tarik."

"Who's Tarik?"

"That's another long story. I'll have to tell you later," Zax said looking down at the floor. "What are you doing in here? I told you to stay outside?"

"You did. I didn't listen," Cole said unapologetically.

"Some friend you are," Zax said, shaking his head.

Cole shrugged. "You're not the boss of me." As he waited for a rebuttal, Cole saw Zax's face light up like someone had put his finger in an electrical socket.

"Cole!" Zax screamed.

His peripheral caught an object that had jutted past the doorway to the kitchen. Without thinking, and in one swift motion, Cole brought the bat down and struck a hand holding a revolver right at the wrist.

The gun fired with the bullet striking the floor a few feet in front of Zax.

Cole wasn't sure if Zax had bounded to the doorway or just leaped from where he stood. All he knew was that the big guy was now in the kitchen. A hard slap and a whimper later, Zax stepped out. "I think that's all of them, but you wait here while I check it out."

Zax went down the hall and checked the bedrooms. He came out less than a minute later. "All clear. Now, we need to find our way to the basement."

Mr. Buddy partially laid on a big rug that had Zax's interest. He moved the janitor to the side and pulled back the rug.

"Bingo!" Cole said.

"Is that what you call a door on a floor, *bingo*?"

"No. It's a game. It's...we don't have time for this. I'll tell you later."

The wood on the floor had been mitered to recess a latch. Sliding back the bolt, Zax lifted the false flooring, revealing a narrow ladder. "I don't think I'm going to fit."

"Move aside, then. I got this," Cole said stepping forward.

"What if someone else is down there? You know, a bad guy."

"Doesn't matter. I'll yell and let you know. If I can't take him, you find someway to get down there and rescue Charlotte. Don't worry about me. Just make sure she's safe."

Zax moved aside and got on his knees by the opening.

Cole left the bat on the floor and stuck a foot down the hole and onto a rung of the ladder. "You shouldn't be here when I bring up Charlotte. When I find her, I'll give you a signal. Go outside and hide. We'll make it out okay. I'll come and see you tomorrow." He began his descent on the ladder.

When Cole's head lowered to meet Zax's gaze, the big guy said, "Be careful."

"Okay, *Dad*," sarcasm laced Cole's words.

"Hey! I'm your friend. I just don't want you to get hurt," Zax said, obviously offended.

"Are we in *beast mode* or are we not in *beast mode*? Don't get mushy on me," Cole said, making his point.

"Just hurry up," Zax said with half-open eyes. "Kids…what to do with them."

Zax's words trailed off as Cole's feet hit the floor. He pulled a thin chain hanging from the ceiling, and an overhead light came on.

Near the opposite wall, the floor in front of a metal shelf looked scoffed up like something had been dragged across it. He stepped over and grabbed it by the frame. There were a few boxes on the shelves, but they appeared to be empty. Without too much effort, he was able to slide it aside.

Behind the shelf, he saw a door. Across the door was a plank of wood set in place to keep anyone inside the room from coming out.

This was it. This was another one of those moments of truth. In just a few seconds, he would either get the relief of his life or a disappointment that would last for all eternity. This moment would be forever sealed in his mind.

Taking a deep breath, he lifted the plank from the hooks it rested on. He pulled the door open and looked inside the room.

A young boy sat by a coffee table. He was watching TV but then turned to look his way.

The room was small, with a bed over by one side of the wall.

An empty bed.

There were boxes stacked up in front of one corner and a mini-refrigerator by another wall.

But there was no Charlotte.

He didn't know what had gone wrong, but he had failed.

The four corners of his mind started to fold inward.

The back of his head felt cold and numb.
Cole's reality started melting.
He had lost his place in the universe.

CHAPTER 23

"Cole! It's you!" Charlotte screamed with surprise.

"Charlotte!" Pulled from his quagmire, Cole couldn't believe his very eyes. Charlotte had been in the room, hiding behind some stacked boxes in the corner.

Something was in her right hand, and she was careful to keep it away from his head when she flung her arms around him. "Thank God that you're here!"

He felt her arms wrap around him, and it was the most blissful moment in his life. He had found her! It was up to him to make it so. He believed in himself and knew that the only way this moment would come true was if he never gave up!

"Where are the police? I heard a gunshot. Did they get that sick man? I hope they lock him away forever," Charlotte said so fast the words sounded like one run-on sentence.

"No, the police aren't here." Then Cole remembered Zax waited for his signal. He turned his head a little toward the open doorway, and said loudly, "No, the police aren't here, CHARLOTTE."

"Why are you yelling my name?" she asked, turning her head and raising a wary eyebrow.

"Uh, I guess I'm just so excited to see you," Cole said. "Come on. We need to leave."

"Let's go, Raymond," Charlotte said.

"Can I wait for my cartoon to end?" Raymond asked.

"No, I'm afraid not. If we leave now, we can see your parents soon," she said.

"Yay! Let's go."

"That's Raymond Jones, isn't it?" Cole asked.

"Yeah. He's been down here the whole time."

Charlotte took her arms from around him. He gazed deeply into her eyes. "They didn't hurt you, did they?" Douglas and Mr. Buddy were still unconscious on the floor. Whatever they had done to Charlotte, he was going to do to them ten-fold.

"No. They didn't hurt me or Raymond." Charlotte brought the object she had in her right hand into view.

"What's that?" Cole asked.

"It's sort of a knife I made. I took a soda can and bent it back and forth enough to where I was able to tear it in half. From there, I shaped it the best I could with my bare hands into a knife blade. I rolled up some cardboard to make a handle."

"That thing sure looks deadly. Great job!" Cole said, genuinely impressed. This said a lot about Charlotte's character. The girl was like him. She was in for the fight until the bitter end.

But there had been no bitter end this time. "Okay, let's go." He turned to Raymond. "Little guy, lead the way."

Raymond stepped forward and headed out the door. Cole followed close behind him up the ladder in case he fell. There were no incidents, though.

He and Raymond waited as Charlotte emerged to the living room.

She looked at the two bodies on the floor. Her eyes widened, and she gasped. "Mr. Buddy? What's he doing here?"

"He was in on it. That's old man Douglas. They were partners. There's another guy in the kitchen. He's the driver that was going to take you and Raymond away," Cole said.

"Are they...dead?" she asked.

"No, but I might have come back and killed them if they had hurt you."

"Cole...you did this to them?"

"Yes!" he said without flinching.

"How?"

"See that baseball bat over there? It's not just for hitting fastballs," Cole said, at least that statement wasn't a lie. "We can talk about all of this later."

Unclipping his phone from his belt, he called Brennon as fast as he could. He didn't check on the boy earlier when he and Zax arrived at the farm as he planned. He hoped to goodness Brennon was near and they didn't have to wait on the police.

After two rings, Brennon answered, "Cole?"

"Brennon! Thank goodness. Drive over to Douglas' now! I've got Charlotte!"

"You do?"

"Yeah, man! And I've got Raymond Jones too. We're heading down the driveway, and we'll be by the road in a couple of minutes. Get your butt over here now!" Cole didn't wait to hear what else Brennon had to say. It was time to leave.

"Brennon's going to pick us up in his Mustang. Let's go and wait for him by the road."

Raymond led the way, and Charlotte followed behind. As the three kicked up dust, running down the driveway, Cole looked behind and saw Zax by the barn. The big guy gave him a wave.

Cole furtively waved back.

Just before they reached the end of the driveway, the red Mustang streaked up the road and skidded to a stop.

Cole dashed ahead of the other two and opened the passenger door.

Raymond entered first, and Charlotte followed.

Cole plopped down in the passenger seat and tapped on the dash. "Let's go!"

The Mustang made a wide turn and headed back toward town.

The bright red car diminished to a small point as it chewed up black asphalt. Leaving the horrors of the real world to await final judgment.

*

The day before seemed like a blur when Cole thought about it. Really, how often was it that someone gets to meet a genetic hybrid of bigfoot and man who had traveled from the future and then rescued two abductees from human traffickers?

Brennon had a thousand million questions on the way to the police department, as well as Charlotte.

Raymond pretty much just sat in the back seat and made car noises mimicking the Mustang's throaty engine, and giggled. He said he liked to go fast, and at one point, asked Brennon if he could drive it some day.

The police and FBI had a thousand million questions, and his dad had a thousand million and one.

Cole couldn't remember a time he felt so tired when he finally was able to crawl in bed that night. He slept peacefully, too, even though he dreamed. There was no bigfoot in his dream that night. Instead, the night terror had given way to a dream about a baseball game. He was on the pitcher's mound in a game, but there were no other players on his team on the field. The batter was in the box, but no catcher behind the plate to do the job. It was just him against the other team. He had to throw a perfect game and hoped to hit a homerun to win. Despite the odds, he was up for the challenge. In fact, he remembered the feeling he had in the dream when he was up on the mound. It was a feeling of confidence, and he had a yearning to take it on to prove he could win.

Marvin 'Dougie' Douglas, William 'Mr. Buddy' Johnson, and Nathan Fortenberry were arrested and taken to the hospital where they all awoke and had a fantastic tale of how a bigfoot broke into the house and knocked them all out. Of course, they denied they had any connection with Charlotte's and Raymond's abduction. The FBI found one of their malware tracking programs embedded in Douglas' computer that had all the evidence needed to put the three criminals away for a very long time. Not only that, but Cole overheard that the computer contained some solid leads to other criminals in the network.

Cole was exhausted that day from telling his side of the story over, and over, and over again. From the beginning, he was careful the way he told the event, keeping it simple and not embellishing the facts. Yes, he and Brennon skipped school and found the handkerchief where Charlotte was kidnapped. Yes, he and Brennon broke into Mr. Buddy's house and then followed him to Douglas' farm. Yes, he went alone to the farm the next day and kicked in the door and took the three men down with his baseball bat. That's it, he told the same story the same way and never once wavered—no matter how crafty his interrogators became, he just looked ahead and dryly repeated what he had said before.

With the criminals in hand and the victims safe with their parents, there was really no point in finding a crack in Cole's story. The authorities just felt it almost impossible to believe that Cole could take three men down with a baseball bat. Cole countered one time with, "What, you'd rather believe that bigfoot broke in and knocked them out instead?" Of course, that shut the questioner up pretty quickly. It was easy to understand why the three criminals came up with such a cockamamy story. Why would three grown men want to admit that a fourteen-year-old boy had beaten them in a fight? The police said the men had been drinking that morning, too. That fact gave some explanation of their delusional statements and how they were physically overwhelmed.

"I ought to have my head examined for bringing you back here," Mark Rainwater said as he drove his truck toward Douglas' farm.

Cole sat in the passenger seat next to him. He had been looking out his side window but saw only images of the previous day in his mind. "I can't leave my four wheeler out there in the woods. Someone might steal it."

"You should have let me bring the trailer. I can't say I'm very comfortable with letting you ride it all the way back home."

"But I like taking long rides through the woods. It helps me unwind. After a day like yesterday, I need to do something to take my mind off what happened." Cole wasn't lying, but there was no way he could fully disclose his intentions.

"There's no way I can argue against that. You're a hero, son. I'm proud of you," Mark said. Then, he added quickly, "I'm mad at you too." He let out a sigh. "What you did was wrong. You and Brennon put yourselves in danger. Face it, son. The worst thing that could have happened is that you could have been killed, and Charlotte and Raymond would both still have been sold. You should have gone to the police when you found that handkerchief."

The fingers on Cole's left hand mindlessly tapped on the center console. "Maybe. But I was afraid they wouldn't believe me. See, if we had gone to the police when we found the handkerchief, and they went and searched Mr. Buddy's house, they wouldn't have found anything either. It's only because Brennon and I saw him driving to Douglas' when he should have been in school that gave us a clue where he had taken Charlotte."

"You could have told that to the FBI when you got back to school," Mark said.

"What? Tell them that Brennon and I skipped school and broke into Mr. Buddy's house?"

"Hmmm. I get it."

"Plus, things just weren't all that black and white. There's a whole lot of stuff that's been going on in my head. The ride back home will help me sort things out."

Mark chuckled. "There has always been a lot of stuff floating around in your head. But hey, who am I to deny the wish of the town hero?"

Cole turned his gaze toward his dad to see if he could read if he were being made fun of or not.

"You know, I think two of the greatest things I've ever seen in my life were yesterday. When Raymond's parents entered the room, and he ran to them. I almost couldn't stop myself from breaking down and crying a river.

"And after Lori showed up and met Charlotte, she hugged you so hard that your face turned red."

"Yeah, she really latched on. She kept kissing me too."

"I know," Mark said. "I'm jealous."

"Dad!"

"I'm kidding, Cole." He reached over and patted Cole's hand on the console. "I'm very proud of you, and I'm so glad that you weren't hurt. But please, in the future, don't put yourself at such great risk without talking to me about it. Things went well for you this time, but next time the outcome may be different. I'm not always going to be around, son. So, you better make use of your old dad while I'm here."

Cole's dad knew just how to play him. If his dad had used threats, Cole just would have tuned him out.

"I'm still laughing how that TV reporter got your name wrong. I guess she was so intent to get the story out first, she didn't pay enough attention when the police chief read your name when he gave his statement. I guess I *could* have named you *Cold* Rainwater. In this day and time, it wouldn't be all that unusual."

"I don't know, Dad. Sounds kinda gimmicky or like I'm some movie star's kid. It kinda sucks that I get my fifteen minutes of fame, when they showed my school picture on TV, and put *Cold Rainwate*r beneath it."

"Eh, I wouldn't worry about it. I'm sure the newspaper will get it right," Mark said. "We're just about there."

The truck slowed, and Mark turned up Douglas' driveway. He pulled up as far as he could before coming to a stop.

There was yellow police tape around the house and the Benski truck, but no officers were on site.

"I'll see you back at the house in a few hours," Cole said. He opened the door and stepped out, and then grabbed his pack filled with water and snacks from the floorboard.

"I love you, son. Be careful," Mark said.

"I love you, too. I will." Cole closed the door and headed toward the barn.

A new chapter in his life was just about to begin.

*

Walton Finch entered the forest right as the sun rose Sunday morning. He knew old man Douglas was a mean old cuss before he drove up his driveway and asked to see the huge footprints a couple of days before, but he didn't suspect him to be involved in something as nefarious as human trafficking.

He was shocked that such a recluse had such lofty plans. There wasn't a whole lot of information that had come out about the case. Walton did hear one FBI agent, in a brief statement, say that Douglas used something called the *Darknet* on the internet that connected him to international human traffickers. Walton didn't know a lot about computers; just enough to do bigfoot research, buy hunting supplies, and look at scantily clad women in compromising videos.

Equally as shocking was learning that a long time employee of the school system had been involved too in both of the kidnappings. *What some people would stoop to for the almighty dollar*, he thought.

After he had left Douglas' on Friday, he planned to wait for him at the bar, Lost Times, Douglas frequented. There, he would buy the old codger a few drinks and see if he could get him to loosen up a little and agree to let Walton come on his property to inspect the footprints. That ship had sailed, though, and his connection with the local police informed him it would be in his best interest if he stayed away from the property for a long while.

Walton didn't need any trouble with the law, but there was no way he could ignore the great mystery of the footprints. He had been traveling on foot and had made it north of Douglas' property after a few hours' hike through the forest from a remote road.

Going *squatchin* was his favorite pastime in life. Walton had planned his vacations around bigfoot hot spots over the last several years. Washington State was known as the *squatchiest* state in the US and his favorite place to hunt the elusive creature, having made the trip there three different times.

Walton was also a member of The Bigfoot Field Researchers Organization. BFRO, founded by Matt Moneymaker, one of the stars of his favorite show *Finding Bigfoot*, connecting him with like-minded people across North America. Visits to the website allowed members to report their personal experiences with the hominoid. The site included maps, photos, and even sound recordings. He had purchased his hat, with the *Keep it Squatchy* moniker emblazoned across the front, from the BFRO gift shop.

Nothing would satisfy him more than being the first to find actual proof of a North American bigfoot. Walton had endured years of taunting from his friends and family over his obsession. Romance for him was as elusive as the creature itself. He never could find the girl who equally shared his passion, or could stand to be around him after one date. Finding bigfoot would gain him international fame and command respect. He'd have the last laugh then and would laugh the loudest too.

Something unusual and high in the sky caught his gaze. At first, he thought it was sunlight reflecting off a small cloud, but the object wasn't a cloud. The object didn't travel at a great amount of speed either. Walton had seen jets travel across the sky much faster. There were no wings, tail, or fuselage on this aircraft. It was disk shaped, and it was traveling down to Earth like it was going to land!

This wasn't the first time Walton had seen mysterious objects in the sky. Of course, all of his other sightings had been at night. This was his first daytime sighting of a UFO, and it was going to land within walking distance.

He kept his gaze steady and drank in every moment, recording everything in his mind to recount accurately later. When the object's trajectory brought it past his field of vision, he pulled out his compass and noted the direction.

What luck! This was a once-in-a-million chance for him to be at the right place at the right time. Walton's heart beat faster, and he felt numbing excitement surge through his body.

The hunter checked the safety on his rifle out of habit. After a deep breath, he hurried toward the alien landing site.

*

Cha'nu, the female bigfoot, had spent the morning foraging on select buds, shoots, and tender foliage. She also had her fill of grub worms and thought about finding a safe place to nap.

The possibility of attracting the mysterious stranger as a mate kept her in the area. If by tonight he hadn't made his move, she was going to head back to her home the next morning.

The dance two nights before was an invitation, and she had left a trail easy enough in the woods for him to find her. It was imperative for the male to pursue her at this point, as it was unheard of to offer one's self to a potential suitor a second time.

She had mixed emotions about the stranger. It wasn't just his smell. There were physical characteristics about him that set him apart from every other male she had met. His oddities were intriguing, though, and not repelling. How would other members of her community receive him if they did become mates? Would other males challenge him?

The stranger certainly looked strong and healthy enough to hold his ground. But what if more than one male attacked him at the same time? The stranger *was* different. The community might ostracize both him and her.

These were things not to be concerned with so much right now, though. There had been no evidence that the stranger had an interest in her. This made her feel sad, as his uniqueness compelled her to desire him more.

The wind carried the scent of a Stealer, along with an odor that bristled the hair on her back. She had seen more than a few Stealers over her lifetime. The odor came from the long stick that barked thunder that they carried.

At least there was only one Stealer in the area. Still, the interloper was a threat to her and the stranger. If the stranger had been lured by her invitation, he might be looking for her right now, distracted by the raging fires of courtship that she had hoped to ignite.

No Stealer would deny Cha'nu a chance to be happy again.

She quickly bounded through the forest, determined to decisively end the threat.

*

Cole slowly approached Zax's cave and shut down the four wheeler. He slipped off the seat, and his helmet, taking his bag of supplies with him.

Zax stepped out of the cave with the rangefinder in his hand. He stretched out his arms and contorted his back, and then opened his mouth and let out a big yawn. "I wasn't sure you were coming back."

"You think I'd rather stay home and play Xbox than spend some time with a bigfoot time traveler who is going to save the Earth from an alien invasion?" Cole said as he approached.

"I'm not a bigfoot. I'm a Nu-Man, and, I don't know what an Xbox is."

"An Xbox is a game machine. I don't think they make any controllers big enough for your hands to fit them."

"Eh, I don't much care for games anyway." Zax put his left hand on the small of his back and leaned backward. "I have got to get a mattress to sleep on."

"Maybe you could come over to my house for a sleepover. I can make popcorn, and we could sit on the couch and watch movies and stuff."

The brow over Zax's left eye lowered. "Are you being sarcastic?"

"Do you think you could actually fit in my bed?"

"Are all humans this rude to strangers?"

"No, only to bigfoot time travelers who are going to save the Earth from an alien invasion," Cole dryly said, and then widely grinned.

The Nu-Man burst out in laughter. "You had me going there. I like you, Cole Rainwater."

Cole reached out his hand. "I'd like to thank you for what you did yesterday. If I had gone snooping around Douglas' place by myself, I doubt I would have been able to save Charlotte."

"And you would have probably ended up just like her." Zax reached out his hand, totally engulfing Cole's hand in completing the shaking of hands gesture. "I saw the girl, but there was a little boy too. Who was that?"

"That was another kid who went missing a couple of months ago. He's actually the nephew of my baseball coach."

"Uh, were...your girlfriend and the boy...hurt in any way?"

"No, thank God," Cole said while shaking his head, trying to keep the bad thoughts out of all that *could* have happened. "Their parents were really happy to see them."

"I guess you're quite the hero around here."

Cole blushed. "Well…I have been getting a lot of attention. On the news this morning, the reporter said President Trump got word of the story, and he might be coming here to give me an award or something."

"President Trump. Yeah, I remember reading about him. He proved himself to be the most unique president in American history."

"In a good or bad way?" Cole asked.

Zax paused a moment. "Do you read the ending of a book and then read the beginning?"

"No, why?"

"You'll just have to wait and see how the president performs. The whole point of living is to endure the experience, both the good and the bad." Zax leaned against the cave's outside wall. "Now, you were able to convince the authorities that you singlehandedly overcame three grown men with a baseball bat?"

"It wasn't easy, but I finally convinced them of that. I was careful to tell the same exact story over and over. They finally gave up."

"The criminals, what did they have to say about yesterday?"

"They said a bigfoot had attacked them. But, they had been drinking, so that didn't help their story," Cole said. "One FBI agent tried to get me to admit that a bigfoot broke into Douglas' house and that I went in when it left. Then he suggested that it might have been a bear that broke in. I don't know if he was serious or not. I think he was just trying to see if he could get me to change my story."

"You did well," Zax said. "I did have some worries last night that you might not have kept our secret. It was my head that worried with doubt, but my heart told me that I could trust you. Still, I had my rangefinder set to scan when you arrived, and I saw that you were alone. I was prepared to leave from the cave's rear entrance in case you had brought others."

"I had a hard time convincing my dad to let me take my four wheeler home through the woods, but he finally gave in." Cole opened his bag and pulled out some bananas. "Here, I brought you some food from home. It's not much, just a few things I thought you might like to try."

Zax took the bananas, and said, "Come on in and let's sit down."

Cole followed the big guy and sat on matted pine straw.

"What else is in the bag?"

"Here, try this." Cole pulled out a soda can and opened it. "It's called Mountain Dew. Try it."

Complying, Zax took hold of the can with his thumb and index finger, bringing it to his lips, and drank. "Hey, this is good. Cuts through some of the slime that's been building in my mouth." He drank more, swished it around in his mouth, and swallowed. "I don't suppose you have a toothbrush and toothpaste in that bag, do you?"

"Afraid not. I can bring them to you next time." Cole pulled out a plastic bag and opened it. "Try these. They're called Cheetos. I like them a lot. They go good with Mountain Dew, too."

Zax held out his hand while Cole shook some in. The big guy put some in his mouth and crunched away.

Cole ate a few and had some bottled water he brought with them. "What do you think?"

"Salty and cheesy. Two winning combinations." Zax brushed his hands. "This orange stuff sticks to your fingers."

"That's called *cheetle*."

"It even has a name," Zax said as if to himself. "Anything else in the bag?"

"I've got some gummy worms and some granola bars. Try some gummy worms next." Cole had the bag of candy out and ready to pour into Zax's hand.

The Nu-Man took a serving and tasted a few. After several chews, he said, "Wow, these are sour. Good, though." He ate the rest in his hand and continued to chew. "Sticks to my teeth. I really wish I had a toothbrush now."

"Do you want any more?"

"No. I've had enough for today." Zax's tongue probed his teeth, searching for trapped pieces of gummy worms.

"Zax, I have been thinking," Cole said, not knowing if he should even bring this up right now. "Sure, uh, I can get you a couple of blowup mattresses to sleep on. I can go to the store and buy you food and other things you might need. But I think it's going to be hard for you to live out here in the woods. You said that you were used to living better than what we do now. Have you ever thought, that once you complete your mission, that you might reveal yourself to the rest of the world? I mean, there's no way you wouldn't be treated like royalty. You could live anywhere you wanted, I bet, for free even. I'm sure the government would give you anything you wanted. They'd have to believe your story. Just look at you. You're living proof that a hybrid human-sasquatch exists."

Zax scraped his front tooth with a fingernail, flicking the gooey substance gathered toward the ground. "Yeah, I've thought about all of that too." He shrugged his shoulders. "Sure, I'd love to live in a nice house with a pool. Eat the finest food and drink the best wines. But for some reason, that style of life doesn't feel right. Not now. This isn't my time period. This isn't my world. There's no telling what might happen if I give myself over to the authorities. My fate may not include luxuary of any kind."

"Because you aren't human?"

"Partially, but that's not my main concern. You've accepted me rather rapidly. I'm sure most others would too," Zax said, and rubbed the side of his nose. "Beyond being probed for genetic research, I'm more concerned with what they would want to know about the Skinks' advanced technology. I could give them information that might be used to alter man's timeline. I could, in fact, do some of the things I'm trying to undo here in the first place."

"You think so? I don't see it that way. Science will always advance. So what if you tell them some things that will make advancements come quicker?"

"And what if I do and somehow or another it alerts the Skinks of Earth's existence? I know that's a stretch, but not impossible. But even if that never happens, you know man will use any science I pass on to make deadlier weapons. I've been reading the news. The planet is in grave danger right now with all the nuclear weapons all over the world. What if China, or Russia, or India, or whoever gets worried that I might be helping the United States build a superweapon and they make a preemptive nuclear strike? You know, I might rather the Skinks come and take over the planet than mankind poisoning it and taking all other life with it."

Cole sighed. "It's all so complicated. Like you said earlier, I guess we'll just have to endure the situation and see what the future has in store for us."

The rangefinder *beeped* its alert once more.

Zax snatched it from the ground and acknowledged the alarm. "The Skink probe is leaving orbit. It will be setting down shortly. Let's go. We've got a planet to save."

*

Sweat trickled down Walton Finch's forehead, stinging his eyes, as he trodded up the ridge to get a better view of where the UFO had landed. He held his rifle in one hand and used the other to remove his cap, briefly wiping the sweat away with his forearm.

His breathing slowed to normal as he walked the last several yards to the lookout spot. Avoiding tree roots, he peeked beyond the trees to the land below.

There it was.

In a small clearing.

An alien spaceship.

Walton felt the numbing excitement threaten to paralyze him. Again, this was the time when he needed his full senses to work for him. Telling himself to remain calm, he brought the rifle to his shoulder and viewed the spaceship through the hunting scope.

The craft was about one hundred yards away. From his estimate, it was less than twenty feet in diameter and rested directly on the ground. There were no doors, windows, or seams of any kind on its matted, coal-black skin.

Something reddish-brown moved by one side of the craft. An animal, of some sort. Just as he thought it might be a bear, Walton realized that it was not. He saw only the head and part of the left arm, but there was no mistaking what the animal was.

Sasquatch!

The impossible became even more impossible. An alien spacecraft and a bigfoot in the same location. Was there a connection? Of course, he had heard theories about UFOs and bigfoot having some sort of connection, but he had never given those theories any credence. He'd have to rethink that now. There might be a lot of things he'd learn today.

Then another movement caught his gaze. In front of the UFO, a young boy was rounding to the side, right about to come in contact with the bigfoot monster!

Walton wanted to yell a warning but knew that would be a waste of time. His finger went immediately to the rifle's safety, of which he clicked to *off*. With a finger on the trigger, he began to squeeze gently, making sure he waited until the last moment to take his best shot.

The boy stopped and pointed at something. The bigfoot looked toward that direction and moved its lips like it was speaking.

Confused, before Walton removed his finger from the trigger to consider what he saw, something large hit him on the back of his head.

The rifle thundered on impact, and the world spun around as he landed on his back.

When he looked up, he saw blue sky and a massive bigfoot towering above him.

The bigfoot's fist rose before it plunged downward, turning the bright blue of the sky to the dark of night of Walton's unconscious.

*

The alien probe landed two miles away from Zax's cave. Just like the day before, Cole found himself alongside the Nu-Man heading for a world-changing event.

This time it was for more than the fate of one young girl. The future of all of mankind rested on Zax's shoulders. The big guy would try and save a world that may have no place to offer him refuge.

Cole had been told the day before how he was a *hero* and how *unselfish* his act was, risking his life the way he did. Right now, it all seemed like such a small thing, realizing the sacrifices Zax had made and what the future would bring for the Nu-Man.

When the alien probe came into view, Cole had to veer off from the straight path toward it because of obstructions. By the time he arrived by the probe, Zax was already there.

The Nu-Man had his hands on his thighs, trying to recover his breath. He waved Cole to stay back after the boy shutdown the four wheeler.

Taking off his helmet, Cole said, "What? I'm not waiting here."

"Just a minute!" Zax's tone let Cole know he meant business. Uprighting his body, he left his blaster on the ground and examined the underside of the disk's edge. He stopped and walked to the opposite side, where he ran his fingers over the bottom side of the disk in a certain pattern.

Nothing happened, but Zax stepped away, and said, "Okay. You can come over here now."

"What did you do?" Cole asked as he hurried forward.

"The probe has a self-defense mechanism. It's not designed to use force first, as the Skinks would like nothing more than indigenous creatures to check out their probe. We're going to access the probe's data storage. Even though I know the codes, I'm just being over cautious. I don't want either one of us to end up dead because I didn't take every precaution."

"Oh, okay." Cole stopped as he reached the disk and looked underneath the edge. "What were you looking for under here?"

"Look to the left. See that mark?"

Searching, Cole found something etched in the disk's skin that looked like the letter V, and then said, "Yeah. What's it mean?"

"It's a proximity mark. It gives you an idea where the hardware components are located. I turned off the defense system from the other side."

"How did you turn it off? I don't see any buttons or switches."

"Come over here. I'll show you."

Cole meandered around the disk and reached Zax's side.

"Watch." The big guy ran his fingers along the smooth underside of the disk, just as he had done a few minutes earlier.

Nothing happened.

"Hmm."

"*Hmm*? What do you mean, *hmm*?"

"The other code worked. I just expected it to work here too. Don't worry, there're other codes." Zax ran his fingers across the skin again, with the same results as before.

"I don't get it. How are you punching in a code?"

"This probe is made of transmetal. It senses my touch, and I'm giving it a code to allow me to access the data storage."

"It's not working."

Zax huffed out a breath of air and pursed his lips. "I'm not finished, am I?"

Cole kept his mouth shut, the stress evident in the Nu-Man's tone.

After two more sets of finger patterns, a seam appeared in the transmetal, opening up to electronic equipment housed in the disk.

"See? You were all worried over nothing," Zax said.

"I wasn't worried."

"You're one of those people who always has to have the last word, aren't you?"

"No."

"*Yes*, you are. Why don't you just admit it?"

"No, I'm not," Cole was capable of getting a little aggravated too.

"Then, don't say another word until I'm finished."

"Okay."

"That's another word."

"I thought we were here to save the world?"

"I'll save the world when *I* have the last word."

Cole went to speak but stopped short as Zax raised a finger of warning at him.

Satisfied at the minor victory, the big guy took off his backpack and pulled out a domino-shaped translucent object. "This is the data crystal. All I have to do is remove the one that's in place now and replace it with this one."

"You know how to do that?" Cole asked.

"Yeah. I trained alongside Tarik. He was supposed to be the one doing this. I just trained with him to help him learn the sequence. It is a bit more complicated than the way I made it sound. I have to remove a few components out of the way to get to the original data crystal. There are codes I have to swipe in that allows the components to be removed. It shouldn't take long, though."

"Okay, I'll stay out of your way." Cole watched as strangely shaped panels, that looked nothing like any circuit board he had ever seen, came out of the disk and were placed on the ground.

"I'm just about there." Zax reached in the access port, soured the expression on his face, and gritted his teeth. After several minutes of obvious frustration, he said, "My hand is too big to pull out the data crystal."

"I thought you said you'd done this before, in training?"

"Well, you know, thinking back, I never actually changed out the crystal. I learned how to do everything to get me to it, but I never changed it out. Tarik was the one going back in time, not me. I've watched him do it many times. Looks like I'm going to need your help."

"Me?"

"Yeah. You're going to help save the world, too. Come here." Zax motioned Cole over. He used the light from his rangefinder to illuminate the access port. "Over there to the right. In the corner...see it? There's a switch right next to it. You'll have to run your finger around until you feel a bump. Push the bump, and the data crystal will release."

It felt weird reaching into the access port. Cole's mind produced an image where the disk's skin closed tightly, severing his arm from his body. But this was no time for his wild imagination.

Doing as instructed, worrying that he might push the wrong switch and screw something up, he finally felt the bump. The data crystal released as soon as he pushed it. "Got it!" He snaked his arm out of the port and held the crystal for Zax to see.

"Great job." Zax handed him the new data crystal. "This one will just snap in where the old one came from. But if you don't have the new crystal back in place in thirty seconds, the probe will explode and kill us both."

"What!"

"I'm just kidding. You like kidding me. Well, I can kid back. Don't be mad."

Cole breathed a sigh of relief. "I don't get mad. I just get even. Now, hold my beer and watch me do this."

"I have absolutely no idea what you're talking about."

Cole smirked. "I know, but one day you will." He stretched out his arm, felt the data crystal near the slot, and pushed it into place. "Fits just like the one that came out." Stepping back, he massaged his right hand with his left.

"Okay, just give me a few minutes, and I'll have this thing buttoned up tightly." Zax went to work putting the rest of the electronics in place.

With a little time on his hands, Cole walked around the disk, looking for the three other perimeter symbols. There was no telling the level of technology inside this probe. He tried to imagine what powered it and hoped maybe one day Zax could explain enough about it that he would understand. That is, if Zax trusted him enough with that information. Cole didn't see the harm it would do since the big guy wouldn't tell him how to actually build such an engine.

A few yards away, there were some large, flat rocks under two shady trees. Cole thought that would be a great place to sit and have some water and maybe a granola bar or two.

"Hey, Zax."

"Yeah?"

"You about finished?" Cole said, stepping where he could see the Nu-Man's head sticking above the disk's edge.

"Just closed the access panel. It's ready to go."

"Let's go sit on those rocks and have some water and snacks," Cole said as he pointed.

Zax turned his head to look, and said, "Looks like a nice place," and then fell straight backward to the ground.

The *crack* from a high-power rifle sliced through the moment, bringing with it the realization that Zax had just been shot!

"Zax!" Cole screamed and dashed over to his friend's side.

Lying with his back flat to the ground and his arms vulnerably splayed to either side, the Nu-Man showed no signs of life.

Frantically, Cole called Zax's name over and over and looked for the wound. Then, he noticed above and over to the side of Zax's left eye, right at the temple, blood started oozing from a shallow furrow about a half inch wide. He parted the hair near the wound and was relieved that the bullet had only grazed his friend's skull. Cole was even more relieved when he noticed the big guy was still breathing.

Who had taken the shot? Cole's head popped up on a swivel and gazed around. If they were in someone's sights, then they were both in danger.

The alien probe sat in between the direction of the bullet and where Zax lay. Hopefully, the probe would shield them from any further gunfire until he awoke. "Zax, you need to wake up. We need to get out of here."

It was no use. The Nu-Man was out-cold and would have to sleep it off.

Zax's backpack laid within reach. Cole pulled it over and dug past packaged foodstuffs until he found a pouch that looked like it contained medical supplies. Opening a square packet, he removed a disposable wipe that he hoped had some germicide on it, and cleaned Zax's wound.

Amazingly, the bleeding stopped. Cole watched, and the wound started to skin over. Whatever evils the future under the Skinks had to offer, the benefits probably equaled them as well.

"*YAHAHHH!*"

Cole's external anal sphincter quivered, and electric fire ran down his spine at the startling cry from a beast. He had been squatting near Zax's head as he tended to the wound but fell to his butt when he whipped around to see what rounded the alien probe to attack.

There it was in broad daylight.

Bigfoot.

The beast was more terrifying than when he remembered from his first encounter and his dreams. This one was different, though. It was obvious this bigfoot was female.

She opened her mouth again, showing canine teeth that looked two inches long. "*YAHAHHH!*" After her warning, she raised both arms in the air and rotated them in small circles.

Zax's blaster lay on the ground between Cole and the bigfoot. Even if he could get to it before she reached him, he didn't know how to use the futuristic weapon. He was completely at the beast's mercy. Cole didn't know who shot Zax, but now wouldn't be a bad time for them to take down this bigfoot.

The bigfoot's ire intensified. She leaned forward and screamed again. Then, she waved the air between them with her right hand.

Cole felt like he could feel her hot breath on his face. Her message came through loud and clear. She wanted him to move away from Zax.

His options were few. He could either move from Zax's side, or he was certain that she would move him herself.

Keeping his gaze toward her, Cole crab-walked backward using both hands and feet, giving the female her space.

Complying with her wishes immediately calmed her down. She ambled over to Zax's side and knelt. Bringing her face over Zax's, her nostrils flared in and out as she examined him. Then the bigfoot made an unusual sound similar to a cat purring.

The bigfoot shot a steady gaze over at Cole. He took it as a warning that he needed to keep his place and not interfere.

Standing from Zax's side, she then reached down and picked up his right arm. With her right hand, she placed it under Zax's left armpit. In one smooth move, she lifted the massive Nu-Man and slung him over her shoulder.

Cole was in awe of the incredible strength displayed by the female bigfoot. She and Zax were nearly the same size, with the female being slightly larger. Now, she had taken claim of the Nu-Man. All Cole could do was watch as the cryptid carried his time traveling friend into the hidden secrets of the great forest.

Once the two were out of sight, Cole was left with the gentle breeze as his only companion. Zax was gone. Just as unexpectedly as the Nu-Man appeared in his life, he had disappeared in the same manner. Cole sensed that the female bigfoot had no intentions of harming Zax. Still, once the big guy awoke, Cole was curious how Zax would react to his new environment. One thing was for sure, Cole would visit Zax's cave often to see if his friend had decided to live on his own or remain with the other bigfoot creatures in the wild.

The alien probe in a way reminded him of the monolith from *2001: A Space Oddessy*. Inside, the probe contained science that once deciphered could exponentially advance mankind. It was a shame to let an opportunity like this go. But what could he do? There was nothing for him to learn from it. He could call the authorities and have them try and disable it so it wouldn't leave the Earth, but Cole knew the consequences of that. There was probably no way to prevent the alien probe from leaving when it was ready anyway.

Gazing around, Cole saw no clues as to who had fired the shot that hit Zax. Time was moving on. If he was late getting home, his dad was sure to worry. The shooter would have to remain a mystery for now.

Zax's backpack and blaster lay on the ground. The alien probe would leave Earth soon enough, but Cole now had the responsibility to care for the personal items until if and when the big guy returned.

After loading his four wheeler, Cole pulled out his phone and took one photo of the alien probe. When he looked at the screenshot, he thought he'd seen more realistic looking CGI UFOs in movies.

He took the photo just for keepsake, as he had no intention of ever telling anyone, and he meant anyone, the fantastic tale of the gentle giant from the future who saved mankind from total destruction.

CHAPTER 24

Cole sat on the bench next to a handful of teammates, chewing away on a snack. It was Friday night. A week had almost passed since he and Zax rescued Charlotte and Raymond.

It had been a whirlwind of a week, for sure. Monday at school turned into a *Cole Rainwater* appreciation day. Or, perhaps he should have called it *Cold* Rainwater appreciation day. It seems that the mispronouncing of his name by the reporter had stuck, and now Cold was his new nickname.

He had been forced to recount his heroic story in every class of how he singlehandedly took down the three evil men. His self-conscious did begin to weigh on him, as it was an out-and-out lie that he continued to tell. But what was a boy to do? Say that a *bigfoot time traveler did it who came to save the Earth from an alien invasion*?

He smiled to himself when he had said that line to Zax and remembered the Nu-Man's reply. *I'm not a bigfoot. I'm a Nu-Man.*

Cole really missed Zax, but had a feeling that wherever he was right now, he was content. At least, content for now. Who knows what the future might bring? What if the female bigfoot chose Zax as a mate? Would they be able to have children? Who would the offspring take after, Nu-Man or sasquatch?

Of course, after he rescued Charlotte and Raymond, he did have to confess to the police and FBI what led he and Brennon to believe Douglas held her prisoner. On Tuesday, the principal sat him and Brennon down and gave them a strong talking-to on the wrongs of leaving school without permission. After reading a list of the dire consequences, the principal, because of his *forgiving nature*, let both boys off with just a warning; suspension or detention had been waived.

Tonight had been a good night for baseball. Dent County High played Calhoun High, an arch rival. Dent County led in the bottom of the 9th. The bases were loaded, but there was only one more out to go now that the last batter from Calhoun had struck out.

Calhoun had a lopsided winning record against Dent. What was so surprising about tonight, was that half of Dent's team were off sick with a stomach virus. There were only three pitchers available, and Cole was number three! For a while there he thought he might get a chance to go in the game. The second pitcher, Brent Roy, came in at the bottom of the 7th and looked like he found his groove again and was going to cruise the team into a narrow victory. The score didn't matter. A win is a win.

At least Cole learned the identity of Zax's mysterious shooter. He had read an online story from the local newspaper how a guy named Walton Finch had a hunting accident where he received trauma to the head. His memory of the event was blurred but claimed he remembered someone big standing over him at one point. Police had no leads, and anyone with information on the incident was encouraged to contact the authorities. There was no mention of bigfoot or a UFO, the latter which surely Finch saw when he shot at Zax. The female bigfoot must have hit him on the head hard enough to erase his memory.

The pitcher for Dent, Brent Roy, shot one off the mound into the catcher's mitt.

"Ball," the home plate umpire called.

Cole took the last bite of the nutrient bar. He had eaten half before the game and waited for the 7th inning stretch to start back on the rest of it.

When Cole arrived home on Sunday with Zax's backpack and blaster, he quickly had to find a good hiding place. Handling the blaster bothered him because Zax had never shown him how to use it; not that he had any reason to. Cole didn't feel comfortable with the weapon just stuck behind some junk in the garage. So, on Monday after school, he wrapped the blaster and the extra ammo that was in the backpack, in plastic bags and took them into the woods and buried them. He covered the freshly turned earth with rocks and made a mental note right where he knew to find it.

Roy threw another pitch.

"Ball," the umpire repeated.

The rest of the items in the backpack went in his room. The survival knife was really neat. It had a burning laser that he had to be careful with.

The rangefinder was the most interesting, but he still didn't really know how to use it. He kept it in his closet, in a box with his old Nintendo game machine. His dad would never go looking in there and accidentally find it.

The medical supplies in the pack might come in handy one day. When time allowed, he thought he might *play* with some of the wipes and ointments to see how effective they were on humans. That one wipe he used on Zax healed him like magic. The bandages in the supplies weren't much different than the ones he could buy at the drug store.

As far as the packaged food, Cole tried one that had baked chicken and mashed potatoes. He had MREs before, and the Nu-Mans' packaged food was far superior in flavor. His favorite items, were the nutrient bars, as Zax had called them. He had said they were meant for Nu-Mans. But when Cole took a bite of one, he thought they tasted okay, once you got past the smell. They did give him a lot of energy too. The nutrient bars pepped him up more than two energy drinks.

Roy delivered another pitch. Before the ball hit the catcher's mitt, he grabbed his right elbow and winced in pain.

The crowd from Dent moaned in disappointment.

"Ball," the umpire said.

Coach Jones ran from the dugout toward the mound, followed by the catcher.

Cole looked up into the stands and saw Charlotte and her mother sitting in front of his dad. Charlotte had taken the week off school but came out tonight to watch the game. She and Cole had spoken every day, and things between them were slowly warming. They weren't boyfriend and girlfriend yet, but Cole's hopes were high. The last thing he wanted from her was some misplaced gratitude. Their relationship should be something heartfelt and not out of obligation.

Overall, Charlotte had put the ordeal behind her. She had a few counseling sessions with a state worker and said that had helped her a lot. A couple of days ago, Cole brought her some school work to do at home so she wouldn't fall too far behind. She was kind of down in the dumps, so he gave her one of Zax's nutrient bars. Funny thing, she had said she liked the way it tasted. The nutrient bar really lifted her spirits too. So much so that he had given her one before the game started so she'd get up for it. Whatever horrors remained in her subconscious were subject to time's healing powers. Hopefully, nothing would stick around and haunt her like Cole's dreams of bigfoot.

Coach Jones approached the dugout with his arm around Roy. The poor boy's face was red, and tears streamed down his cheeks. "Rainwater, get on the mound."

Cole felt like he was just hit in the face with a wet fish. "Huh?" *Oh, yeah.* He was the only pitcher left on the team. He'd forgotten that for a moment. "But I haven't warmed up, yet."

"Throw a few balls to the catcher, and let's get this over," Coach Jones said.

Unsure if that was a vote of confidence or if the coach had resolved himself that they would lose the game, Cole sprang off the bench and trotted toward the mound.

The Dent High fans yelled in support, and then chanted, "Cold! Cold! Cold!"

Blood rushed to his face making his ears feel hot. The combination of the crowd's cheers and the nutrient bar made him feel bulletproof.

"Don't worry, man. You got this," Brennon said in Cole's right ear and slapped him on the rear with the back of his glove. The boy had left right field to give him words of encouragement and headed back to his position.

He worked his arms around a bit and tossed a few balls to the catcher. Feeling like he was good to go, he gave the umpire a nod.

"Play ball!" the umpire said.

It was time to compose himself. Tune out all the outside noise, and avoid praying to an *eight-pound-eleven-ounce blonde hair blue-eyed infant baby Jesus*. How stupid was it to pray to an almighty God over some silly high school ball game anyway? God would probably be more likely to make the team lose with the most prayers offered for wasting his time.

Throw the ball with your arm and feet. Turn and shuffle, pull, snap. Feet and wrist. He knew what to do. Pitching was all in the execution, though.

Cole went through the windup and let the ball rip.

The batter never moved a muscle as the ball slapped the mitt. He looked bewildered at the umpire, and then turned his gaze to the catcher as he pulled the ball free from his glove and tossed it back to Cole.

The crowd roared and chanted, "Cold," again.

Another windup and pitch sent a fastball right over home plate.

The batter swung this time, though the ball hit the catcher's mitt long before he tried to hit it.

This was almost too easy. Right now, Cole felt like he could walk out on any professional baseball field and hold his own.

"Come on, Cole! Just one more to bring us home!" Coach Jones was on his feet and cheering like the rest of the crowd.

The batter, narrowing his eyes and gritting his teeth, took a few dummy swings and rested the bat on his shoulder.

As Cole delivered the pitch, the batter started swinging before the ball left his hand.

No matter.

The batter swished through empty air as the ball went over his bat.

It was over! Cole had won the game!

The Dent crowd jumped to their feet, cheering, and calling his name. Cole's whole body was electric! He had never felt so high before in his life.

But the crowd noise slowly gave way to a disturbance growing inside his head. All of a sudden, he felt dizzy. His vision started to lose focus.

As if all the muscles had been removed from his bones, Cole collapsed to the ground, and everything went dark and silent.

*

Coach Jones dashed from the dugout and slid by Cole's side. The boy's eyes were open, but he wasn't responding. "Cole, can you hear me? Cole!" He patted him lightly on the cheek and felt his neck for a pulse.

The crowd had gone silent, and a woman in the stands cried, "Oh, no!"

There was no pulse, and Cole wasn't breathing. "Doctor! I need a doctor."

No time to panic, Coach Jones knew how to deliver CPR. He began chest compressions and started the count.

*

Cole opened his eyes and gasped deeply for breath. He was lying on the ground but didn't remember why. Coach Jones was sitting next to him wearing a huge smile on his face.

"Cole! Cole!" Mark Rainwater ran and fell by his son's side. "Son, are you okay?"

Cole cleared his throat and paused. He remembered winning the game, now, and then feeling sick. "Uh, yeah, Dad. I feel fine."

"Get the EMTs over here to check him out," Coach Jones said.

Feeling his energy return, Cole sat up.

"Try not to move too much until the EMTs get here," Mark said.

"But I feel fine."

"Cole..." Mark said with parental warning.

"Really. I don't wanna sit on the ground anymore." Cole hopped to his feet, and the crowd came alive again. He saw Charlotte and her mom jumping and clapping.

"Cold! Cold! Cold!" the chanting continued.

Cole took off his cap and raised it high in the air, waving at the crowd. His inner core had transformed in some way. He felt so strong that he thought he could crush a coconut with his bare hands.

As he continued to wave his hat in the air, he noticed hairs growing from his knuckles and the palms of his hands.

Cole felt like a new person.

He felt like a *new man*.

EPILOGUE

Cha'nu watched with the rest of her tribe as Zax and Kam'bu circled each other in the *ring of honor*.

The tribe's chief, Rik'us, was a fair ruler who demanded honor and equality for all.

Zax had awoken in Cha'nu's care sometime later the day he had been shot. He wasn't entirely sure what happened but did notice that the wound on his head had been treated with a wipe from his medical kit. He could only imagine that Cole had been the one to do so.

At first, Zax was fearful that Cha'nu had hurt the boy when she had found him injured. Though communicating with her was crude, through drawings he made in the dirt and simple sign language, he was able to piece together part of the story.

A hunter had taken the shot that grazed his head. Cha'nu attacked him just as he took the shot. When she came to rescue Zax, she found Cole and let him go unharmed because he posed no threat. Zax was relieved when he learned that.

At that point, Zax was curious to meet members of Cha'nu's tribe. He realized the risk he was taking by following her there. But was that any less risky than staying where he was so close to humans? He'd already taken a shot from one hunter. The next hunter might not miss.

The Holder's language, what he learned they called themselves, was simple and a mixture of broken, spoken words and grunts. In a few days, he carried on basic conversations with Cha'nu, though he was careful not to speak any words of English. He had no idea how she would have responded to that.

When Cha'nu presented Zax to the tribe, the males of the group had an instant distrust of him. Though Zax couldn't tell if distrust was the right way to think of it, as it could have been more that they had less respect for him. Zax was more the size of the females, with the males being a good six inches taller or more. Plus, he was an intruder with a strange smell.

It helped that Cha'nu was a well-respected member of the tribe. She had vouched for Zax, and that was good enough for most. They were also happy to see that she had snapped out of her depression over losing her mate.

Only one member of the tribe, though, felt strongly enough about giving him a chance to fit in to offer a challenge in the ring of honor. There was no way Zax could refuse.

Kam'bu probably outweighed Zax by a hundred pounds. Not an ounce of that weight was fat.

Zax would have to use speed to counter the difference in sizes.

Tiring of the dance, Kam'bu made the first move as he lunged forward, trying to grab Zax using both hands.

Zax slapped Kam'bu's hands aside and darted around him as he lost his balance.

Once behind him, Zax pushed both arms under Kam'bu's arms and brought his hands to the back of his opponent's neck.

Kam'bu roared in frustration and tried unsuccessfully to reach behind his head and hit Zax.

In full control, Zax wanted to swiftly end the match without either one of them suffering any major injury. Using all his strength, he pushed down on the back of Kam'bu's neck, buckling his opponent's legs until his knees hit the ground. Not stopping there, he pushed more until Kam'bu's forehead touched the earth.

Turning a quick gaze toward Rik'us, he waited for a ruling.

"*Cha'pa!*" Rik'us declared.

The victor, Zax released his grip and quickly stood.

Kam'bu rose slowly, probably his pride more injured than his body. He turned and locked gazes with Zax.

Extending two open palms toward Kam'bu, Zax offered a sign of respect.

Though Kam'bu hesitated, he placed both of his hands on top of Zax's.

The tribe howled with approval.

Cha'nu first went to Kam'bu and touched her forehead to his chest, to let him know she respected him too.

The Chief gave a wreath made from mistletoe and placed it on Zax's head. The crown didn't declare him a winner of the match. It was a sign that he was now part of their tribe.

The females took turns touching their heads to Zax's chest, and then the males offered him the open palm acceptance.

Later that night, they all gathered for a final feast before heading back to their individual territories.

Zax felt more alive now than any other time in his life.

He no longer had the dread of being a bigfoot abomination.

THE END?

www.ingramcontent.com/pod-product-compliance
Lightning Source LLC
Chambersburg PA
CBHW071504170626
46811CB00007B/2736